LOVE IN A SUNBURNT LAND

ANTHOLOGY VOLUME TWO

RHONDA FORREST   LOUISE FORSTER

LEANNE LOVEGROVE   SUSAN MACKIE

EMMA POWELL

THE SUNBURNT LAND TEAM

Five Australian authors, **Rhonda Forrest, Louise Forster, Leanne Lovegrove, Susan Mackie** and **Emma Powell** joined forces in 2020 to create an anthology of rural romance stories that would encompass various unique Australian rural and small-town settings.

Love in A Sunburnt Land, Volume One was published in June 2021. By publication day the group had formed a great friendship and continued meeting to support each other in their own writing and publishing goals. This gave birth to the second anthology.

The Sunburnt Land authors hope you enjoy their stories as much as they loved working together to bring you laughter, tears and most importantly – *Love in a Sunburnt Land Volume Two.*

FIVE FABULOUS STORIES

All My Heart by **Rhonda Forrest**

A new job in a small town. She only has to last six months.

A short-term teaching position in Tranquil Bay, North Queensland is an exciting option for Tess. Warmer weather, slower pace and a change of scenery are just what she is looking for and will add skills to her resume for moving back to Canberra at the end of the year. A romance with a burly footballer adds spice to her stay, however she soon realises that not everyone can be trusted. Will the complexities of a small town and new school send her home sooner than she anticipated or will she discover a reason to stay?

The Green Place by **Louise Forster**

Magic can happen anywhere but in this small country town, it's extra special.

International journalist Grace Taylor has in the past handled many dangerous assignments and is ready for any situation. Joe Mathews has a passion for sustainable farming. How can two such diverse people get on? And why does writing a feature on a reluctant Aussie farmer have her questioning her very future? He wants nothing to do with being a feature in a women's magazine that his sister arranged, with her parting words, 'it's time.' He and his nine-year-old son have been on their own for two years, and happily so. Is he ready to deal with the reaction they both have when Grace blows into their home and community?

Love in Between by **Leanne Lovegrove**

Finding community, and love, in the most unexpected place.

Caleb Stirling has never had it easy, but he's worked hard and is a stellar chef of his own five-star restaurant in Sydney.

Over one fateful week his world crumbles around him and he finds himself in an outback country town where everything he's ever known is threatened.

Bridie Finch is the lifeblood of *Bellethorpe*. Need something done? Give it to Bridie. She's so busy looking after the community, her father and their strawberry farm, she fails to care for herself.

Now, Caleb must care for his orphaned niece. But Bridie needs a chef for the annual Bastille Day Festival and, unwillingly, he lands the role. But there's no place to hide in town and soon the locals discover who he really is. Instead of rejecting him, they rally with support and quickly both Bellethorpe and Bridie get under his skin.

A sweet small-town story of community, being accepted and finding love in the most unexpected of places.

Meggie & Max by **Susan Mackie**

He's the new Vet with something to hide. She's got a wedding to organise.

Meggie's in Barrington for her brother's wedding, local Vet Angus Hamilton. After working overseas for years, she hasn't told her family she's not going back. And she hasn't told them why.

Max is the Locum Vet hired to help out in the lead up to the wedding and during the honeymoon. But he doesn't arrive alone.

They each need to move on from their past. When their secrets are revealed, will it empower them, or tear them apart?

The Song by **Emma Powell**

Tina Lombardi is a star. But something is missing.

After winning Sing to Win Tina became an overnight home-grown Aussie sensation. Running away to the US after a very public meltdown she built a career there. But something is missing. When she returns to Australia to judge on the same show she realised what that was. Connection. Not just to home but to another person's heart. When she meets Clay, the local singing farmer and his equally talented daughter the connection is strong. But will she end up choosing stardom over her own heart?

ALL MY HEART

RHONDA FORREST

A small town and a new job.
She only has to last six months.

all my heart

RHONDA FORREST

To the Sunburnt Land authors
Louise, Leanne, Emma and Susan

A great team filled with fun, friendship and support.
How lucky we are.

Rhonda Forrest

1

Tess held the glass high, the bubbly liquid cool on her throat as she drank the last of her champagne. It was expensive and French, and she smiled as the young man next to her promptly re-filled her glass. 'Can't have it empty now, can we,' he said, sending a cheeky wink her way.

She held her glass out, drawn in by his charismatic eyes and mischievous smile. Today was the first time she'd met handsome footballer, Tom. She had heard he was one of the best sportsmen in the district; his well-known identity splashed across billboards wearing his footy attire, his face on the television ads nightly. All that meant nothing to her. She knew as much about football as she did about North Queensland. The men she'd dated in Canberra—where she'd lived all her life—were more used to attending the theatre, strolling through the art gallery or spending a relaxing day sprawled on a picnic blanket in one of the pristine parks in the city.

Tess had only been in Tranquil Beach for just over a month, but it was obvious that not only was the weather and the school she was teaching at completely different to what she was accustomed to—and anything but tranquil—but the men also, were a very different breed. It wasn't that she hadn't previously mixed with country people. Some of her relatives lived on farming properties and she'd spent holidays with them, riding horses, helping round up sheep and getting her hands dirty. She wasn't precious, she kept reminding herself. It's just that this was vastly different to the country lifestyle she'd been familiar with.

Tom held his glass high to clink against hers. She gazed at his arms; bulging muscles, a tight-fitting collared shirt showing off a fit, strong body. He poured the contents of the flute down his throat. 'Bit bloody fancy this French stuff. I usually drink beer, but when you're at the races you have to go with the flow.'

'It's delicious. I can't believe everything is free. It was nice of Miranda to ask me,' she replied.

'Corporate invites are the best. Don't pay for nothing. Bloody big marquee, perfect shade.'

She cringed a little at his colloquial language. Every second word was *bloody*, and he missed out words when he spoke, or said them in an incorrect order. She reprimanded herself. Don't be stuck up or judgemental. Besides, Tom's looks made up for his slang. His dark hair was wavy, his skin tanned from hours in the sun. He'd already told her he was a car salesman who spent any spare hours not playing or training for footy, at the beach. He'd made a beeline for her the minute she'd arrived and her worries about not fitting in or feeling out of place were now forgotten. She'd come with a group from work, most of them young, single, and female. At thirty-five she was a bit older than most of the other girls, but she reassured herself she didn't feel any different than she had at twenty-five.

Tom wasted no time sharing his personal details. 'I'm thirty-two and I've spent all my life up here,' he'd added, 'wouldn't live anywhere else. Best place in Stralia.'

She wanted so badly to correct him. 'Oh, you mean, Australia,' she said it slowly.

He'd laughed and thrown a charming look her way. 'You're cute. Are you an English teacher or something? I can tell you right now, not much use trying to change my language. Born and bred here. Tranquil Bay local, through and through.'

She'd taken another sip from her glass. 'I need to get used to the local accent. It's noticeable. I never knew there would be a change in dialogue, from south to north.'

'We're a different mob up here. Footy, mates and having a good time is what it's all about.' He leaned towards her, his dreamy eyes looking straight into hers. 'And of course, a bit of romance, fishing and making sure beautiful girls like you are looked after and shown around. Are you pleased you've made a change?'

'I am, thank you. It's …' she paused, 'different. It's never easy at the start, especially with the students at school. I'm sure I'll settle in quickly though. Miranda and the others at work are super helpful and friendly. They've made it easier for me.'

The change she was seeking had been easy to arrange. Schools in the north of the country were keen to take on teachers, particularly someone with experience. They'd warned her that it would be quite a different setting than the elite private school where she'd taught for the last thirteen years. She might find it difficult to begin with, but teachers who arrived in north Queensland—often from the city—had a track record of settling in, finding their feet and usually loved the casual life-style and busy social life. Most of them stayed and never left.

She wasn't convinced about the last part, but she needed a change after the last relationship breakup. She wanted to get away from Canberra, plus the weather in the northern regions was inviting and the opposite of what she was accustomed to. She was after sunshine and warm weather. A year or even six months in the remote area would suit and hopefully she would get a promotion or two under her belt before heading back to the more competitive nature of private education in Canberra. Who knew, perhaps opportunities would pop up while she was at Tranquil Bay. Her contract was flexible and she could always leave and return to a higher position. Her attention was drawn back to Tom as he rubbed his arm against hers.

His voice was deep and his words rolled slowly. 'Miranda said you're single?'

'I am. Yes,' she replied, taking another sip from her glass.

'Good. Me too. Only recently broke up but it wasn't meant to be anyway. Miranda told me you'd be here today. I've been keen to meet you. She said you were new to town. Where you from?'

'I'm from Canberra. It's where I've always lived and where I went to university. I've taught there for a number of years but my parents have taken off in a camper van to travel the country, so I decided I'd make a move somewhere different as well.

'What do you think so far about our little town.'

Tess took another long sip from her glass. 'It's very pretty and I like the way everything and everyone moves at a slower pace. I'm a bit shocked I can't swim in summer though. It's hot now and it's July, the middle of winter!'

'Easy fixed. Stick with me. We've got a pool at our place. A few of us boys have a house on the beach. Great for cooling off.'

Miranda came up behind Tom. 'It's a party house. Always something happening and where everyone gathers.' She kissed him on the cheek. 'I knew you'd hit it off with Tess.'

Tess giggled. 'Tom's definitely looking after me. I haven't seen the bottom of my glass since I got here. I've had way too much to drink. The bubbles go down easily. I need to slow up.'

Tom placed his arm firmly around her waist, his body rubbing up against hers. 'Fill her glass up, Miranda. We've only just started.'

* * *

Tess left them both chatting. 'I'm just going to the bathroom. I'll be back soon.' She passed her glass to Tom as she left. Her head was starting to spin and she was unsteady on the high heels that she wore. Everyone at the races was dressed up, just as much as they would be at the big meets down south. The other girls had warned her and although she thought she'd be overdressed, now she was pleased she'd worn her best outfit. The emerald green dress was tight and short, revealing toned legs and a shapely figure. She'd left her blonde hair loose, just adding a bit of chic with a stylish clip that pulled one side back. Her hair had grown long and was down past her waist, the rainwater she used at the tiny flat she was renting, adding an extra shine and bounce.

As she made her way to the toilets her thoughts turned to the flat that had been provided as teacher accommodation. It was a lot smaller than the photos had shown, the fittings were outdated and the shower and toilet were actually on the outside of the building. At least it was secure, as promised, although she'd already had some scary encounters with large toads and grasshoppers that made their way through the slatted timber that closed in the outside area.

The racetrack amenities she entered now also had a variety of bugs flying in and out and a huge green frog stared back at her from the corner of the room. The area was messy and she kicked aside paper towels that were strewn across the floor. Typical race day she thought, no different to any other part of the country. Flowing alcohol and the mixture of drinking, betting, and socialising in the sun, always a potent mixture.

When she came back out of the cubicle, she had to wait to use the sink. Two young girls were trying to hold each other up, their laughter and conversation, loud and raucous. They turned around as she also tried to stand straight without swaying.

'Bloody good champers,' one of them said, swinging her arm in the air as the other girl tried to help fix her hair.

'Stand still you idiot. Your hair is all over your face.'

Tess laughed with them, eventually stepping in and holding their glasses while they both attempted to fix themselves up.

'Thanks muchly,' one of them said. 'We need to get back out there to watch the horseys go around.'

The other girl took the empty glasses back off Tess. 'Who watches the horses. Are there horses here?'

They laughed again before staggering out through the exit. The door slammed loudly behind them as Tess leant against the wall. Her head was really starting to spin, the frog in the corner blurry as she closed her eyes. Usually, she was careful about how much she drank, but today the atmosphere had been carefree and fun, enticing a feeling of freedom and new adventures, the flowing champagne too good to refuse. Miranda's group consisted of about twenty men and women and the excitement of meeting new people coupled with the nervousness of being the newcomer made her disregard the number of drinks that she'd downed.

She opened her eyes, the frog coming into focus, its bulging black eyes blinking at her as she straightened the front of her dress. The top part was low cut and showed off her figure, her slender waist and hips accentuated by the shimmering silky fabric that flowed smoothly over her body. Green eyes stared back from the mirror and she checked that she still looked half decent. Thank goodness she wasn't one for fussing about makeup. It only ever took her a few minutes to get ready and she reapplied some lip gloss, reassuring herself that she had made some sort of effort.

'Not bad for thirty-five,' she said out loud, smacking her lips as she held onto the basin for support. No more alcohol, she admonished herself. She didn't want to be remembered as the drunken teacher. This was a small town and no doubt there could be parents of students attending today or perhaps even some of the students. The first few weeks at her new high school had not been a smooth start to her teaching position and she didn't want to add ammunition for any gossip or false misconceptions.

* * *

CAREFUL TO WALK STRAIGHT AS SHE EXITED THE RESTROOMS SHE FOLLOWED a path that led back to the main marquee. When she tried to push her hair back behind her ears her sunglasses fell off the top of her head. The concrete path was cracked and uneven and as she bent down to pick them up she stumbled forward. Concentrating hard she tried to stay upright, the concrete looming towards her. She flinched as a strong hand grasped her arm just in the nick of time, saving her from face-planting into the ground. A man's voice said, 'Easy there. You nearly went A over T.'

Tess steadied herself, grateful that the man standing next to her had stopped her from falling. She looked up. 'Thank you. My heel got caught in the crack.'

He raised his eyebrows. 'Or maybe too much champagne.'

She frowned. 'Perhaps.'

He placed his hand out for her to shake. 'The name's Joel. You're with Miranda's group. We were introduced when you first arrived.'

She looked hard at him, trying to stop the spinning in her head. He was a bit older than most of the others in the group and she vaguely remembered being introduced to him. 'Yes. Joel. I remember. Thank you again.'

He took her sunglasses from her and wiped them with his shirt. 'You've got dirt all over these. Anyway, nice to meet you, Tess. I'll let you get back to the others. I'm headed for home. Sun and beer aren't a great mixture for me. I'm going to get my son to pick me up. Payback for all the times I've done it for him.'

She smiled, drawn in by his friendly face and piercing blue eyes. 'Thank you. I agree. I don't normally drink so much but...' She looked down, mortified when she noticed that a string of toilet paper was attached to the heel of one of her shoes. She kicked her foot to the side but the paper was stuck. Wishing the ground would open up and swallow her, she pulled her foot upwards, reaching out to hang onto Joel's arm to steady herself. He laughed loudly as she tried to explain that it wasn't used toilet paper.

'The bathroom was a mess. I should have checked that nothing was attached. It's not used, it's just rubbish that...'

Joel chuckled and shook his head. 'You're having a bit of bad luck, aren't you?'

He watched as she straightened up, her lips pursed, her face burning. He looked straight into her eyes, his lips curling up in merriment as she stuck out her chin and glared back at him.

'It's no big deal. It's not toilet paper, it's the hand towel stuff, you know what you dry your hands on. You pull it out of the tin, metal dispenser thing, you know it's on the wall.'

'Yep,' he replied, still staring at her.

'What? What are you laughing at?'

'Turn around.'

She turned, berating herself for simply following his instructions and not thinking about her actions before doing them.

'What?' she asked again.

He crossed his arms as she tried to look at where he was staring. She swivelled around, glimpsing the back of her dress and suddenly feeling that not everything was where it should be.

Joel reached over and pulled gently, untucking the back of her dress from her full-size underpants. 'Wouldn't want to be walking into the crowds looking like that, would you?'

He laughed loudly as she closed her eyes. Granny knickers, she thought to herself. She had worn her full-size knickers so you wouldn't be able to see any pant lines under her dress.

He held her by the shoulders and turned her around. 'All shmick. Off you go. Don't worry I won't tell a soul.'

She felt sick. Toilet paper and now granny undies. What a great introduction to the local crowd. She slid her hands over her dress, straightening the front and back, ensuring everything was in place.

'You better get back, he said, with a slight laugh. 'They'll be wondering where you are.'

Her head lifted and met his gaze as her words seemed to get stuck in her throat. 'Thank you,' she murmured.

Tess made her way along the footpath, trying to walk straight and upright. She wasn't brave enough to look back until she was about to enter the marquee. The noise from within the canvas shelter had increased and a quick glimpse told her that everyone definitely had their fill of alcohol. Loud music bellowed from a band that was playing and the dance floor had instantly become a moving, gyrating mixture of patrons, most of the girls now holding their shoes in one hand and their drinks in the other. The men joined in, dancing wildly with untucked shirts and dishevelled attire. She clenched her teeth. Just get into it. You're still young, you can keep up with the pace. She looked backwards over her shoulder. Joel sat on a concrete wall, his hand raised high to give her a wave as he talked on his phone. She waved back before disappearing into the marquee, spotting Tom who had obviously been looking for her.

He leapt over a couple of chairs and grabbed her hands. 'Thought I'd lost you in the crowd. Come on and I'll get you another drink. The party has just started.'

2

———

I f Tess thought her presence at the races had gone unnoticed, she was mistaken. Within the first half an hour of lesson one on Monday she was questioned by half a dozen students. 'Saw you with Miranda and Tom Lette at the races on Saturday, Miss. You looked pissed,' a tall, lanky student called Hamish said.

'That's Miss Owens, not Miranda, to you and please watch your language,' she looked down, sorting her papers and getting ready for the lesson.

'Youse were getting into it. I saw ya dancing with Tom. You know he plays footy for the team?' quipped Alex. 'Looks like he has the hots for ya.'

'Please Alex, pronounce your words correctly. It's you not ya, and you, not youse. Try and speak properly. This is an English lesson.'

Alex and Hamish both rolled their eyes dramatically, before embracing each other and doing a thrusting gyrating movement with their hips, obviously what was supposed to be, an imitation of how she had been dancing with Tom.

The other students laughed loudly, one of the girls called Sarah sidling up and fluttering her long false eyelashes that were thickened with heavy mascara. 'You know he just broke up with his old girl-friend. I'm not sure she'd be happy if she knew he was all over you.'

'Thank you, Sarah, for your advice. Now you need to present your-self to the office to remove some of the makeup that is plastered all over your face, plus you have five earrings in your ear. You know you're only allowed two.'

'They don't care. I been up there already and told them I can't get the makeup off and the piercings are new. Can't have them closing over just because of some stupid rules. They cost me a heap to get done. You weren't the only one dollied up on the weekend.'

A few of the other girls laughed, the students finally taking their seats, their bags carelessly tossed down on the floor beside them.

Walking through the middle of the room Tess tried to remain composed. It wasn't a great start to the lesson and the more they carried on, the harder it would be to gain and hold their attention.

A student called Matty appeared beside her, taking a chair out of her hand. He continued down the row, putting the chairs on the ground that had been left stacked on the desks. Matty didn't walk, he strutted, his school shirt undone, revealing a bright t-shirt underneath that was not part of the school uniform. The girls loved Matty and he jumped over the row of desks, handing her a couple of books that she had placed down when she first arrived at class. 'Thank you, Matty. You'll go a long way with the girls, using those beautiful manners.'

He did a bobbing, dancing movement, looking around ensuring he had the full attention of the class. 'Oh, I already have, Miss, believe me I've gone a long way.'

The class erupted into laughter and she glared at him, her gratitude for his help withdrawn.

'Sit down, Matty'

She tried to remain composed. This was her fifth week with her new classes and to say she was struggling was an understatement. Other teachers at the school had warned her that picking up someone else's class mid-year was never easy. The classes she had been given had already gone through two teachers since the start of the year. That meant there was no fixed routine and their behaviour would need reigning in. That information hadn't daunted her to begin with. She was experienced and had always had a good rapport with students at her old school. Those lessons were friendly, full of instruction with great feedback from students and parents. These new classes were nothing like she had experienced before, and she likened them to being in a jungle with wild animals. The one-hour lessons that were supposed to be preparing students for their assessment piece were more like a continual argument with mouthy, rude and disrespectful teenagers and she despaired at how little content she was actually getting through. She spent most of the lesson checking the clock that hung on a tilted angle above the board, hoping for the time to pass quicker.

She wasn't game to comment on the clock's crooked placement. In her first week she had spoken out loud, remarking that it was not perfectly straight and she'd have to get the janitor to fix it. Before she even finished speaking, two of the boys stacked a chair on top of a desk and one stood on the chair and righted it for her. The other shook the desk, tilting it back and forth while the boy on the chair balanced like a trapeze artist. She had demanded that they stop. No students were allowed to stand on desks or chair, never mind one of top of the other.

It was typical. Whatever she asked them to do, they did the opposite. Her patience and cheery disposition that she had arrived at her new school with, was wearing thin. The conversation this morning about her day at the races was the longest interaction she'd had with this particular class of year twelves. With some of them already turned eighteen and only less than six months to go, they were counting down the days until they finished, most just going through the necessary steps to get their final certificate.

She'd been told right from the start that this was the low English class, full of behaviour issues and students who just wanted to pass and weren't considering going on to further study.

Casting her eyes around the class she signalled for a couple of the boys to take their hats off, closing her eyes as both threw their hats over their shoulders without a backward glance.

'Piss off you dickhead,' a short rotund boy called Fred called from the back. 'You nearly took my fucking eye out.'

She pulled herself up straight, her eyes narrowing.

'Fred, come here to me. Immediately!'

Fred glared back at her. 'You should say please.'

She held her breath before replying, her words coming out through clenched teeth when she finally replied. 'Please come here and see me, Fred.'

Fred rolled around in his chair before standing up. He cast a look across the class who were now silent, waiting to see what her reaction would be. She waited for him to come to her desk but he stood sullenly behind his chair.

'Can you please stand outside the door and wait for me. I won't have that language in here.'

'What language,' his face was surly, his tone disrespectful.

She kept her voice level, her anger in check. 'Thank you, Fred. Wait outside.'

She sighed with relief as he turned and walked out through the door. Handing out the work sheets as quickly as she could, she ran through the lesson for the day. In between her instructions she asked Matty to turn around and stop talking to the girls in the seats behind him, could Ashton please sit on his chair properly and Aleisha, put the gum she was chewing in the bin. Ben needed to put the can of coke he was drinking away, Vera to stop talking as no-one needs to know about your date last night and all of you, put your phones away.

For a moment there was silence and most of the class were listening. She had spent hours trying to make the lesson for today as interesting as she could and at least the topic of writing resumes and covering letters held some sort of connection to the real world. She'd gained their interest for a short while last week by letting them know what they would be working on would be useful for when they left school. She would ensure the documents were of a high standard and please employers. It was also helpful that she'd remembered to book the laptops out and now each student had one in front of them, ready to work on something that was about them.

It suited them best. No handwriting, no worrying about spelling and they could use the internet and waste time in between if they got bored. Apart from walking around and checking on them individually, there wasn't really any other way she could know what they were doing. It was clear that as soon as her back was turned they were on car sales dot com, or looking at the fishing report or just about anything else they could waste their time on that wasn't blocked by the education department. That wasn't her problem. If the school didn't have the spyware software in place that she'd used in her previous school, there wasn't much she could do.

As her new boss had said, 'Just get them over the line, you know, a pass. That's all most of them need. This time next year they'll be in a trade or working in the mines. They'll earn more than you and me by the time they're twenty. So don't stress over the little things.'

It was an entirely different game compared to St Markel's in Canberra. The boys she had taught there were in the extension English class and could quote the literary classics, analyse poetry and Shakespeare, and write in calligraphy style handwriting with impeccable spelling. They were destined for the top universities, to be lawyers, doctors and even politicians like their parents.

The students she cast her eyes over now did not wear blazers and long trousers, or skirts that came down to the top of long white socks with black polished shoes. They wore crushed uniforms, sports uniforms, mis-matched socks and shoes with the shortest skirts she had ever seen, matched with tight blouses, often the top buttons undone with not a tie or badge to be seen. The girls' hair was not back in neat braids or buns but long and free with a variety of colours and styles. She sighed. It was what it was. She couldn't change everything and no-one else seemed to be worried about it. Her main priority was to keep some sort of order and try and improve on their English before they went out into the big wide world. Now, she thought, next mission, to sort out Fred.

Twenty minutes had passed since she had sent Fred outside and she had to admit she had become side-tracked with getting the rest of the class on task. As she moved around the class, checking on the students' progress she thought carefully about what she would say to him. Even a minute spent outside could allow for further disruptions inside. At the moment the rest of the class were on track, their fingers tapping on the keyboards filling in the structure she had supplied them for their resume. She felt like she was tiptoeing as she made her way to the door, closing it gently behind her, hoping that the rest of the class wouldn't even notice that she was no longer standing over their shoulder. Fred stood just outside the door and she prepared herself for another argument.

He looked straight at her, his messy hair half over his face, his body odour causing her to wriggle her nose. She bit her lip, trying to ignore the strong smell and making a mental note to email the Guidance Officer about having a chat to some of the boys about body hygiene. It wasn't even summer, but this was the tropics.

She smiled at him. It was an awkward age and she knew Fred copped a bit of teasing from the other students. He wasn't part of the 'in' crowd, he was new to the school and she'd often spotted him in the library at lunchtimes, no doubt the air-conditioned room a drawcard compared to the searing heat outside at that time of the day.

To her surprise she received a half-smile back. She ignored the urge to tell him to push his hair back from his face, focussing instead on his words and the fact that he was meeting her gaze. His words were mumbled. 'I'm sorry, Miss. I shouldn't have sworn. I don't want any more detentions after school. It means I miss work.'

It wasn't what she expected and she found it hard to hide her surprise. Perhaps the time that had passed had given him time to think. 'Thank you for your apology. I won't have swearing in the room. If you can assure me it won't happen again I'll let it pass.'

He smiled broadly and she wondered how sincere he was and if letting him off would work. She was supposed to refer him to the office, but she'd already sent so many students in the first few weeks for swearing. 'It won't happen again. Thanks Miss.'

She nodded and smiled back, relieved not to have another argument. 'Where do you work?' she asked.

'I got a job at the mill in the afternoons. I work in the office with the technology side of things. They say if it works out they'll put me on after I finish school. I have to have my senior pass though.'

'You're only just scraping through English. You're going to need a B at least to pass overall. I've seen some of your work. You're a good writer.'

'The last teacher was sh..' , he paused, 'the last teacher didn't really help us. He was hopeless and let us do whatever we wanted. Everyone mucked up, did no work and now everyone has bad grades.'

'That's easy to fix. Just put in the work and you'll pass. It's not a hard course. Just remember once you finish this year, that's school done for the rest of your life. Unless of course you decide later to go on to university.'

Fred laughed. 'I don't think I'll be going to uni.'

She gave him another encouraging smile. 'You can do whatever you want. Uni, work, apprenticeship, it's all up to you. My job is to get you through and why not aim for the As, you're definitely capable enough.'

'Thanks Miss. Everyone always thinks we're stupid because we're in the low class, but really most of us are smart.'

Fred followed her back into the room, sitting down quietly and beginning his work.

* * *

Tess spent the rest of the lesson roaming the room, helping each student with the wording and structure of their resume. The fact that she hadn't reported Fred to the office added a sense of calm to the room and for the first time since she had started she felt like she had achieved a rapport with a student.

Before the lesson ended she reminded the class that her job was to help them, that they all needed to pass and she was there to work with them. What she wanted though was no swearing, no yelling out and for them to be quiet while she was talking. As the bell sounded and they filed out through the door, she breathed a sigh of relief. One class down, four to go.

Her relief was short-lived as the next class attempted to line up outside the classroom. They were her year 9 English class and with the class at maximum capacity of thirty they presented a variety of different learning capabilities, diverse behaviour problems and every other issue she could think of.

Today however, she was ready for them, having spent hours on

Friday night creating a lesson that would keep them busy and quiet. Last week she had nearly walked out on them, questioning if she was really cut out for teaching or if she should admit defeat and quietly make her way back to the well-ordered, civilised private school where she didn't have to break up fights, solve bullying problems or work out how to accommodate all the different learning problems in her class.

As she'd said to Miranda, it wasn't that those problems didn't exist in her old school, it was just that there was someone else to pass the problem onto and support educators who dealt with the trickier kids in the class. Now the problems were all in her face. These kids weren't sneaky or didn't try and hide their problems. They said it like it was and let her know in no uncertain terms what they did and didn't like.

She waited until the pushing and shoving stopped, until they were quiet. 'Right, let's go in.'

3

———

She'd been packing up her books after the last lesson of the day when Delvene, a girl from her senior class, entered the classroom. Looking up, Tess attempted a smile. She was exhausted after the day of teaching and wondering what the young girl might have forgotten. Tess had picked up from day one that Delvene was a ringleader, one of the popular girls who flitted around in her short skirt and tight blouse, trying to look as good as she could while organising the social events for the weekends. Her boyfriend Layton was also in her class and Tess had spoken to them on several occasions, threatening to separate them if they couldn't keep their hands off each other in her classroom.

Now the dark-haired attractive girl spoke in a polite voice, and if Tess didn't know better she might assume that Delvene was trying to speak properly, in a manner that Tess had been drumming into her classes since she took them on.

'Good afternoon Miss Barber. Would you have a moment to talk to me?'

She was suspicious. This was unusual. 'Of course, I do. What would you like to know?'

Delvene pulled her shoulders back and held her head high. 'Fred said you told him you could help him get good grades and pass Year 12. I don't usually talk to him but I sit next to him in Science.'

'I did say that. But it will be up to him to work hard to achieve them.'

The young girl hesitated. 'Layton needs help also. No one in our class has gotten good grades this year. The teacher wasn't very helpful. He wasn't an English teacher. They couldn't get anyone else.'

'It isn't, *gotten*, it's *received* good grades.'

Delvene screwed her face up and put her hand on her hip. 'Well, nobody has received high grades and Layton is smart. He wants to be a policeman, but he needs to pass English.'

'It would be helpful for him to receive a pass. There isn't much use sitting in class for twelve years to receive a fail mark. Why don't you ask Layton to come and see me. Perhaps some extra tutoring or even some more effort from him might help.'

'Trouble is his dad doesn't want him to join the police. He's dead against it.'

'It is a stressful job and it's difficult to get in straight from school. But there are different ways we can help to find the right pathway for him.'

'His mum was a cop. She left.'

'Well, that's not uncommon. Sometimes we are in jobs that we think we'll like but then once we're in the situation we might not like that career at all.'

'No, I mean she left the family.'

'Okay. I see. Perhaps Layton needs to come and see me. I'd love to talk to him. You can come with him if you like.'

Delvene's face lit up. 'Thanks so much Miss. He'd probably come if I did as well.' She turned to go. 'You know everyone reckons you're stuck up, but Fred reckons you're okay and I do too now.'

She ignored the insult of apparently being stuck up, deciding this was as good a time as any to try and develop some camaraderie within the class group. 'I feel as if Fred gets picked on a bit by some of the others. I'm surprised someone like you doesn't stick up for him. Sometimes it only takes one other person to back someone up.'

Delvene sighed. 'I feel sorry for Fred. He's not into what most of the other boys are. He's a loner.'

'I can see that, but everyone is different. You know Delvene, it doesn't take much to be nice to someone. Everyone has feelings and you don't have to be best friends, just a few words now and then can make all the difference.'

'I'm not a nasty person. Do you think I've been mean to him?'

'I didn't say that. I'm just saying to think about it a bit. It's obvious to me when a student is pushed out or feeling isolated. It's difficult being a new student also and he only arrived earlier this year. To me, you seem like a leader who other students look up to.'

Delvene laughed. 'Me? Are you kidding? Why would they do that?'

Tess gave her a smug look. 'You have a strong personality. Make sure you use it correctly and also make sure you and Layton come and see me about English.'

Delvene looked down at her feet, almost as if she wanted to keep talking. She hitched her school bag over her shoulder and turned to walk out. 'Thanks Miss, we'll come and see you after school on Monday.'

'See you then, 'Tess replied.

4

———————

Tom arrived to pick Tess up right on seven. It was one of the things she admired about him. They'd been on a few dates since the races and he was always on time. He was also an immaculate dresser and her heart raced as he leant in and kissed her on the lips, his hand wrapping around her waist as he pulled her in close. She giggled, 'I'm not even out the door yet.'

'Can't keep my hands off you. God, you look gorgeous.' He held at her arm's length, his eyes roaming over her body. She felt the heat rising in her face. It was only a few weeks since they'd met and he'd tried several times to either get her to come back to his place or for him to come back to hers after their outings. So far she'd managed to say no, knowing exactly what he wanted. It was however getting harder to resist him and he'd already told her he didn't want to waste time. He spent so many nights at training and then footy games on the weekend. There weren't that many evenings when it was just the two of them alone together. 'I want to make love to you under the stars,' he'd told her last week as they lay on the beach together. His strong hands had roamed over her body, his touch sending sensations through her that she hadn't experienced in a while.

It was early days though and although he was very good looking, fun to be with and told her he was madly in love with her, she wasn't going to rush in.

Tonight, he was taking her to a special dinner at the football club. Miranda and a few of the others from work were going and she was looking forward to a fun night out. The locals were friendly and welcoming and there was no shortage of social activities to attend. Classes at school had started to get a little easier and she was learning to manage the behaviour problems a bit better. There was no use trying to use the strategies she'd used at Saint Markel's. Now she used a different approach, still with high expectations and consequences, but an added extra effort that allowed her to constantly monitor the students' activities in class and keep them on track.

'A cattle prodder, that's what we need,' one of the older male teachers commented. 'Lazy and a lack of motivation. I tell you what though it's always a different story once they're out of here. Being a small town, you keep track of where most of them end up. There are a lot of opportunities for young ones in the industries up here. We need them to stick around and fill the jobs around here.'

Another teacher added, 'They make good money. Wait until they're coming back to visit you with a family in tow.'

Tess couldn't imagine sticking around in the area long enough to see those results, but she did feel like she was starting to get to know the students. She joined in the conversation. 'They've been hard to crack to start with. Almost like they don't trust me, but once they know I'm keen to help plus I'll listen to their home problems, well I feel like there has been a turning point.'

* * *

As she sat at a long table at the football dinner, she thought about the problems some of the students had shared with her. Music from a live band thumped loudly throughout the room and raucous laughter and chatter were a noisy background to her thoughts. She looked up as a waiter asked if she wanted her drink topped up.

'G'day, Miss. Would you like another glass of wine?'

She looked up to see Layton, the boy in her English class, dressed up in a waiter's outfit holding a wine bottle ready to top up her drink.

It was lovely to see a familiar face and she smiled broadly. 'You look different all dressed up, Layton. Thank you, I will have another one.' She admired how neat he looked, his dark curly hair combed and sitting neatly, unlike the unruly mop it was when he was at school.

He tilted the bottle and slowly filled her glass. 'How come you're sitting by yourself?'

She gazed around the room. 'Sometimes it's nice to just sit and watch everyone. I'm quite happy, thank you.'

He looked over to the dance floor. 'I know you're here with Tom. He's over there, with all the boys.'

Layton sounded annoyed and she made sure her words sounded upbeat. 'He's socialising with his mates. I'm happy here.'

Layton shook his head and she could tell by the look on his face that he thought Tom was not where he should be, but didn't want to speak out of place. 'Do you want me to remind him you're here, sitting by yourself?'

She took a sip of her wine before replying to him. 'It's okay Layton. Look, here's Miss Owens, it's fine, she'll sit with me.'

Layton smiled as Miranda flopped down into a chair beside Tess, holding her glass up for Layton to refill. 'Can't go anywhere here without running into someone from school,' she said. 'The joys of living in a small town.'

* * *

Although the music was pumping and there was flowing wine and food, Tess did not particularly enjoy the night. Tom spent most of the time talking to his mates and when she joined him, although she had contributed to the conversation, she didn't feel like he cared less whether she was there or not.

As the night wore on he became louder and drunker and when she told him she was ready to leave he suggested she catch a taxi home and he'd catch up with her in the morning.

She'd happily grabbed a lift home with Miranda and her partner, thankful to leave the noisy bar and a very drunk Tom. At least her tiny unit was quiet and gave her time and space to herself. She sank into her bed, lying awake for a long time, thinking about home and friends, her family who she was missing. Lifting the corner of the curtain she peered through the window to the beach across the road. The ocean shimmered in the moonlight, the wind pushing through the huge fig trees that grew along the esplanade. Curlews called out, their long cries mournful and eerie. Had she made the right decision moving to such an isolated northern place? The weather was hot, the school life was difficult and Tom, well, tonight he had annoyed her. She didn't need him to sit or be with her continually all night, but he was the one who had asked her to go with him to the dinner. Why had he bothered when he'd hardly spoken to her? Plus, she didn't like being told to make her own way home. The girls at work were friendly and fun to go out with but she hadn't known them that long. They weren't like her friends back home who'd she'd known since primary school. She missed those old friends tonight. It would have been good to have one to talk to, to get their feedback on what they thought of Tom and her new school. She lay back, mulling over the events of the previous night and weeks, before finally falling asleep.

* * *

IN THE MORNING SHE WAS WOKEN BY A BANGING ON THE DOOR. IT WAS Tom and he pressed a large bunch of flowers into her hands as she let him in.

He kissed her on the cheek, his face smooth and a whiff of an enticing aftershave, a pleasant scent so early in the morning. 'Had a bit too much to drink last night. This is to show you how much I care about you. Grab your gear and I'll take you for a spin in the boat. The tide's good and if we go out past the islands there are whales jumping everywhere. Hurry up. I've got the entire day.'

Tom pampered her all day and by the time they came home late in the afternoon she had forgiven him for the night before. That was the trouble, he was charming and seemed to know what to say and how to get around her. In the past she hadn't been so patient or tolerant, but the day out on the water had been fun and romantic. There had been an esky packed full of food and drinks to entice her, the tasty selection waved in front of her while Tom ensured she was well looked after. They'd relaxed on the beach and soaked up the sunshine. With no one in sight they lay on a picnic rug, their legs entangled, their bodies pressed up against each other. Tom's hands were warm and his touch sent her mind and body reeling, his caresses, kisses and words romantic and heartfelt. She was falling for him and as much as she tried to remind herself to go slowly, she knew it was only a matter of time before she asked him to stay the night.

5

———————

Over the next couple of months Tess settled into a routine at work, arriving early in the morning and leaving late in the afternoon. The extra time and work she put in allowed her to keep a firm handle on her classes. The frustration she'd experienced earlier in the year had levelled out and she accepted there was only so much she could do in the limited time she had a class. She'd worked her butt off and was looking forward to the last two weeks of school, before the September holidays. The plan was to do nothing except sleep, eat and read for two weeks. It would give her time to recuperate from the hectic term.

Tom also suggested that they go away for two nights. He had a break in between training and games and it would give them a chance to be together, away from the town. It was the final step in their relationship and she carefully considered his proposal. 'I just want to be with you away from everyone,' he whispered in her ear as they lay together on the lounge. He'd tried hard to be invited to stay the night on several occasions, but she'd held tight to her decision to make him wait. He was persistent though and the more time she spent with him the more she wanted to see him. Kissing up and down her neck he muttered vows of love. 'I adore you babe. You mean the world to me. Don't make me wait any longer.'

She laughed as his hands roamed over her body, her skin on fire where he touched. 'Okay, okay, I'll go away with you.'

He'd smothered her in kisses, excited and happy as he pressed up against her. She'd nearly given in right then and let him stay the night, but the lounge was uncomfortable and her bed was narrow and lumpy. From what he said it would be romantic where they were going and as he'd added, he'd make sure it was a night to remember.

She'd driven to a larger town further north and bought sexy new underwear and a tiny pair of new bikinis that showed off her body. It would be the start of a different stage of their relationship, and she was excited to be throwing herself once again into an ongoing and serious romance.

* * *

THE LAST WEEK OF SCHOOL PASSED SLOWLY AND SHE COUNTED DOWN THE hours until they went away. Tom had booked a secluded cabin on one of the nearby islands, telling her not to bother putting in too many clothes; they would be able to walk around with nothing on if they wanted.

Her skin tingled at the idea of being naked with him and she tried to regain her thoughts and bring them back to the reports that she was methodically entering into the computer. Her senior class had done well and with a lot of encouraging and prodding, including sitting some of them at her desk and prompting them through the entire lessons, they had all passed, with most improving their marks from the previous terms. If they could keep up the work they would gain good marks and finish the year with grades that would look impressive on their reports and resumes.

She looked up as Layton entered the room. Along with Delvene he had achieved A's on his exam last week, the marks a direct result of the many afternoons she had spent with them both after school. They'd jumped up and down and hugged each other when she'd told them their results and she'd tried to remain calm as they both threw their arms around her and included her in their group hug. This kind of behaviour would have been totally unacceptable at her old school and certainly her students would have refrained from such action and been calmer in their responses.

Here at Tranquil Bay High, there was something about the students' spontaneity and genuine thankfulness that made her warm to them, and she found herself becoming protective, wanting the best for each and every one, like a mum with a brood of teenage chickens. Even the ones whose limited conversations were grunts and nods, were starting to have a rapport with her and she marked it as a success when one of them actually said a few words in response to a question. They were after all teenagers and sometimes this was as good as it was going to get. As long as they were respectful and doing their work, she was happy.

She smiled at Layton as he entered the room, his backpack slung over his back, his hat in his hand. It had taken her nearly an entire term to teach the boys to take their hats off before coming into the classroom and she noted that most of them did it now without being asked.

He looked bashful and shuffled his feet as he stood in front of her desk, holding out a box of chocolates in his hand. 'Good afternoon, Miss. I just wanted to give you this.'

She took them from him, sending a warm smile his way.

He ran his hand through his hair, spirally curls springing out wildly across his head. 'Delvene said you'd probably eat chocolate. It's to say thank you for all the extra tutoring that you helped us with. Well, helped me mainly. Delvene's smart, she doesn't need any help.'

'Thank you so much, Layton, and yes I love chocolates. Delvene is smart but you are too. You have great writing and knowledge skills. You can take on any job you decide on. I know you have your heart set on joining the police service, but keep your options open.'

He twisted his mouth, a frown on his face. 'I'm having a hard time with my dad about my choices. He's dead against me being a police-man. All we seem to do is argue. I'm thinking about moving out of home as soon as I can. He's on my case all the time.'

She sighed. 'Parents only ever want the best for their kids. Your dad probably has a good reason for wanting you to look at other options. He'd only be thinking of you.'

'He does have reasons but that's not my problem. Him and I were always close but not anymore. I need to do what I want to do.'

'It is important you do a job that interests you. There's not much use going into something just for the money or because someone else wants you to.'

'Do you like teaching, Miss? I mean it's not easy. Look at the trouble we caused when you first came.'

She laughed. 'You're showing your maturity now. Yes, I do love it. I loved the kids where I used to teach too. They generally come from very wealthy backgrounds and most go into academic or professional jobs. That's not to say they don't have their own problems and things in life to deal with. '

'We must seem like a rough mob compared to them?'

'The students here do come from a variety of different backgrounds. But now that I've been here a while, and, since everyone is being more respectful and behaved, I've grown to like it here also.'

'What do you reckon the difference is between us and them? Are we really that different?'

'Not at all. In the end you're all teenagers, trying to work out where you fit in, what you're going to do after school and wrestling with parents, girlfriends, boyfriends and everything else that's out there that a young adult life throws at you.'

He stood and thought for a while. 'We are all the same, hey. You think if you had a lot of money life would be easier but maybe those kids have more demands, expectations on them from their parents.'

'That's often the case. I'm telling you though, the main thing is that you're happy. Stay out of trouble and have confidence in yourself.'

'Thanks Miss, I feel better than when I walked in here. Dad's really bringing me down. I need to be confident in my choices.'

He picked up the bag that he'd put down on the floor. 'Have a good holiday, Miss.' He turned to walk away.

'I will. I'm actually going away for a few days, so I'm looking forward to that.'

Layton turned around. 'Are you going away with someone?'

She stood up to see him out. 'I am. I'm going with my boyfriend Tom. It will be nice to go somewhere I haven't been before. I'm not supposed to tell anyone.' She laughed, 'So don't repeat it because he asked me not to mention it to anyone. I think he wants to get away and just disappear for a while.'

Layton stared hard at her. He had piercing blue eyes and they narrowed before he looked down at his feet. She waited for him to leave but he stood still.

Eventually he looked up. 'It might be out of place for me to say this. You know with you being a teacher and all.'

'Well, if it's something you shouldn't say, don't say it. See you after the holidays.'

Layton stood still.

'Thank you for the chocolates,' she repeated, making sure she was standing in the open doorway to the room next to her. There were dividers between the classrooms which were open and she could see the teacher in the next room organising her posters on the wall. Layton was a good kid but it had been drummed into her to ensure she was never in a classroom with a student alone. It was just common practice to not put yourself in that position. Layton also looked at the teacher next door, giving her a quick wave when she looked back. He turned back to Tess as the teacher returned to what she was doing.

'Look, Miss, this is not something I'd normally do. But you've been really good to me and Delvene and I don't think I would have lasted this term if it wasn't for you.'

'That's fine. You don't have to thank me. The chocolates say it all. Now off you go and enjoy the holidays.'

'I think you need to know something. About Tom that is.'

She went to speak but the look on Layton's face changed her mind. He was wanting to tell her something. He'd turned red and kept looking around making sure no one else was in earshot.

'What?' her voice came out squeaky.

'His old girlfriend lives across the road from me. He's there a lot.'

She laughed. 'Oh, that's fine. I'm sure they've kept in contact. They went out for a long time before they broke up.'

Layton scowled, his voice low and angry. 'I didn't want to say anything before, but Tom's a liar if he's telling you they're just friends. He stays there probably four nights of the week. Comes there late, I'd say after training. She lives straight across the road. He parks his car at the back of the house where no one can see it and he doesn't leave until the morning. It's a known fact around town that he's back with her.'

It was a long speech and he spoke slowly, his gaze never leaving Tess's face. 'I'm sorry Miss, but you can ask Delvene. We thought you must have broken up in the last couple of weeks.'

Tess was speechless and she looked everywhere except at Layton.

Layton looked at her one more time, his words mumbled. 'I'm sorry. I have to go.' He turned and walked down the stairs, turning to give her a quick wave before disappearing down the path.

6

Tess slammed her books into her bag, her mind reeling, her chest heaving with anger. Tom had played her for a fool. Romancing, dining and wining her while all the time he'd been seeing his ex-girlfriend. She believed what Layton had told her, his words hitting her with a thud. Tom had sounded different over the phone when she'd talked to him the last couple of weeks and there had been a number of occasions when he hadn't returned her message or calls. She never tried to contact him when he was at training or there was a game on, but she'd sometimes wondered why he hadn't responded to her calls at night.

He'd also been making up excuses why he didn't want to call over to see her after training, like he had in earlier weeks. She should have been onto it. She'd let him draw her in emotionally, trusting they were in a relationship and he wouldn't be seeing anyone else. Who did that? Why do it? She thought long and hard. He had made sure of an exciting build-up to escaping to the island getaway. Had that been his plan all along. Thank God she hadn't given in to his pleas and slept with him.

Now she needed to work out what steps to take next. She shoved student papers into her bag before slamming the windows shut and pushing chairs in under desks. Rage filled her and she swore out loud. Why couldn't students pick up their own rubbish, straighten their desks or put their chairs up. What was the problem with them? Was all her work trying to turn them into responsible, organised adults a waste of time? Had all the time she'd spent here been for nothing? Why waste months of her life on students who didn't care about anything except themselves? What had been the point of wasting not only her time, but demoralising herself over a man who was seeing someone else?

She shoved some books that had been left on students' desks into a pile on the back shelf. She wasn't even going to neaten it. Why couldn't one of them have done that? Shoving the wiper over the board she paused for a moment to read the messages some of them had left for her, wishing her a lovely holiday. Ha, she thought. As if they meant it. They didn't care about anyone except themselves. They were all just like Tom.

She picked up another stack of books and papers and slammed them down on a table, kicking a chair out of the way as she made her way back to her desk. She knew she needed to calm down and think straight. Being angry like this was out of character for her. A note that one of the girls had left for her, wished her a happy holiday and a card from another student thanked her for everything she'd done during the term. She cast her eyes over it. *'I wouldn't have made it through without you Miss. Thank you.'*

She reminded herself it wasn't anyone else's fault. Certainly not her students. The fault was hers. The trouble was, Tom had made a complete fool out of her. If Layton and Delvene knew what was going on, it meant the entire town probably did too. She glanced down at her phone, the ringing distracting her from her fury. Picking it up she tried to sound calm. It was the office and it was unusual for them to ring this late in the day. Most teachers would have left already, keen to start their holidays.

Hannah, the office girl sounded rushed. 'Are you still at school?'

She tried to keep her voice even. 'Yes, I'm just about to leave.'

'There's a parent at the office. He wanted to see if he could have a quick chat with you. He's worried about his son and doesn't want to wait until after the holidays to talk. He said he wouldn't keep you long.'

'Oh, sure,' she said, curious because the entire time she had been at the school, no-one had bothered to contact her with any concerns and the dozen or so parent requests she'd put in for interviews never replied.

'I'll come straight up.'

'Thanks so much,' Hannah said. 'I'll see you in a minute.' She hung up, leaving Tess standing with her phone held to her ear. She threw it in her bag. It would have been good if Hannah had told her whose parent it was or what it was about. She hadn't given her a chance to ask. No doubt Hannah was keen to get down to the pub, to celebrate the end of another term.

Tess walked quickly to the office, the grounds empty apart from a few of the cleaners who gave her a friendly wave. She was still furious about the situation with Tom and she tried to calm her angry thoughts and keep her mind focussed until the conversation with the parent was done. She'd deal with what she was going to say to Tom afterwards.

* * *

Hannah was waiting for her at the front desk. 'He's down in one of the meeting rooms. Can you make it a quick chat because I can't go until you both leave. I'm the only one left, the others will already be at the pub.'

Tess was in no mood to be amicable. 'It will depend on what the parents want to know. I can't rush them out. You'll have to just wait until I'm finished.'

Hannah glowered at her. 'Bloody rude, requesting to speak to you on the last afternoon. Didn't even make an appointment.'

'It's fine Hannah. I'm sure they wouldn't have asked unless it was important. Now, you didn't tell me, who is the parent?'

'Layton's father. Layton Barton. He's in your Year 12 English class.'

Tess refrained from rolling her eyes. 'I know who Layton is. Thank you.' With that she strode down the hallway, looking for the right room to enter. In the first room she came to she saw a man seated at the table, his back to her. He turned as she entered, and she was shocked to see it was Joel, the man she had met at the races—the day she drank too much champagne.

He stood, his cap in hand, a smile across his face.

'Hi Joel, sorry I'm looking for a parent of one of my student's. Apologies I've come into the wrong room.' She went to walk out but stopped suddenly as he spoke.

'That's me. I'm Layton's father.'

She blinked a few times before turning around. Joel put his hand out and she shook it. 'He said he had a lady teacher who was new to the school. He's never mentioned your name but I figured that it might be you.'

She sat down behind a desk in front of him, realising that she didn't have any of Layton's work with her or even a report to show. Suddenly she felt exhausted. The term had been long, the work hectic and now to top it all off, the predicament of being made a fool of by Tom.

'I didn't realise you were his dad. You don't seem old enough to have a son that age.' A sudden realisation came over her and her body tensed. Joel had come to tell her about Tom. Layton said they lived across the road from his ex-girlfriend. Was it common knowledge throughout the town that he was taking out two girls? They would all presume he was sleeping with both of them.

Joel leant back in his chair, his blue eyes gazing straight at her, his dark curly hair tousled and much like Layton's, needing a good cut. Of course, she thought to herself, they were similar. The same handsome features, a strong stocky build and that distinctive mop of dark curly hair and blue eyes. He smiled at her and she remembered how friendly he was. She also remembered that he had observed her at an unpleasant moment. For goodness sake, what if he'd repeated the toilet paper story to Layton. She felt her face turn red.

Sitting upright she tried to gain her composure. 'I think I may have an inkling about why you want to see me.' She tried to keep her voice even. 'Layton stayed back this afternoon to talk to me.' Fatigue pressed down on her body and suddenly it felt like everything in her world was crashing down. Her words were barely audible. 'He told me about Tom.' Joel's eyes widened. 'Layton said you live across the road from his ex-girlfriend and that he's been staying there quite a lot. Thank you for coming to let me know. I'll admit it was a shock to me but I'm grateful that your son was decent and mature enough to politely give me the facts. No doubt everyone in the town would be aware of it. That is, everyone except me.'

Joel played with the cap in his hand. He leant over the desk, resting his hands on the surface. 'I'm sorry to hear that. Well, that you had to find out from someone else. To tell you the truth I didn't realise you were still seeing Tom.'

'Was Layton right? Is that what's been happening. Please tell me.' She bit her lip, keeping her emotions in check. She was tired and defeated, but there was no way she was going to spill any tears over the relationship.

'They live right across the road from us.'

She snapped, annoyed with herself, with Tom and with everyone in this town who had let her be sucked in by an obvious player. 'I know that!'

'Look, don't take it out on me. I've come to talk to you about Layton. But if you're asking me for honesty, well, yes, Tom has been visiting across the road for a couple of weeks. We just assumed that he was no longer with you and the old relationship was back on. It's usual standard for Tom. I'm surprised...' he stopped talking as she held her hand up to stop him from saying anything further.

'Thank you. That's all I need to know and I'm even more mortified that I assumed that's why you were here to talk to me.' She straightened her shoulders and tried to look as professional as she could, even though she could feel her face burning. Couldn't she get anything right? Why had she jumped to that conclusion? Think straight, she reprimanded herself. She used her most professional voice. 'Right, let's move onto what you want to know.'

'I'm sorry to see you upset. Don't let it get to you. No one is probably aware that you were still going out with him. They are possibly like we were and assumed you had moved on.'

'It's only two weeks ago that I went to a football function with him. And...', she scowled, her voice angry, 'he's supposed to take me away for a couple of days. We were going for the weekend.' She straightened up in her chair, pushing her hair back behind her ears. Professional, keep it professional, she reminded herself. At least she could try and recoup the last of the meeting. Save some face and get on with the reason why he was here. 'Anyway, that's my problem. I'd rather not discuss that anymore. What is it about Layton that you'd like to talk about?'

She'd put her teacher voice and attitude back on, pushing the other matter to the back of her mind as much as she could. When Hannah appeared in the doorway, pointing to her watch, Tess was curt and definite in her response. 'You'll have to wait Hannah. Mr Barton and I are discussing Layton's education. I'm not going to rush this.'

* * *

ONCE THEY STARTED TALKING IT WAS OBVIOUS TO TESS THAT JOEL NEEDED to offload a variety of doubts and worries. He was divorced and had been a single dad since Layton was ten years old. Layton was his only child. It was just the two of them and they'd always been close. The last six months, however, Layton had turned into a different person and his father had lost the open communication they'd always had. His son had become surly, moody and spent a lot of afternoons and nights away from home. He told Joel that he was at Delvene's house, but Joel didn't believe it and was concerned that his son was out drinking. His other big concern was that he might be taking drugs. Joel's mood swings were unpredictable and he wouldn't listen to anything his father said. He'd also lost the ability to have conversations with his father and resorted to mainly grunts and one syllable replies. Joel was at his wit's end what to do with him and when he'd come up to pay a bill at the school, decided to see if he could talk to one of his teachers.

Tess had been the only one left, and he appreciated her time and the fact she'd agreed to talk to him at such short notice.

Once they started talking Tess found it easy to discuss the changes in Layton over the last term. Her observations were the opposite of Joel's and he sat back in his chair, listening intently as she explained how Layton and Delvene attended tutoring most afternoons. His grades had improved, his attitude was more mature and respectful than a few months ago and she appreciated his direct, no-nonsense approach to everything at school. She'd watched him playing handball with some of the younger students last week and admired his role modelling and the way the younger kids looked up to him. In her eyes he was a polite, conscientious young man who seemed to have a direction in life.

'I've also observed him making sure a student who was a bit on the outer and being bullied by some of the other boys, was protected and included. Just a few words here and there, but small efforts that have made a lot of difference.'

Joel listened carefully, some of the stress easing from his face as he took in all the positives that Tess offered. 'He was always kind as a kid. Looking after others and making sure no-one got left out. He has a sense of righteousness and justice. I'm pleased to hear that he might still go by those ethics.'

'From what I see here he definitely does. I hope that my observations have put your mind at ease a little. Of course, I have no idea what he does after he leaves here, but from picking up on their conversations I think that he spends most of his time with Delvene. She's a strong character but with good morals and I would be very surprised if she was involved in drug taking or anything too risky. I mean none of them are angels, but to me, and going from what I see and hear, I'd say they are normal teenagers doing the regular things that teenagers do. I don't see anything that would lead me to believe they are doing drugs or involved in anything illegal.'

Joel leaned forward over the desk. 'I guess being a teacher you would have seen it all before.'

She sighed. 'Unfortunately, I have. The students at the last school I taught at came from a high socio-economic area but there were some who were involved in hard drugs. Drug addiction and mental health issues don't discriminate, they have the ability to affect kids from every walk of life.'

He looked straight at her and she could feel his concerns, the angst that came with bringing up kids. His voice was deep and she watched him as he shuffled in his seat, his mannerisms and voice so similar to Layton's. 'You have no idea how much your words and insights into my son's school life have helped. Once these kids get to high school you lose touch with what's going on. At primary school you're there for the parent interviews, the sports days and chatting to their teacher when you pick them up. I guess I've always stayed away from the high school. I mean they have to work things out for themselves and I've always encouraged Layton to speak up and become independent.'

'You've done a good job. He is independent and like I said, he's a natural leader. I understand your tactics. We also try and make them think for themselves and not lean on us too much.' She glanced at the clock at the wall. 'I hope that this has helped ease some of your concerns.'

'It has. It's like a weight has lifted from my shoulders. I can't thank you enough. The kids are lucky to have you as their teacher. I hope you're going to stick around for a while. Sometimes this school has been like a revolving door with teachers. They come, they transfer out, they get promoted. The word is they come here to get the country points and then leave for better and higher positions.'

'I must admit, I'm not planning on staying long term.' She hesitated, looking for the right words without appearing to be just the same as the teachers he had just described. 'I only came for a short stint. It's not that I'm trying to climb the ladder, although my aim is for higher positions.'

He gave her a wry smile. 'Ah, so it is only a steppingstone?'

'Well not exactly but it was meant to fill in a gap and to give me a change of scenery. I think perhaps teachers have left previously because it is a tough school. It was also very difficult for me at the start, but now…' She paused thinking hard about how she really felt about the school now that she'd got through this last term. 'Now I'm getting close to the kids. I want to make a difference. That's why I chose this job.'

Joel stood up. 'It's a shame you're not going to stick around. Thanks for this meeting, you have no idea how much it's helped to hear that he is going okay. I don't really have anyone to talk to about this sort of stuff.'

'Layton's a great kid. I believe he has a wonderful future in front of him.'

Joel went to reply but Hannah appeared at the door again, tapping her fingers on the wall as she asked how much longer they would be. They laughed and cut the conversation where it stood. Tess probably hadn't solved everything for Joel, but she had put his mind at rest a little and he said he'd appreciate having another meeting once school resumed after the holidays. They'd only touched on the fact that Layton wanted to go into the police service and she'd recognised the immediate bristling at the mention. That topic would wait for another day. For now, it was the end of the day, the end of the term and her mind hopped back to the present, the end of another relationship.

7

The problem of what she was going to say to Tom was solved when he rang that afternoon. She hadn't long been home, her bags of books and schoolwork piled on the kitchen table, her computer bag and more books stacked on the floor where she had thrown them down. She reclined on the lounge, stretching her legs out and relishing being in a room that wasn't a classroom. She'd changed into a pair of old denim shorts and t-shirt and in her hand was a large cold glass of wine. It was the second one. The first one went down without hitting the sides and she reminded herself to go slow. She wasn't going to drown her sorrows or waste her time commiserating on a piece of shit like Tom.

She clicked the answer button, his deep voice causing a tightening in her chest. 'Hey babe. You're on holidays.'

'I am,' she answered, trying to keep her voice even.

'I just thought I'd ring and let you know I'll pick you up early in the morning. About six?'

'Really?' There was so much she wanted to say, but the words stuck in her throat.

'Yeah. Does that suit. I'll have to be back early on Monday. At least that will give us two nights together.'

Silence echoed through the phone.

'Are you still there?' he asked. 'I can't hear you.'

'Yep, I'm still here.'

'What's up. You don't sound happy. I thought you'd be pleased the term is finished. Plus, you're going away with me.' He made a rumbling noise, a growling sound that he would have thought of as a sexy overture. She closed her eyes. How had she been so stupid. He continued to talk. 'I can't wait to be with you. We may not leave the bed all weekend. I'm dying to touch you, everywhere.'

She so badly wanted to hang up on him, but she forced herself to stay on the phone, her voice sweet when she replied, 'Is there anything you need to tell me before we go away tomorrow?'

'What do you mean? Like what food or drink to take. I told you I'll bring it all. I've got lots of bubbles for you.'

It must have seemed so easy for him, or that she was easy, Tess thought, as she took a deep breath before continuing. 'I think there is something we might need to talk about before you start planning any more for this little holiday.'

'Geez, Tess. I've got to go to training in a minute. Can't it wait until tomorrow.'

She'd had enough. 'Are you still seeing your ex-girlfriend?'

There was a gap of silence before he replied. 'What do ya mean?'

'What I said. Are you in a relationship with your old girlfriend?'

'Who said that?'

'It doesn't matter who said it. I want the truth.'

'Sometimes I still see her. That's not got anything to do with you, or us though.'

'Really, you don't think so? Answer me straight. I just want a yes or no and don't give me any of your bullshit. Are you seeing her, in a relationship, sleeping with her?'

She waited but there was no reply. Her words came out loud, louder than what she wanted. 'How did you think I wouldn't find out in such a small town.'

His voice was wheedling, his words jumbled as he replied. 'Look, Tess, babe, Tess. I might have weakened a couple, just a couple of times. We went out for ages, a long time. But you're who I really want.

I promise I won't see her again. Let's just have the weekend together and sort it out then. I love you babe.'

'So, is that a yes? Your answer to my question?'

'Like I said, it was only a couple of times and that's in the past now. You mean everything to me. I promise I won't slip up again. C'mon I've paid for a beautiful, secluded cabin on a remote island. I've spent heaps just to spend some time with you. I won't make a mistake again. It's you I want and who I really care about.'

Tess left the silence hang in the air for a while.

'Are you there, babe, are you thinking about what I've said, because you know we're great together.'

Did he seriously think she would give his words any consideration? She spoke slowly. 'No, you won't make a mistake with me because I don't want to see you again. Enjoy your weekend. I'm finished. Goodbye!'

She hung up and turned her phone off.

Gripping her glass in her hand she stood up, pacing up and down inside the unit. She wanted to throw the glass against the brick wall, smash it into a thousand tiny pieces. What a bastard he was. How long would he have continued seeing both her and his ex. If it wasn't for Layton she would have spent the weekend with him, slept with him, been sucked in by his promises of love and loyalty and been the idiot everyone around town talked about. No more men. That was it. She'd made an oath to herself before she arrived in Tranquil Bay to not become involved with anyone the entire time she lived up here. Why had she slipped up? All men were the same. No more. Single life suited her fine. She could concentrate on her classes and she had plenty of female friends to go out with. Besides she enjoyed time by herself and she was only staying in the town for a short while. How had she been so gullible. The tropical heat must be getting to her.

* * *

SURPRISINGLY TESS SLEPT WELL THAT NIGHT. WHEN SHE KICKED BACK THE covers and jumped out of bed in the morning she was re-invigorated and felt like she could take on the world. She didn't need a man in her life, particularly a burly, muscle-bound one who couldn't even pronounce his words correctly. She thought about getting back to a purposeful routine so she could enjoy the two weeks of holidays by herself; leisurely walks, reading, relaxing, and sitting for as long as she wanted on a sunchair on the beach. It was good to be in control again and not worry about anyone else. There was a lot to be said for being single.

The sun filtered in through the window and she watched the seagulls in the park opposite, fighting over scraps of food that someone had thrown to them. A clear sky stretched above the horizon and she closed her eyes, a salty breeze cooling her face. She questioned herself about the fact that she wasn't upset. She was annoyed that she'd been taken for a fool, but not being with Tom anymore didn't bother her in the least. Thinking about it objectively, she realised she hadn't been invested, she'd held back, not just physically, but emotionally. She was thankful the relationship hadn't developed and grateful to Layton for bravely telling her the truth. It was a genuine act of kindness. It had been the right thing to do and she was proud of him, despite the initial shock and embarrassment. The start of her holidays, while not what she'd planned, would be the start of a new attitude. She drank the last of her cup of tea, standing up and stretching her arms high in the air. The next two weeks would be her own.

* * *

WHEN SHE'D GONE FOR A WALK IN THE AFTERNOON THERE WAS A SPRING IN her step and a smile on her face. She waved back to a group of teenagers, all of them from school. A few of them were students who had been surly and rude to her over the term and she hoped they didn't yell out something inappropriate and spoil her walk. They'd spread out picnic blankets under the sprawling fig trees that lined the foreshore, their laughter and chatter drifting across the beach where she walked. A couple of them raced towards her, boisterously greeting her and asking if she'd like to join them. 'We're about to have a game of beach volleyball. We've got a net up. Join us,' said Evelyn, a pretty red-haired girl who had given Tess a torturous time when she'd first arrived.

'It's nice to see you, Evelyn. I hope you're enjoying the holidays?'

'We are Miss. Fred, Charles and Jacob are all over there. C'mon and play volleyball with us.'

She was taken aback at the genuine offer. 'Thank you. That's lovely of you to ask me. I'm off for a walk though. Too much sitting and eating. I need to regain some of my fitness.'

'Miss, you always look good. Join in if we're here when you come back.'

A tall, boy whose name was Richard sprinted up behind Evelyn. Richard was one of the biggest troublemakers in her senior English class and she had come close to tears a few times when he had called out what he considered funny comments and sent the entire class into chaos. She eyed him warily, remembering how hard it had been to reign the class back in after one of his outbursts.

Now he held his hand out towards her. 'Hey Miss Barber. I bet you're glad you're on holidays and away from school. I don't know how you put up with us.'

She shook his hand. 'It is good to be on holidays, thank you Richard.'

'Come and play volleyball with us,' he added. 'We're a different mob out of school.'

She raised her eyebrows. 'Really? I'm not convinced.'

He laughed loudly and jumped around on the sand, making jabbing punches with his fists in the air. 'We can't let off steam at school. It's like being cooped up in a jail. I just can't sit still for that long.'

She allowed herself a small laugh. It was hard to stay angry and she appreciated that both students bothered to come and talk to her.

'It's nice to see you all out together and being active.'

'Come and join us Miss,' Evelyn said.

Tess's earlier suspicions disappeared. Evelyn's words were sincere. She smiled and held her hat tightly, the wind threatening to tear it away. 'Thank you. It's lovely of you to ask. I'm set on walking though, so I'll give it a miss this time. Enjoy your holidays.'

She watched them as they ran back to the others, turning every so often to wave to her. Richard did a couple of somersault flips and then jumped in the air, waving boisterously at her. 'Have a good walk, Miss,' he yelled out. She waved back and continued walking, looking back at the group a couple of times.

It was refreshing to see them all jumping around and playing volleyball instead of complaining about sitting properly on a school chair or writing in a style that made sense and could be deciphered. They looked so much happier. A couple of them waved at her and she waved again, enjoying the feeling of being a part of a small community. A sense of excitement washed over her as she looked along the golden stretch of beach in front of her, empty apart from a couple walking hand in hand and two men fishing, their long rods poking out across the tiny waves that lapped at the beach.

Further out, diamonds sparkled across the top of the ocean. Seagulls squawked and chased each other, a flock of them diving in and out of the water. Out further, small islands dotted the horizon, the blue of the sky stretching out beyond them, its vastness large and bright compared to the often dull, grey skies of Canberra this time of the year.

The water's edge was inviting and she felt like a kid as she dipped her toes in the clear water, jumping over small waves that lapped languidly on the shoreline. The granules of sand were pleasantly rough beneath her feet and she looked upwards at the seagulls that dived in and out of the water. It really was paradise and there was no way that Tom and his infidelity was going to spoil her day or the weeks ahead. Thank goodness she had found out at the start of the holidays and not at the end.

8

———————

Tonight, she was going to celebrate the beginning of the holidays and splurge on dinner by herself at one of the local cafes. She twirled in front of the mirror, happy with the way she looked. Her legs and arms were nicely tanned and her flowing knee-length dress and strappy sandals were perfect for the warm weather. The casual outfit and flat shoes were a welcome attire after living in a city and she appreciated the fact there was no need to wear make-up. At school she always wore her hair up but on holidays she let it down, long and shiny after the touch of the sun and a wash in soft tank water.

She'd chosen the café because she knew she'd be safe from running into Tom or anyone else in that group. It was a little bit out of town and not one of the regular haunts of locals. The thought of Tom left hanging on the phone yesterday caused her to briefly feel angry, but she spoke harshly to herself. *Get on with it. Don't waste any more time on him.*

The café only had a few customers dining in and she requested a table tucked away in the corner. Those who were already seated looked like tourists and so far, including the staff, she had not seen anyone she knew. Perfect, it had been a good decision to come to somewhere a bit out of town. Her mouth watered as she looked over the menu and she didn't look up as the waitress ushered another guest over to a table not far from where she sat. Perusing the wine list she concentrated on what she wanted to drink. She'd driven, so one drink would be the limit. A quiet groan escaped her lips when someone said her name. Was there nowhere to go in this town where she could be alone?

The voice was familiar and she turned around to see Joel staring down at her from where he was seated at a small table near her. 'Hi, Tess. Second time I've seen you this week.'

'Oh, hello. Nice to see you.' She put her head down and continued to study the menu. She had been a bit short with her greeting but tonight she wanted to be alone with her thoughts. That would be her luck though. There was probably a whole truckload of other locals who would drift in and sit at the table with Joel, right next to her. No doubt they'd all know what had happened with Tom. She gritted her teeth, determined not to let anything ruin her night.

The waitress chatted to Joel and she blocked out their conversation, focussing on what she wanted to order. A male waiter appeared beside her. 'Hey Miss. How good is it to be on holidays?'

Her heart sunk as she looked up. Timothy was in her English class and was often coarse, surly and loud, calling out when he wasn't supposed to and ignoring her instructions throughout the lessons. She'd had to speak to him on several occasions about his language and lack of interest in school. If only he'd concentrate on his schoolwork. Another wasted talent. The only thing he was interested in was sport and the female students; he was a popular personality. She looked at him now, dressed neatly, standing tall and talking like he was in charge of the entire place. He was a stocky boy with a rugged face and she knew he came from a farm further out behind the hills.

She sighed. 'Yes, thanks Timothy. I didn't know you worked here.'

He smiled at her. Unusual she thought. The entire time she'd taught him she couldn't ever remember him smiling. 'Yep, me and Millie. Well as you've taught us, I should say, Millie and I.'

She couldn't help but laugh. 'So, you have listened to me this year.'

His face crinkled up in an even bigger grin. 'Of course, Miss. We love you. You're the best English teacher we've ever had.'

Her eyebrows raised high on her forehead and she blinked several times before she spoke. 'I'm in shock. That's not always the impression I get.'

'Yeah, it's true. Here, ask Millie. We drive in together. She lives out where I do, so they give us the same shifts.'

Millie sauntered over. 'Hi Miss. Fancy seeing you here. None of the teachers from school usually come here. They go to the Regatta in town on a Saturday night. You could always eat here and then go and join them. They're always there until late.'

'Thank you, Millie. I'm quite happy to be here by myself. It's lovely to see you both out of school. Can you take my order?'

* * *

MILLIE AND TIMOTHY STAYED AND CHATTED UNTIL THE CHEF CALLED OUT from the back of the café. Timothy patted her on the shoulder and Millie gave her a little hug before whispering in her ear. 'I'm glad you pissed that arsehole, Tom, off. You deserve someone better than that.'

Tess looked at her in surprise. 'News travels fast in a small place. Thank you for your concerns.'

She watched the two of them as they collected plates and glasses from other tables. They were so close to finishing school, on the cusp of adult life. It would be interesting to know what they ended up doing. There were still students who she hadn't become close enough to know their background stories, particularly what they did outside of school or where they worked. At school Timothy never opened up to her about too much, although like many of the others he had softened over the last few weeks and she'd managed to get him a pass for his last assignment. As she watched him serving customers tonight, she was proud of the way he spoke and interacted with adults, vastly different to the side of him that she often witnessed at school. Seeing him in a different environment was refreshing and perhaps he would find his pathway once he left school.

She watched Millie with interest. At school Millie was often roughly dressed. Her uniform was never ironed, her hem always loose and Tess continually supplied her with safety pins, paper and pens throughout the term. She'd also hemmed Millie's skirt for her and brought in a bag of clothes that she no longer needed. Millie was much the same size and had been surprised at the offer. 'I have plenty of clothes. Why are you giving them to me?' Her face was fixed in a scowl and nothing Tess offered or provided seemed to win Millie over. Tess knew from the personal information she had access to, that Millie's home life was somewhat difficult. Her mum had left years ago, and her father was attempting to bring up the family alone. Although Millie had older siblings, they had left home a few years ago and now as the eldest it appeared that she was also responsible for younger brothers and sisters who were also at the high school.

Tess had tried to contact Millie's father a few times regarding her absences, attitude and grades. She'd managed to have a quick conversation with him and he sounded supportive and understood her concerns. From talking to him Tess could tell that he was a gentle caring man who was trying to do his best, but work and looking after younger kids was full-time. He worried that Millie, being thrown into a carer role, had missed out on his attention and also had taken on extra adult responsibilities to help him out. 'I try to take the burden off her with the younger ones, but we've got no other family and often she's the only one I can turn to. She's a good kid and she works hard and helps me out with money. It's not easy though.'

Tess was sympathetic to the dad's problems and tried to talk to Millie to see if there was anything else she could do to help. 'Don't try and pry into my family.' Millie was defensive, her eyes glaring and face angry when Tess talked to her after class one day. 'And what did you ring my dad for. He's got enough to worry about. Now he's asking a heap of questions. Just leave us alone. I'm fine.'

The conversation twirled in her mind. Tonight, Millie was neat, her hair back in a high ponytail, a black skirt and pressed collared green shirt sitting nicely on her neat figure. She walked confidently, the tray held high as she waited on the tables, smiling and chatting to the customers as she went. Tess found it interesting to see the changes in her students when they weren't at school. They were completely different, both in how they looked and how they acted.

Her eyes wandered around the room, stopping when she came to where Joel sat, sprawled back in his chair, a beer in his hand as he gazed out the window. He must have felt her eyes on him and he turned around, looking directly at her.

'You'll never find anywhere to go around here where someone doesn't know you. You're a local now,' he said.

She smiled. 'They're good kids. All of them. I don't mind chatting to them.'

'It's a tricky age. I remember it myself. Thinking I knew exactly what I wanted to do, but really another path might have been better.'

'It's true. I was the same myself. I guess you have to try different jobs to work out what you really want in life.'

They chatted for a while across the space between them. Mille interrupted them as she placed a cocktail in front of Tess. 'There you go, Miss.' Millie looked from Tess to Joel and back again. 'Miss, this is Joel, Layton's dad. You know Layton in our class.'

'Thanks Millie. Yes, Joel and I know each other.'

There was an awkward silence as Millie left to attend to another customer. 'Are you waiting for someone to join you?' Tess asked.

Joel sat up straighter, turning his glass in his hand. 'No, I came here for probably the same reason you did. To not run into anyone else.'

'Oh sorry. I didn't mean to intrude.' She frowned, feeling that she had interrupted his quiet time.

'You're not intruding. I didn't mean you. Just the usual crowd. I need a bit of a break from them.'

'They're all lovely but I'm a bit the same. I'm a bit older than most of them, so the late nights and drinking don't really hold a great attraction for me anymore.'

He laughed and took a sip from his drink. 'I know exactly what you mean. Half the time I tag along for a bit of company and then to drive some of them home. If you think you're older, how do you think I feel.'

How old are you? You seem young to have a son Layton's age?'

He swivelled in his chair. 'Thank you. I was only twenty-two when he was born. I turned forty this year.

They continued to chat, the conversation flowing.

Tess leant back in her chair, choosing her words carefully. 'You can say no. But do you want to join me. It's silly that we're talking across the tables.'

Joel's face lit up and he nodded. 'That would be great. I was going to suggest it myself but figured you wanted to eat alone.'

He got up and came and sat opposite her. 'You know the entire town will know we've dined together before we've even left the place.'

9

The conversation continued long after the meal was finished and the table was cleared. Joel was curious about her life before she came to Tranquil Bay and she enjoyed reminiscing about the years in Canberra and teaching at St Markel's. 'You sound like you miss it,' he said, leaning back in his chair, his legs stretched out in front of him. Timothy placed another beer on the table. 'That will put me over the limit', Joel said.

'I can give you a lift home if you want. Millie and I go right past your place,' Timothy offered.

'Thank you. I might take you up on that. I'll pick my car up in the morning.'

Tess spoke up. 'I can drop you home if you like. Layton told me once that you live down past the showgrounds.'

His eyes crinkled in the corners as he grinned at her. 'Thank you. That would be great and save me waiting for these two. It's not worth the risk of driving myself. I've been here a while, but I'd be over the limit.'

Timothy finished clearing their table. 'We're shutting up soon. I don't want to rush either of you but you can sit outside if you like, to finish your drink. Just leave your glasses on the table when you're finished. Here's your coffee, Miss.'

* * *

A FULL MOON ROSE OVER THE TOP OF THE COCONUT TREES THAT LINED THE street. Beyond that the surface of the ocean shimmered golden, a balmy breeze filtering through the trees, cooling the night air. It was quiet out the front of the café, the other diners had left, those who were out for a big night jammed into the pubs and bar in town.

'Thank you for such a lovely night,' Tess said, peering over the top of her coffee cup at Joel.

He smiled. 'It's funny how things work out. You were supposed to be away on holidays and I thought I'd be having dinner with Layton tonight at home.'

'You have to remember what we talked about over dinner. He's eighteen, he has to make his own decisions and learn by his mistakes.' Joel looked up as Timothy and Millie walked out of the café. They flicked the lights off behind them and locked the front door of the cafe. 'Have a good night, 'Timothy said, 'and make sure to blow that candle out before you leave.'

Tess watched the two of them as they walked towards Timothy's green car. They held hands, laughing and talking, Millie squealing as a bat flew low above her head. They waved as they drove out of the car park and she thought what a nice young couple they made.

'They're good kids,' Joel said. 'They all work hard. Talking to you has reminded me what it's like to be that age. I'd forgotten. For months I've felt like my gut is continually twisted every time he tells me what he has planned. All we've done is argue and I never realised until talking to you, how much I've been on his case.'

'I told you. You think he's getting into trouble and not doing what he's told at home but compared to others, he's a really good kid. I'm not saying he's perfect, but I've worked with hundreds of kids that age and he's up there with the best of them. Well mannered, considerate and mature. You've done a great job with him.'

'Thanks Tess, and as I said last time at our meeting, you have no idea how much that means to me. I haven't had anyone to talk to about what's been going on. The fellas at work have little kids and I don't have family nearby. Layton's idea of becoming a policeman only came up in the last six months and because I opposed the idea right from the start, our relationship had a massive shift.'

'He's a young adult and you should be pleased that he is looking ahead and has a goal.'

'I guess so. I always thought he'd do a trade. I've got a good carpentry business with three fellas working for me. We mainly do renovations but there're often new houses to build or one of the larger commercial projects around town that come up. I'm never out of work and the money is good. It's a great lifestyle and the work's outside, using your hands. I'd hoped he might want to do an apprenticeship with me.'

'Why are you so opposed to the police force?'

'His mother was a copper. She should never have gone into that sort of career. Always thinking she could save everyone and solve their problems.' He drank the last of his beer, looking down into his glass. 'She became involved with a fella she worked with. They both had issues with some different situations at work and at the time her stress levels were through the roof. Her priorities weren't with me or Layton. Everything revolved around her work and I guess someone who she thought understood her better than me.'

'Does Layton ever see her?'

'Rarely, and as he gets older it's become less and less. She remarried and had two other kids.'

The moon rose higher in the sky, the beach cloaked in a golden glow. They sat in silence, both with their own separate thoughts.

Tess broke the silence. 'I guess we should get going.'

Joel placed their empty glasses in the middle of the table. 'I guess so.'

* * *

JOEL SAT IN THE PASSENGER'S SIDE OF THE CAR. HE STARED AT TESS, HIS voice gentle with a lovely unrushed pace that she'd come to appreciate. 'Are you sorry that your relationship with Tom didn't work out. When I first met you at the races, I wondered what the hell you were doing with him. I only spoke to you briefly, but you seemed a very ill-fitted match.'

'I don't know what I was thinking.' She shrugged and shook her head. 'I guess because I was new to town and then someone paid me attention, I lost my head. I was up for a bit of fun. There's been a run of bad relationships.'

'Ha, ask me about bad relationships. I know how you feel.'

She turned to him. 'I hope I'm not being too forward, but it's been lovely talking tonight. Would you consider meeting here for dinner again next Friday?'

He grinned and sent a smouldering look her way. 'Did you just ask me out on a date?'

Her face burned. 'No, not at all. Just as friends.'

He laughed, his eyes crinkling at the corners. 'It's been good to talk to you. I haven't felt so relaxed in a long time. Sure, why not. I'll pick you up, that way you can have a couple of drinks.'

Tess started the car, a warm feeling washing over her. There was something about Joel that made her feel excited, alive, and after tonight she badly wanted to see him again. Be careful, she silently chided herself, Tom had seemed exciting also when she first met him and look at how that ended up.

'I'll look forward to it. I hope that everything settles down for you in regards to Layton.' She tried to keep her voice level, to not make it so obvious that she was super excited to get another chance to talk to him.

'It was interesting to hear how he is at school. It makes me feel that perhaps I have done something right over the years.'

'You definitely have. You should be proud of him. Parents often don't realise how great their kids are.'

'I'm still not keen on the police idea, but you're right, he's eighteen, the decisions are now his.' He shook his head and ran his hand through his hair. 'It hasn't been easy bringing him up by myself and as you said, I still think of him as a kid.'

She steered the car out of the car park, pressing hard on the brakes as a police car followed by an ambulance rushed past, sirens blaring and lights flashing. Joel steadied himself, holding onto the dashboard as the car came to a sudden halt. 'Sorry,' she said, 'those cars came from nowhere. It's unusual to see emergency vehicles around here.'

'It is,' he replied, peering ahead through the windscreen, trying to see where they were headed. 'I don't like the look of that.'

It didn't take Tess and Joel long to find out where the emergency vehicles were going. By the time they got to the showgrounds, the whole area was lit up by flashing lights. Tess pulled over to the side of the road, the way ahead blocked by police and fire trucks.

'Shit, Layton's out somewhere tonight,' Joel said, 'Delvene was going with him.' He craned his neck trying to see what had happened.

Tess turned the car off. 'No, oh no. That's Timothy's car. I can see from this side.' She unbuckled her seatbelt and jumped out of the car. Joel followed her, both arriving at the first police car together. In front of them, firemen were already working on the car, the front of the green Mazda squashed front on, a light pole slicing through the middle of it. Joel grabbed Tess as she tried to rush forward. 'You can't go in there.'

Her chest heaved and she tried to move towards the car, but Joel's arms wrapped around her. He spoke calmly, tightening his grip as he held her back. 'We can't go any further. Timothy and Millie are in the car. I can see her green shirt from here.'

10

———————

The sounds that night would stay with Tess forever. Not only the groans and cries from the two trapped in the car, but the crunching noises of metal as the fireman used tools to pry open the top of the car. Once Joel managed to calm her down and make her promise she'd stay where she was, he'd walked down the road a little towards the accident. His mate Pete was one of the policemen who was standing guard, ensuring no one neared the crash site. Pete's son was also in Tess's class and he also knew the two occupants of the car. The two men spoke while she waited, her heart in her mouth, fearful of what he would find out.

When Joel returned he placed his arm around her shoulders, rubbing her arms as she tried to stop herself shaking. 'They're both alive,' he said. 'Millie's in a bad way and Pete said one of her legs is broken. He's not sure about Timothy. They're worried about spinal injuries. They're going to airlift them both to Townsville Hospital. Their parents have been contacted and they're going to make their way straight to the hospital.'

Tess turned as someone called out behind them. It was Layton and Delvene, and just like she had, they went to go towards the crumbled car. Joel stood in their path, grabbing Delvene as she tried to push around him. 'You can't go in there. You need to stay back.'

Delvene's voice was hysterical and Joel held her tight. He tried to talk to her but she wasn't listening, straining against his arms as she stared at the car, calling out Timothy's and Millie's name.

Layton stood beside Joel. 'Dad. What are you doing here? Are they okay? What happened?'

'I had dinner at the café,' Joel replied. 'They were both working there and only left a short while ago, just before we did. I'm not sure what happened, but I just spoke to Pete and he said they're alive.' Delvene struggled against his arm and Tess stepped in, pulling the young girl into her arms. She hugged her tightly, continually talking and calming her. 'Delvene, listen to me and calm down. Stay here. We can't go any closer. We have to let the police and ambulance do their work. There's nothing we can do.'

The young girl sobbed and clung to Tess, the flashing lights of the rescue vehicles reflected in her shocked eyes. Eventually she calmed, Tess's words finally getting through her initial shock.

The four of them stood together, the area now full of onlookers who also recognised the car and stopped to check what had happened. Tess moved from one group to the other. They were mostly kids from school and she hoped her familiar face was a soothing voice of authority, as they listened to what she said, asking questions before thanking her for letting them know what was going on.

Pete found her in the middle of a group, Delvene still clinging to her arm as Tess talked to the kids about what had happened. 'You can let them know they'll be on their way to the hospital soon.' Pete said. 'The chopper is about to land so it would be great if they all moved back to the other side of the road. Right out of the way. Can you get them to move over there? I've asked several times but no one seems to be listening.'

She nodded before gaining the group's attention. They quietened when she spoke, nodding and responding with wide eyes and frantic looks. 'Thanks for your help,' Pete said as he returned to give her some more information to pass on. 'The last thing we need is for them to try and help or get in the way. They mean well but we need to give these guys room to do their job.'

She moved across the road with the group, Delvene still clinging to her arm. Layton appeared with Joel walking beside him, his voice raised to be heard above the noise. 'Here comes the helicopter. It will land in the park there. Thank God they're alive.'

The group stood silently, clinging to each other as the noisy motor and flashing lights of the helicopter added to the lit-up area. Delvene squeezed Tess's hand as the two stretchers were loaded in, the doors secured and the pilot prepared for take-off.

She checked that everyone was okay. A couple of the boys gave her a hug and thanked her for being there. A small group of them sat down on the grass, watching as the emergency services continued to clean up the area, the flashing lights of a tow truck arriving in the street.

'There's not much use hanging around,' Joel came up beside her, 'How about we drive back to my place with Layton and Delvene. I think they need to sit and talk.'

She shivered, the enormity of what they had witnessed, sinking in. 'Do you think they'll be alright? Did Pete tell you anything else?'

'He said they wouldn't know any more until they got them to the hospital. At least they're alive and in the best of hands. There's no point surmising.' Layton and Delvene stood nearby. 'I think the best thing is that we all go back and have a cup of tea together. He put his arm around Tess's shoulder, ignoring the quizzical look from his son as he guided her back to her car.

'Follow us back home,' he called out to Layton. 'Your teacher and I had an unplanned dinner together tonight, so if you're wondering why we're in the same car, that's why.'

* * *

THE FOUR OF THEM SAT IN JOEL'S KITCHEN, MULLING OVER THE ACCIDENT. A strong cup of tea helped Delvene to settle down, although her attempts at not crying were not successful. 'I'm sorry,' she stammered,

'Millie's my best friend and the car was so crumbled. I can't see how they've survived. What if she dies in hospital? I need to go to her.'

Joel's voice was calm as he reasoned with her, passing tissues and telling her not to apologise. It was only natural for her to be upset. The scene had been shocking for all of them. He proposed they wait until morning and then work out if they should drive to the hospital. Layton poured Tess another cup. 'I'm curious how come you and my dad were at the accident together. Did you come from the pub?'

Joel cleared his throat. 'We were at the café at the same time. Both sitting alone at separate tables that happened to be near each other. We joined forces and ended up having dinner together.' He smiled at Tess. 'We'd had a lovely night and Tess was driving me back here, dropping me home when we came upon the accident.'

'Talking about home,' Tess said. 'It's after midnight. I might get going and try and get some sleep.'

Joel walked her out to her car. 'I'll be in contact,' he said. 'Hopefully I can find out some information early in the morning.'

She looked up at him as she started the car. 'See you in the morning. I might drop back over here if that's okay.'

'That'd be great. Drive carefully and I'll see you then.'

11

The next morning the sky was overcast and dark heavy clouds gathered on the horizon. Unlike Canberra, the clouds didn't cool the air, the humidity pressing down as she prepared to drive over to Joel's. The events of the night whirled around in her mind. Hopefully Joel would have news on Timothy and Millie's condition.

Tying her hair up in a messy bun, she looked at her reflection. She didn't look as fresh as she had yesterday morning and she pinched her cheeks, trying to restore some colour to her face. Sleep had not come easy last night and she lay awake for hours, worrying not only about those in the car but also the effect on their friends.

* * *

A row of vehicles lined the footpath outside Joel's house. P Plates adorned the variety of utes and cars and she waved to the person getting out of the car in front.

It was Fred who looked just the same as he did at school. His hair hung over his face and baggy shorts and an overlarge t-shirt draped loosely on his body. His feet were pushed into large thongs and he walked with sagging shoulders and a slow stride. He did however look up and manage a smile as he greeted her. 'G'day Miss.'

'Good morning, Fred. It's nice to see you. It looks like there are quite a few students here.'

He stood waiting for her to get out of her car, pushing both sides of his hair back behind his ears, before shoving a tattered straw hat on his head. 'They said you were there last night. Delvene rang me and let me know that a group from school was coming over to have breakfast. It was nice of her to include me.'

Tess gave him her warmest smile. 'Let's go inside then, shall we.'

* * *

JOEL GREETED HER AT THE DOOR, STEERING HER TOWARDS THE KITCHEN AND showing Fred the way out to the backyard. 'They're all out there. Layton's got the barbeque on and they're cooking up a storm. Delvene's father is the local butcher and he's sent plenty of meat to cook up.' He shut the door behind Fred, turning his attention back to her. 'Come and sit in the kitchen with me before you get inundated with their questions.'

She was surprised how his smile and welcoming manner eased her mind, the touch of his hand on her arm as he greeted her, like one good friend to another. 'How are they. Have you had any news?'

Pulling a chair out, he looked at her with concerned eyes. 'Sit down and I'll fill you in. Let me boil the jug first and I'll make you a cup of tea. You don't look like you've slept much.'

She settled into the chair, grateful not to have to face the crowd from school as soon as she arrived. Joel moved around the kitchen, preparing her tea and remembering exactly how she had it from the previous night. Unlike how she felt this morning, he looked great. He was dressed in casual shorts and a t-shirt, his bare feet brown against the old lino of his kitchen floor. Wishing she had half his energy, she watched as he moved around, bringing her a bowl of cut up fruit before serving her a cup of tea.

'Have you eaten anything yet?' he asked.

'Usually I have a good breakfast, but this morning for some reason I've actually forgotten to have anything. I'm not thinking straight.'

Start with this and after we've talked we'll join the others out the back.'

She sipped her tea, the warm sugary drink a soothing familiar start to her morning. 'Thank you. This is lovely.'

He sat down with her, placing a glass of orange juice next to her fruit. 'I've been on the phone to the hospital this morning and both kids are stabilised. Their families are there at Townsville with them. Millie has a broken leg and a couple of cracked ribs as well as plenty of bruises and cuts. Apart from that everything else is okay. She's having surgery on her leg this afternoon.'

'And Timothy?'

'They were worried about spinal injuries but so far that is looking more positive than they originally thought. I spoke to his father and he said they can't find anything majorly wrong with him. He has plenty of cuts and bruises and some stitches for a cut on his face but other than that it appears he also will be okay. He might even get released from hospital tomorrow.'

Tess breathed a sigh of relief. 'From what the car looked like you would think they'd both have more serious injuries or even not survived.'

'I know. I really thought the worst last night. Millie's condition is not great but it could have been far worse. Apparently Timothy swerved to miss a dog wandering across the road. He overcorrected and that's when they hit the pole.'

Tess leant back in her chair and closed her eyes. 'Thank goodness they're okay. How quickly circumstances can change.'

Joel took the empty plate and glass from in front of her, pushing the cup of tea forward. 'I'm glad you came over, you need feeding. Drink this up and then you'll have to face the gang out the back. They've all been asking when you're arriving. I told them you would need breakfast first.'

'That's very thoughtful of you. It's funny how you don't think you've been affected by things but when you stop and think about it, like I have this morning, I've sort of hit a brick wall.'

'It's also your first day of school holidays. It's often the way if work has been busy, you don't stop and then when you do, you really come to a crunch. You'll probably want to catch up on some sleep.'

'Layton and Delvene as well as all the others must be relieved. That was a terrible sight for them to witness. It was the sounds also.'

'They were all asking about you this morning. Checking with me to see if I thought you'd be okay.'

She laughed. 'Sometimes they're so dramatic. Of course, I'm okay. The main priority is Millie and Timothy.'

'They think a lot of you. I was listening to them earlier.'

'Unbelievable really,' she said. 'So many of them gave me such a difficult time when I first arrived. Now they actually speak to me like a human being.'

Joel laughed. 'Bloody teenagers. Up and down like an emotional rollercoaster. I don't know how you put up with them in class. I'd throttle them in five minutes.'

She smiled. 'I love kids. When I first taught this lot I thought I'd never get through it. They're so different to the classes I'd taught down south. They just took a lot longer to win over.'

'Well, you're the most loved teacher in Tranquil Bay at the moment. They said that you help them, not only in their schoolwork but also with personal matters. Delvene said you made her realise how some kids feel left out. She told me this morning about how changing her attitude towards one person and going out of her way, just a tiny bit, she'd come to understand why it was so important to make sure everyone is included.'

'I didn't say much.'

'Well, whatever you've been talking to them about, it's sunk in. They might not listen to their parents, but they've listened to you.'

* * *

THE BREAKFAST WAS IN FULL SWING BY THE TIME JOEL AND TESS FINISHED talking and joined the group who filled the backyard. It seemed like everyone in the grade was there plus extras. Delvene was the first to give her a hug. 'Did you hear, Miss? Did you hear they're going to be okay?'

'I did. It's the best news we could have hoped for. Who would have thought they'd only have those injuries, considering the condition of the car.'

Layton passed her a bacon burger. 'Here you go Miss. Our mate Fred is a great hand on the BBQ. He took over the cooking as soon as he arrived.'

'Thanks. Layton. Your dad just made me breakfast, but I won't say no to this.' She looked over to the cooking area, where Fred was flipping eggs and shuffling mushrooms and onions around like he'd been doing it all his life. 'It's nice to see Fred included.'

'Yeah, Delvene took him under her wing. As soon as she started talking to him, he opened up and started talking to us. He's actually a pretty cool guy underneath all that hair.'

She laughed. 'Fred found it hard to make friends because you had all gone to primary and then high school together. It only takes a small effort to reach out to people.' Another group of students from school came to say hello and she chatted for a while, checking they were all okay and asking what their plans were for the holidays.

Out of the corner of her eye she saw Joel, talking to a couple of the boys from school. Layton followed her gaze. 'It's weird to see Dad mixing with everyone. Normally when my mates come over we don't bother talking to him.'

'All you're interested in is going out,' Delvene added. 'You should give him some more time. He's done a lot for you, and he doesn't have anyone else to talk to.'

Layton shrugged and stared again at Joel. 'All he ever usually does is get up me about something I haven't done, or he disagrees with what I want to do. I'd given up on him. It's easier to stay out of his way.'

Tess turned to him. 'I sense his loneliness and it's not from being alone without a partner. I'd say all he really wants is for the two of you to communicate and maybe for you to let him in on part of your life. Doesn't have to be about everything, but it's hard for parents to bring kids up. It's extra difficult when you're doing it by yourself. Let him in a bit. You'd be surprised.'

Layton nudged her with his elbow. 'Have you two been talking about me? How come you seem to know what he might be like?'

She raised her eyebrows. 'We've been talking about a lot of things and yes we have been discussing you. What parent doesn't want to talk about their kid? I probably spend more time with you and the other students in the class, than anyone else at the moment. I'm a great believer in second-hand gossip so I don't feel like I'm out of place to say that he's worried about you. He's also proud of the person you've become. Mostly what he says about you is positive, not negative like you might think.'

Delvene linked her arms through Layton's. 'No wonder he's worried about you. You never tell him where you're going or what you're doing. He's probably thinking the worst.'

'I spend a lot of time at the gym and down at the beach running.' Layton flexed his muscles making her and Delvene laugh. 'I need to be fit if I'm going to join the police. He wouldn't know that's where I go. He probably thinks I'm hanging out drinking or doing drugs. He'd be so far from the truth if that's what he's thinking.'

Tess finished the last of her burger, her stomach full and her energy returned. 'How is he supposed to know what you're up to if you don't talk to him.'

'Layton doesn't tell him stuff because once they start talking they always end up arguing about him becoming a policeman,' Delvene quipped in, 'and usually his dad comes up with plenty of negative comments.'

Tess looked to make sure Joel wasn't looking their way; he didn't need to know they were talking about him. 'It is true that you should avoid people who bring you down with negativity, but you need to remember that you're all he's got. Most of his life he's spent bringing you up. He probably does need to let go a bit, but you also need to let him in. Anyway, here he comes, so end of conversation.'

'Talk about a lecture,' Layton mumbled.

Joel came up next to them, his eyes searching as he looked from one to the other. 'What are you three talking about?'

'Oh, you know Dad. Delvene and I just love to talk about English with Miss Barber. It's our favourite subject.'

Joel's eyes sparkled and his smile made Tess's heart beat faster. What was it about him? Why did she have the urge to link her arm through his, the way Delvene and Layton were standing together. His deep voice startled her thoughts. 'Bloody liars. I could tell you were talking about me.' He looked towards Layton. 'I hope you weren't complaining about how cranky I've been lately?'

'Never,' Layton replied.

Tess spoke up, now was as good as time as any. 'Layton was saying how he's getting so fit from going to the gym regularly.'

Joel's face fell and his eyes narrowed. 'I didn't know you went to the gym. Why didn't you tell me?'

Layton stood tall and looked his father in the eye. 'I'm getting fit so I can get into the police force. I never told you because I knew you'd only go off about it being a stupid choice.'

She pursed her lips and threw a stern look Joel's way, hoping that their previous talks would have had some effect.

It took a long time for Joel to answer and for a long while he looked down at the orange juice he was swirling around in his glass. Finally, he lifted his eyes, speaking directly to Layton. 'You know, I've been giving your idea some thought, and,' he paused and threw a wink her way, 'Tess, ah I mean Miss Barber and I have discussed how you're progressing at school and what your plans are for the future. I've come to the realisation that I'm not going to be able to change your mind and if that's what you really want to do, then who am I to stop you. I made my own choices at your age and some worked out and some didn't.' He wrapped his hand around Layton's arm, squeezing it affectionately. 'All I could think about last night was what it would have been like if that was you and Delvene in that car instead of Timothy and Millie. I can't imagine how their parents would have felt getting that phone call.'

Layton's face was covered in a wide grin and he wrapped his arm around Delvene's shoulders. 'Thanks Dad, you've just made my day. I have only ever wanted to do one job and I'll pursue it no matter what. It's a big deal to me though, that I have your approval.'

Joel's words were shaky. 'Excuse me girls for getting a bit soppy, but you have to remember that you mean everything to me, and lately I haven't been that great at talking or telling you how proud I am of you. I want us to get back to what we once were. A close father and son.'

Layton let go of Delvene and wrapped his arms around his father, the two hugging before drawing apart.

Joel cleared his throat. 'I think your teacher here has done more than just help you kids. She's also given me some stern words of wisdom.'

Delvene wiggled around and moved her shoulders up and down, a comical look on her face. 'And that's my next question. Exactly how did you two meet? Surely it wasn't through school. Parent teacher interviews? I think not.'

Tess pushed her sunglasses down from the top of her head so that they covered her eyes. 'That, my dear Delvene is another story and not particularly one I want to share at the moment.'

'Ahh come on,' Layton added as another group of students came up to listen in. 'Look, we're all interested to find out.'

Joel linked his arm through hers. 'Miss Barber and I met at the races a while ago. Let's just leave it at that. C'mon Tess, I need you to listen while I make a phone call to the hospital. We need to work out what Timothy and Millie might need help with.'

She gave the group a winning look, her lips pressed tightly together as she smiled and waved goodbye.

12

———————

y the time Joel and Tess talked to the hospital and Millie's father, the group out the back had packed up and gone their separate ways. Layton came in and gave his father another hug. 'Just going to the gym and then over to Delvene's house. I'll be home for dinner.'

She watched them both, pleased at Joel's response and relieved that the relationship with his son seemed to have repaired somewhat. It hadn't taken much. Just someone laying out the facts and making Joel look hard at himself and what he was expecting from his son.

Reluctant to leave, Tess slowly stood up. It was time to go. Joel had put some plans into action to help the families out. Between the both of them they had sorted out how to make life easier for those involved. Arrangements to help Millie and her father, Colin, out with the rest of his kids had been easy to organise. Joel knew Colin, they had both lived in Tranquil Bay for many years. He let him know that the kids at breakfast this morning had started a fundraiser, with over a thousand dollars sitting there waiting for him to collect. That was just a start, to help him out with items his family might need.

Colin was overwhelmed and thanked them both for reaching out and making life easier for all of them as Millie recovered. 'I don't know what to say. Just, thank you. It's been tough and to have everyone helping me and Millie out, well it's brought tears to my eyes. The main thing is that she's also going to be okay. I'm bloody proud of her, she's one in a million. She has a new attitude to school this year because of your classes. She's made her mind up to be a kindergarten teacher and I know she'll be great at it.'

'She will be,' Tess added. 'And if she needs any help then I'm more than happy to do that.'

'Thanks once again. The entire family appreciate what everyone has done.'

* * *

JOEL WALKED HER OUT TO HER CAR. THE MIDDAY SUN WAS HIGH IN THE sky, its heat searing and the humidity causing her to breathe in sharply. 'I can't believe how muggy it gets here. Canberra has a dry heat, nothing like this.'

'It's gearing up for the hotter months. Wait until that kicks in.' He opened her car door, turning to face her as she sat down in the driver's seat. The tone of his voice changed and a concerned look returned to his face. 'You said once that you were only staying in town for a while. Are you planning on going back to Canberra?'

She pulled her hair back, twisting it around her hand before tying it up in a messy bun on top of her head. Thank goodness she'd worn her denim shorts and singlet top. It was too hot to wear anything else and she had also grown accustomed to throwing on rubber thongs or flat leather sandals. Anything to keep herself cool. 'No wonder women have short hair up here,' she said, looking up at Joel who hadn't moved from where he was standing leaning on the door of her car.

He went to say something but stopped again.

'You asked about Canberra. I'll see the end of this year out and then decide. Perhaps another year but it was never my plan to stay.' She waited for his response, but he just stood there staring at her.

She giggled, 'You're staring.'

Shaking his head, he stood upright. 'Don't ever get your hair cut. It's beautiful.'

Her face burned and she knew it would be red and flushed. 'Thank you.'

'See you whenever,' he replied as he shut her car door.

* * *

FOR SOME REASON SHE WAS UNSETTLED. IT WAS HOLIDAYS AND SHE SHOULD have basked in the relaxation and late morning sleep-ins. Usually she loved the days to herself. Time to read books, go for walks or watch a movie. Now however, reading made her cranky, walks were boring and she had no desire to turn the television on. Whatever was wrong with her? She had caught up with some of the other teachers for lunch a couple of times and made numerous trips out to Millie's house to drop off food and other items, including money that the kids were collecting. Fred had fixed up some old laptops and this morning came with her to help out.

Millie was not long out of hospital and sat with her leg in a cast, her arms and face showing an array of cuts and bruises. Apart from that her recovery was going well and she was grateful to be back at home. They sat and talked along with two of her siblings while Fred was kept busy installing some technical products that had been donated. Now the family's internet connection would be stronger and quicker.

Fred had struck up a conversation with one of Millie's younger sisters who was in the grade below at school. She also was interested in technology and when it was time to go, Tess had to ask him several times to finish up what he was doing. Not that it mattered. She had nowhere to go or no-one to see.

Millie thanked them profusely, overwhelmed with the support for her and Timothy. 'Your help has made such a difference to my family. This community is amazing and my dad is like a different person. The lines of worry have gone from his face. When some of the local organisations found out how hard it's been for him, they put all sorts of things into place for us kids. He won't have to worry about school costs or other bills that were stressing him out. He's always hidden that we were struggling so much. He would never ask for help.'

'It's a shame it took a car accident for them to notice,' Fred said. 'I guess we're all the same, not looking beyond what we see. It makes everyone happy, to give and to receive.'

'Wow,' Millie's sister, Jan, was wide-eyed and besotted by his words. 'You're so deep and your words are like poetry.'

Tess and Millie gave each other a quick glance, both trying to not laugh. 'C'mon Fred. I need to get home. I have people to see and places to go.'

* * *

FRED LOOKED OUT THE WINDOW AS THEY DROVE BACK TOWARDS TOWN. SHE noticed that his hair had been trimmed and his clothes now fitted a bit better. 'Delvene has been trying to do a makeover on me,' he told her. 'She thinks she's my sister or something. Bloody bossy she is.'

'You look good,' Tess said as they neared his house. 'You're really keen on computers aren't you.'

'It's my thing. The mill is putting me on after school and their plan is to get me working in the technology section. I don't have the stamina or the desire for physical work but there's plenty to do in the IT section. They're impressed with what I know.'

'Well done. I'm really pleased for you. It seems like everyone has a plan for when they finish school.'

He chuckled. 'And now I've got a date. Millie's sister, Jan, is picking me up tonight and we're going to the movies. Jees, what next?'

She smiled at him. 'You're all growing up. Soon you'll all be gone and the next lot of year 12s will be moving in.'

'I hope they're nicer to you than we were.'

Steering the car towards the side of the road, she pulled up outside Fred's house. 'I'm not sure if I'll be at the school next year. My contract is on a six-monthly basis, and that time is nearly up. I know they want me back for another twelve months but I'll have to see.'

'Teachers always leave our school. Only a few loyals stick around. Anyway, thanks for taking me with you today. Now I have a date. I'll ring Delvene and get some help on what to wear.'

'She'll love that. I'm pleased that you've made some friends.'

'I never bothered talking to them before. I guess I was just as unfriendly towards them as they were to me. I thought they all hated me. Now we're getting on fine.'

'Everyone has come together. It's lovely to see. Everyone needs someone.'

She pondered on her words for a long time after she arrived home. Lying on the couch she thought about what she really wanted to do next year. Only yesterday an email arrived offering her a Head of Department position back at her old school, St Markel's. The pay was a big step up and it was the position she had always been chasing. A promotion and a return to the comforts of the city and her old life. Back to the choice of shopping centres, flash eateries and places to go. The art galleries, museums and theatres. Back to civilization.

She closed her eyes, rubbing her forehead that was starting to ache from too much thinking. If the job offer was so wonderful, why wasn't she jumping up and down for joy? Why hadn't she emailed straight back and accepted the position? Why had it taken her until this morning to accept their offer. A hollow sensation pounded in her stomach, a lethargy and crankiness with who knew what.

The sound of her phone ringing stirred her from her apathy and she put down the chips and ice-cream that she had mixed together. If all else fails, eat what you feel like, she reminded herself as she ripped open another chocolate bar, placing it in her mouth as she pressed answer.

A rush of excitement filled her as Joel's voice sounded from the phone.

'Hi. It's Joel here. Delvene gave me your number. She said she's not supposed to have it, but you gave it to her when you were working out how to help Millie.'

Her mouth was full of chocolate and she mumbled her reply. 'Yes… I told her I'm not..'

'Are you okay? Joel asked. 'You sound like something is wrong.'

She quickly finished the mouthful of chocolate. 'Sorry, I was eating chocolate.'

'What are you up to?' he asked.

'Oh, you know, the usual. Out with the girls, dinners, lunches. Just what we normally do on holidays.'

He sounded dejected, his voice flat. 'I guess you're too busy to go out to dinner then?'

She tried to keep her voice level, to not show the excitement or to let it be known that she was standing on her tiptoes, trying to stop herself from jumping up and down. 'I could possibly fit that in.'

'You don't sound that keen. It's okay to say no.'

No longer able to contain her enthusiasm, she shouted, embarrassed after she realised how loud and rushed her words were. 'I would never say no. I'd love to go out for dinner with you. I have nothing on, I mean not clothes wise just no other events to attend.'

She envisaged his smile on the other end of the phone. 'See you at six. I'll pick you up and book a table at the resort. It's about half an hour out of town.'

Fabulous. Wonderful. 'I'll see you then.'

As she clicked the phone off, she did a dance, jigging around and punching her arms in the air. Stop it, she thought, it's only a date.

13

———————

Joel arrived early and she called out for him to come in. 'Just putting on my shoes. I'll be two seconds.'

He stood in the kitchen, leaning on the bench, looking around the small space that she called home. 'It's not a very big place,' he called out to where she was in her bedroom, trying to find the sandals she wanted to wear.

'It's fine for me. The Education Department supplies it for minimum rent, so I'm not complaining.'

When she came out into the kitchen, he stopped talking, his eyes wide as he looked at her.

'What? she said, looking down at her feet. 'What's wrong?'

He laughed as he walked towards her. 'Are you always worried you've got something hanging off your shoes, or something tucked in wrong at the back?'

She glimpsed over her shoulder. 'Just the way you looked at me, like something wasn't right.'

He looked her up and down. 'You look amazing. That's why I stared.'

She bent down and fixed the clip on her sandals, straightening the fitted floral dress as she stood up. It was an old favourite, a reliable go to, that accentuated her slim figure and showed off her legs. Even though there were always parts of her body that she was unhappy with, she actually loved her waist and legs. His eyes met hers as she looked up. He had dressed up for the occasion and his fitted jeans and collared white shirt showed off a fit muscular body, tanned from fishing and working outside.

'You look good,' she replied. 'You're lucky your work is physical and keeps you fit.'

'It does but the heavy work can sometimes take toll on your body. I've slowed up a bit.' He offered his hand to her. 'Shall we go?'

* * *

SHE HADN'T WANTED TO LET GO OF HIS HAND. IT WAS LARGE AND COVERED hers as he led her out through the front door. She let go of him, locking the front door before following him to the car. He held the door open, his eyes locking with hers before he closed it gently.

Her stomach twirled and nervous flutters ran through her body. Stop it she admonished herself. Whatever is wrong that you keep falling for every guy that comes along. Had she felt the same about Tom at the start? She reminded herself that she had only fallen for him because he was persistent, wining and dining her, apologising for his ways and coming back after every mistake. At the time she was struggling to fit in and make new relationships. He happened to come along at just the right moment. When she was vulnerable.

With Joel it was different. She didn't want to get into a relationship with anyone. She had pretty much decided that she would leave at the end of the year and return to Canberra. There was no way she would let anything develop. She'd need to be honest with him and let him know what her plans were. She smiled at him as he started the car, for now she was going to enjoy being with a very polite man, who had intelligent conversation, was interested in her and her life and just happened to be very handsome.

14

The dinner was everything a date should be. The resort was five star and Joel had booked a table away from other diners. Their seats looked out across the harbour, the twinkling lights of the yachts and other boats tied up creating a colourful wonderland; a romantic backdrop to the glistening silverware and low candles that flickered on their table.

The conversation as usual, flowed easily, and they talked about their jobs, families and funny stories from childhood. He laughed at her anecdotes about the kids at school and didn't seem to notice when she avoided the question of what grades she'd be teaching next year. When they finished the meal he took her hand and led her down to the far end of the beach. Fairy lights adorned the bushes that edged the beach and they sat at a table and chairs that looked out over the water.

A full moon rose above the masts of the sailing boats and a sailor called out to another person on a boat nearby. She peered out across the inky water. 'It would be such a different life, living on a boat. The kids tell me that some of these yachts sail around the world.'

'They do. A lot of these anchored here, have arrived for racing season. They come from a range of different countries.'

They talked for a long while before Joel grabbed both her hands.

'Let's walk along the beach a bit. Look at that moon, it's lighting up the entire area.'

She laughed and undid her shoes, holding them in her hand as Joel held the other one. His hands were rough from the carpentry work and her hand felt small and secure in his. When he stopped and wrapped his arms around her she looked up into his eyes, closing hers when his lips pressed down on hers.

His kiss was long and passionate and took her breath away. She pushed her body against his, tingling sensations running through her as his hands caressed her back. When their lips finally parted, he looked straight into her eyes, his hands reaching up and stroking her face. 'I've fallen for you, Tess. I haven't been able to get you out of my mind.'

She pushed herself against him, leaning forward until her lips were once again on his. They kissed until she pulled away, resting her head on his chest. His hands moved through her hair and he tilted her head up so that she was looking straight at him.

'Do you feel the same way or am I reading the situation wrong?' he whispered.

She took a long time to answer, averting her eyes when she spoke. 'I do feel the same way, but I have to be honest with you. My contract is up for renewal at the end of the year however I've decided to return to Canberra. I've been offered a promotion.'

His body stiffened and he held her at arm's length. 'Right. I see. Well, I guess I read this all wrong. There's not much use starting something if you're not going to be around much longer.'

'I don't go for a while. We could still see each other until I go.'

'What's the use of that? I'm not interested in short-term relationships.'

They stood apart and she gripped her arm with her other hand, her eyes downcast. 'I don't want a short-term relationship either. I don't know why I even suggested that.'

* * *

THE DRIVE BACK WAS AWKWARD, WITH NEITHER OF THEM SPEAKING UNTIL they pulled up outside her unit. She sat in the passenger's seat, confused and feeling guilty. She could see he was hurt. 'I'm sorry. I never meant to upset you,' she said, her voice quiet and lacking its usual energy.

He smiled at her. 'It's okay. I understand. I wouldn't have been so open and talked about how I felt if I'd known you were leaving. Maybe it's for the best. I've been married before and already had my family. You've still got all that in front of you.'

'That would never concern me.' She screwed her face up. 'I would never worry about something like that. It's just that I've agreed to take on this new job. I've already said yes.'

He patted her arm and she tried to ignore the sensation of his hand on her skin as he responded. 'It's okay, Tess. Wrong timing that's all.'

Tears welled in her eyes and her mind swirled. Why did everything happen at the same time.

Emotion flickered in his eyes and his voice was husky when he spoke. 'Goodnight and good luck with everything. You've made a difference to a lot of young lives around here.'

She went to speak but her chest ached and her words wouldn't come. Finally, she whispered, 'I'm sorry. Goodnight.'

15

The holidays flew past and before she knew it, she was back at school, preparing the students for their last term of the year. Final assessment kept her busy as she worked with the senior students to complete their end of year pieces. There were formals to get ready for, graduation dinners to organise and other end of year events to organise and attend. Joel had not contacted her since their dinner and although she watched for him on the roads or hoped to see him on the beach, she had not glimpsed him over the last six weeks.

St Markel's sent a continual flow of emails through regarding the new Head of Department role and what was expected of her. There was going to be a lot more responsibility with the new position and they'd already warned her there was extra work that would need to be done at night and on the weekends. It was what she had always wanted, wasn't it?

Extra curriculum on Saturdays, Literature Clubs, Sports coach and debating and speaking committees to join and be an active member of. The commitment was intense and she was reminded of the difference to the busy, but more relaxed style of Tranquil Bay High.

Next week she'd have to start packing up her belongings and get ready for the move down south. As she looked out her small window onto the beach, her chest tightened. She'd grown attached to the small town, the beautiful ocean just across the road and the teachers who were now like her family. Although the humidity was sometimes unbearable, she loved the heat of the day followed by the balmy tropical nights. Like the night she'd had with Joel at the resort. A full moon, a sky full of stars and a shimmering ocean that stretched as far as the eye could see. She tried to push it from her mind, to forget how her body ached when he kissed her and how she dreamt about his arms around her before she went to sleep at night. When they talked it was like they'd known each other forever. She didn't worry about what she said or looked like. She could be herself, plus he made her laugh.

* * *

IT WAS ONLY TEN O'CLOCK IN THE MORNING, BUT IT WAS A SATURDAY AND with no motivation to do anything she curled up on the lounge wearing an old t-shirt, comfortable attire for sleeping.

She'd slept for an hour, the busy weeks of the last term catching up with her. A loud knock at the door woke her up and she remembered that Miranda had said she'd call around this afternoon. She thought she'd be later than this though. When she opened the door she tried to hide her shock that it was not Miranda but Joel standing there, smiling warmly at her, saying something about a note she wanted him to get.

Her hair was all over the place and she wiped her eyes, still trying to wake up properly. She pulled her t-shirt down, ensuring it was covering her. It was good to see him, even in this half-dressed state. He wore faded board shorts and a t-shirt, his dark hair, trimmed and neat. 'You've had a hair-cut,' she said.

He ran his hand through his hair. 'Um, yes. I have.'

'It's nice to see you,' she said, her heart in her throat as she stared at him. So many times since their dinner she had thought about him and now he was in front of her. All she wanted to do was throw herself in his arms and feel his lips on hers. 'I haven't seen you for ages.'

He cleared his throat, one hand resting on the side of the doorway.

She couldn't help but stare. He was gorgeous, the way he spoke, the way his eyes met hers and the cute way he shuffled his feet when he was trying to get his words out.

'You left a note with the kids for me. Thank you. It was nice what you wrote and yes, I'd love to take you to the falls before you leave? I'm glad you asked me and yes it's important that you see it before you go. It's one of the top spots to see around here. How did your phone get broken?'

'I did?' she scrunched her face up. 'What note? I didn't leave a note and my phone isn't broken?'

'Layton gave it to me. He said Delvene took the message from you and you'd ask for her to pass it on to me. My phone's been out of action also so I figured that you'd tried to ring but couldn't get me.'

'Really? Delvene said that, did she? I never asked that.'

'Right,' he said. 'So, you didn't want to go to the falls. The message got mixed up somehow. How come you wrote the note.'

She shook her head. 'There was no note left and I'm not sure what's going on.'

He frowned for a moment. Their eyes met. Realisation hit them at the same moment and they laughed. 'Bloody kids,' he said. 'I think we've been set up.'

They stood looking at each other. 'They made all that up. Wait until I see them.' She looked up at the sky. 'It is a beautiful day.'

'How about we go. You don't look like you're doing much and considering you're leaving, I might not see you again. How about it. It's bloody hot and I'm ready to cool off.'

Grinning, she ushered him in. 'Wait a sec and I'll get my togs on. I'd love to go for a swim.'

* * *

They'd talked the entire way. The Falls were a series of deep rock pools situated in the gorges about half an hour west of Tranquil Bay and were popular swimming holes for the locals. It had been weeks since they had seen each other and the conversation flowed easily as they caught up on what had been happening. Joel was excited about Layton's acceptance into the course that would see him join the police force. Millie's leg was healed and they were planning a party at Joel's the following weekend for everyone who had helped out. 'You didn't reply to the invitation,' he kept his eyes on the dirt road while asking the question.

Her voice was quiet. 'I didn't think you'd want me there. I didn't want to spoil it for you. I know you've done so much to help the family out.'

'Rubbish. You make sure you come. I don't want to part on bad terms. Maybe I was a bit abrupt that night at dinner. It's not your fault you're leaving. It sounds like you've finally landed the job you've always wanted.'

'You had a right to be abrupt. I should have told you before we went out what my long-term plans were. I didn't want to spoil the night though.'

He hadn't added any more to the conversation about their date and she changed the subject to safer topics.

* * *

Heavy rain in the last few weeks ensured the falls were flowing, the water deep and perfect for cooling off. She followed Joel along a narrow path that led in and around huge boulders that lined the creek. Thick rainforest closed in on either side, the cool shade of the towering trees a welcome relief after the heat in town.

She looked skyward. 'It's beautiful. The palms are so tall and the trees are covered in so many different ferns. Look at how thick those vines are.'

He waited for her to catch up. 'It's a shame you haven't been here before. There are so many places to visit just in this local area. You've probably seen all the coastal attractions but once you head inland there are just as many incredible places, like this.'

They stopped at a clearing, a small pool beckoning them. 'This is where I usually swim. It's safe and the water flows through so it's always clean.'

She slid into the pool, her tiny bikini colourful below the clear water. 'Who do you come with?'

'I just come by myself. It's a great place for floating around and contemplating life.' He strode into the middle of the pool, his chest bare, the water streaming from his hair when he came up after submerging himself under the water. Standing up he beckoned her to come out to where he was. 'There's a sandy bottom and you should be able to stand here.'

The cool water was refreshing and took her breath away as she swam towards him. Lying on her back she kicked off and floated across the pool, looking up at the clear sky above. A waterfall sounded in the background and the musical notes of tropical birds called out from the rainforest.

She swam back to where Joel stood on the sand, watching him as he dived below the surface, her eyes fixed on his bare shoulders and broad back when he stood back up. He shook his head and droplets of water scattered through the air. When she stood next to him his blue eyes stared into her and she wished that he'd kiss her just one more time.

'I'm not going to kiss you,' he splashed water at her. 'If I kiss you now, it won't stop at that. Not with you in that tiny bikini.'

She stood still, tears threatening to come. Ducking under the water she wiped her eyes, speaking sternly to herself to not cry. Whatever was the matter? She was not weak and the last thing she wanted was to break down in front of him.

He stood and stared as she resurfaced. 'Are you okay?' His voice was gentle and she wished he hadn't spoken so softly. He was breaking her heart.

She bit her lip, unable to speak.

Reaching out he held her hand, bringing it to his lips and kissing it.

Her words came out jumbled and she tried hard to talk straight. 'I don't want to go. I think I've changed my mind.'

He raised his eyes, still hanging onto her hand. 'Really? You *think* you've changed your mind.'

She moved closer to him, reached up and touched his chest, closing her eyes as his head bent forward and his lips pressed down on hers.

His hands held her around her waist, her body trembling at his touch. Eventually he pulled away, ducking under the water again, resurfacing a bit further away. She swam towards him, the cold water swirling around her body. Although he could stand where he was, she wasn't as tall and she tried to tread water before giving in and hanging onto his shoulder.

'You can't stand here, can you?' He squeezed her tightly around her waist and lifted her up. Wrapping her legs around his waist, she pressed up against him. 'Did you lure me here to change my mind?' she whispered.

His hands caressed her back. 'No way. I had nothing to do with it. Some interfering teenagers set this up with a forged note demanding that I take you for a swim.'

Leaning forward she kissed him, not letting go or taking her lips from his even when he floated on his back. Holding her tightly he kicked lazily around the rockpool, her body relaxed and resting on his. When they floated back to the sandy bottom where she could stand, he placed her down kissing her passionately as they stood together.

She looked straight at him. 'I've made a decision. I'm going to stay. If I stay would you consider being a couple. I sound like a school kid, but are you interested in going out with me?'

He twisted her hair through his hands, twirling it high and piling it on top of her head. 'Are you sure that's what you want. You're throwing away a career move, more money and city life for...' he cast his eyes around the area, 'for this and all the other places that I'm going to take you to.'

'Now I feel like I'm making a decision that's right. I'm going to stay. I'm not going to go. I'm going to stay here with you.' She threw herself at him, wrapping her legs around him again as they both fell back in the water.

16

———

The first thing she'd done when they finally returned to her unit was to type up an email. At her request, Joel sat beside her, listening as she read over it, ensuring everything was correct. When she hit the send button he'd kissed her again and they'd cracked open a bottle of champagne and made a toast to what was to come next.

When she rang her principal at Tranquil Bay he'd whooped and yelled in excitement through the phone. 'What changed your mind?' he'd asked. 'I thought we'd lost another great teacher. I know it's a tough school but you're just starting to settle in.'

'I love the school and the kids and it's somewhere I feel like I can make a difference. There's also someone special I want to stay for.' She looked at Joel who sent a smouldering look her way.

* * *

SHE'D SEEN JOEL EVERY NIGHT SINCE SHE'D MADE HER DECISION. THEY were inseparable and she didn't think she could be any happier. The planets were aligned and for once she was calm about her decisions, taking in her stride any obstacles that arose at school and feeling excited for the new classes next year.

On Saturday she'd driven over to Joel's to attend the party for Millie and Timothy. Both had recovered well and there were tears and hugs all around when they made speeches and thanked everyone for the help that they'd given. Drinks flowed and Fred cooked burgers for everyone on the barbeque. Jan stood beside him the entire time and Tess laughed as she watched the young girl gather Fred's hair and tie it up in a high pony-tail. She finished with a long kiss on his lips and a few of the other boys clapped, cheering as Fred's face turned bright red.

School was nearly finished and they all had plenty to look forward to. Tess stood with Joel, his arm around her waist as they talked to some of the kids. Layton raised his eyes. 'Geez Miss. I thought you were going to go back to Canberra and your old school. Dad must have done some fast talking.'

'Someone,' Joel playfully poked Delvene in the ribs, 'Someone set us up. A series of forged notes and concocted demands. Is that right, Miss Delvene?'

Delvene wore a smug look. 'Fred and I devised that plan. Layton said it was a stupid idea but we thought it was worth a try. And look! It worked didn't it.'

17

Joel booked the same table at the resort for dinner. Tonight, she was totally relaxed, her mind at ease with no more decisions to be made. The year ahead was sorted and hopefully, the ones to come after that. When they'd finished dinner, Joel lifted his glass high, clinking with hers as he made a toast. 'To us and what's to come.'

She looked at him across the table, his blue eyes staring into hers. 'I'm so happy I could burst.' she said.

'I feel the same. I feel so content,' he leaned over towards her, taking her hand in his, 'and excited.'

She squeezed his hand, holding it tightly. 'It's so strange how things work out. If I look back over the last year it's been an up and down time.'

'Nothing is ever straightforward. I'm just so pleased you're not going.'

'So am I.'

He put his glass down and took both her hands in his. 'Let's go sit down near the water. The moon is up and there should be a breeze down there.'

* * *

THIS TIME THERE WAS AN EASE AS THEY WALKED TOGETHER, A FAMILIARITY and trust.

Joel wrapped his arms around her and drew her to him, his lips pressing down on hers.

He kissed the top of her head and turned her around. 'Look at that ocean. How could you ever leave Tranquil Bay?'

'I can see myself staying here for a long time,' she sighed. 'It's different when you have a reason for staying.'

She turned around and faced him, her hands reaching up to stroke his face.

His words were soft. 'Everything in life is different once you have a reason. You're my reason, Tess. I love you.'

'I love you more,' she replied as his lips pressed down on hers.

THE END

THE GREEN PLACE

LOUISE FORSTER

The green place

Louise Forster

For all volunteers
who keep this country safe and operating, thank you!
Where would be without you?

Louise Forster

1
____

Grace believed she'd made the right decision.

Heading into the highland farming country during drought for an interview with a man whose reputation for sustainable farming practices was the ultimate test, wasn't it?

With tension mounting in her hands, shoulders, and back, she continued driving behind the cattle truck. She'd had plenty of experience driving under difficult conditions, like a Red Cross van through a sandstorm. But during a terrible drought, following the massive, double-trailer beast hurtling along the dirt road was far worse than she'd imagined. Her car windows were shut tight, and the tiniest particle of talcum-powder road dust wasn't supposed to pass through the best air filters on the market. Perhaps their trials hadn't included dung and the stench of urine.

As a journalist, Grace had travelled to many countries; one of her most memorable trips was interviewing Desert Bedouin Women and their changing environment, where she learned a thing or two. These beautiful women insisted she use camel's milk for her face and Argan oil to gloss her hair. Not that she cared a lot, but Grace let them do their pampering all over her, including a mashed fig and honey face mask that made them giggle. Perhaps to the Bedouin women, she looked a bit—alien, unlike theirs; her skin was quite pale.

The truck hit an extra pulverised section of dirt that obliterated everything around her; she leaned over the steering wheel as if that would help her see…something. Squinting, she was suddenly reminded, was terrible for the complexion, but today was an automatic response she couldn't help. The cloud enveloping her once super shiny vehicle looked more brown than red. A stone rang out sharply as it bounced off the bonnet. Grace flinched, and so did her heart when the stone shot up like a bullet just missing the windscreen. But she wasn't about to pass something that she thought was longer than a city block without a clear view of oncoming traffic or, god forbid, stray cattle. Though the car's satnav clearly showed where she was going, no one drives with their eyes glued to the tiny screen lit up with an arrow. Not that she had a choice; this was the only way to Binowee, the First Nations People's name for *The Green Place*. Better, she thought, to stay put where she could see the ghostly trail of the truck's taillights.

Grace had fought with her brand-new agent, Harry Ricardo Bennet, to get him to agree to this assignment. The fight was not necessary as he'd been told by Vogue management to trust her judgment. He was close to giving her the okay until he got one look at the successful farmer, Joe Mathews and, with a face that said, *holy cow*, decided she was not to go. His argument was, you're going to the back of beyond to interview a farmer for Vogue —their editors will not be interested. She knew that was untrue; they *had* signed her contract for this assignment and were *very* interested. Instinct told her something else was going on with her agent, but she hadn't been able to put her finger on it, yet. Was it that Joe, a strapping, wide-shouldered athletic bloke, was also a hot, good-looking guy? He could very easily grace the front cover of GQ, wearing a pair of snug-fitting jeans and a casual white shirt rolled up to expose his muscled forearms. Oh yes, she'd pictured Joe doing precisely that for her article.

She'd first laid eyes on Joe at a seminar attended by agriculture students. Later, wading through the crowd of young women and men, desperate to ask more questions, she was able to approach him. Joe was Hot with a capital H. His good looks didn't daunt her in the slightest. She introduced herself and asked whether they could chat over a meal, her shout. He declined but agreed to have a coffee. Sitting opposite each other in a plush Melbourne restaurant, Grace told him of the planned Vogue interview and asked if she could come to his farm and do it properly, on-site. He flatly refused.

He'd pushed his chair back and laughed. 'Vogue?' then laughed again as he left. Which made this trip even more interesting, Joe's sister, Leigh, had been her contact and told Grace to ignore his attitude, that she'd take care of it. A stickler for due diligence, her research was thorough. Amongst other things, Grace had watched Joe's interview with a Sustainable Agriculture group, where he'd explained how he'd turned his inherited dust bowl farm into a productive green oasis. Ten years of changing his father's mindset from the old ways to the new was a battle. A battle that many of the younger generations had fought and won. Joe was allocated the worst half of the vast cattle station and given five years to prove that his new-fangled ways were better for the farm and economically viable. Fifteen years later, his father had retired, and the farm was Joe's. The Drone video was proof he'd worked a miracle.

Grace jumped when a British woman's voice on the satnav filled the confines of her car with, 'After eight hundred metres, you will have reached your destination.' Perhaps the announcer dared not try to enunciate Binowee Station, which was dead easy compared to some of the strange cattle station names in Australia.

Grace slowed her car at about two hundred metres, thankful to leave the truck to its road. It motored on like a massive beast, its rear end surrounded by a pale grey, swirling cloud. She was relieved driving behind it was over, her shoulders, arms and hands relaxed as she turned her car toward the farm's drive. Eyes on the prize in front, she admired the stunning granite pillars and black, curly wrought iron arch high overhead with an impressive sign hanging from a set of short chains in the centre.

'Welcome to Binowee.'

Leaning forward, Grace peered through the dusty windscreen and whispered, 'Binowee, The Green Place.' Oh yes, she was a stickler for doing her homework. Settling back, she noticed the cattle grid and eased her car across. The rattle-clang of the steel bars took her by surprise, renewing her body's tension. Unable to see much, she automatically turned on the washers and wipers and sighed with an 'Oh God, really?' Mud smeared in an arc across her vision. Frowning at her own stupidity, she pumped water over the windscreen and waited until there was a wide arc of streaks she could see through.

Eager to get some fresh air, she opened the side window, stuck her head out and breathed in the hot mountain air. The sun was out in full force, birds sang in the trees, and the aroma of cattle dung made her smile. She looked to her left and saw the empty cattle yard, and left behind, was a gardener's dream, piles of dung. Thankfully, a soft breeze sent a hint of sweet-smelling flowers into the confines of her car. Sun filtered through the trees, and a glint caught her eye. Curious, she eased her car forward, and there in the dappled shade leaning against a tree was a kid's battered blue bike. 'Must belong to Joe's nine-year-old son Finn,' Grace whispered to herself and moved on but did wonder how she would feel interacting with a child. 'Just fine,' she told herself firmly.

Shoving her long auburn hair off her face, she glanced down at her designer dress, a gift from Vogue for the occasion, which she knew was a mistake. No amount of explaining that people on the land don't usually wear designer gear to a farm helped change their minds. As Grace was on the assignment under their logo, Vogue decided she had to look the part, no argument. Knowing Vogue expected photos, she shrugged away their heavy-handed attitude about presentation and turned her attention back to the long undulating driveway lined with ancient gnarly pines.

A couple of kilometres in, she rounded a corner and slowed the car down to a crawl. Leaning over the steering wheel, she studied the homestead, glorious in the morning sun. Built in the early 1800s out of local stone, the house was surrounded by acres of beautiful long-established, lush gardens and trees. Perhaps her designer dress would fit right in after all. She could just make out white rail fences behind the house where horses grazed in grassy paddocks. Beyond that, the country's soft rolling foothills slowly rose to join the Great Dividing Range further back. She imagined that the higher peaks would be covered in snow come winter. Just seeing it made Grace's heart swell. Her voice, barely a whisper, seemed loud in the confines of her car. 'Wow, stunning doesn't even come close.'

2

That same morning, Joe Mathews had waved at the bus carrying his son, Finn to school. Turning back to jog along the driveway, his phone buzzed. He dragged it out of his jean's back pocket, and not knowing the caller, he thought it was most likely someone needing farm advice, which happened often, so he clicked to answer.

A high-pitched voice came through, and the woman immediately went into her spiel.

He listened carefully as she introduced herself, every vowel enunciated perfectly. 'Trinity Westlock. Editor of our new editorial, stories of interest at, the aptly titled, Connect.

It will be a monthly contribution where readers can discover how a visionary such as yourself is attempting to change farming practices across the country. Changes that will benefit us all, and a new direction for *Vogue Magazine*.'

She gushed with appreciation that he'd okayed the interview. Lost for words, he took a moment and forced himself to remain calm. The woman jumped right into the silent gap and told him how excited they were at *Vogue*. When he did find his tongue, Joe politely but firmly told Ms Westlock he didn't know what she was talking about. Then she went on to say, 'But it's all been arranged.' His reply was a short sharp emphatic NO. At which, Ms Westlock dropped all niceties and continued in a very business-like manner. 'Your sister, Leigh Gardner, briefed us on what your reaction would be, Mr Mathews. She told us to take no notice. Ms Gardner is your silent partner — but only to a point.' Trinity sighed, 'I can assure you, your interview won't be the least bit painful. Your story will be the first for the magazine and will most *definitely* get maximum coverage in ads on all media. Besides, Ms Grace Taylor is a professional, and therefore the whole interview will be over before you know it. So please be kind to a top, award-winning journalist, the best in the country. We are fortunate to have been able to contract her for this opportunity about the amazing work you've done to turn your farm into a showpiece. The in-depth article will show others how to manage their properties, large or small. They'll benefit from your years of expertise. Word of mouth is a powerful thing, Mr Mathews, I suggest you prepare yourself. All of us at Vogue have complete confidence in Ms Taylor, an investigative journalist in high demand. She will do justice to your fabulous farm work.'

Oh, she's good, Joe thought, *gets tough, then strokes your ego.* But he knew that name, Grace Taylor, and it bothered him that he couldn't remember from where.

Trinity took a breath but wasn't about to waste any time getting back to her point. Only Joe jumped in first, his tone calm but firm. 'Ms Westlock, anything you want to know about how Binowee operates, you could've asked Leigh. I include my sister in all decisions on the farm. In fact, with everything that happens here. So, I suggest you call her back and arrange your interview with Leigh.' When there was no response, Joe added, 'And if that doesn't work, get in touch with Food Tank, Australia's sustainable food industry. They've listed about seventeen organisations that can answer all your questions regarding sustainable agriculture—If I were you, I'd start with the one called *Kiss The Ground.*'

'Sorry, what was that?' Ms Trinity asked, sounding distracted. 'Who should kiss the ground, Mr Mathews? And are you being insufferably offensive?'

'Geez,' Joe muttered. Frustrated, he shoved his hat back, roughed up his hair, and added, 'As an editor looking to educate the public on what the rest of the country is doing to save the planet from destruction, it might be a good idea to become better acquainted with what is going on. *Kiss The Ground*—are a legitimate Agri organisation.'

'Whatever—' Trinity's curt brush-off told Joe she was getting shirty, and he couldn't help but smile. Her tone didn't change as she continued, 'Listen carefully, Mr Mathews—as I said, Grace Taylor is a much sought-after, freelance, investigative journalist. And a very professional colleague who is on her way. We've tried to contact her on another matter, but she must be in a black spot or something. There's no stopping her now! Not that I would.' But before the phone went dead, he heard Trinity mutter, 'Honestly, some men are a pain in the….'

Joe immediately rang his sister and let fly with, *what the hell are you playing at?* But his rant had no effect. And when he finished having a go, Leigh calmly said, 'It's time, Joe. And you know it.'

But he insisted he would find love again when he was good and ready. And setting up an interview to get him seen in a women's magazine was a ridiculous idea. Especially readers of a fashion magazine who aren't in the least bit interested in where their food comes from or how it's grown. No matter, he was *not* doing it. But she was his media-savvy manager and told him that, to push his passion for sustainable agriculture, he had to shove his ego in a barrel and lock it up real tight. *Ouch.* But as far as he was concerned, he pushed his farm ideas in all the right places: farming papers, magazines, tutorials on their farm, and Town Halls all over the country. All these places were worthy of his valuable time. Happy to bend someone's ear and educate people on the importance of leaving the land in a far better condition than before was his lifetime goal. Joe was fair, he listened to counterarguments, and then he'd explain his proven methods with slide shows and drone videos. The simple changes he introduced were cost-effective and brought maximum yields. Leigh took care of all the social media platforms and his schedules. He argued that Vogue was not going to work. But Leigh had come back with a better argument. What if even one farmer or partner happened to pick up a magazine at the dentists, doctors or hairdresser with accompanying photos and got in touch for a chat. How could that be a bad thing? Besides, Binowee's website always needed updating to keep the interest ongoing. Leigh's final words had him thinking. 'Let me remind you, Joe, you're the one who mentioned having coffee with Grace Taylor, telling me what a ridiculous idea it was. So yeah, I thoroughly looked into it.'

Joe knew she was fed up with him because she hung up without their usual banter, a toss-up on who could get in first when she'd call him gorilla face, and he'd call her a fluff-bucket.

Suddenly, his son's dog Luna became alert, her ears twitched, and her tail wagged.

'Enough, Leigh,' Joe muttered at the clear blue sky. 'You've got your way. I'm not happy, but it appears there's nothing I can do unless I politely order Ms Taylor off the farm. She's here.' With a last look at his phone, just in case Leigh left a message, he shoved it into his back pocket. 'Looks like my argument didn't go down well,' Joe quietly grumbled as he ruffled Luna's ears. 'But hey, it wouldn't be the first time.' Running his hand over his dog's head, he added, 'Or the last.'

Even though Leigh's heart was bigger than the outback, and she meant well, pushing for him to move on with his life annoyed him no end. Joe could deal with the pain of his wife, Maeve leaving him, but to abandon Finn, he would never forgive her for that. So, Leigh and his parents had better get used to the fact that he was not in any hurry to find a lifetime love partner again. Besides, he had plenty to occupy himself with, as there was considerable interest out there to get more information. Many people on the land were acknowledging climate change was real, asking for assistance to bring their beloved farms back from the brink. Some had been in the same family for generations. All Joe wanted was to be left alone and get on with his passion for changing outdated, often damaging, farming practices that hadn't worked for some time.

And now, here she was. It couldn't be anyone else but the journalist person, slowly inching up his drive. The only noise her car made was the crunch of tyres on his gravel driveway. He could just make out the car's logo, 'Tesla' an electric car. Hmm, okay, he pulled his hat further down to shade his eyes, muttering to his dog that his sister should be here instead. Left to his own, anything could happen. But then, as the car drew ever closer, remembering the spark between Grace and himself at their first meeting sent an unexpected flurry of anticipation through him. *Shit!* He took his hat off and, using his fingers, rubbed his skull, then pushed his hair back before shoving his beaten-up Akubra back on, adjusting it for comfort. His, or rather Finn's dog, a weird mix of who knew what, but mostly a large breed of some sort, sidled closer then sat on her rump next to his feet. And this was exactly how she behaved when Finn was due home from school. She'd wait, wriggling with anticipation, front paws dancing until she saw the bike appear out of the shade-giving pines, and then she was off, making a crazy dash to greet him.

But this wasn't Finn, and Luna always barked, alerting Joe if they had a visitor—strangely, not this time. She sat on her rump and kept sweeping the driveway with her tail.

'What's up with you?' Joe asked, reaching down to ruffle her ears again, but she didn't make a move. Didn't even look up at him, just gave a quiet little whimper. Not knowing what to make of it, Joe shrugged, took a deep breath, and sighed.

Barely able to see inside the dust-covered car with a streaked muddy windscreen, he directed her to park under the carport. She flashed her lights and slid the silent car under the shade. Out of the opening door, a pair of shapely legs came into view, and then the woman herself....

The Grace Taylor.

Her Christian name suited this elegant woman perfectly. Then Grace smiled, and Joe thought he'd never seen anyone more stunning; every thought evaporated, there was just an all-encompassing sense of euphoria. He didn't know how to handle the emotional and physical reaction of a tight gut and a thumping heart and decided to just ride the wave. She called across the wide driveway and turning circle, 'Won't be a sec.' Her voice was rich, a mellow tone that would surely make grown men take a second look. With a quick wave, she bent over and ducked back into her car to gather her things, her movements fluid as she straightened, then closed the car door with a swing of her hips. With waves of auburn hair hanging past her shoulder, she strode towards him with a gentle smile and killer heels. All Joe could think of was *holy smoke*. His chest tightened, taking his breath. Nah, he told himself, not happening. But his body had other ideas as she walked towards him, elegant, like poetry in motion. He had a vague thought, a phrase he'd read somewhere. Or were they words in a song; it didn't matter, it fit her perfectly. Her silky, blue dress in the softest shades of a summer sky with equally understated flowers in the palest pinks and greens rippled and fluttered around her legs to just below the knee.

Briefcase in one hand and handbag strap over one shoulder, she sang out, 'Is everything okay? You were expecting me, yes?'

Joe came to his senses. 'Yes, absolutely, just not sure why Vogue readers would be interested in a farm and how it operates … you know?'

Standing in front of him now, her subtle perfume had a similar scent to their lemon tree. The blooms, a heady mix of sweet citrus that … go on Joe, that what? Yeah, that Maeve would bring into the house, filling it with their fragrance? Is that it?

Joe firmly told himself, she's gone mate — not coming back — ever.

Grace is a journalist, a city girl, here to do a job and then she'd be gone as well. Wouldn't see her for dust billowing off the back of her expensive car. He pulled himself together and faced his issues head-on. Whatever his sister Leigh tried, he was *not* going back for a second shot at happy families—not happening *ever* again, not to himself, but especially not to Finn. His son would bear the emotional scars for the rest of his life.

3

---

ell, feast my eyes.

There he stood, Joe Mathews, calmly waiting in the blazing sun, a cowboy hat shading his face, hands resting a fraction below his narrow hips, snug white T-shirt that stretched across a powerful chest, shoulders, and biceps. He was _way_ better looking than she remembered when they had coffee in the city and where he seemed to wear a permanent frown. Like this, in his natural surroundings, his Green Place, Joe was something else. And then he started to stride towards her. She'd never seen anything like it, except in the movies. Farmer Joe had a natural, very relaxed shoulder swagger happening. His long legs, muscular thighs straining under the denim, cut the distance easily. Grace had the weirdest sensation; one she'd never felt before. Her legs were not under her control. She imagined someone under the influence of several wines had legs like hers felt right now. So, what the hell was that all about. But then logic told her that spending a good part of the day in her car, of course, her legs would feel wobbly. Ah, but her physical reaction, heart, chest, her complete body were all on high alert. Holy cow, this was the stuff of books, not real — not real, Grace tried telling herself. But her surroundings, the air she breathed, everything slowed down, it felt like her walk towards *him* took forever. But then she blinked, and suddenly there he was, standing directly in front of her, the remarkable but challenging frowning man, Joe Mathews.

So, with years of dealing with stressful situations, she forced a steady hand and slowly lifted her sunglasses to rest on top of her head. Holding onto a calm composure, she spoke in her best telephone voice. A voice, she was once told over the phone by a client who heard her say, *good morning, Grace Taylor speaking. How can I help you?* made the guy forget why he called.

'Hello, Mr Mathews.' Grace purred, doing her best to ignore the enormous dog stretching its neck in her direction but not moving any closer as it sat at Joe's feet, which she was grateful for. Joe swept his green-eyed gaze over her, and she'd bet her favourite Prada shoes that he liked what he saw. She wondered what his hand would feel like; was it rough, strong from working on the land? Grace extended hers and couldn't help but notice his hesitancy as he grasped her hand in his and gave it a firm but gentle squeeze. Openly assessing him, she could feel something was brewing behind his soft eyes, not to mention his body language, his masculine aura that overwhelmed her thoughts. She didn't know where to start, so she put those feelings aside for another time.

Perfect, her mind decided for her, not waiting to get better acquainted.

His grin went up a notch; it slowly became an almost shy, sexy one-sided smile. Grace gave herself a mental shake…again. She had to interview this bloke, spending days in close quarters, so ignoring his effect on her was the only option — and a priority. But he kept smiling, all the way to his eyes. *Perfect,* her mind was at it again. Unable and unwilling to take his scrutiny anymore, she slipped her sunnies back on to cover her eyes. After all, with the right person, the eyes could easily give you away and leave you emotionally naked.

'Lovely to meet you, Grace,' his baritone voice rumbled deliciously, playing havoc with parts of her body. He let her go and rested a hand lightly on the dog's head, adding, 'This is Luna. We've only just changed it from Go-Nuts, my son Finn's idea for a pup who would.'

She nodded and gave him a blank expression partly due to her instant attraction, but also, where's the rest of the info. 'Would?' *There you go, Grace; like all women, you can multi-task.*

'Okay, my apologies. I imagine you wouldn't have had much experience with dogs or animals of any sort ....' he trailed off.

Grace jumped in with, 'Only the two-legged variety and go-nuts would've been the ideal name for some,' she smiled sweetly.

Joe laughed, full-bellied and honest. 'Touché.' Grinning, he rubbed his jaw. 'I'll explain. As a pup full of energy, she would go nuts, full of excitement, running around, chasing a ball or bugs as all pups do. Until they mature, their job is to piss you off at every turn, be out of control, until they figure out, at your direction, they can round up cattle, which is a hell of a lot more fun than chewing someone's shoe. She loved it, but she also needed to settle and be a good companion for Finn. Go-Nuts was a mouthful. So, Luna was it.'

'I see.' Grace's glance at his dog was swift. 'She's behaving beautifully right now.'

'Hmm ...' Joe peered down at Luna. 'Yes, but I have to say her behaviour right this minute is totally out of character. I get a strong feeling she's very interested in you.'

'I couldn't imagine why,' Grace muttered nervously. And that threw her for a loop because she didn't do nervous and then blurted out for no reason at all, 'I had a dog once.'

'Okay, what breed?' Joe asked and seemed genuinely interested.

Genuine, her brain threw into the mix of feelings. Grace wasn't sure how to handle or which box to shove them into, shut the lid down, lock it, even sit on it if necessary. At least that's what a friend accused her of doing anytime something came up that Grace didn't want to deal with.

Grace noticed Joe slant that handsome head of his again, then his brow furrowed, and a concerned look entered his eyes.

'Grace ... er ... Ms Taylor?'

'I-I don't know.' An anxious feeling gripped her stomach. With difficulty, she mastered her emotions and changed the subject. 'It's very nice out here....'

'Nice?' Joe frowned on a smile as if amused and confused all at once.

'Oh, Mr Mathews, your ego is showing. You and I know your farm is way more than nice, but I'm starting to melt, and….'

'Really?' Shaking his head, Joe laughed and then apologised. 'Sorry, I should think before I speak. And yeah, it's a bit warm, but it's also a beautiful day.'

'Would you mind if we went inside, somewhere cool?'

'Of course, follow me.' Joe slapped his thigh, and Luna ambled alongside. As they headed for the veranda, he called over his shoulder, 'I don't know how long you'll be staying, but I'd be getting a hat pretty quick.'

'Not a problem. I have one, just haven't stopped by the B+B to unpack yet.' Grace managed to get her legs moving and joined him on the opposite side of where his dog walked. Driving through Myrtleford, I noticed an excellent range of shops. Can you recommend a good place to buy a few groceries?'

'You cooking for yourself?' Joe looked puzzled.

'Yeah, I enjoy cooking, nothing too fancy. As I'm going through the process, I'm also mentally going over my notes and prioritising them.'

Heading up the granite steps, onto the wide, shady veranda and out of the searing heat was a blessed relief. The old stone colonial homestead, majestic and very well looked after, was even more stunning close-up. All the paintwork around the sash windows and the timber railing along the veranda looked as if they'd just been added.

'Take a seat,' Joe offered, pointing to the chunky rattan chairs with thickly padded cushions in a colourful flowery fabric. 'You thirsty? Would you like a drink?'

'I would love anything cold.'

'Coming right up.' Joe toed off his boots at the door then disappeared, his footsteps thumping along a hall runner as he headed deep into his house and into a distant kitchen. Interestingly, Luna stayed by her side, and then, to her surprise, lay at her feet, which made her feel a little anxious. Grace had been in life-threatening situations where fight or flight was off the scale. This dog taking an interest was hardly a concern — yet it was.

She took a deep breath and slowly let it out. Luna laid her chin on

Grace's foot. Grace stared down at the dog, hoping she'd move away, but she took no notice and closed her eyes.

Joe returned, took one look at his dog, and tilted his head as the softest, warm smile eased into his puzzled face. He gave a slight shrug and, ice blocks clinking, handed Grace a tall glass. 'Lemonade, thanks to my sister, Leigh.' He took a long drag of his and licked his lips. 'But you two have probably met, yeah?'

'We've only spoken on the phone.' Grace smiled – just a little; wouldn't want things to get too friendly. Then out of the blue, her inner voice snapped, *but why the hell not?*

'How long are you staying?'

'What's the matter Mr Mathews, sick of me already?' *What a stupid remark, Grace.*

'Not at all. On the contrary, but ...' and, with a lopsided grin, he made no bones about looking her up and down. 'I hope you've brought gear appropriate for a farm?' Grace opened her mouth to speak, but Joe got in there first. 'If not, there're a couple of places in town, nothing fancy."

Were her journalistic capabilities questioned solely on her attire? And damn it, her feminine side thought he was eyeing her because he liked what he saw. Grace's disappointment flared. *How flimsy is my ego?* She should have known better and insisted on wearing light-weight pants and T-shirt. But her boss at Vogue said she was representing the famous magazine and wanted her to make an impression by dressing fashionably.

Well, she was no wilting violet ... except perhaps today she was, but hey, give a girl a break.

Grace let the icy cold lemonade slide down her parched throat. 'Delicious, thank you.'

'You're welcome.' Joe downed the rest of his drink and set his glass down. Leaning back, elbows on the armrests, relaxed fingers entwined, hands resting on his flat torso, he asked, 'So when do you want to start?'

Grace could read people well, but with Joe's tone, she had no idea whether he was keen or just wanted to get it over with. She'd never been indecisive; doing that could get you into very sticky situations and bad for all concerned. Thankfully her experience dealing with people kicked in and what followed was more in control than her thoughts.

'Hmm, I've had a long day. I need a shower, some decent food and a good night's sleep. Let's start tomorrow. I'll get up early and be here around nine. Is that okay with you?'

'We're up at about six, so yeah, for us, that's a late start.'

Ouch, Grace could almost feel his disapproval.

'Where are you staying?' Joe asked.

She cleared her throat and firmly replied, 'At White Rose BnB.'

There was no mistake, Joe's eyebrows shot up, but he quickly controlled his surprise. 'Super snazzy. You'll like it there, suits you … I reckon.'

Another backhanded appraisal. Grace didn't hide her disappointment and annoyance.

'Mr Mathews,' Grace leaned forward; she'd been told often enough that her look of determination worked. 'It's a BnB. But let's move on. Let's make this a positive experience, right? An editorial that will make readers think twice about where their food comes from and how much work time and effort it takes to bring it to their restaurants, supermarkets and homes through sustainable farming. Then you'll have to stop making judgments about everything I say and do and trust that I know my job.' She waited for a response, but Joe simply looked even more relaxed and added an I've-got-you-pegged smile. She almost got up and left him to his farm, his problems with journalists and his life.

4

Oh, bugger. He'd stupidly just annoyed the feisty Grace by suggesting she needed a super snazzy place to stay. What was he trying to do? Why was he treating her like shit? Ugh, he was an idiot because he liked what he saw, but more to the point, he admired her take-no-bullshit attitude. So, he'd better pull his head in and behave. So yeah, he felt his grin tweak up a notch, a point for Grace, and he was happy to surrender … for now.

'How about you come early and join us for breakfast? That way we can get an early start.' Joe studied her reaction and got nothing but a couple of blinks on a deadpan, beautiful face and the bluest, crystal-clear eyes he'd ever seen. 'According to my son, I make a mean scram-bled egg.'

'Toast and coffee?' Grace asked, head tilted to one side.

'Absolutely,' he answered calmly, while inside, he felt anything but a clever grownup.

'I'll be here at seven.' With that, she started to get up, making Luna jump. Grace fell back into her chair. 'Bugger, I forgot your dog was there.'

Joe immediately stood. 'Hey, Luna girl.' He patted his leg to encourage his dog to move. Holding out his hand, he gave Grace a genuine smile, on the verge of grinning stupidly but in the best way. She just had that effect on him, and he hoped he didn't look like he needed medical attention. Grace took his hand and rose out of her chair; now, she was barely inches from his side. She started to pull away, and Joe instantly felt the loss. He gently squeezed her hand, saying, 'See you in the morning.'

Tail wagging, Luna jumped down from the veranda. Ears pricked, looking very alert, she watched the driveway. Then body wriggling with anticipation, she took off at full speed to greet her best friend, Finn.

Joe glanced at his watch. 'Finn's home from school.' He moved to the railing. Beside him, laughing softly, Grace turned towards the driveway. Legs pumping, Finn burst out from the shady, old pines. Luna, tongue hanging out, and looking up adoringly at Finn, ran along at his side.

'Your dog is amazing,' Grace murmured, her words tinged with emotion.

'Yep, when Finn came home with her, I thought, she's going to be trouble, but turned out nothing more than any pup. Luna is smart, but because of her size, she doesn't have the stamina of a Kelpie or Collie. Nevertheless, she does a great job rounding up cattle until I see she's had enough and then I'll call her off. We don't have our own Kelpies. My neighbour, John Murray and I help each other out when moving cattle. He's got the dogs, and I've got horses. Together, we make a great team.'

* * *

GRACE FOLLOWED JOE STRIDING ACROSS THE DRIVEWAY TO GREET HIS SON. Finn pointed at her car and looked questioningly into his dad's face.

'Finn, this is Grace Taylor. She's a journalist and here to ask questions about how we manage Binowee.'

Finn nodded and stuck out his hand to shake hers. 'Hi,' the nine-year-old said brightly. 'Dad's the best farmer in the state and the country! Are you staying for dinner?'

Laughing, Joe reached down, put an arm around his son and kissed the top of his head. Finn complained, grumbling, 'Ugh, dad! Yuck!' but his grin said otherwise.

'Thank you for the invitation, Finn, but maybe another time.'

'Sure,' he grinned and waved a dismissive hand. 'Anytime. We've got lots of food.'

'Much appreciated.' Grace thought he was an adorable and very confident kid. 'But I'm here because people say your dad knows quite a lot about good farming,' Grace explained.

'Sustainable farming.' Finn wagged his finger. And Grace didn't have to wonder where he learned that from.

'Beg your pardon, Finn. Since you live here and help your dad on this farm, it makes you very special. I'd go so far as to say, you probably know as much as your dad.'

'I do; I know heaps!'

'So, if it's okay with your dad,' Grace glanced at Joe, who shrugged, but his wary, alert eyes studied hers and seemed to say, there's a proviso. She wondered what that might be. 'I'd like to include you in my article.'

'Don't forget, Luna. She's very important.'

'Oh, of course, and Luna.'

* * *

Joe spent a restless night of stupid scenarios and wild dreams about a stunning woman approaching him wearing a beautiful smile and very feminine sexy dress, the cockerel crowed heralding a new day was about to start—with Grace. His body and mind felt frayed like he'd only had half an hour's sleep. Hopefully, a shower would wake him up.

Dried and ready to get dressed, he pulled on his favourite jeans and dark blue T-shirt inscribed in red with the words that said, *If Not Now? Then when?* that he often wore at talks throughout the country. Looking down at the words, he chuckled, realising it could mean a hell of a lot more—today. Rubbing his hair dry, Joe didn't want to, but he had to admit, he looked forward to meeting up with Grace again. Part of him resented feeling this way, and another told him to relax and enjoy her company. Continuing his inner dialogue, he strolled to the kitchen; she was a journalist doing her job, and then she'd be gone soon enough. *Yeah, too soon.*

Muttering those feminine ways couldn't be trusted, Joe pummelled the sourdough he'd prepared the night before, dropped it into two loaf pans and slid them into the hot oven.

'Dad-dad, you were right. The hens really like their new pen. I found ten eggs!'

'Wow, that's great, Finn. You've got happy hens. We'll share some with Aunty Leigh. Can you give them a clean-up in the laundry?'

'Sure.' And his son was off, dashing to the laundry with his basket of fresh eggs.

Smiling, Joe dropped bacon into a skillet, chopped fresh chives and grated a hand full of tasty cheese, peeled a few mushrooms, and sliced them to sauté in butter.

'Right, my man,' he rubbed his hands and smiled at his son. 'We're ready for our city guest who probably never tasted food as fresh or good as this.'

'Yeah,' Finn laughed and ran down the hall, Luna at his side. 'Hey, Dad,' he called out from the veranda, 'Grace is here.'

Luna gave a couple of happy-yodel-whoofs, then Finn sang out, 'G'day, Gracie!'

Joe strolled down the hall just as Grace replied, 'Morning, Finn. How're you?'

'I'm good, thanks. Wait till you see our breakfast. The hens laid ten eggs this morning, and they're real big too.'

'Gosh, I hope you're not giving me all ten.'

'Nah, even I couldn't eat that many.'

'Probably just as well,' Joe offered from the veranda. 'Morning, Grace. Come on up. I see you brought a hat and changed from the… erm dress to jeans.'

'The dress thing is a long, boring story.'

'Don't mind, Dad. He gets nervous around women.'

Thankfully, Grace replied with a little advice. 'You know, Finn, sometimes grownups don't like their foibles to be pointed out.'

'Foibles?' Finn peered up, his nose wrinkled in question.

Grace explained, and Joe couldn't help but find them both endearing. *Shit*, he thought, *careful*, his inner voice warned. *She's here to work, not staying.* But *he* was an adult, and though he liked very much what he saw, that should be the end of it. There was a risk of Finn becoming too attached to Grace when it was inevitable that she would leave. He'd then have to watch his son deal with yet another heartbreak; he didn't want that to happen again.

The timer went off in the kitchen. 'Can I take your briefcase,' Joe extended his hand. Looking a little taken aback, she handed it over. 'Okay, got to get the bread before it turns to charcoal.'

Finn offered his arm to Grace, which made his dad grin from ear to ear—and worry.

'Thanks, Finn.' Grace slipped her arm through his son's. Another tick for the stunning journalist…*Shit!*

'I think Dad should take a chill pill.' Finn muttered.

'I heard that,' Joe called over his shoulder.

'Oh my, that smells so good. You're baking bread!?' Grace called to his back.

'Dad does this nearly every morning. And I collect the eggs.'

'Nothing's too good for our guest from the city, fresh eggs and all the trimmings too.' Joe put in.

* * *

Joe looked very comfortable in his country kitchen with all the bells and whistles to make cooking a pleasure and not a trial.

'Your kitchen looks brand new. State of the art, as they say.' Grace stroked the beautiful mellow timber breakfast bar and slid onto a stool as Joe lined up their plates near the stovetop.

'Yep, it's pretty good. The benchtop you like so much,' he gave her a cheeky wink, which even *he* didn't see coming. He ploughed ahead as if nothing had just happened. 'The timber comes from an Ironbark tree uprooted during a wild storm. Had it milled on-site and dressed it myself.'

'Dressed it?' Grace asked, head to one side. 'How does someone dress timber?'

'Lots of sanding until it's silky smooth, much like…like any timber, you need to work it, bring out the grain, oil it, then sand it some more and oil it again.'

'Sounds like quite a process, but well worth it. Love the beautiful red sheen.'

Finn plopped himself onto a stool next to her and grinned up at Grace before turning to Joe. 'Gave Luna her breakfast,' he informed, sounding pleased.

'Okay, let's eat.' Joe turned to the stovetop. Though it was by no means difficult, Grace was mesmerised by a man beating eggs for crying out loud. But hey, his forearm muscles bunched up all the way to his shoulders.

'Are you on the grid?' And now, her question came out shaky.

'We're mostly off-grid, so needed to make sure whatever I put in didn't drain our battery too much. During the winter months, I use the AGA. It warms the house and heats our water.'

She knew her next question was a silly one but asked anyway. 'So, you're not concerned about wood-smoke pollution?'

He grinned at her as if he knew this was coming. 'If you burn old, dried logs and do it correctly, there's very little or no smoke, plus we have a particle filter that prevents pollutants from entering the atmosphere. We use fallen timber off the property, and though there are fireplaces in every room, we don't use them. They're blocked off at the top. Nothing can fall down them, which happened a few times when I was growing up.'

'Yeah,' Finn dived in with more info. 'Dad woke up one night with a frightened mountain brushtail possum running around his room.'

Joe laughed, 'Yeah, I sat on the bed hugging my knees and yelling for help. It gets bitterly cold up here, and that night it was pouring rain. The possum was probably looking for a warm, dry place. To live a comfortable life and not want to migrate to sunny Queensland for it, we need to keep the entire house warm so the plumbing doesn't freeze, and we end up with burst pipes and water everywhere.'

'I knew that. Just testing you.' Grace laughed softly.

'I knew you were. You're not that ill-informed,' Joe added with a knowing, quirky half-grin.

'Okay, so we've got that out of the way,' Grace replied. 'You know me, and I know you.' And quickly added, 'In a professional sense, of course.'

Chuckling, Joe carried three loaded plates, one in each hand, the third resting on his forearm as a waiter would in a restaurant. 'Where to? Indoors or the back veranda?'

'The back veranda sounds perfect.' Grace followed him out.

Finn was already there setting the outdoor table. His last sweet touch was a vase of yellow and pink tea roses. Grace leaned over to smell their subtle, beautiful perfume. 'They bring me back to my grandmother's house. Nanna-Rita loved her garden, and it showed.' She quickly blinked away the tears that threatened. Joe pulled a chair out for her; she thanked him, took a deep breath, and sat almost opposite Finn, who didn't hide his concern for her.

'Grace? Are you okay? Is your Gran alright?' he asked.

'Wow, your house evokes memories. Unfortunately, my Gran passed away five years ago. It's another long story for another time.' She glanced at her watch. 'We'd better eat up. You have a bus to catch.' She surprised herself; that wasn't something she'd say to a child she hardly knew. Perhaps this house brought out more memories than she cared to have right now. Grace reached across the table to pat Finn's hand. 'Don't know about you, but I'm hungry. And the best part is, I didn't have to cook. I'm going to enjoy your dad's delicious breakfast with you.' Finn flashed a big happy smile, and Grace immediately thought, *shit, I went too far.*

'Finn collected the eggs this morning,' Joe stated around a mouthful of buttered toast.

Quickly swallowing, Grace replied, 'One of the first things Finn mentioned, ten, I believe. Hmm, this is delicious, and I love the bread.'

Finn babbled on about the farm and school and how he was on the soccer team. They had a home game coming up this Saturday, and would she like to come and watch.

'Sounds exciting. I'll have to see how fast I can work.'

'Oh…' his crestfallen expression was enough to melt granite, let alone Grace's defenceless heart. Hang on, she was hardly defenceless. She'd worked with and interviewed the toughest people. Amazing how a sweet boy could demolish the barriers of keeping *personal* shit out of work time.

'Finn, I'll get your dad to jot down the where and when, and I promise to do my best to be there.' She wasn't going to let his half-hearted smile slide. 'Finn?' when he looked up from his plate, Grace added, 'I won't make promises that I may not be able to keep. That wouldn't be fair on you—or me.'

Finn's nod of acceptance was genuine in that he understood. But that didn't mean he liked her answer or explanation.

5

Joe smiled across at his chatter-box son, who held court and often made Grace laugh, which he had to admit was contagious and had him joining in. But it was time to break this up…unfortunately.

'Finn, you'd better get ready; you've got half an hour, and make sure you brush your teeth *with* toothpaste.'

'Yeah, Dad,' his ho-hum tone didn't go unnoticed as he sauntered off.

'Hey,' Joe called out to his retreating back, 'I bought your favourite strawberry flavoured toothpaste, so don't give me a hard time!'

'Finn poked his head around the door. 'I bet you guys are going to have fun, and I just want to spend time having fun with you. But I'll be stuck in a stuffy classroom.'

Joe took a deep breath, pushed his chair back and headed over to talk to his son. 'Have you forgotten all about your clay modelling project?'

Finn's face lit up, his mouth a big circle and eyes round he darted off, yelling, 'I'll be ready in a sec.'

'Teeth, Finn, otherwise you'll end up like Gramps!'

'*Ooh noo!*' Finn wailed.

'That always gets him,' Joe chuckled as he sat down and glanced at his watch. 'He's got twenty minutes before we take off.'

'Oh, you're taking him to school?'

'No, but we usually cycle to the gate. It's something he enjoys, we chat along the way, and I watch him get on the bus. Happy to give him some freedom getting home. But Luna and I always wait for him to emerge out from under the old cypress pines.'

'You seem to have it all figured out.'

'Yeah, it works,' Joe said brightly. 'I'd better fill you in on today's plans. I have to check on the stock on the far south paddocks. All up, it's about an hour's ride. So, unless you come with me, there's nothing much for you today. Sorry, but I've had it planned for over a week. I've already put it off twice. Have to go and get it done.'

'Ride?' Grace's endearing expression melted a corner of his heart. How was it at all possible that a well-travelled, experienced journalist could look so innocent?

'Yes, ride on a horse.'

'Oh … I'd love to see it.'

'Sure,' Joe grinned, happy in the prospect of showing his prized horses, but if he were honest, it was more than that. It was the opportunity to spend time with Grace. No harm in that…surely.

He pushed his chair back and gathered the empty plates, saying, 'I'll just clear our breakfast, then we can go.'

While Joe cleared the kitchen and stacked the dishwasher, Grace moved around his open living and dining area. She checked out family photos and a few keepsakes, and Joe answered Grace's questions, including where and what time the soccer match started.

'This is a lovely photo of you and Finn.' As he wiped down the bench, he noticed she peered closer at one photo. 'Why are you the only one soaking wet?'

'It was during a school fundraiser. Finn's teacher was on duty at soak-the-sad-parent. You hit the bullseye to flip the seat, so the seated person or parent gets dumped, which was me. Mind you it cost the person throwing the ball five bucks. See, humiliating a person doesn't come cheap.'

Laughter bubbled around the room, and it felt good, *too* good. Boy, was he in trouble? No-no-no—he was going to fight this too-good feeling surging through him, yes, fight it all the way, wasn't he? 'Come on,' Joe called out a little more abrupt than he'd wanted. 'I'm done here. Let's go, Finn!'

Grace gave him none too happy questioning eyes that said, are you okay? Or maybe you want to change your tone? And now he felt like such a heel and should apologise. 'Sorry, didn't mean it the way it sounded.'

'Sure,' Grace shrugged, 'I guess you're not used to having a stranger wandering around your house, looking at your stuff. I do understand.'

Luna sidled up and gently nudged her. Grace let her hand rest on the dog's head.

Finn came charging down the hall, backpack bouncing. 'I'm ready!' He waved at Grace and took off for the carport and his bike. 'Hey, Dad? Grace can come too!'

Joe looked down at his boots but found no answers there. He took a deep breath, which didn't work to settle his nerves, and turned to Grace. 'Would you like to ride with us down to the bus?'

Looking troubled, Grace left him hanging as she took a moment to decide. And then Finn yelled,' C'mon Gracie, it'll be fun.'

'Thank you, Finn.' She swung around to face Joe. 'I'm not so sure that it's okay with you though?'

'It's not that…never mind.' He moved deeper into the carport and returned with a women's bicycle. 'Please join us.' Surprising himself with how sincere he was.

'Thank you,' Grace swung her leg through and took off.

Finn yelled, 'Yay!' Then gave Luna a quick cuddle.

Once on the way, Joe relaxed and told himself to stop being an arse to a woman who, through no fault of her own, was making him react without thinking things through. He hugged his son goodbye and considered himself lucky to get the occasional show of affection in public. Finn's face appeared at the back window, grinning and pulling faces.

After waving Finn off, Grace called out, 'Race you back.' And she was off, long legs pumping, jean-clad bum off the saddle. She sure meant business. Tongue lolling out, Luna raced beside her.

And Joe laughed like he hadn't in a long time, which meant he was breathless and useless at trying to catch up.

Back at the house, the bikes stored away in the carport, Joe noted, 'You're fitter than you look.'

'I'm not sure how to take that.' Grace's steady gaze made him feel like she could read his mind. 'But I'll take that as a compliment.'

Yep. 'As it was meant.' And he tried hard not to grin.

'Just let it rip, Joe. Why hold back on happy, you know?'

'Sure…but time to get some work done. Finn will be back before I know it. I've got to get going.'

'Well, am I still invited? Or would you rather I leave?' Grace tilted her head and waited as he headed for the door. 'I can always come back tomorrow. Maybe you'll be in a better frame of mind, you know, let loose and laugh a little.'

'I know what you're saying—look,' and heart hammering, he decided the direct approach was best. 'I'm going to be brutally frank.'

'Good. Go for broke. I won't turn into a blubbering mess. I promise.'

'I've been alone for nearly two years.' He levelled his gaze on her stunning, clear blue eyes that gave nothing away, nothing to encourage him to open up. But damn it, his feelings demanded to be heard. 'I like you, Grace…a lot.'

Grace laughed, short, soft, and sweet. 'Thank you, Joe,' she said through a smile. 'And I appreciate you being honest.'

'Okay, but hey, give this bloke a break, stop laughing at me,' he chuckled. 'C'mon, let's go for a ride, assuming you can?'

'Oh, I think I can manage to sit on a horse.'

'Excellent, it'll be good to show you what Binowee's all about.' He took her hand and breathed a sigh of relief when Grace didn't pull back.

'Hang on a sec, I'll just get my camera…if that's okay with you?'

'Yeah, sure. Lots of people, farmers mostly have taken shots, helps spread the word back home. While you're doing that, I'll get us some water.'

Carrying a small cooler bag, Joe waited at the bottom of the steps.

Grace rushed down from the house, carrying an expensive-looking camera. She took a few shots of the house before stowing it away.

'Luna, come.' Joe called out.

Joe strode off to the paddock beyond the back of the house and with a simple hand signal, told Luna to sit before letting go a piercing whistle, calling his distant grazing horses to come his way. He hoped they wouldn't let him down. Sometimes they were too content and didn't budge until he rattled a bucket of oats, but thankfully not this time. The horses immediately raised their heads, and ears pricked, eyes in his direction, they turned and trotted towards him. Feeling like a teenager who proved his masculine prowess to the fair damsel felt bloody amazing.

But did Grace notice, or was it just run of the mill stuff for a seasoned investigative journalist who travelled the world. And as if on cue....

'Hey, I'm super impressed.' Camera to her face, Grace called him out. 'Just saying.'

'Yeah?' Joe couldn't stop the silly grin spreading across his face.

'*Yes,*' came out in a weird but endearing giggle.

'You'll keep,' he chuckled as he sauntered off to open the gate.

* * *

AFTER TAKING SEVERAL PHOTOS, GRACE LOOKED BACK OVER HER SHOTS. There were a few of Joe. Well, what could a girl do? He just happened to walk into her viewfinder. Joe was handsome but modest. A passionate man about sustainable farming. She had to admit she enjoyed his company. His comment earlier that he liked her, still resonated. She didn't let on at the time, but her heart raced. And though it scared the crap out of her, she liked him—a lot. Acting blasé, Grace leaned back against the whitewashed post and rail fence, attempting to look busy, making sure her camera settings were doing the job, when she felt a warm horse's breath over her shoulder near her ear. She smiled and faced the gorgeous chestnut mare.

'I think Oddie likes you,' Joe said.

'Oddie?' Grace asked, keeping her voice on the quiet side. The horse whickered softly, then lipped her hair and nuzzled her neck. 'Hey, girl,' she murmured and rubbed her blaze. 'You're adorable.'

'Unbelievable,' Joe pushed his hat back and rubbed the top of his head. He shoved his hat back on and opened the gate.

Trying hard not to smile, Grace enjoyed the easy-going state of affairs right now. Joe clicked his tongue, and the horses lumbered after him. 'By the way, my bay gelding is Bill. They're both Australian Walers. Great riding horses.'

'They are beautiful.'

A short time later, Joe came out of the shadowy barn with the horses bridled and saddled. His t-shirt sagged, bulging with something both horses were very keen to get at.

'Oh see, they love what you've got there. Whereas they just love me because I smell good.' Grace took Oddie's reins while Joe yanked his t-shirt up and, clutching two apples, passed one to Grace then grabbing the other with both hands, he twisted and snapped the apple in half.

'Now you're just showing off.' Grace pursed her mouth against a grin.

Joe laughed, and it was so good to see. He sobered and asked, 'You said you can sit on a horse, but can you actually ride one—merry-go-rounds don't count.'

While Joe fed the horses half an apple each, Grace told an edited version of her story. 'I'll let you in on a little secret. Where I come from, most youngsters know how to ride, me included. On an assignment in a Middle Eastern country, a prince, and I hasten to add, 'prince' was a dubious title, suggested I ride his camel, and no, it wasn't a metaphor.' Pulling a face, Joe shook his head. 'He said if I rode this cantankerous beast straight down his private racetrack without falling off, I could choose a horse from his stable.'

'Holey shi-cow!'

'You can curse in front of me, Joe. I won't be offended. Anyway, this guy loved to bet, but he wasn't a good loser. I knew the dangers, but hey, what could he do with a cameraman and sound operator making sure this interview went *live*. His camel, Al-Harib was lovely, I sweet-talked her, and she was fine. We won the bet. Inside the prince's magnificent stables, he took me aside. We agreed that I wouldn't accept the offer of one of his stunning Arabian horses if he would….' Emotions got the better of Grace. She pulled herself together and said, 'And the rest can wait for, let's say, a night over dinner and a glass of wine.'

Trying to soothe her, Joe rubbed her upper arm. 'Crikey, Grace, you went to dangerous lengths. I hope the outcome was worth it.'

'Hmm, I'll probably never know.' She gave a disappointed shrug. 'C'est la vie. The world has changed dramatically, and for me, that was my last trip into dangerous places. I'll sit quietly somewhere and write about my experiences.'

'Grace, you are fearless. I'd very much like to hear more over a glass of wine.' Joe said as he mounted Bill and leaned down to open the gate and let Grace through before doing the gate dance again to close it.

'Sure thing, Joe.' Grace hoped her little video of it worked out well enough to use. 'Gotta say, that was very impressive, more like a beautiful dance. You have to stop. This girl can't take much more.'

'Yeah, okay, I'll take credit.' Bill whickered. 'Sorry, Bill will take the credit.' Joe leaned over and quietly said, 'Actually, it's all, Bill. He's very clever.'

'Gotcha,' Grace stood on a log, mounted Oddie and made herself comfortable.

'C'mon, Luna girl,' Joe called and at a slow trot, he headed for the back hills.

Oddie was not going to be left behind and, without so much as a nudge, followed at Bill's side.

The land was dotted with trees, and long swales, obviously man-made, were contoured across the vast slopes, with dams at strategic places to attract birdlife. The grass along the swales looked so lush for this time of year. Joe took off to check his stock and fences while Grace took the opportunity to take photos of the work Joe had done to change his farm and make it sustainable for his animals, the environment, and his family.

Luna stayed with her and sat on her rump in Oddie's shade.

Lost in a daydream, enjoying the valleys, hills and mountains beyond, Grace jumped when Joe called out.

'Stock and fencing looking good. This way now, Grace.'

Oddie followed as Joe took them further up the foothills where the tree line thickened and granite boulders looked like they'd pushed themselves out of the ground. They came to a shaded, grassy glen and a swift-running stream glistening in the dappled sunlight.

Joe swung off Bill, and before Grace knew it, he'd reached up for her.

She gave him a look that she hoped said, *really?*

'C'mon, Grace, the ground is uneven, there're hidden rocks under the grass, and Oddie is sixteen hands.'

She slung a leg over and reached for his shoulders while his hands went around her waist. He eased her down. With her hands on his chest, she could feel his heart thumping under her palms. Grace looked up into his worried yet hopeful face.

'Grace?'

'Yes,' came out unexpectedly breathy, which she couldn't quite understand.

'Um…you hungry?'

Sadly, his hands slid away, and so did Joe, their beautiful moment *gone*. He stepped away and removed the horses' bridles, leaving them to graze the patches of lush grass.

'Hungry? Yes, I am, actually.' Grace made light of the moment.

Joe spread a picnic blanket over the ground. He pulled out two neatly packed sandwiches from the saddlebags, handing one to Grace.

'Thank you.' Grace sat cross-legged on his tartan blanket, opened her sandwich, and took a bite. 'Hmm, this is amazing, delicious!'

'My grandmother's pickle recipe, now Mum's and Leigh's. A show winner every year.'

'No wonder it's delicious.' Grace took a sip of water and asked, 'I understand the strategic placement of trees, the dams, which you seem to have a few of. But tell me how the swales work?

'Okay, without the swales when it rains, the water runs straight down the hillsides and doesn't get a chance to soak in. Swales stop that from happening, and the water soaks into the ground feeding the grasses and whatever else is planted.'

'Yeah, that makes sense.' Grace took another bite, chewed and asked, 'Aside from your dams and house tanks, are there any other ways you source water?'

'When there's no other choice, I can pump up groundwater. Had to do that this year to keep the cattle alive. Even had to bring in hay bales. So, although I practice sustainable farming, mother nature can be brutal.'

'I can see your land is well looked after.' Grace patted his knee. 'You can be proud of your achievements.'

Joe smiled. 'Thank you. The farm is a work in progress. Before we go home, I'd like to show you our favourite place.'

'I would love that. Let's finish off and go.'

The climb was steep as they rode up a hill that rose quite dramatically. On reaching the crest, Grace feasted her eyes on the stunning vista before her. The magnificent Great Divide appeared to never end. On and on, hills became mountains far to the horizon.

'I've never seen anything so gobsmacking beautiful. And there's just no end, a three-hundred-and-sixty-degree panorama.'

'It's amazing and my favourite place. Three thousand and seven hundred kilometres of mountain ranges stretching from Queensland down to Victoria.'

Grace felt a tear trickle down her cheek. She scrounged for a tissue but couldn't find one and swiped her face with her sleeve.

'Grace?' Joe's voice rumbled deep with understanding.

She turned to see his outstretched hand offering her a bunch of folded tissues.

'Thank you. I don't know what came over me.' She wiped her face and blew her nose.

Joe's infectious laughter echoed around them.

It made Grace laugh and cry at the same time.

Joe drew his horse closer and, reaching for her, leaned across. 'You've got a bit of tissue stuck to your cheek.' And with the utmost care, he peeled it off.

Grace caught hold of his hand and pressed it to her cheek, then pulled it away to study his palm before tenderly kissing him there. Their eyes met, and Grace knew something very profound had just happened between them. So much was conveyed without a word spoken. But at that moment, she knew exactly how Joe felt, and her heart skipped, and her breath caught.

'Um…I don't know why I just did that.' Puzzled, she frowned at him. 'Not in my entire life was I ever compelled to kiss the palm of another human being.' She still had his hand in hers; peering at it, she placed it on his thigh.

Joe smiled a curious one-sided tilt to his mouth and then softly murmured, 'We keep this up, I'll run out of tissues.'

Grace's laugh was soft but short. 'What are you doing to me, Mr Joe Mathews?'

'Goes both ways, Ms Grace Taylor.'

'Did we just get married?'

Joe threw his head back and laughed hard, making his horse side-step away from the noise.

'Now look what you've done. It'll take me weeks to regain Bill's trust,' she said, dripping with wry humour.

'Weeks, huh. I like the sound of that…weeks.' He looked at his watch. 'We'll catch up on this conversation later. Right now, I've got to head back for Finn.' He nudged Bill to move on and over his shoulder, warned, 'Careful, going down is tricky.'

'Yes, of course.' Grace answered, raising an eyebrow with her mouth skewed to one side.

Trotting back through the paddocks, Joe slowed his horse, turned to Grace, and asked, 'Would you like to stay for dinner?'

'I would enjoy that, thank you. It'll be lovely to catch up with Finn and his day at school. Is it okay with you that I include him in my piece, just a short interview?'

'I don't see why not, but you'll have to ask him yourself. It'd be an interesting life experience for him. And he's not a bit shy. But in the end, it's his decision.'

Taking it easy, Grace leaned back in the saddle as they walked Bill and Oddie down the dappled sunlit driveway. The bus came into view just as they reached the gate. Joe slid off his horse as a very excited boy leapt off the bus. He waved at his friends and ran the short distance to greet his dad. Then Finn hugged Bill and Oddie. The horses whickered their greeting. Such a lovely sound, Grace thought.

Craning his neck, he grinned up at Grace. 'Hi Gracie, you're still here, are ya staying for dinner?'

'If it's okay with you, I would love to.'

'Whoohoo, Yay! Let's go!' Finn ran to his bike, yelling, 'race ya to the house, last one is a rotten egg!'

'C'mon, Gracie, you heard him.' With Joe's nudge, Bill stopped prancing about and eagerly took off.

'What do you reckon, Oddie?' And with the slightest touch of her heels, she was off galloping. Grace let her horse have her head while she tipped forward to lift her behind. Around the first bend, Finn and Joe were neck and neck.

Grace caught up, and Joe gave her a wink and a smile. And though Grace wanted to beat Joe, she didn't want to outrace Finn and thought to hell with it. She was having such a good time, it wasn't the least bit important who won the race, so Finn reached the veranda steps first.

Grace let herself go and laughed. 'That was so much fun!'

She flung a leg over Oddie's rump and was about to slide off her back when a pair of large hands wrapped around her waist and set her down on the ground. This was becoming a habit. She wanted to thank Joe, but he'd already moved away and was leading both horses to the tables.

He called out to his son. 'Hey, Finn, wash up and change—'

Finn cut in, 'Dad! I know-er. You don't have to tell me every time.' And then from the side of his mouth, 'Especially not today, Dad.'

'*Oh*…sorry son,' Joe mouthed. Then in a normal voice, he added, 'Okay, soon as I'm done with Bill and Oddie, we'll have cold drinks out back.'

'Yippee! Can I have a chocolate milkshake!'

'Sure, but I'll make it.' Joe gave his son the all-important, I know everything face familiar to all kids. The funny thing about it was, when those kids grew up, they used that very same, I wasn't born yesterday, face. Something Grace had experienced often while growing up.

Grace followed Joe and held her hand out for Oddie's reins.

'It's okay, Grace. You can go in where it's cool if you like?'

She waved her fingers in a hand-em-over gesture. He pursed his mouth against a grin and put the reins in her hand.

The barn was stifling; how on earth were the animals going to cope. But after the horses were unsaddled, he took them straight through to the horse yard where there was shade and a light breeze and hosed them down. Grace found a squeegee amongst the tack and went over Oddie's beautiful coat removing the excess water. Then used the squeegee on Bill while Joe removed their bridles and hung the saddle blankets over the railing. It occurred to Grace that without having to say a word, they worked well together.

Hmm, interesting and a little unnerving.

'Thanks, Grace. You did great. And don't think I didn't notice you easing back with Oddie.' His soft eyes and endearing lopsided smiles really were a turn on. No matter how much she tried to deny it, she had to admit, he had that effect on her.

She shrugged and said, 'Finn is a terrific kid. The best. A few of my friends have children, and they're adorable. But I don't have a clue when it comes to games and whether adults should even compete with a nine-year-old. I just went with instinct.'

'Your instincts are good. Of course, there will come a time when such things have to change. A kid can't go through life thinking they can win at everything all the time.'

'Painful, but true.'

6

───────

Grace hugged Finn goodnight and said she'd probably see him in the morning.

'Thanks for helping me with my homework, Gracie.'

'It was my pleasure; glad I could help you nut out the math problem. And I tell you what, it put my brain to work.'

'Yeah, I saw that,' Finn chuckled.

'Take Luna out the back for her business. And get ready for our show. I'll be right in.'

'Okay, Dad.' Finn took off, yelling, 'See you tomorrow, Gracie.'

Smiling, Joe shook his head. 'I love that kid; his enthusiasm is limitless.'

'I've noticed.' Grace extended her hand. 'Well, thanks for a very informative day, a great dinner and wonderful company. You can't beat that. If it's okay with you, I'll be back tomorrow?'

'Yep, looking forward to it.' Joe held her hand. 'I-I hope….' He brought her hand to his chest. 'Grace, I would very much like to kiss you.'

'Hmm…you would have to be *the* most polite bloke I've ever met.'

And then he gave her the wickedest grin that made his calm grey eyes twinkle.

'Well, Joe. I'd say, go for it.' Grace moved closer. 'What're you waiting for?'

'I'm savouring the moment.' His gaze slowly roamed over her face.

'Uh-huh,' Grace reached up and cupped his jaw. 'Now please, Joe.'

As it was, the wait was worth it. This man could *kiss*.

* * *

GRACE CHOSE TO STAY AT ROSEWHITE HOUSE, JUST TEN MINUTES FROM Myrtleford. Beautiful views from her balcony made it the perfect place. Plus, the trip to Binowee was easy going and short. Gazing out at the distant hills while sipping a glass of juice, her phone rang. She swiped it off the table and read the name Trinity. Grace let go a frustrated sigh and answered, 'Hi Trin, what's up?'

'I've asked you not to call me that. It's Trinity. Please remember.'

Grace paused. 'I've asked you not to call, visit or email while I'm on an assignment. Distractions are a pain. What is it that couldn't wait until I got back?'

Trinity cleared her throat. 'Well, we certainly wouldn't have bothered, but it's important that you know.'

'Okay, I'm listening.'

'Your lawyer called, as you had instructed he should if your agent Harry Bennet decided to pay *you* a visit.'

'Hold on a sec, *Trinity*, he's not *my* choice. It was Vogue who suggested Bennet.'

'Whatever,' Trinity waved it off. 'Fine, nevertheless, he intends to visit and nothing I said was going to put him off.'

'Damn the fool. He's been getting way too personal. The so-called dinner to discuss my trip etc, turned into too much touchy-feely and cheesy innuendo. I let it go, thinking I've told him there's no chance of anything other than a professional partnership, he'll stop. But dropping in on me means he's an idiot and will keep trying.' Grace let go a heavy sigh and said, 'I'm not happy about this whole thing. Bennet is a creep.'

'Sorry about that, but he was recommended,' Trinity complained.

'Who by?'

'Management. But apparently, no one had time to check.'

'I can handle it. Trust me and my lawyer—and no one else. I've got it covered. I have to go now, or I'll be late. Anything else, quickly?'

Trinity Westlock—sounded nervous or stressed—which Grace had been told was something Trinity was incapable of feeling. Right now, Grace begged to differ. Women in management, surrounded by men, always had it tough. Grace felt guilty for snapping at her, but at least she managed to mollify Trinity that everything was working out well. She had some exceptional material for her feature article and, to add more interest, she was off to a local soccer match. There she was going to meet and chat with locals to ask about their farming practices and what they thought of Joe Mathews and the way he transformed Binowee.

Grace followed the posh voice of her satnav, explaining how to navigate to the soccer field, when her phone rang. 'Hi, Sam, what's up?' she greeted her lawyer cheerily.

'Hey, kiddo, letting you know Harry Bennet is on his way. Don't know what he's up to, but I've spoken to Trinity, explained everything regarding Mr Bennet and his peculiar demands and made sure the contract was in her hands and that she was happy. Don't know why Mr Bennet wanted me to hold off, I scoured the fine print and it's all good. Even had a colleague look it over.'

'Thanks for letting me know, Sam.'

'Hey, I've pulled you out of many scrapes. This guy is just an annoyance. I'll always have your best interest at heart, always will.'

'Thank you, Sam, appreciate it.'

'No worries, talk soon.' And he was gone.

She found a place to park under the shade of an old eucalypt, grabbed her hat and phone and strode the fifty or so meters towards the clubhouse. She spotted Joe standing at the railing as he looked across the field, giving his son a wave and a thumbs up.

Grace sidled up next to him and tapped his shoulder. 'Hi,' she said, unable to suppress a grin. 'Have I missed much?'

Joe swung around. 'You made it. Fantastic, Finn will be blown away.' Smiling, Joe rubbed her upper arm, then quickly dropped his hand and added, 'They've only been on the field for about fifteen minutes. So, plenty of time for Finn to show off his soccer skills.'

Grace's peripheral vision had vanished because suddenly, two boyish arms wrapped around her waist.

'Hey, son, take it easy.' Joe ruffled Finn's hair, then hitched a thumb over his shoulder. 'I won't be long, just need to chat with Barney about the northern fence. Back in a sec.'

'Finn,' Grace gently took hold of his hands and hunkered down to talk to him. 'Wow, you look amazing, love the soccer gear. How's the game going?'

'No goals yet. I think we're all a bit rusty.'

'Oh, sure. That can happen to the best of us. Before you know it, you and your teammates will warm up and start flying around the field. Anyway,' she plucked dry grass out of his hair and said, 'what matters most is that you're all having fun, right?'

'Oh yeah, heaps of fun. And guess what?'

'Okay, you've got me, what?' His bubbling enthusiasm had Grace giggling.

'Aunty Leigh is here too,' he said through an infectious chuckle.

'Hey, Finn,' a soft voice sang. With a smile adding to her lovely face, the tall woman reminded her of Joe. Dressed in comfy capri pants and a form-fitting T-shirt, with her long sun-bleached hair tied back in a high ponytail, she held her arms out for her nephew.

'Aunty Leigh!' Finn ran to her and flung himself at her for a mighty hug. She didn't even have to take a step back, impressive. Looking up into her pretty face, Finn asked, 'Where are Phillie and Tom?'

'With their dad on the play equipment.'

'After the game, we're all going to stuff our faces at the sausage sizzle and then eat lots of ice cream,' Finn nodded vigorously, thought about it, and added, 'maybe even two lots. One vanilla and one choco-late. Can they come too?'

'Sure, but remember they're still little, so one sausage sandwich is more than enough. And take Uncle Jim with you.'

A whistle blared, and Finn ran off yelling, 'See ya!'.

Laughing softly, Grace stood, and hand extended, she greeted Leigh. 'It's lovely to meet you face to face at last.'

'Same here.' Leigh grinned. 'You're perfect.'

'Pardon, what do you mean?' Grace queried, head to one side.

'*Ah…* Don't mind me.' Leigh shook her head. 'No, bugger it. You *are* perfectly gorgeous. And a breath of fresh air. How do you like what you've seen so far?'

'First of all, I want to thank you for getting my assignment off and running.'

'My pleasure, but you know, it's for everyone's benefit. There's a lot riding on it for us and our area.'

'Yes, true, and as I understand, this soccer match and everything that goes with it has all been donated by businesses in town to raise money for the hospital?'

'Yep, we need a new x-ray machine and a lot more, but that'll do for starters. What do you think of the farm?'

'Well, having seen the before photos and now ridden over the farm, I can say Binowee is truly amazing. Joe has worked miracles. I believe once my assignment goes live, it *will* be very successful. The important thing is getting sustainable farming out there to people who want to know where their food comes from and how it's grown. The best part of this agreement is once Vogue has had my piece in their magazine for a month, I'm free to spread it around. It's in my contract. At least it better be.' Grace took a moment to gather her thoughts on how to ask her question.

'Don't hold back, Grace. I'm not the type who needs pampering.'

'Good to know. Okay, here goes. Do you think Joe would agree to do a live interview?'

Leigh threw her head back and laughed.

'Oh, that bad, huh?' Grace felt the worm of disappointment.

'No, not at all. He'll talk the legs off an iron pot when it comes to proper farming practices. But what he and I, will be asking, is where will the interview be shown?'

'All over, as many places that will take it on, like *Food Tank* and *Kiss The Ground.*'

'Just ask my brother. He'll do it for the right reasons.'

'Okay, wish me luck.'

Shouts and cheering ended their conversation as happy voices filled the air.

Leigh kissed her cheek then pointed to the play area, yelling out on the run, 'Hope to see you again soon.'

Grace yelled back, 'I would love that!'

She heard but took little notice of footsteps thumping up behind her, drawing closer.

A familiar voice called out, 'Yo, Grace!'

Grace stopped in her tracks and looked over her shoulder. 'Harry!'

'Damn it,' he started, breathing hard, 'I thought that woman would never leave. I was melting in this heat; it's burning up my nose and lungs.'

'That woman's name is Leigh Gardner and Joe Mathew's sister. Trinity let me know you were coming. Why are you here!?'

'I'll tell you, but not here among the um…farmers.' His nose wrinkled with distaste before adding, 'Let's have dinner with a few wines, and we'll talk. I can offer you way more than this lot can.'

'You have to be kidding me?'

He shook his head. 'No, deadly serious. After you're done with this,' he waved a dismissive hand, 'I've got information on Trinity and the mob she works for, and it's not good. So come on, let's get out of here, grab a bite.' Harry looked around, 'I'll tell you all about it but not here. I found a great place to have lunch, and we can celebrate. You know, just us two, not a crowd of gossiping onlookers.'

Astonished, Grace took a couple of steps back and raised her hands, palms out facing him. 'Unbelievable!' She was shaking with anger. 'Okay, Harry, I know what's going on here. *You* are a useless, self-centred, misogynistic idiot!' Absolutely livid and not caring who saw her rage, she stepped forward. Her index finger jabbing into his chest, she growled. 'You've blown it. By the time I'm finished with you, you'll be lucky to get a job anywhere in this country, and—'

Harry cut in, adopting an arrogant posture. 'Oh no you don't! I am and will remain your agent until the contract you signed ends three years from now.'

Arms folded, Grace collected her thoughts. She raised her eyes to meet his, and in a dangerously quiet voice, advised, 'You think I don't make sure I'm covered when taking on someone new? You think I just blithely jump in and sign a piece of paper that binds me for three years without protection?' Harry looked both shocked and worried. And Grace cheered inside. She couldn't remember who said it, but it always stayed with her: *There's nothing better than assuming your opponent has a few hidden secrets that one could draw on when needed for one's protection.* She didn't have anything on Harry but showing how he'd reacted to her accusation there had to be something.

'I don't know what you're talking about,' Harry blustered.

'Never mind—*Harry*. My lawyer has everything I need in safe-keeping.'

'Right, that's it?' he snarled. 'That's all you've got, gossip? You won't hear the end of this *Grace Taylor*.'

'Oh, but my lawyer will make sure it is the end; there is no doubt. What he has is solid information and nothing to do with gossip. You are an opportunistic sleaze.' And just for good measure, she bluffed, 'We were just waiting for you to show your hand, and here you are. Human nature is so predictable. And another thing, with my connections to back me up, know this—*we are done!*'

Shouting, whooping, and hollering echoed across the field. Grace glanced over to see Finn being surrounded by his teammates as they gathered around, and she'd missed whatever he had just done.

Gone was the delightful, easy-going day where she could watch a boy and his teammates play soccer on a grassy field surrounded by loved ones cheering them on.

'Leave now before I lose my temper,' she threatened.

Her peripheral vision was well and truly on alert. She turned to what caught her attention. Joe at the fence line, grinning like a very proud dad. He'd been there the whole time during her altercation, with one eye on the soccer field, the other on her and the heated exchange with Harry. But he didn't step in and get into a chest-thumping competition with her so-called agent, which Grace thought was considerate and very much appreciated. *Yeah.*

'Go Harry! Get lost! Don't *ever* bother me again! Be proud of the fact that you successfully crapped all over what should've been a brilliant day, with amazing, wonderful people.'

Red-faced, Harry strode off, muttering, bitch.

Grace was relieved to see the back of him.

Grace needed to pull herself together because Joe was striding in her direction. Not stopping, yet being polite when friends wanted to chat.

Once at her side, he greeted her softly and with meaning, 'Hey Grace.'

'Hey, Joe.'

'You okay?'

'Am now.' She looked up into his handsome, concerned face. 'It's one of those need to explain over a bottle of good wine moments.'

'Gotcha. I'm gonna make sure we do that. Cos, I want to bottle the exchange I just witnessed and sell your amazing control on eBay.'

Grace's laughter cut through the general hubbub. Happy, cheery faces turned her way, saluting her with all manner of signs; boy scout, girl guides, military, you name it was there, and Grace had never felt such joy and … dare she believe … a sense of belonging.

'Gosh…'

'Grace…' Joe tentatively placed an arm around her shoulders. Feeling the overwhelming wave of support, she leaned into him and soaked up his comfort, but not for too long. That would only make her feel…weak.

Grace pulled away. 'Thank you, Joe. That was all a bit tense, and in future, I'll look for my own agent, regardless of the "trusted" person who wants to recommend one.'

'Though mine was recommended,' Joe grinned. 'Or I should say, I was told. Leigh made sure she would be the one to look after both our interests.'

'Sounds like the perfect partnership.'

The game continued, and Finn kicked the ball, passing it to a player whose swift legwork sent the ball flying into the net for another goal. The crowd went berserk. Setting the altercation aside, Grace joined in, jumping up and down on the spot, clapping and calling out, 'Go Finn—Go Finn!'

Oops, perhaps she was a little over the top, but at least the day's crap was momentarily forgotten. And standing to the side, arms folded, happily gazing at her, was Joe.

She gave him an innocent look and honestly said, 'This has been the best day I've had in a very long time. Thank you so much for inviting me, Joe.'

'Hey, I would've, but Finn got in there first.'

'True, he did. And here he comes surrounded by his team.'

Finn called out, 'Dad-Dad! Did you see Azim kick a goal?'

'We sure did. A brilliant shot. Did you see Grace jump up and down yelling…' Grace clasped a hand over his mouth, but Joe carried on anyway, with a muffled, 'Go Finn.'

'Nah, sorry Gracie, we were busy celebrating. And we're starving, so can I go get a sausage?'

'Absolutely. I've paid for the whole team to have one.'

Finn's eyes lit up, and arms wide, he slammed his little body into his dad and hugged his waist. He looked up, his adoring face all smiles, and said, 'Thanks, Dad,' then raced off with his teammates and headed straight for the sausage sizzle stand.

'They'll be wanting ice cream next,' Grace informed him.

'Yep, but that's not my department. Azim's dad, Khalil and I have an understanding. I get the sausages organised, and he gets the ice cream.'

'So, Azim and his family, do they come from Iraq, Afghanistan … or somewhere like that?'

'According to immigration, they come from somewhere in Saudi Arabia, but no matter how often we've asked, they won't go into specifics, possibly out of fear. They settled here a couple of years ago. Azim has an older sister who insists her name is Jasmine. They're a beautiful family and part of our community. All we know is the kids had a tough start in life, and if you love your kids, it's even tougher on the parents. The important thing is, they're all thriving now.'

Overwhelmed, Grace felt light-headed and ready to…to, she wasn't sure what, but this couldn't be. They couldn't be. Azim was a very popular Arabic name, but not Jasmine.

'Don't move, I'll get you some water.' Seconds later, Joe was back, took her hand and placed a glass of water into her palm then wrapped her fingers around the cool glass. He helped her lift it to her mouth. She took several long sips. Then Joe guided her to a quiet place, a shady bench under the trees.

7

———————

Joe had only known Grace for a short time. Nevertheless, he knew she was strong in mind, spirit and body. But to see her face drain the way it did was unnerving. She sat silently sipping water and staring at the ground.

Joe waited.

He looked across the oval and saw the boys were on their second sausage sandwich. And it wouldn't be long before Finn came running up with his ice cream, ready to go home.

'Hey, Grace?'

It felt like a lifetime before she answered. 'Yeah?'

'Are we saving this one for a glass of wine and a talk?'

'Definitely. Looks like it's going to be a long night sometime soon, yeah? You deserve nothing less.'

'I wouldn't go that far, but … sure, I'll take it.' Grace splashed a little cold water on the back of her neck. 'Just so you're not freaking out, and by the way, thank you for helping me with the water and finding somewhere to sit, but if I'm right, then this last little episode is definitely worth celebrating.'

Eyes on Grace, Joe leaned forward, propped an elbow on his knee and, resting his chin in the palm of his hand, whispered, 'I'm in awe.'

'Not me, surely. It's got to be Finn. After all, he kicked a goal and instigated another. Truly awesome.' Grace tried to smile, but Joe didn't miss the ever so slight mouth tremble.

'You know, Grace…' he let his hands drop to his knees, 'I want to hold you real bad right now.'

'Oh, interesting…too late. Finn is running a race to get here with two ice creams and a paper bag.'

And then, there he was, and to Joe's way of thinking, his son got the vote for man of the match.

'Dad, Grace, I bought you a couple of sausage sangas.'

'Thank you, Finn, that was very thoughtful.' Grace said, 'I'll eat mine in a moment. Just want to get some shots while the light is perfect.'

'Sure, but don't wait too long,' Finn declared, 'they're much tastier hot.'

Joe kept his eyes on Grace as she wandered off, taking photos of the oval and surrounds. He knew it was all a ploy to get some breathing space and not let Finn see she was dealing with a crisis. Concerned, Joe determined to find the cause. God, how he wished his situation was different. His son came first and foremost. Finn needed protection from any more devastating disappointments, especially when they could be avoided. So, what was he doing saying shit like, *I really want to hold you right now?* Besides, what would Grace do in this town, beautiful as it was, with amazing people, when she could travel all over the world for her fabulous career.

'Dad…' Finn tugged at his sleeve. 'Dad!?'

'Yeah, Finn,' he answered and gave his son undivided attention.

'You should ask Grace to the dance next month!' Finn announced, bubbling with excitement.

'I'm sure Grace has plenty to do rather than go to a country dance.'

'Like what?' Finn asked, all innocent. 'She's done everything, pretty much. I bet she's never been to a country dance, for – for all that hugging and kissing day, Val-Val… C'mon Dad you know the one I mean.'

'Valentine's day.' Joe answered dryly.

'Yeah, that's the one,' Finn fidgeted with enthusiasm, 'and if you don't ask her, I will. Grace can be my date. Whoohoo!' He jigged about, grinning from ear to ear.

'There's a dance?' Grace appeared behind them.

'Yeah,' Finn piped up, 'At the RSL hall.'

'Where is this hall?'

'It's in town. You can't miss it!' Finn squealed with excitement.

'But it's not until February fourteenth. You'll probably have way too much going on back in Melbourne.' Joe hoped he wasn't right—yet there was a problem. Which made him think, bloody hell, why is this so damned hard.

'Depends, but yeah,' Grace began, 'it's often someone's birthday or anniversary, even if it's the anniversary of their broken—'

'Marriage?' Joe cut in.

'Dad!' Finn yelled, his face suddenly red with anger and heartbreak.

'I was going to say, broken toenail,' Grace added, 'Sorry Finn I didn't mean to upset you.'

'You didn't—Dad did!' Finn cried out, then angrily scrubbed the tears from his face. 'Mum's coming back. I know she is! She said she loves me. You can't just leave someone you love!'

Joe hung his head and clasped his shaking hands until his knuckles turned white. His heart ached for his son; it broke him every time this happened. Maeve was not coming back. She'd filed divorce papers so that he could move on. 'Finn, please.' When he had his son's undivided attention, he put his arms out. 'I'm sorrier than you'll ever know. Come here, please.'

Finn hesitated, then ran to Joe, who wrapped his arms around him...in public. Which showed just how much his son was hurting, and Joe's heart broke a little more. He felt movement and looked up to see Grace quietly edge away. As if he dared not ask yet was compelled to, he voiced just above a whisper, 'Please don't leave, Grace.'

Finn pulled away from Joe's neck, used his dad's T-shirt to wipe his face and echoed what his dad had said.

'How could I possibly ignore such an exemplary request.'

'Exemp–exempla,' Finn tried through his hiccups as he studied his dad's face. 'Our new friend uses a lot of big words.'

'Hmm....' Joe made eye contact with Grace, hoping they under-stood each other without having to say a word. She gave a little, I'm okay shrug, but Joe's barely perceptible nod made her smile.

A shrill cry, 'Dad!'

'Yes, Finn, I'm sure Grace knows a lot of big words. That's her job. And that's a good thing. You can learn stuff even outside school hours. The word is e-x-e-m-p-l-a-r-y. Meaning, excellent, admirable.'

'Grace, *you* are exemp-alary.' Finn told her earnestly.

'That *is* high praise, Finn. And coming from you means even more to me. Thank you.'

With an arm wrapped around Joe's neck, he said. 'Can we go home now?'

'Sure.' Joe stood, grabbed Finn's forearms, and then swung him up to sit on his shoulders.

'Whoa!' Finn cried out through sniffles, 'I haven't done this for a long time.'

'No, and is it any wonder, no more pancakes for you.'

'That's alright. I know how to make 'em,' Finn shot back.

'I'll see you two, maybe tomorrow. I'll ring first. And I'm putting my order in for pancakes. I'll bring the strawberry jam, maple syrup and ice cream.'

Finn whispered in Joe's ear; his question worried him. Neverthe-less, he asked Grace. 'Finn's asking if you'd like to come...' and he nearly said home, 'over for dinner?'

'I'd love to, Finn. But hey...' Joe clenched his teeth at *but* and braced himself for the rejection. 'It's been a big day. How about I shout your favourite meal.'

'Yes!' Finn launched his hands into the air. 'Fish and chips and potato cakes.'

'I'll order it right now and bring it around to Binowee while you freshen up.'

Joe swung Finn off his shoulders, held his son's face with a gentle touch and asked, 'You okay?'

'Yeah, Dad.'

Wrapping his arms around his son's small frame, Joe made a silent wish that he could heal his son's pain.

* * *

JOE'S DEEP FATHER AND SON CONNECTION AND UNCONDITIONAL LOVE WAS the stuff of a Disney movie, except so *very* real—real life, real trauma, real pain. Her heart ached for them both and for herself. She'd never experienced a connection like theirs first-hand.

By the time she arrived at Binowee with the steaming fish and chips package, it was early evening, and the sun's rays streamed up from behind the mountains casting everything in its warm glow.

Grace barely had room to open her door, let alone get out. Luna was right there, greeting her with happy woofs and warbles. 'Hi, Luna girl. C'mon move over.' She eased the door open, ruffled Luna's ears, then grabbed her shoulder bag and the wine.

But before she could get to their food, Joe came up and insisted, 'Grace, I'll get the food.'

Oh, lordy, he smelled great. She didn't know what it was but caught the scent of citrus, pine and…leather? His hair was still wet from showering. Grace breathed him in as they walked back to the house.

Coming to her senses, she asked, 'How's Finn?'

'He's okay. Maeve leaving will always hurt.'

'Maeve being his mum, your wife?'

'Yes, soon to be ex…she's filed divorce papers, said it's so I'm free.'

'Oh. I'm sorry, Joe. I don't know your situation, but if Finn has a rough time, then so must you be.'

'I have to be honest, saw it coming twelve months prior to her leaving.' Joe stopped abruptly.

'Yay!' Finn yelled from the veranda, 'Dinner's here, I'm starving!'

Joe added quickly, 'I came to terms with it eight months ago. Finn may come to terms with it when he's older and better able to process what happened. Unfortunately, he's far from ready.'

'I feel for him…I feel for you both.'

'No need, I'm good. And Finn has me.' Joe stopped walking and turned to face her. 'There's more to the long story.'

'There usually is. Including mine, I'm sure, but all I have is the sensation that overcame me at the oval, which was weird. I have the feeling your situation, or perhaps Finn's, has brought back foggy memories of something that I can't put my finger on. But something's brewing.'

'Relax, it'll pop in one day. It has too.'

'Well, I brought wine, two bottles, you think that'll do?' Grace frowned, 'Of course, a couple of glasses could have a positive or negative effect. When I become a blubbering heap that you don't know what to do with, I suggest you throw a bucket of icy water over me.'

Joe's laughter rang out across the yard.

'Perhaps I should've brought a case?'

'Not to worry, Gracie, we have a cellar full of wine.'

'Ooh, I can't wait to see what's down there.' Forget about the cellar. Joe just called her, *Gracie?* But there was no time to work that one out; fish and chips were getting soggy.

As they entered through the front door, Finn came thundering down the long hallway with Luna by his side. Freshly showered, wearing shorts and a T-shirt with a dragon on the front, arms wide, he thumped into Grace, wrapping her up in a fierce hug. The force made her take a step back, or they both would've toppled.

'Wow! What a greeting, thank you. I've never had a hug quite like that. 'She wrapped her arms around him. 'You smell good too.'

'Too?' Joe fished, giving her a crooked, I'm not smiling, smile.

Grace changed the subject. 'I hope the oven is on like I asked?'

'Sure, we've got a tray ready and everything,' Finn happily informed.

'Well, I'll be? I'm impressed.' Entering the kitchen, Grace kissed Finn on the top of his head.

'Dad needs one of those as well. There's no favouritism here, ya know.' Finn stated firmly.

'Um…well, Finn, I think your dad is old enough to find his own… erm, kisses.' Grace felt heat rise into her neck and up her face. She made a hasty retreat. 'I just need to use the bathroom.' She hurried down the hall, found the bathroom, closed the door behind her, and muttered, 'Good lord. I've dealt with rowdy cat calling blokes, with Kings and Princes who carried enormous knives, with intimidating corporate giants who thought they could demand anything and that they were above the law. But these two, father and son, have…have what Grace…have…bugger it, they've filled a big part of my heart. It's like a slow flood growing, taking over. Shit!'

'Everything okay, Grace?' Joe called from the other side of the bathroom.

'Just a sec, Joe.' She splashed cool water on her face, dabbed it dry with the hand towel, then swung the door open, barely inches away from his face, her words rapid-fire, 'It's another one of those chats to add to our list. And I'll be damned if I leave anything out. Warning Joe, it's going to be a bumpy night.'

'I can't wait.' Joe's chuckled, and then on a cheeky, sexy grin, he called out, 'Finn, I think you embarrassed our new friend.'

'No, you did not!' Grace yelled, striding down the hall.

'Sorry, Gracie, didn't mean to embarrass you,' Finn said, giggling.

'Oh sure …' Grace muttered as she moved back to the kitchen and casual dining area just as the tray of crispy fish, chips, and potato cakes came out of the oven.

Nose in the air, Luna hovered, hoping a treat might fall her way.

Using tongs, Joe grabbed a few chips and put them aside. Looking at their dog, he explained, 'They're hot, wait.' Tail wagging, Luna sat on her rump. 'Finn, did you wash your hands after you fed Luna?'

'Yeah,' as if to say, of course I did.

'Finn, could you put some plates out?' Joe indicated with a sideways nod. 'We'll eat on the deck.

'But Dad,' Finn began, wearing a frown, 'we always eat off the paper.'

'Yeah,' Grace agreed, 'that's how we used to….'

Dinner was great, relaxed even with the thoughts bouncing around in her mind of promised tell-all chats and the sudden burst of memory of eating fish and chips off butcher's paper.

Finn scooped the last of his ice cream into his mouth and asked, 'Can I have a game before bed, Dad?'

'Sure, but take Luna out for a short walk first while I clean up.'

'Yep!' Finn rolled his eyes, 'don't I always do that?' He patted his leg to encourage Luna to follow.

'Yeah, you do. You look after Luna like she's yours,' Joe quipped.

The sound of *'Hardy-ha-ha-ha,'* disappeared outside.

Twenty minutes later, Grace watched, father and son play a game of chess. Though she wasn't a bad player, she doubted whether she could keep up with Finn.

Game over, Finn triumphed over his dad. 'You're getting too good for me,' Joe told him, smiling proudly. He looked at his watch. 'You've got Facetime in ten minutes. Get ready for bed. Go on,' Joe hugged his son, 'You know the routine.'

Finn came to Grace's side. 'Night Gracie, thanks for coming to watch me play and for the best dinner I've had in *forever!*' Which he finished off with another eye-roll.

'Oh sure, Finn. But I know otherwise. I mean *really*, going by break-fast, your dad's a pretty good cook.'

'Ah, but that was because you were coming. Other days, it's a bowl of muesli and a banana.'

'No…' Grace squeaked. 'But when I was invited, I'm sure I heard you say, wait till you see breakfast, and the hens laid ten eggs. And that he always baked bread.'

'Oops.' Finn chuckled and raced off.

Joe didn't say a word. He simply smiled and gathered plates, happy enough, it seemed, for Grace to have his back.

'C'mon, I'll show you the cellar.'

Grace followed through a door in the butler's pantry. Joe switched on the lights, and Grace was amazed at the size and scale of the spiralling, brick stairs, taking them down to a cavernous room filled with racks of dusty bottles.

'I'm gobsmacked. This is enormous, and so are the racks. What's that down there?'

'That's Leigh's domain. She's a mushrooms expert. Her produce is in high demand in Melbourne restaurants mostly. She doesn't produce enough to go national, and she's more than happy with that.'

'Your farm is capable of so much. I'm surprised you haven't gone into cheese.'

'We have, or rather her partner Josh has. He was a city lawyer, met Leigh through a friend and asked her out. Gave up city life, became our local lawyer and cheesemaker. It wasn't until Leigh was satisfied with his cheeses that she approached the same restaurants and offered a taste. One bite, and they were sold.'

'Dad, dad!' Finn called down.

'On our way!' Joe took Grace's hand, led her through the vast cave-like room to the stairs, and then ushered her back to the kitchen.

'What is it, Finn?' Joe asked, arm around his son's shoulder.

'Mum wants a word.'

'Okay, tell her I'm coming.' He turned to Grace. There was no doubt in her mind, Joe was troubled.

'Listen, I think I should go. We'll do the wine thing another time. Or not.'

'No, Grace, we're going to talk tonight. Doesn't matter about the Facetime with Maeve. It'll take a couple of minutes, no longer. Please, pour us a glass each, get in a comfy chair out on the back veranda, and wait for me.'

'Okay, but any longer than a couple of minutes, I'm gone.' Feeling the heat, she flipped her hair off the back of her neck. 'I…to be perfectly frank, Joe, there is something.' She waved her hand back and forth between his chest and hers, indicating the two of them. 'You still have issues you need to sort and a son who needs you. Not some stranger from the city. Though he has been a perfectly charming young man for a nine-year-old.'

'Fair enough, and I totally understand. But please, let's do this. I'll be back before you sit down.'

'Okay, Joe. I'll wait.'

He leaned in and took his ever-loving time kissing her cheek. 'Thanks,' he murmured sweetly and strode down the hall.

Grace grabbed a bottle of her favourite Sauvignon Blanc and began twisting the top. It wouldn't budge. 'Oh, you've got to be kidding me,' she muttered. Bending over, she held the bottle between her knees, hand around the neck she attacked the screw top lid. Growling with effort, she still couldn't crack it.

'I was looking for you out on the deck,' Joe chuckled.

She yelped with fright. Luna came running, and so did Finn.

Straightening, she held the bottle out to Joe. 'And no cheating.'

'How am I going to cheat?' Joe effortlessly removed the cap and handed the bottle back to Grace with a wicked smile.

'Smartypants,' Grace rolled her eyes.

Chuckling, he turned to Finn. 'Did you say goodbye to your Mum?'

Finn squeaked, 'Yeah,' sounding a little offended by Joe's question.

'Can't wait for his voice to break,' Joe mumbled, adding, 'Okay, I know it's Sunday tomorrow, but mate, it's nine-thirty.'

'I'm going. I came to see what the commotion was about. And say good night to Gracie.'

'Aw…thank you, Finn. Sleep tight, don't let the bed bugs bite.'

Finn wrinkled his nose, pulled a *what-the* face, and told Grace emphatically, with big eyes, 'There are no bugs in my bed, Gracie.'

'I'm so sure there aren't. It's just an old saying.'

'And don't forget you're coming to that dance in a few weeks,' Finn instructed.

'It's in my diary,' Grace replied, 'I've even reminded myself a week in advance. How's that?'

'Just checking. Sounds good to me.'

'Okay, I know I'll enjoy it once I get amongst it.' Grace eyed Joe, saying. 'But I'll have to shop for something appropriate to wear.'

'Not really,' Finn declared, 'our celebrations are laidback, and you don't even have to wear a dress.'

'Grace has the perfect dress….'

'Okay, it's all settled.' She turned to Finn. 'Unless I'm on a deadline or rushed off to report on something, I would love to come to your dance next month.'

'Stop the delaying tactics, Finn,' Joe said with a smile.

'O-k-a-y…' and with a little wave, Finn left.

'I'll be there in a minute,' Joe called after him.

When the house had fallen quiet, Grace took a tray out to the back veranda and placed glasses and the opened bottle of Sauvignon Blanc on the table, plus what she found in the fridge, cheeses, chilli humous and avocado dips. In the butler's pantry, crackers and nuts.

And then the moment when they'd both tell all.

8

____

Joe stooped over Finn's bed. And kissed his forehead. 'You did great today, so proud of you.'

'Thanks, Dad,' Finn's voice croaked with sleep.

'Night, son.' Joe murmured, and leaving the door ajar, he left the room.

Knowing who was waiting for him, he took a deep, steadying breath and strode through the house to the back deck, ready to take on Grace's questions.

'Nice spread, thank you.' He poured them both a glass of wine. Passing one to Grace, then sat in a chair opposite so he could see her lovely face. He took a mouthful of his wine, a little Dutch courage, possibly. 'I'll start and get things rolling before we're too drunk to watch our words.'

'Well, you know what they say, drunk talk isn't just nonsense.'

'Yeah, I've heard some people get too drunk to care. But I do care, and as I'm quite sober, I'll start—*not* with the easiest, but *the* most heartbreaking.' He lifted his glass and drained it. Joe was painfully aware, Grace waited, poised for his revelations?

'Joe, stop looking so nervous. I'm here to work, but somehow, you and Finn have... how can I explain.' Watching Grace grope for the right words was interesting and showed she cared. 'I hope we're friends, the type who won't be offended with how the other feels.'

'Yes, of course.' Joe thought it was going to be a hell of a lot harder. He took a deep, breath. 'Okay, I'm starting. My soon to be ex-wife, Finn's mum Maeve, left. She went back home to Ireland, where she's much happier.' Grace's reaction was not what he'd expected, remaining calm, at least on the outside. But when he focused on her eyes, her emotions were just as he thought; there was a great deal going on behind the scenes. But Joe ploughed on. 'Maeve became homesick. That might sound like a copout, but I witnessed a slow but profound change. When she knew I was looking, she'd put on a happy face, but you can only do that for so long. Depression settled in, and everything became a daily struggle; that's when she started self-medicating with alcohol. At first, a nightcap, and then an afternoon drink as well. You get the picture.' He twirled the remains of his wine. 'Sadly, Maeve knew it, I knew it, she was headed for disaster. She told me that she couldn't take the heat, the flies, the creepy-crawlies, the isolation was intolerable—in the end, everything piled on top of her. The way I dressed, talked to Finn, talked to her, ate an apple, anything. Maeve was utterly miserable and lashed out any way she could. She loves Finn; there is no doubt. But this place was way too alien. She's happy at home in Ireland. The drinking hasn't stopped altogether, but it has significantly reduced to a social level. She's working and studying to be a counsellor. She chose that subject to better understand what Finn is going through. So, when Finn and his mum Facetime, she is better equipped to handle his questions fairly. Not that she wouldn't anyway, Maeve was, *is*, a great mum, but in the wrong country.'

'I know what it's like to spend time in a foreign country,' Grace began, earnestly. 'For me, it's work, so I'm kept busy investigating, interviewing, keeping dates, no one to watch out for except my crew, who are all adults and know what they're getting into. And I know exactly when I'll be going home, which works fine nine out of ten times. Occasionally there's a hiccup.' Grace angled her head to one side, deep in thought. She faced him again and added, 'I know I'd be devastated if I had to live somewhere else other than here...um Melbourne.' She lifted her glass and took a long sip before setting it back on the table. 'Something else occurred to me just now. I know you're aware the most important years in a child's development are the first three, some say five years. Who was his primary caregiver?'

'Maeve was. Though we were both acutely aware of Finn's development.'

'Seems to me, Maeve stayed as long as she possibly could…got most of her work done. I can only imagine how conflicted she must've been and still is.'

Joe stared at his hands, turning his glass around and around. Fingers under his chin, she tilted his face, unwavering, he looked into hers. 'Grace…' Joe shook his head, trying to come up with an appropriate and deserving reply. 'You are an extraordinary person.'

'Thank you; I'll take that as a compliment.'

'Exactly how I meant it.'

* * *

Grace picked up her glass, hoping to break the awkwardness, of the heavily laden atmosphere, she downed the remains of her wine before placing the glass back on the table.

'My turn.' She sat back in her comfy chair, wanting to know yet so afraid she might be wrong. 'Okay, this is difficult to ask, but if I don't, I'll always wonder.'

'Just let it out,' was Joe's suggestion. 'What's the point of wondering about the what-ifs. Will saying it hurt someone?'

'No, not a bit.'

'Well, go ahead. I can't wait to hear what's so damned difficult.'

'Yes, you're right. You know about the Arabian prince and his horse. I *wasn't* just there to interview him because he was *allegedly* a 'Prince', he was a person with enormous power. When I politely encouraged his highness to release a teenager sitting alone, isolated in jail I got his polite, yes, yes, such a tragedy, and that was it. He'd smoothly move on directing me to something of greater importance to him. I'd draw him back to the young woman who was in serious trouble for supposedly attending a women's rights demonstration in the public square. Yesmin was simply walking home from school. But it didn't matter what anyone said. Even though the investigation showed she'd never been affiliated or attended anything like a demonstration. Yesmin was studying music at the time. Her school categorically stated she was an exemplary student who happened to be in the wrong place at the wrong time. They had witnesses and proof that she took that route every school day. Her extended family praised her trustworthiness. All of it fell on deaf ears. Which is exactly how I felt about my discussion with the prince.' Grace took a deep, steadying breath, and forced herself to stay focused. 'We got wind that she was being transferred to a women's facility—'

'Who is we?' Joe cut in.

'International Women's Rights groups, Amnesty, the UN. Tremendously brave people working tirelessly undercover, and in the background. But here's where it gets tricky. A couple of months after the arrest, her family got wind that a person of high rank may have intervened. It *is* just a rumour. And then suddenly there were all kinds of rumours and wild conspiracies. No one can really tell why or how it happened, but suddenly, without notifying her parents, Yesmin was moved.'

'Yep,' Joe murmured, 'throwing more rumours out there is an effective way to lead people off a trail.'

'You're not wrong, whoever they might be, organised that Yesmin was to be transferred at night. I know there was a group of people who were hellbent on saving her and her family. Whatever happened, it worked. The thing is, no one knew where the family ended up. If they did know, they weren't telling.' Grace sipped her water, letting the cool liquid slide down her throat.

Joe patiently waited.

'And then there was a soccer match in an Australian country town.' Grace gritted her teeth forcing herself to stay in control.

'Grace,' Joe murmured and reached for her.

She quickly stood and moved away, not wanting to be comforted, believing, though she gave it everything, she may have failed at saving Yesmin and her family. Something that haunted her daily. And now there was a grain of hope that she may have stumbled across the family she so desperately wanted to help and that they were safe and in a *good* place.

Grace pressed the cool glass to her face and continued. 'I spent over eighteen solid months trying to help Yesmin. I wrote to her, knowing the letters would either be heavily censored, or she wouldn't get them at all. Amnesty gave me a copy of her school photo, which was lovely, so I'm sure if I met Yesmin, I'd immediately recognise her. Hoping the Prince was the key to her and her family's survival, I wrote my piece on the Prince in a favourable light. He was charming, and exceptionally well mannered, so it wasn't difficult. My interview with him was published, which included photos of him, his camel, and his amazing horse. He was most impressed and sent me a cryptic card that I interpreted as he hoped my family were safe and well. His close, trusted people are thorough at delving into someone's private life. Their research is impeccable and correct. He knew I didn't have a 'family'. I hope I'm right about the Prince and not just whistling in the wind.' Grace felt as if she stood with her toes gripping over the edge of a clifftop. 'My question, who is Azim's sister, Jasmine?'

'She's a high school student who happens to be studying music.' Joe gave her a wary gaze. 'Grace, this is most likely coincidental. Her family have a stall at the farmer's market every Saturday, both their kids help out for short periods so their parents can go purchase food, wander a bit and join the locals in a chinwag. We can drop by and see what happens, what do think?'

'I would love that. But even if the family isn't the one I'm hoping for, it's awesome that they've found a safe place.'

'What we know about Jasmine and her family is sketchy, but then I have little to do with them on that level. I only know that Finn and others think that they're terrific people. Our country would've been totally alien to them, but they joined our community with everyone's help.'

'Thank you, Joe. I'm still looking forward to next Saturday.' Grace moved to get her bag. 'It's very late. I'd better get going.'

'There's nothing else you want to shake off?'

'Only my new agent who I've let go. He never did feel right, but he was recommended. He tried to force me to take my editorial, your story to a different magazine. I'll sort it out with Trinity.'

'Um, Grace, I don't think you should drive home. You've had wine, you're not familiar with the roads. It's dark, no street lighting here. It's cloudy so moonlight isn't going to help.'

'I'll be fine.' Grace smiled.

'Grace—I won't be. Please stay. We have plenty of rooms available. I keep one fresh and clean for Leigh and her husband Jim.'

'Okay, you're right. I'll stay. But I don't have my bathroom stuff, like a toothbrush.'

'We country people buy in bulk. There's no running low on anything. I always get extra. You'll find everything you need in the ensuite.'

'Thank you.' Grace smiled, 'I'm looking forward to one of your breakfasts. Can I charge my laptop somewhere?' She hefted it out of its carry bag.

'In my office, follow me.'

Down the dimly lit hall, Joe opened the timber panelled door and ushered Grace through.

'I'll clear a space on my desk for you,' Joe sounded apologetic.

'Hey, don't apologise. I'm well aware people have their own ways of filing.' She looked over his workspace. 'I'm sure you know where everything is.'

His, 'Umm…yeah,' sounded more like, he probably didn't.

Having plugged her laptop in, Joe ushered Grace into the hallway. 'Your room's down here.' And he opened the door wide to a luxurious time capsule. The room looked to be recently decorated but keeping to the style of the eighteen-hundreds. A bay window with a box seat, warm colours in the muted floral drapes and a four-poster bed big enough for a whole family.

Grace turned to take in the whole room and asked, 'Are you sure, isn't there something smaller? I could get lost in here. It's beautiful. I'm never lost for words, but I am now.'

'I'm glad you like it. And there isn't anywhere else. Besides these rooms should get used. This is a home, and it should be lived in, not kept as a museum.'

'Oh, you are so right. Okay, I'll happily sleep in this like the queen I am.' Grace laughed, softly.

'Good. We did make modifications; this door leads to your ensuite. There's stuff in there that Leigh and her brood including her husband Jim use when they stay for weekends. There's a walk-in closet through this door.'

'Thanks, Joe.' Grace walked up to him, almost touching. He looked…worried, at a loss. 'Joe, if it's okay with you, I'd like to kiss you good night.'

Suddenly she was in his arms, his soft lips on hers and she melted into him. Nothing mattered, no peripheral noises, there was just Joe, his kiss, his hard body against hers, and he smelled great! The kiss lasted and became more urgent, deeper. His hands slowly moved up to cup her face. Oh, yes that was nice.

He pulled away, but only far enough so he could speak, 'Grace,' he murmured low a whisper away from her lips, 'This would have to be the hardest thing to do right now. He stepped back a little more and eyes meeting hers, he added, 'But it's not just me I have to keep in mind, it's you and there's Finn. I can see he's growing attached to you. I'm already there, best if I leave now before…Good night my queen,' his tender smile, warm and apologetic. He kissed her briefly. 'See you in the morning.'

9

———————

Sleep was a long time coming as Grace agonised over various scenarios, then finally dropped off wondering, what if?

The rooster crowed and cursing, she grabbed the bedding and pulled it over her head, swearing that she'd only just shut her eyes.

A careful knock on her door and she threw the covers back, quickly pulled on a pair of pants and opened the door.

'Hey, Finn. Good morning, did I sleep in?'

'Nah, Dad made us breakfast, all we have to do is cook it. And he left you a note.' Finn dug the mangled piece of paper out of his shorts pocket and handed it over.

After opening it with care, Grace read it out loud. *'Morning, Grace. I knocked on your door, but you must've been fast asleep. My neighbour, John called early this morning, a section of fence is down, and his cattle have wandered onto Binowee. We'll help each other out should only take a couple of hours. If it's a problem, please let me know and I'll call Leigh to pop over. When issues like this crop up Finn usually comes with me. He asked to stay home and promised to finish his homework. I said if he had a problem, to wait and ask me when I get back. Feel free to use my office. Joe.*

'Gosh, I must've been out like a light.'

Finn gave her a crooked smile and nodded his agreement.

'Excellent, just give me a moment, Finn. I need a shower.

'Cool, I'll get started on my homework.'

Reluctantly, Grace turned off the shower that fell on her body like warm rain. She dried and dressed for the day in the clothes she had on the day before, which wouldn't be the first time. She headed for the kitchen, where Finn sat on a stool, studiously bent over his sheets of homework.

'I'm impressed, Finn.' She rubbed his back in passing while moving around the island into the kitchen proper. Bowls were lined up with whipped eggs and chives, grated cheese, and slices of his homemade bread. Grace made their breakfast, herself a coffee, and slid a glass of juice under Finn's nose. They took their plates out to the back veranda, with Luna lying at Finn's feet.

'It's great having you here, Gracie.'

'Thank you, Finn, I enjoy your company too.'

'What're you gonna do now?'

'I was thinking of opening my laptop to check my emails. What about you?'

'I'm going to check on my chickens and collect eggs with Luna. She loves watching them. I've let her in the chicken run a couple of times. She doesn't do anything just watches like she's really curious, even lies down with her head up and paws crossed. The hens got used to her pretty quick.'

'Wow, that's amazing. Luna is a very cool girl-dog.'

'Yeah,' Finn smiled full of love and pride for his dog, his pal. Pushing his chair back, he collected their plates and took them to the kitchen where he piled them into the dishwasher. Grabbing his basket and kitchen scraps, he took off, calling, 'C'mon Luna, let's go.'

'Wait!' Grace called, 'Do not go anywhere else unless you tell me first.'

'I won't!' was Finn's sharp reply.

Grace entered Joe's domain, his timber panelled, masculine home office. It was still early, but she could tell it would be a blistering hot day. Grabbing her azure blue singlet top she yanked it away from her chest a few times to fan air around her body and did the same with the white calf-length skirt that right now she wished was made from cheesecloth rather than heavy fabric. At least her bare feet were cool on the polished timber floor. Joe had told her to use his office as often as she liked. After all, other than her phone, it was the only room in the house where she could connect to the outside world with her laptop. A sudden warm breeze ruffled the gauzy cream drapes on either side of the sash windows and she hurried to close them. Pulling back her hair she scanned his library for books on sustainable farming and gardening. One stood out from the rest, the book by Permaculture guru Bill Mollison. Some of his books dating back over twenty years or more. She smiled, having read a couple for research purposes as many followed his doctrine of caring for the land. Checking further, she found Joe's, *The Green Place*. She had her copy, but pulled his off the shelf, opened it and wondered whether his edition had info inside revealing more of the man, Joe Mathews. She read the dedication again.

To Maeve, you'll always have a place in my heart and my home.

Hand over her tightening chest, she whispered, 'Hmm, what was that?' A rush spread into her chest, pressing on her heart. After a couple of deep breaths, she reminded herself that she was on an assignment, and a heart flutter would not stand in her way.

Lovely sentiment, though, and she couldn't help but wonder how Maeve was coping. No amount of research on Joe's life brought her name up. There were plenty of family pics in the dining and living room, and Grace recognised a few photos of his farm on Joe's website and Facebook page.

'Maeve, I really do hope you're okay,' Grace whispered.

She shrugged and made herself comfortable in Joe's office chair, careful not to mess with his piles of paperwork. Then arranged her notes and laptop on his cluttered desk and settled in for some serious writing.

Grace set up her notes with photos to the side, including ones she'd taken at the soccer game. Re-reading her email with her article attached, Grace was satisfied that she'd done her best. Especially the before and after farm photos Joe said she could use.

A scream for help cut through the air. Grace shot up and accidentally hit the send button. *'Finn!'* Grace grabbed her phone, as she was trained to always do in emergencies. She was out the door in seconds, thundered down the hall and out to the veranda. She called out to him, searching the garden and grounds beyond for his location.

'Finn — Finn! Where are you!'

Gracie! Come quick! It's Luna — *SNAKE!'* Echoed across the narrow valley in one long, panicked cry.

Quick, clear and concise thinking was Grace's reputation under stressful conditions.

Hands bunching up her skirt, barefoot, and legs flying, she ran to the sound of his voice and found Finn and Luna in the dam. Grace knew that the dam and wooded area beyond were a no-go zone for Finn without an adult. Especially this time of year when snakes were about. His boyish arms were holding Luna's head out of the water; thankfully, both were able to stop from going under. Knowing her clothes would restrict movement and weigh her down, Grace immediately tore off her skirt and top. In her bra and undies, she ran into the dam, but when the muddy bottom started to suck at her feet, she made a shallow dive, hoping her body weight would pull her out of the sludge. Thankfully it worked. She swam hard as she could toward Finn and Luna. The dog's large frame dwarfed the worried nine-year-old as he slipped and struggled to keep his and Luna's heads above the water.

'Hang on, Finn!' Grace yelled.

Though distraught, he paid attention. 'You've got to help her—got to!' His pale face and fearful eyes focused on hers as he disappeared with Luna under the muddy water.

She was there in no time and ducked down to feel around for his body. Fingers groping, she latched onto his T-shirt. Finn was still holding onto Luna, and he wouldn't let go. With a mighty kick, Grace heaved him and his dog to the surface. She wrapped her arm around his chest. 'Hold onto my arm. Finn! Do as I say!'

'No! I can't let go. Luna will drown!' He coughed and spluttered.

'She won't drown. I have Luna. I've got you both.' Grace urged, 'Stop fighting me. Trust me. I wouldn't let either of you go. Lift your legs so you can help me kick. That's it, kick as hard as you can.'

Grace couldn't help but notice that Luna only used three of her legs. Something was very wrong. Nevertheless, the sweet girl was trying hard to swim all the same.

'You can let me go now!' Finn announced, panting. 'I'll show you where to get out.'

Trepidation filled her, but Finn put his trust in her. Now she must do the same. She eased her arm off him and watched closely as he swam to the edge.

He clambered onto a grassy ledge. 'Over here!' he called. 'There're boulders right here, so you can climb out.'

She hung onto Luna's chest, and with one arm outstretched for balance, she pulled through the water to where Finn waited. With a couple of meters to go, she struggled with the pain in her feet but kept swimming. Nothing was going to stop her now that she was so close.

'What's wrong? I'm coming in!' Finn yelled.

Grace forced air into her lungs, pushed harder, and yelled, 'No!' Finn was up to his chest in the water but waited. *Smart kid.*

Reaching the smooth but slippery rocks with her toes and still holding Luna up off her front legs, Grace took a moment to catch her breath.

'Gracie, are you okay?'

'Yeah, got a cramp, is all. I'll need your help. You take Luna's butt, and I'll carry the rest.' She silently pleaded with the dog not to struggle. This gorgeous girl seemed to know, and together they carried her up the grassy bank and laid her down.

While she massaged and stretched her calf muscle, Finn fussed over his dog. Grace closely studied Finn; he looked exhausted but otherwise okay. He scooted closer and eased Luna's head onto his lap. Stroking her, he talked soothingly to his much-loved companion.

Grace held his chin with thumb and index finger, forcing him to look at her. 'Okay, listen carefully. Do you know, was Luna bitten and if so, where?'

'No—I don't know!' he cried out, anxious. 'She saw the snake up near the house, probably headed for the chickens, and went crazy. Now she's being weird with her front leg right here,' he sobbed and swiped the tears away with the back of his hand.

Grace searched but couldn't see any puncture marks or grazing… nothing. Perhaps the water had washed the wound clean, but if Luna was struck, then Grace had to hurry with first aid. All she could think of was to treat the dog the same as you would a human. She grabbed her T-shirt and, beginning at the seam, started ripping. She also needed access to Luna's leg. 'Please, Finn, let her go,' she pleaded with the boy she'd come to love, urging him to let go while tugging at his arm.

Suddenly, forgotten memories surfaced, and Grace immediately stopped trying to force Finn to release his dog. She was back at age seven, hugging her sweet puppy, Rosey, while her uncle, her guardian, yelled at her to shut up and pulled Rosey out of her arms.

But this was not the time to lament past trauma, she shook the images out of her mind and told herself to concentrate on Finn. Nothing else mattered right now, least of all a time in her life that she'd rather forget and could do nothing about anyway.

'Finn,' she tugged at his arm again, this time he did look at her. 'If you don't let go, I can't try and help. If she was bitten, the poison will take hold. Please trust me and let her go enough to see where I need to start. There's no time to waste.'

Hiccoughing through his sobs, Finn eased back and searched Luna's leg for the spot the snake may have struck. 'Here,' he pointed to a barely visible mark, just above the ankle. 'The snake reared and struck just as Luna jumped sideways, she fell badly, her legs kind of crumpled under her and she yelped really loud. She rolled down the embankment and ended up in the dam. Luna nearly drowned because she couldn't use her leg properly.'

'Oh…' Grace peered at what looked very much like a badly sprained ankle or worse. If she didn't treat it Luna's recovery could be very difficult and last much longer. 'Listen carefully, Finn.' He nodded and waited. 'See how her paw is kind of swollen?'

'Yes…l-looks horrible,' Finn stammered.

'I need to wrap the whole leg, and it will hurt—a bit.'

'H-how do you know what to do?'

'Ah, that's a long story for another time. Right now, I want you to be very brave, hold Luna firmly, stay calm …' Grace tried to think how best to help Finn and his dog while she nicked the edge of her shirt and ripped it up for a makeshift bandage. 'I've got an idea; sing a gentle song. Hopefully, your voice will distract and soothe her. I'll do my best to work fast.'

It was all over in seconds. Finn sang a lullaby, and an exhausted Luna closed her eyes.

Using her fingers, Grace felt around the ankle, then gently held the dog's leg. Luna yelped and struggled to get up.

'Sorry girl, so sorry, Luna.' Finn nuzzled her head.

She bound the ankle tightly, covering the possible snake bite area, and continued bandaging further, right up her leg and down again to her paw. Luna licked her hand before letting her head flop down again.

'Finn, I'm not a vet. I won't lie to you; we've done our very best to save her.'

His tear-stained, distraught face broke her heart. Finn hung his head and mumbled, 'Yeah, I know.'

Grace grabbed her phone to call Joe. 'Finn, while I try to get hold of your dad, you can tell me all about Luna.'

'I came home from school one day, and Aunty Leigh's car was parked in the carport. I got excited cos she usually brings Phillie with her, and we always have heaps of fun together.'

'Unusual name, Phillie. Is it short for Philomena?' The ringing timed out on her call to Joe, and Grace left a message for him to hurry home.

'Yeah, Aunty Leigh calls her that when she's annoyed, and Phillie hates it.'

'I can't imagine why.' Grace gave him a little shrug.

Finn chuckled and buried his face in Luna's neck again, mumbling, 'Phillie hates being called Philomena, Josephine, Bolt.' Lifting his head, Finn looked at her with teary eyes that melted her heart and said, 'Please don't call Phillie any of those names, not even Bolt.' Deadly serious, he shook his head.

'Oh, I would never. But what a deliciously perfect bunch of names. Thank you, Finn, for letting me be part of that. And by the way, you are so very brave.' She just wanted to hug and reassure him, so she put her arm around his shoulders and gave him a little squeeze. 'Your dad's not answering. I'll keep ringing while I race up to get the first aid kit in my car. I'll be a couple of minutes.'

'No, Gracie, don't leave me. *Noo!* You can't leave me!' Finn cried out on the edge of panic.

She cupped his face and looked directly into his frightened eyes. 'You have such a close connection with Luna. She can feel your emotions. Believe me, Finn, it's a powerful thing you have. Please stay calm so that she can feel it. You'll help her so much if you can do that, okay?'

He nodded ever so slightly. 'You will come back?'

Heartbreaking for the boy she had so quickly grown to love, Grace chose her words carefully. 'Hey,' she smiled at him, 'I, Grace Taylor, do honestly swear that I will not leave you, Finn.' She extended her hand. He looked at it and grasped it firmly with a tentative, teary smile. 'Good, now stay calm.' she affirmed and messed his hair.

Still looking worried, he agreed, closed his eyes, and took a few deep breaths.

"That's the way, Finn. You can do this.' Grace pushed herself up and took off, racing back to the house while listening for Joe's answer, but there wasn't one. She left another message, then hurried to her car. 'Shit! Keys!' she cried out, voice strained. She would not fail sweet Finn, ever. Grace ran into the house straight into the office, grabbed her bag, found her keys, and headed back to her car. Jumping in, she slammed the door and didn't think any further than getting to Finn and Luna as fast as possible. She drove her car as if it was an off-road SUV, through the garden, over flowerbeds, through the roses, and cursed the hardy shrubs that wanted to slow her down.

Reaching them, she noticed Finn's shoulders were shaking, his head buried in Luna's neck.

'No-no-no, I'm not too late! *No!*' filled the confines of her car. She parked as close as possible and jumped out with her first-aid kit. Kneeling next to them, she tore open the bag of bandages. Talk to me, Finn?'

'She's…she's tired,' Finn managed through a sob.

Luna was panting way too fast, obviously in distress.

'Finn, think calm. Luna can feel how worried you are and will want to help *you*.' Grace urged softly, and hands shaking, she unpacked her kit but kept on with her soothing talk. 'I know it's hard, but take a few deep breaths and try to calm down again, like you did before. I promise this will help her. I'm going to bandage her leg again bit by bit with this elastic bandage and do it nice and firm. This is what you're supposed to do with people, so it will work on dogs too.' Grace hoped she was right.

Breathing deep, Finn whispered, 'Okay.'

Grace eased her ripped T-shirt off bit by bit, quickly replacing it with a proper bandage, wrapping it firmly up and down Luna's leg. She kept wrapping until she'd used the complete roll. Grace put her head on Luna's chest and listened to her rapidly beating heart. She searched in her kit and found antihistamines. Try anything was her catchphrase, so on top of venom, if there was an allergic reaction, antihistamine had to help. *Yes!* Grace affirmed in her mind. She up-ended the kit, walked into the dam and filled it with water. Then back to Finn and his dog. She put a couple of tablets down Luna's throat and carefully held her head, hoping she would drink. She managed to lap at the water, which was a good sign.

'Finn?' When she had his attention, she said, 'We've done all we can. Now we must keep her as quiet as possible. Are you okay sitting like that? Your knees must be getting sore?'

'No, they're not—I'm not moving,' he insisted.

Luna raised her head enough to look at Finn, then licked his face.

'Good girl, Luna. We're doing all we can. Brave girl,' Grace cooed.

And then, without warning, she was thrown back in time again. At least she had an idea why it was happening. Rosey was ripped from her arms, and she relived that traumatising moment again. Grace had no idea why her dog was taken from her. All she had was a feeling of fear and loss and utter devastation. But most of all, anger. Rosey was the only thing she had that gave her comfort after her parents died.

'Hey, Finn.' Understandably, he was terrified of losing his dog. It showed in his face as his body trembled. Grace gave him a reassuring smile and felt for the dog's pulse. 'She's not panting so hard, and her heart isn't racing like it was earlier.'

'Yeah, that's good, isn't it?' At the sound of Finn's voice, Luna shifted ever so slightly.

'I'm not a vet, but yeah, she's strong, healthy and loves you, and she knows you love her. That makes a huge difference. She won't give up without a fight.'

The roar of Joe's four-wheel-drive echoed down the embankment and stopped a few feet away. The driver's door swung open, and looking like any father would, under the circumstances, Joe hurried to Finn's side.

'Hey, I see you two ran into a bit of trouble.' Joe said, keeping his tone light.

'Sorry, Dad.' Finn buried his face in Luna's fur and cried.

'Son,' Joe put his arm around Finn's shoulders and spoke softly. 'There's nothing to be sorry for. And hey, looks like Grace did an amazing job. I don't think anyone could've done better.' He kissed Finn's wet face, cupped his cheeks, and swept his thumb across to wipe his son's tears. 'Stay quiet now, for Luna. Grace can tell me what happened.'

An emotional wreck, Grace stood back to give father and son some space. She grabbed her skirt, hauled it on over her head and thought it wasn't a bad idea to leave it hanging off her breasts.

Joe approached her, briefly glancing back over his shoulder to make sure Finn was okay. 'You did a fantastic job with Luna's leg. Were you a nurse in another life?' He smiled affectionately.

'Um…no. Not by a long shot. I'll explain another time.' She gave him a tentative smile.

'Sure, I'll hold you to that. We'll make time over several glasses of wine.' Concern filtered into his handsome face. 'Please, tell me what you know? Did you see the snake?'

'No,' Grace answered. 'I was at your desk reading through emails when I heard Finn calling. I ran down here and helped them both out of the dam. Finn told me he hadn't seen the snake at first, but Luna had and went after it. That snake must've been close because he said Luna got between him and the snake and barked and possibly got too close a few times when she tried to bite it.'

Finn called out, 'Yeah, I yelled and yelled for Luna to stop, but she wouldn't listen. And Gracie, you couldn't see what was going on. And Luna wouldn't stop. She just kept on chasing. And she really likes you, so she might have tried to protect both of us and tried even harder to get the snake,' Finn ended on a heavy sigh.

'What happened next,' Joe asked.

'She just kept going for the snake,' Finn muttered. 'And then it slithered down this way. Luna was at it the whole time. It was like she was really angry and wanted to bite it dead.'

'Yeah, brave girl is very protective.' Joe stroked Luna's head. 'Then what happened?'

'The snake reared, ready to strike, and Luna jumped up and backwards out of the way, so I couldn't tell what happened. But she did fall badly like her legs crumpled. She couldn't get up and kinda rolled down into the dam. When I caught up, the snake was gone, and Luna was swimming in a circle. Grace helped us both from drowning. Then I swam to the rocky slope and showed her where to get out. And now I'm trying to keep her quiet, but I don't think she wants to get up right now anyway.'

'I don't suppose there's a vet available?' Grace whispered.

'Sadly, no. I did get to talk to Jack, our local guy. He said if Luna had been struck and the snake injected venom, he would *not* get here in time with an antivenom. He's seen dogs go down fast, less than fifteen minutes, half an hour.' Joe lowered his voice, 'and they're gone.'

Eyes welling, Grace turned to look over the dam and, for the first time that day, noticed the azure native water lilies, made brighter by the afternoon sun and thought, how beautiful and such a contrast to what was happening on the bank. She took a few deep breaths, pulled herself together and focused on Joe. 'Okay, it's wait and see then.'

'Yeah…I'm just glad no one else got bitten.'

She followed his gaze to her feet. Hmm, yep, okay. Without a care, she went careening down the slope barefoot. Sure, there was blood, some of it already drying. She knew that they needed attention but curled her toes, perhaps trying to hide that she'd hurt herself. Before she could reach the scattered first aid supplies, Joe was on it.

'Grace is something, isn't she?' he murmured into the afternoon air, at no one in particular, but he did give her a warm, soft look. He bobbed his head once, in respect, or acknowledgement, whatever; she didn't care because she had to admit coming from Joe, his response felt too good. Joe was an exceptional man. And he was going to attend to her grazed and cut feet.

He rummaged through the pile of first aid strewn on his lap and found what he wanted. And with a handful of swabs, a bandage and isopropyl alcohol, he approached her feet. Being highly skilled in first aid, Grace knew this was necessary.

'Oh great,' she muttered. 'I know what I have to do. Let me do it.'

'Uh-uh—this is a farm where animals wander about dropping crap, so what I'm about to do will be thorough, and I can see the bottom of your feet better than you. I'll wash your feet with clean water first; get the dirt off. Just grit your teeth.'

'Sure, that'll work.' Her sarcastic response couldn't be missed. And Grace knew what he was up to when he started talking and asking questions.

'When I spoke to the vet, he said to ring him tomorrow if he was needed.' Joe splashed water out of a flask onto her feet, adding quietly, 'Do you think Luna's ankle is sprained or worse?'

'I'm pretty sure it's a sprain,' she whispered, 'but only an x-ray would show if anything needed…you know, fixing.'

Bending right over, Joe dabbed her feet dry and swabbed them liberally with the antiseptic. Grace's eyes watered, and she grasped his hair as it was the only thing within reach. He didn't flinch or cry out, and she could almost hear his smile.

Holding a flask of water, Joe said, 'Take these,' handing Grace a couple of painkillers. Not bothering to straighten his hair, he asked, 'Is the pain subsiding?'

'Yeah,' Grace managed to breathe out. 'Sorry about the hair clutching. Thought you might enjoy it.'

'Made my day,' he chuckled. With wound dressings on her soles, he wrapped an elastic bandage around her feet to keep them in place.

'Thank you,' Grace whispered.

'You're welcome.'

They sat in silence for a while, listening to Luna's breathing.

'She has a lot in her favour,' Joe said, sounding worried. 'Best not to move her until she starts to stir. Even then, keeping her quiet is most important.' He rubbed his face, 'There's something else. Remember Finn, Luna is allergic to European wasp stings. So that could also be the problem.'

'Um…just on the off chance, I gave her antihistamine. I knew it wouldn't hurt and hoped it would help.'

'You'd have to be the most forward-thinking person I've ever met.' Joe rubbed her shoulder in thanks. 'Grace…do you have a medical background?'

'Not Dr type, bit more than first aid.' Then Grace quietly mumbled what came next, but Joe heard it all. 'More a first responder….' She trailed off.

'First responder?' he repeated quietly. 'And what do they do?'

'I can insert a catheter and introduce fluids, you know, that sort of thing—' And muttered, 'My work isn't about how I respond to someone in trouble. It just so happened that the photographer and sound person vomited at the very idea. I'm a journalist first. I love my work and hope that sometimes I make a difference. Can we not talk about this right now, please?'

'Of course,' Joe responded. *I will get to know you, Grace.* 'You did great. I can't thank you enough.' He took her hand and caressed the back with his thumb. 'I think we'll be here for a while. I'd better ring Leigh on my way to the house for some bedding. Or I'll never hear the end of it.'

'Thanks, Dad,' Finn whispered.

Luna lifted her head at the sound of Joe leaving, but Finn's caring words and gentle strokes soon put her at ease.

Pushing up to stand, it wasn't lost on Joe how Grace patted Finn's back and told him how proud she was. 'I've been to many countries, and I've met many people, but not anyone as brave and caring as you.'

Finn's mouth trembled but managed to say his thanks. On the way up to the house, Joe reminded himself that Finn was a good swimmer, and self-preservation kicks in. But he had to come to grips with the dreadful thought that had it not been for Grace, his son would have lost his much-loved pet. That would've sat heavily on his young shoulders.

Joe shook it off, repeating to himself that it didn't happen. They were both okay.

A full moon meant Joe didn't need a torch as he wandered down from the house carrying a cooler bag with drinks, sandwiches and sleeping bags. He noticed the ploughed-up track Grace had left through Binowee's centuries-old garden. He quietly chuckled that she had the guts to take her car to his son and Luna. The garden hadn't been a factor at all. Grace was formidable. She'd made quite an impact on Finn, and if he were honest, she'd done that and more on him. But this enjoyable companionship would end soon. Grace will head back to her exciting life in Melbourne until another overseas trip beckons. 'Damn,' he whispered into the night, not liking the idea *at all*.

He strode across the grassy strip next to the dam where they'd set up camp for the night. He understood all too well the state his son was in. He could still lose his dog, Finn's only other anchor in life. His son had dealt with enough trauma, and Joe would do anything to prevent that from happening.

'Hey,' Grace's tone felt so good, like a gentle touch. 'Finn's asleep next to Luna. Do those sleeping bags open right up?'

'Yes, I see where you're going with this. He folded one bag and slipped it under his son and Luna's heads. And with Grace's help, they wriggled the other bag under and over their bodies. Finn's hand rested on his dog's shoulder, and neither of them stirred.

'They're exhausted.'

'Yeah, no doubt about that.' Joe sat on the remaining sleeping bag next to Grace, pulled out a T-shirt and handed it to Grace. 'You hungry?'

'Famished, haven't eaten since breakfast.' She took his shirt and asked, 'What's this?'

'I thought you might want something dry to wear,' he murmured, holding back a grin. 'Sorry, don't have appropriate underwear.'

'This is very thoughtful, thank you.' Grace mumbled as she slipped the shirt over her head. 'Jocks, hmm, never tried that.'

'Right, well, I've thrown together some salad sandwiches. Hope that's okay?'

'Abso-bloody-lutely, hand one over.'

Chuckling, Joe gave her a sandwich bulging with goodness.

Holding it carefully, Grace took a massive bite, mouth full she chewed and gave him a crossed-eyed funny face. Swallowing, she mumbled, 'This has to be the best sandwich I've ever tasted.'

'I'll take that with the knowledge you haven't eaten all day.'

'Hmm … wouldn't matter. This is very good.'

'Wine?' Joe asked.

Grace beckoned, cleared her mouth, and murmured, 'You're my hero.' She gave him a wink, took the offered glass of chardonnay, and quickly turned her head to look out over the moon-lit dam.

'Grace?'

'Hmm?'

'I'm not big on personal chit-chat….'

Thankfully she turned back to look at him. He wondered whether she saw his emotion, anxiety, wonder, and admiration. It was certainly how he felt, but hoped she didn't see any of that in his face. For Finn's sake, he couldn't risk another relationship to fail. His son would miss Grace, he was sure of that. But had *he* also invested *his* heart?

'Um…shit.' Dropping his head, he stared at the sleeping bag once used to picnic on with Finn and Maeve. *It's time.* His sister, Leigh's words rang in his head.

'Don't say anything, not right now with all that has happened.' Grace handed him time. 'Your emotions wouldn't be telling the truth of it…if you get my drift.'

'Oh, I do. I'm very aware.' Joe caught her hand. 'You can go sleep up at the house or stay here with me?'

The moment seemed to stretch on for a painfully long time as Grace considered her choices. To his relief, she scooted closer, and he let go the breath he was holding. She lay next to him, head resting on his arm. Joe waited until Grace's rhythmic breaths told him she was asleep. Only then did he allow himself to drop off as well.

* * *

GRACE FELL INTO AN ABYSS, HER BODY SHAKING WITH FRIGHT, INSTANTLY waking her. Heart pounding, she gasped for breath. Her mind had a spring clean while she slept. Memories had flooded in; she knew her parents were journalists who died together in a car crash while driving interstate on assignment. Her uncle and aunt took Grace in. Her uncle hated dogs and would not allow her to keep Rosy. He forced an already traumatised girl to give her up. Grace never forgave her uncle. That memory of Rosy being pulled out of her arms broke her heart all over again. Grace buried her face in the sleeping bag and cried silent tears.

An arm slid around her waist. Joe didn't speak, just held her close to his chest. Eventually, Grace fell asleep.

Finn's rooster competed with the magpies and kookaburras to herald that dawn was on the horizon. Blinking, Grace raised herself on her elbows, gazed at the soft lilac and pink sky, and thought, wow, this country was noisy with early risers but utterly beautiful. She stretched her legs and immediately became aware of how wrecked her body felt. She turned and focused on Luna; her chest rose and fell in a slow, relaxed rhythm. Grace swiped the happy tears from her eyes and almost clapped with joy. Both Finn and his precious pal were going to be okay.

'One of these days, that rooster is going into a pot,' Joe's croaky voice mumbled.

Grace drew back. 'Shit, I didn't realise you were awake.'

Joe curled his arm and tucked her into his chest. 'Are you okay?'

'Yeah, call it brain vomit.'

'That sounds…'

'Gross,' Finn suggested.

Joe laughed and held Grace a little firmer. And she didn't stop him or complain but snuggled into him instead, whispering, 'I had a dog once.'

He kissed her forehead. 'Is it for one of those dinner, wine, talk moments?'

'Yeah. But right now, I would kill for a toothbrush, shower, then coffee and one of your amazing breakfasts out on the back veranda.'

'Coming right up,' Joe mumbled through a yawn. '*And* it's Saturday.'

'Yep…awesome.'

We've got three jobs today, after that we relax. The rest of the weekend is for us.'

Grace replied, trying to sound unfazed, 'The Vet and Farmers Market. What's the third one?'

'Your feet should see a doctor.'

'What!? Grace cried out.

'Dad, Gracie, shush.'

Luna put her two cents in with a doggy yawn.

'Okay, time to get up and get organised.' Joe eased his arm out from under Grace's neck, rolled over onto his knees and stood. Impressive after a hard night, Grace thought and funnily enough, she missed his touch. *Hmm.*

Finn urged Luna up, and the dog hobbled a few meters away to do her business. Once finished, Joe slid his arms under her and carried her to his car, carefully placing her next to Finn. Looking for comfort, Luna propped her head on Finn's lap, who quietly encouraged her to stay calm.

On hands and knees, Grace started to shove the leftover first aid back into her kit while Joe rolled up the sleeping bags and threw them in his car.

'Wait here,' Joe ordered, which surprised her, and the look on her face must've been telling, for he grinned, adding, 'stay off your feet.'

Okay, he had a point, but she tested them out anyway, and other than feeling a bit sore, they weren't too bad. While peering down at them, Joe scooped her up, and to her surprise, she squealed. He took no notice and carried her to his car, mumbling, 'I'll come back for your car later.'

She crossed her arms and let him have his way, defiantly muttering, 'I'm going to the Farmers Market no matter what.'

'Sure,' he eased her onto the passenger seat, kissed her cheek and with a knowing smile, closed the door.

He took the track she'd made through the demolished garden. 'Oh damn, I sure made a horrible mess of the tea roses and…everything.'

'It's nothing to worry about.' And by the tone of his voice, Joe meant every word.

* * *

FEELING REFRESHED AFTER A HOT SHOWER, GRACE SLIPPED INTO A PAIR OF slippers and her dressing gown.

Smiling, she strolled into the kitchen and declared, 'You did a great job with my feet. I assume Leigh brought my bag over from the B&B.'

'We aim to please.' Joe added with an eyebrow wiggle.

Grace pointed at him and laughed.

'Leigh dropped them off while you were in the shower. She couldn't stay, said she'd see us at the market if your feet are up to it.'

Joe was making another of his delicious breakfasts.

Feeling content with her world, Grace wondered how could anything be better than this? Apprehensive she rushed to her ensuite, washed her face, brushed her teeth and pulled her hair into a high ponytail. She stood in her underwear by the open window and let the soothing light breeze whisper over her skin.

Grace had dressed in a pair of loose-fitting cream linen pants and a short-sleeved green top. She was ready for anything, yet nerves played havoc with her heart and state of mind. Not only concerned over Luna's leg and Finn but also a market stall where she hoped to find Yesmin and her family. As they headed off, Grace was over-whelmed with a feeling that this was where she was meant to be. This perfect father and son had, in a short time, become the most important people in her life. And bloody hell, there was no denying it; these feel-ings were something she was very sure of. Especially now, with everyone in Joe's four-wheel drive on the way to Myrtleford as a happy family.

Going into a hairpin bend, Grace automatically grabbed Joe's thigh. It shocked her at how natural it felt. She started to pull away, but Joe gently placed his hand over hers as if this was a normal show of affec-tion on a trip into town. Then, unfortunately, he had no option but to use both hands on the wheel to get safely through the next hairy bend. But she left her hand on his thigh, and the only way she could describe Joe's smile was wicked happiness.

Reaching the vet's, Joe carried Luna and, with a sideways nod, indicated for her to go in ahead. Reluctant and not wanting to intrude on a father and son moment with their dog, she shook her head, saying, 'It's okay, I can wait out here.'

'Grace,' he grunted as he hefted Luna, 'since you bandaged her leg, you have to explain what you saw.'

'I've got to look after my feet.' Grace said, pointing at them.

'Gracie, c'mon.' Finn pulled at her hand.

'Okay–okay.' Grace rolled her eyes and carefully walked into the surgery.

The vet suggested Luna stay in a quiet room with Finn to keep her company until he had the chance to Xray. And told Grace she'd done a brilliant job strapping Luna's leg.

'Thanks, Cam.' Joe shook his hand, as did Finn. 'We'll be at the farmers market; you've got my number.'

Leaving his car at the vet, Joe took Grace by the hand for a short walk to the market. *Hmm*, Grace liked the feeling of his hand, strong, calloused, protective. *Oh my*, the overwhelming sensation of warmth bloomed in her chest, and it caught her breath. Was this love? This feeling came with such a powerful sense of belonging.

'You okay?' Looking across at her, Joe slowed his pace. 'You gripped my hand just now as if your life depended on it.'

Yeah, how true that was. She stopped and looked up at him.

'Now you look like the proverbial rabbit caught in headlights. Is it your feet? I left the car at the vet because finding a park closer is impossible this time of day. Joe stooped, putting an arm around her back and behind her thighs, muttering, 'I should've picked you up earlier.'

'Stop, Joe!'

'What is it. What can I do?' When she didn't reply, he prompted, 'Grace?'

'Nerves,' she blurted out. 'My feet are okay. I've been through much tougher stuff, but meeting Azim's family and hopefully finding Yesmin is something I want desperately to be true. I'm looking forward to finding out, yet it might not be them. See what I mean. Crap, it's tough…and there's more besides, but that will have to keep, for now.'

Joe's *'O-k-a-y…'* sounded drawn out. Closing his eyes, he raised her hand to his mouth and kissed it. 'Let's put one of your anxieties to rest.

I'll introduce you to the Noor family.' As they entered the market, he tucked her hand into his side.

Seeing the colourful tents and array of handcrafts, organic foods, and so much more on display was an absolute delight. The lilting sound of a guitar sent music filtering through the crowd of people, what a joy. Grace could not stop smiling.

Joe headed straight for a stall. Manned by Azim and, she assumed, his parents. In front of them was their display of hand-turned and beautifully carved wood in the shape of bowls, platters, and utensils, plus an array of intricate beadwork.

Joe greeted the family, 'Good morning, Khalil, Farah. Hi Azim, are you ready for the next soccer game?

'I will kick another goal next time,' Azim announced enthusiastically.

'You will, I'm sure of it.' Joe ruffed up his hair. 'I'd like you all to meet Grace Taylor, a journalist who has been all over the world, including in many Arab countries. I don't want to alarm you in any way, but she may have a connection with Yesmin and yourselves.'

'Oh!' Hand on his heart, Khalil turned to face her. His teary eyes spoke volumes. 'I know of this, of you.'

Farah started crying and quickly came to Grace. 'You saved us all.' She whispered. 'Azim, call Yesmin quickly now.' Farah clutched Grace's hand as if she might disappear.

Grace corrected Farah's opinion. 'It wasn't just me. There were many of us, a whole team, trying to get you and others out to safety.'

'Well,' Khalil stated strongly, 'you are the only one here, so do not mind us if we acknowledge what you did for us, and who knows how many more you helped,' he grinned.

'Pappa, Mumma? What's wrong?' A beautiful teenage girl called out, her long jet-black hair flying as she ran towards her family.

'Yesmin, please meet Grace Taylor.' Farah announced.

She took one look, then ran to Grace and wrapped her arms around her. 'Thank you, thank you,' Yesmin repeated, clinging on tightly.

'Oh gosh, I'm overwhelmed. So happy to see you and your family here.' Grace held the girl's shoulders and edged her back to study her face. 'Knowing you and your family are safe makes everything worthwhile. I'm so very happy for you all.'

'How did you find us?' Yesmin asked.

'A soccer match I happened to be invited to.'

'Hi everyone.' A familiar voice sang out.

'Leigh!' Grace called. 'Great to see you again.'

'You met the Noor family. Hi Farah, Kahlil. Azim, Jasmine,' Leigh studied the young girl for a moment. 'What's wrong, Jasie? I saw you watching your brother the other day, he's going to make an awesome player. It's all good.'

Yesmin laughed through her tears. 'I like that you've Aussied my name. My tears are happy ones because we have met this truly amazing lady. Grace helped us come to Australia, and now we're here safe and welcomed.'

Leigh wrapped her arms around Grace and hugged her tight. And for her ears only, whispered, 'The moment we spoke on the phone, I knew you were a very special person, Grace.' Not letting go, she stepped back and searched Grace's eyes, then added, 'Whoever named you knew what they were doing.' Choking back her emotions, she kissed her on both cheeks.

Joe slid an arm around Grace's waist and tucked her into his side, which Leigh didn't miss, of course. She gave him a smile and a wink.

'Yeah-yeah, stop gloating, Sis. Where's Jim and Phillie?'

'They're over at the fairy floss stand. Phillie and the culprit, her dad, will be zooming around for the next couple of hours, and then they'll both fall flat on their arses.' Leigh stopped and looked around. 'But where's Finn?'

'He's at the vet with Luna. She's getting an X-ray on her leg. It's a long story, need to explain over a glass of wine. Come around tonight.'

'Oh, don't you worry, we'll be there.' Leigh kissed his cheek and Grace's. 'Got to go and rescue the boys. You want to come with me, Azim, Yesmin?'

'I would like to go and see Finn at the Vet.' And with a nod from his mum, Azim touched his heart as a sign of respect and took off.

'I would love some of this fairy floss,' Yesmin declared.

'You, my girl, are in for a big surprise.' Leigh hooked her arm through Yesmin's and called out to her parents, 'We'll bring some back for you.'

'Oh, that would be very nice.' Emotions taking control, Farah held her husband's arm and leaned into him. Kahlil looked very surprised, but she told him to relax, that it was not only allowed, but expected of a happy couple.

'Farah, Kahlil, you're welcome to come over tonight. I'll make an Aussie barbeque. We can exchange stories. I'm sure Grace would enjoy hearing how you landed here.'

'Thank you.' Kahlil said, hand over his heart. 'We would enjoy that very much.'

10

B INOWEE

Joe was finally able to relax; the barbeque was a huge success. Everyone heard how Luna ended up at the vet. The X-ray showed no fractures, just a nasty sprain.

Grace was told by Farah Aziz, without naming anyone, how the Noor family escaped. Joe found the story fascinating. That a highly respected man, possibly a Prince, had helped with their escape. They may have met him but their liberating camel drivers always kept their faces covered, so they'd never know. An undercover operation took them through to Dubai. They were given papers and helped board a plane. Eventually, ending up in Australia, where they were granted refugee status. Jasmine's father, Khalil Noor, is a respected builder, and, though a small business, had already helped with several local projects.

Joe sat back in his favourite, man-sized wicker chair, looking over the dam smiling, thinking how great everything turned out. Life was good. He chuckled as a couple of ducks flew in and settled on the dam that could now be seen through the demolished garden. He thought he might just keep it that way.

Grace came out with her glass of wine and sat opposite. 'I just received a text message from Trinity. They love the article that I accidentally sent off when I rushed out to find Finn.

'That's great news.' Heart pounding, he smiled at her, thinking, do it now—say it now! So, he leaned forward, elbows on his knees, and opened his mouth to speak.

'Before you say anything, Joe, let me begin, and if you don't like it, that's fine. But I need to say my piece before I get all tangled up in whatever *you* have to say.'

Joe straightened, and heart hammering now, he sat back, ready for rejection.

'I enjoy my work. I love getting out there and researching in-depth to gather the truth of things happening in the world. I live for that. I love the rush when the tiniest bit of information can make a massive difference in someone's life. I love it all. I love helping people and getting them out of threatening situations. And I'm good at it—'

'Grace,' Joe cut in mouth dry with the fear of having his heart broken. 'I understand—'

'No, please wait.' Grace intertwined her fingers, knuckles turning white. 'I *loved* my life, but I love being here more.'

Joe took a moment for it to sink in. Elation filled his entire being. He tried to speak but kept fluffing his words.

'Slow down, superman.' Grace giggled.

He took a deep breath and found something coherent to say without pushing things too far. 'Does this mean you're moving to Myrtleford?'

'Myrtleford? Why would I move there? When I said *here,* I meant right here. But if that doesn't work out for you ....'

In a flash, Joe was on his feet and just as quickly had Grace on tiptoe, hugging her to his chest. 'I'm right there with you, Grace.' Then mouth on hers, he cherished her lingering, breathtaking kiss.

He slowly pulled back far enough to see her face. 'Grace?'

'Yeah, last time I looked, that was me,' she whispered, smiling.

Dipping his head, Joe rested his forehead on hers. He could feel it; there was movement in the room.

Lips softly touching Grace's forehead, he murmured, 'Finn....'

'Dad, Gracie, why you huggin' and kissin'. It can't be Luna. She's fine, right here, with me. Did the vet say something to you and not to me? Is there something wrong wi–with Luna?'

Arm firmly wrapped around Grace's waist, Joe turned to face his worried son.

'I'm glad you're here, Finn.' 'I've got an idea; we'll sit on the couch, and you can sit opposite on the coffee table.'

'Okay, Dad, but I'm not supposed to do that,' Finn mumbled quietly, sounding concerned. He popped his behind on the table, with Luna at his feet. Both were looking at Joe expectantly.

'Finn, I'll get straight to the point. I hope it's okay with you that Grace comes here to live?'

His face lit up with the broadest grin as his eyes got teary. Arms wide, Finn flew at them. They fell back into the couch, a tangle of arms and legs. Luna joined in the excitement with her whoofs and licks.

Finn stepped back, swiped the tears off his face with his fingers and asked, 'I'm just saying, but talking to Mum yesterday, she said she hoped you...um,' Finn looked at the floor. Joe knew his body language; he was trying to remember his mum's exact words.

'Finn, it doesn't have to be word perfect.'

'Right, Mum hoped you would get married again and be happy.' Finn scratched his head. 'Are you getting married to each other?'

Joe couldn't stop his one-sided smile. He winked at his son, and with a little sideways nod, Finn understood and gave his dad a Mathews quirky grin back. Joe stood and held out his hand for Grace, helping her off the couch.

'Can I just say something?' Grace began. Man, and boy nodded. 'See this here couch.' They nodded again. 'We are never selling this amazing couch, *ever*, or the coffee table. Okay, they're special.'

Finn tugged on his dad's hand. Joe looked down at him, questioning.

'Ask her Dad,' Finn urged and Luna woofed. 'Quick before Gracie changes her mind.'

'Grace Taylor, will you marry me?'

'Yes, but let's keep it very lowkey.'

That's all it took for more huggin' and kissin'.

THE END

LOVE IN BETWEEN

LEANNE LOVEGROVE

love
in
between
Leanne Lovegrove

For Sue,
my fabulous writer friend, thank you for your support.

Leanne Lovegrove

1

Caleb Stirling watched the whirlybird of dust spiral past and thought he must have arrived on the set of a crime show. The squeaking school gate, swinging to and fro, added to the effect.

A cascade of goosebumps erupted across his skin.

Inside the gate, the head mistress of Bellethorpe Primary School, whom he'd successfully avoided the last three mornings in a row, frowned in his direction. Her gaze so intent that he felt trapped like fruit in jelly.

If he avoided her eye, could he slink past unscathed? He'd try.

Taking great interest in Sybella walking beside him, he reached for her tiny hand. In a traitorous move, she dodged his touch and raced away to her friends gathered near the adventure playground. The children's mothers nattered to each other and stared at him too, just like every other day. In time he'd talk to them, but not today. A presence stepped beside him and his heart sank. His luck had run out. He'd avoided contact with anyone at the school, hell, the entire town since he'd arrived in the backwater that was Bellethorpe. Not for the first time he wondered why his sister had lived in the small country town, which on first glance, had little to offer. And in the midst of winter, it was bloody cold.

'Sybella says she hasn't eaten breakfast these last few mornings,' Mrs Ackhurst addressed him. She leaned in as she spoke and then recoiled with her nose in the air. For some reason, he expected her to have grey, permed hair and a chain with glasses around her neck. Prim and proper and sensibly dressed, yes, but she wasn't as old as he'd imagine. Her voice was stern though, and she clasped her hands together as she waited for his reply to a question she hadn't asked.

He thought for a moment trying to remember. He'd seen the kid eat, hadn't he?

'Nor has she had any lunch,' Mrs Ackhurst continued.

'You don't provide lunch?' he enquired.

'There's a tuckshop, Mr Stirling, but she needs money to purchase food.'

Caleb felt his pockets and blew out a sigh of relief as he extracted a couple of gold coins.

'And you need to pre-order.'

Ah. He fondled the coins in his hand.

'Let me escort you. And, on this occasion only, we'll accept a late order. Orders must be in by midday the day before.'

She couldn't be serious. He glanced across at Sybella; each time he looked at the diminutive fragile girl, his heart melted into a pool in his hollow chest. Those black curls, dark eyes; it was like looking at his sister. Sybella sat with a grim expression while her friends laughed and chatted. They were like clones in the identical uniform except their hair was tied into two plaits that ran the length of their tiny backs, their school dresses uncreased and their black shoes, polished. Sybella wore runners with the laces undone and carried a lightweight backpack. It was pink with unicorns on it. The other girls had similar bags but theirs bulged with drink bottles and books.

Darn, Mrs Ackhurst drew him back to the present. Couldn't she let it rest? 'This way, Mr Stirling,' and like the children she taught, Caleb obeyed and followed behind as she strode ahead. She said good morning to each child she passed and their parents. Caleb pulled his cap down lower and hands in his pockets, focused on his shoes

It was only a short walk to the canteen where a bright red sign welcomed you to *Bite Right Inn*. He cringed.

'Oh, thank goodness, Mrs Ackhurst. Mrs Bingham hasn't arrived, and the food preparation isn't complete…'

Mrs Ackhurst held up her flat palm. 'Calm down, Kathleen.'

Kathleen took a deep breath and wiped her hands down her black apron.

'I have the perfect solution. Mr Stirling,' she turned and pointed at him, 'is a chef new to the community. He'll help out, won't you, Mr Stirling?'

What? Uh ah, she had the wrong culprit. He glanced at the basic stainless-steel kitchen with two women hovering near benchtops, knives and other utensils in their hands. 'Don't you simply heat up sausage rolls and make hot dogs and give out lolly bags?'

His words were steady, but his heart hammered fast and his throat constricted. He now regretted that bottle of whiskey last night.

Kathleen smirked and the head teacher replied. 'Perhaps when you were at school, Mr Stirling, but today, it's all about Smart Choices and healthy eating and drinking.'

Kathleen bounced on her toes and jumped in. 'There're categories, you see, there's a poster on the wall over there explaining the details. The top and most important is the green category which is foods you can enjoy in abundance. The amber category is food to select *very* carefully and the red, well, is occasional only.'

What the hell? Someone was pulling his leg.

A nearby door slammed and brought with it a gust of wind down the narrow corridor. Heels clacked on the linoleum floor and broke the silence. The women on both sides of him broke into broad smiles.

He followed their gazes and watched another lady approach. Where were all the men in this town? This woman was different to others he'd met so far. She wore pink heeled boots compared to Mrs Ackhurst's sensible brogues in a muted camel colour. Dark blue jeans matched a bright pink collared tee which featured a large, ripe strawberry on her left breast. She was well-groomed with make-up and long, luscious mahogany locks that curled in slight waves and sat in perfect strands on each side of her face, coming to rest below her shoulders

'Good morning Bridie,' Mrs Ackhurst greeted her. 'How are you today?'

'Fabulous, thank you, Roberta. Hi Kathleen,' she matched their beaming welcome. She paused and stared at him, her smile faltering. He was getting lots of that, too. Were the rumours about small towns true? She threw a quick peek at the two women before asking, 'Is everything all right?' Her smile dropped and her eyes scanned him, starting at his shoes and moving at a leisurely pace until it stalled on his right arm. Most people did that, too. The length of his right arm, commencing at the wrist up to pretty much his shoulder, was covered in art. Black ink.

Caleb removed his cap and ran his hands through his hair and dragged them across his stubble-covered cheeks. God, he must look a sight. He'd been wearing these clothes for days and had slept in them too. At least the black jeans didn't crease but his ratty t-shirt with the portrait of some singer he couldn't even name, hadn't faired so well.

An obnoxious chorus of music blared out through invisible speakers, jolting his thoughts. Mrs Ackhurst let it finish before speaking again. 'That's the start of the school day. I must be off. Mr Stirling, as I was saying, it would be of great help to the school if you could provide some assistance today. It won't take long. We're short and the children need to eat.'

Did she think he was some Jamie Oliver celebrity chef cooking up school dinners? 'I'm sorry that isn't possible. Can she do it?' He pointed at the beautiful brunette, Bridie they said. It was a low act, he knew.

'Are you short, Kathleen? Where's Polly?'

'I don't know, but she's not here and we aren't to expect her.'

As Bridie listened, she was already removing her coat and nodding agreement, her beautiful crystal-clear eyes, contemplative. No doubt her mind was whirring, too. 'I have my own disaster this morning. The chef I use every year for the Bastille Day Festival has pulled out and I need to find another one, pronto. It's only a month away, so I have to get that organised. But of course, that can wait until later. I'll help this morning. We can't let the children starve.'

Mrs Ackhurst observed him again. 'Well, this is timely, Bridie. This is Caleb Stirling, new to town and Sybella's...um... Yes, well, he's a city chef just arrived in Bellethorpe who's sure to help with the festival.'

This time he quickly raised his hand as if that would quell the conversation, but the women ignored him and disbursed. Bridie gripped his wrist, 'C'mon, I'll show you the ropes and we'll get this done in no time. We can chat about the festival too.'

He glanced at his wrist in her grasp. Her fingernails were short but flamingo pink. This woman was a pink powderpuff, all feminine and light and pretty. She was enticing him in all sorts of ways, and his body stirred at the sight of her, but really, all he wanted was to sink back onto the couch and sleep the next few hours away. Forget for a little longer.

Instead, he followed suit, doing what he was told for the second time this morning. In the kitchen she handed him an apron and he robotically placed it over his head and tied the knot at the back; something he'd done a thousand times before. But not since... not in this kitchen either.

'I'm not cooking,' he said, his words harsh and lost on Bridie who was busy gathering lettuces from the fridge and placing them on the bench in front of him. Someone lit the gas stovetop and he jumped at the ignition sound. Bridie paused, her hand on the bench next to his fisted knuckle. Her chest inflated with an intake of breath and her eyes squinted. She moved away to rummage in her handbag before extracting a box. She grabbed a glass of water and collected an apple from the fruit bowl. Without saying a word, she popped out two tiny white tablets, placed them in her palm, waited until he took them and he'd swallowed with a large gulp. When he was finished, she handed him the apple.

How did she know?

2

Well, what a surprise; that wasn't how she'd expected her morning to proceed, it had been a little exciting. First the disaster at school; how could she not pitch in? It had been a rush of prepping salad rolls and fruit cups and baking banana and choc chip muffins. She made a mental note to check on Polly. She might need a homemade lasagne.

Then there was the setback for the festival but what a relief there was a newcomer in town. He'd help. How had she not met him already? He'd been here three whole days. Perhaps they should organise a welcome dinner? Given he's a chef that might not work. A cocktail night or wine tasting at one of their prestigious vineyards? Bridie was sure he'd fall in love with their local produce. Bridie remembered his arm of tattoos and shivered. She hoped he wasn't trouble. Sybella needed him, and the last thing the town wanted was a bad influence. But then, his eyes, they'd seemed sad, his whole demeanour sorrowful and melancholy. But of course, it would be, wouldn't it? She remembered his condition this morning and her guts churned, but instead of judging him she'd turn her mind to how she might help.

But now arriving home, she felt edgy and behind schedule. Always so much to do.

Bridie creaked open the front door, hoping beyond hope that she didn't need to be quiet. But before the door was ajar to reveal their humble living area, she heard the soft snoring.

Her heart sank like a leaden lump to her stomach, and she braced, breathing deeply to calm herself. Taking tiny steps, she entered the room and clicked the door shut. Her father sat hunched over in the armchair he'd slept in last night. She guessed if she was a better daughter, she'd have hauled him into bed and made him comfortable. But really? The man weighed a tonne and for sure her back would ache for days after. There were limits, after all.

Pausing in front of him, she took in his haggard features and sunken skin, the grey whiskers lining his chin. She moved closer, recoiling at the stench of him. Gently, she removed one boot, then the other. Yanking the crocheted rug from the couch, she placed it across his lap and legs. It was cool in this room where the winter sun didn't quite reach through the flimsy curtains.

In the kitchen she put the kettle on to boil and whipped up a batch of her father's favourite cookies. He'd wake later and be ravenous. She wondered if their new celebrity chef baked as well as he cooked. How did she know he was famous? Roberta hadn't said, someone else must have told her but she couldn't remember who. He was certainly an enigma. A tall dark, moody stranger arriving in their town; it was like a scene from a book and Bridie smiled. Her smile slipped as she remembered he'd hardly spoken at the tuckshop as they worked side by side. She'd tried, maybe she talked too much, probably had; she usually did.

In between sips of tea, she placed the tray of biscuits into the oven before filling a glass of water and popping out more paracetamol and placing them on the coffee table to her father's left. She'd place the cookies next to them. A proper meal would have to wait until dinner.

En route back to the kitchen she passed her study. It was a mistake, but she entered and fingered the corners of the manuscript on her desk. Bridie was immersed in this story; she could feel its brilliance and knew it would be successful. You could always tell. She was so excited to be a part of its production. Could she do a little now? Her toes crunched up and she leaned forward, as if the manuscript had a force of its own, dragging her towards it. Oh, she wanted to, couldn't wait to get back into the lives of those characters, live in the world of the words, the French verbs and the joy of translating paragraph after paragraph.

It was mid-week and time to perform her 'day' job. That had always been the agreement. She worked in the farm shop with its assortment of strawberry flavoured produce on the weekends and during the week was her time to work.

But with her father out of action again, the farm beckoned, she could hear it whispering to her. It was being neglected and it was up to her. Bridie glanced out the window. She loved that view, a clear path to the patches of bright red strawberries, row after row. The years had dwindled their patch. In some ways it was a mercy, they could hardly manage what they had. As always, duty called first. It was ironic though, because whilst the berry patch was her first priority, it was the French translation of manuscripts that kept them afloat. And kept her working almost twenty-four seven. No point whinging. With a heavy sigh, she left the room.

The timer on the oven binged and she savoured the aroma of home-baking. Like a real home, a real family.

* * *

Brusque knocking roused Caleb. He shifted his head and groaned as shooting pain raced up his neck. That'd teach him for crashing on the couch. The knocking continued, and he rose out of his chair and laboured towards the door, bleary-eyed and groggy from his deep slumber.

'Well, hello there.'

The voice was too high-pitched, the woman's smile too bright with extra white teeth and flashing eyes.

He squinted at the assault to his senses.

'I'm Jacqueline Kennedy,' she laughed, 'yes, just like the first lady, I'm the first lady of Bellethorpe. The mayor, that is. Welcome to town,' and she handed over a tray of chocolate brownies, the plate still warm.

She bustled past him without an invitation and headed straight for the kitchen where Caleb heard the rattle of cups and the rush of the tap and the incessant talking. 'I can't thank you enough for helping out at school this morning. That's what it's like around here, we all pitch in. But all the better that you're actually a chef. Well, I fancy! Too good for the canteen of course, but the thing is, poor Polly is out for the week, sick, you see, with a stomach bug. We're always stretched to get the help we need, and given you've recently arrived, and I assume you haven't made many arrangements yet, can you help this week? Here's the roster.'

Caleb arrived in the kitchen and put down the brownies. In one hand she shoved a cup of instant coffee and in the other, the piece of paper.

'You won't be alone. There are other volunteers,' she said and took a sip of her own drink. 'And agreeing to cook for the festival, you've made quite the splash into town.'

The taste of the bland, watery instant burned as it slid down his throat. It tasted vile but the heat warmed his insides and he immediately felt better.

'I can see you need some time to sort yourself out, and as you can imagine I have a million things to do. But please sing out if you need anything and the school will see you tomorrow.' With that Jacqueline patted him on the shoulder and left.

Caleb's head spun. This town was something else. He slumped back into the sofa and held the warm cup in his hands. Awake now, he took a moment to examine the room. It was simply furnished but oozed warmth and comfort. It was nothing like his top floor apartment in Sydney with its clean lines and white walls. Here the coloured throws and cushions complimented the lounge which faced a traditional fireplace with stone columns on each side topped with a timber ledge.

Photo frames were displayed on a round silky oak table in the corner with a white vase filled with coloured flowers. The photos were of Sybella with a gummy grin and bright baby eyes. While being chic, the room was also worn and ordinary. But he could picture his sister here. Another shooting pain zoomed across his chest.

His phone buzzed from somewhere and he searched his pockets. The hum sounded nearby, and he moved the cushions of the couch and pushed his fingers in the crevices before retrieving it. His stomach churned as he checked the screen. Marco, his business partner, again. Another missed call and message. He swiped out and the news flashed up. He hated that bloody function. If he wanted the news, he'd read the paper or put on the television. Too late, top story and it was still all about him.

Another knock landed on the door. Jeez, these people didn't leave you alone, did they? But before he could react, the door swung open and Sybella raced in, dumping her school bag in the hall before rushing over to him.

3

Like a little whirlwind, the five-year-old wrapped herself around his torso. 'Uncle Caleb, you forgot to pick me up from school again!' she squealed, pulled back and punched him on the arm.

Shit! He was seriously failing at this parenting gig.

He hung his head, reeling from the embrace and fought the urge to have the waif-thin girl back in his arms. He hadn't had a soul-crunching feel-good hug in ages, and it felt amazing. It'd be weird right, to drag the kid back in for another one. Instead, he collapsed into a heap onto the couch from her light-weight box. Sybella giggled and pummelled him in the chest with closed fists. The force was like a massage against his skin, but he made the appropriate wounded noises.

Bridie wandered into the room and offered a diminutive wave, ceasing their antics.

'You here again?' he didn't mean to sound unkind.

''Fraid so. I was at school anyway. I can pick Sybella up anytime, it's no trouble.'

Was he supposed to thank her for interfering?

'Mummy never forgot to pick me up from school,' Sybella said, her lip wobbling.

'But it's across the road and around the corner, can't you walk home by yourself?' he asked.

'I'm five!' she shouted, 'and mummy would carry my bag and sometimes we'd buy ice-cream.' She stamped her foot.

He was readying his reply when Bridie jumped in. 'Well, let's get some afternoon tea now then. Lucky, because I stopped at the shop and I might just have some vanilla ice-cream. Oh, and strawberries, of course. How about we have ice-cream and berries?'

'Yum!' Sybella jumped up and down on the spot. Okay, lesson number one: you could bribe the kid with food.

'Sybella why don't you take this bag for me and head to the kitchen?' The girl dutifully obeyed.

With her gaze steady on him, Bridie walked over and collected the empty whiskey bottle stashed in the corner crevice of the couch and in a rather robotic manoeuvre with a straight back and dead-pan face, deposited it into her leather handbag without uttering a word.

Caleb swivelled his head left and right for further evidence of his day. There was only the one bottle; he sighed. Clatter came from the kitchen, and he wandered in. Bridie handed him a fizzy orange drink and his eyebrows rose in question. She pointed to the counter and the open packet of Berocca. He nodded and sipped. This woman had a knack for ordering him around. And for having everything at her fingertips.

Sybella served up bowls. 'Want some Uncle Caleb?'

'Absolutely, yes please.' Sybella beamed and he melted a little bit like the ice-cream.

They sat down at the simple timber table and ate. 'These berries are delicious, some of the best I've had.'

Sybella giggled. 'What?' he asked.

She pointed at Bridie. 'Bridie owns the strawberry farm and makes the berries.'

Caleb glanced at her across the table and watched her sit up taller in her chair. His eyes moved to the large berry on her breast. It made sense now. His gaze lingered on her chest (it was quite happy there) but he forced his gaze back to her face. 'These are good. So, you're a strawberry farmer?'

'My father owns the farm. I've left you plenty for later.' She nodded towards the counter where trays of berries were lined up.

'Plenty for breakfast,' he commented.

'I have eggs for breakfast,' Sybella said. Caleb should know that. Lesson number two. Instead of wallowing in his pathetic life he needed to focus on this kid who'd lost her mother. What a twat.

'Guess what ingredients I've brought for dinner?' Bridie addressed Sybella.

'Is it for pizza? Tacos? Fish and chips?' the girl asked but only received shakes of the head.

'Spaghetti bolognaise!'

'My favourite!' Sybella shrieked. 'Thank you, Bridie.'

The kid had impeccable manners.

'Why don't we get started and Uncle Caleb can rest.'

Caleb made to object, but Bridie has risen ending the conversation. Damn, he'd been resting all day. Well, after downing the bottle of whiskey, that is, it had sort of knocked him out. And that had been exactly the intention.

'Caleb, I have some chicken soup for you because it seems you've been under the weather.' She pottered in the kitchen with her back to him.

Sybella turned on him. 'Are you sick? Is that why you've been laying around so much and always tired and your eyes have been so red?'

Bridie turned and leaned back against the bench, smirking. The grin lit up her face, something he hadn't seen before. It made her eyes sparkle and her appear even more beautiful. So, she had a sense of humour, either that, or she was having a dig at him, too.

'Sybella, why don't you tuck Uncle Caleb up on the couch with the television remote. I'll get the chicken soup ready and we'll fix dinner.' It was a ridiculous scenario, but it seemed easier to go along with the idea.

Sybella raced into action and offered her hand to escort him. On the couch, she placed a blanket across his legs and positioned a cushion behind his back. With Bridie's help, she delivered a tray of steaming soup with toast and turned the TV on to a games show.

'Family Feud! That's one of my favourites. Tell me what happens,' his niece said and together she and Bridie whisked out of the room.

He stared at the TV. Family Feud had been one of his sister's favourite programs too. The kid was coping better than he was. He watched the contestants race to beat the buzzer of their opponent and he realised this was the first time he could remember being sober with nothing to do: no rushing to collect fresh produce, no meal prep, no dinner planning. At least drunk he forgot. He could forget that he'd lost his sister and his career in the same week. In only a few short days he'd made the most terrible mistake of his professional life *and* become a single dad.

* * *

Sybella was in bed; tucked up by Bridie, of course. Now she handed him a cup of tea. 'Didn't think you'd sleep if you had coffee.'

'You think of everything, don't you?' he replied.

'I try.' She paused before continuing, 'I am very sorry about Abagail. The whole community loved her, it's such a dreadful loss. You must be going through a hard time adjusting to everything. Please, if there is anyway I can help, let me know.'

He stared. Hadn't she already helped in every way possible?

'You know with caring for Sybella, making meals, housework, whatever.'

'I'm a chef,' he joked.

She didn't laugh. 'Have you been able to get away from work? You run a restaurant, don't you?'

He looked across the room at the blazing fire. The room was warm and suddenly too small. Bridie had lit the fire too, she was exceptionally capable, he'd give her that.

When he didn't reply, she said, 'Have you decided what you're going to do? Are you staying here or taking Sybella to Sydney?'

He shook his head. Caleb was lucky to get through each day at present. When he chanced a glance back at her, he read pity in her eyes. This woman felt sorry for him. Had he become such a pathetic mess that he needed do-gooders helping him out? He'd always been self-sufficient and had prided himself on it. Things had simply got on top of him, that's all. And it would seem in this little backwater it was hard to hide.

She was a damn fine bleeding heart, he had to admit. He thought country chicks wore checked flannelette shirts with dirty jeans and those ghastly workman's boots. Bridie's boots were rather stylish, and she appeared more from the pages of a fashion magazine than off the land. But then, she did say her father was the farmer.

'Here's the information about the tuckshop: the hours, menu and volunteer roster for each day.' She proffered him a piece of A4 paper.

He took it but said, 'Can't you do it?'

She looked at him and her face danced in the shadows from the heat of the fire. Gone was the humour of before, the softness, now she was officious and serious again. 'Yes, of course I can. And I will if you don't. Most mums care for young children in addition to helping their husbands on their properties, so it's not fair to burden them with another job.'

'But it's fair to burden you?'

'I don't mind.' Her response was automatic, but he sensed a hesitancy. She checked her watch and gave out a small, almost indiscernible sigh. He wouldn't say he was a great judge of character, but he sensed Bridie had a fair bit riding on her shoulders.

In a rare move for him, he felt the need to reassure her. 'I'll do it, but only this week while the other woman is sick, and I won't cook.'

Her eyes roamed his face, searching for answers. When she didn't find them, she smiled, and for that it was almost worth it. But secretly his head churned with ideas of how to get out of this ridiculous charade of the school tuckshop.

* * *

CALEB HAD SPENT HIS ENTIRE LIFE IN A KITCHEN. THE EARLY DAYS WERE over a sink of piping hot sudsy water, cleaning stacks of dirty dishes until the soft skin had peeled away from his fingers. Then he'd secured his apprenticeship and spent days cutting only tomatoes. Eventually, he moved on to the next station and cut a variety of vegetables. The first kitchens he'd worked in had been simple and drab with only the most basic of equipment, but later, he experienced elaborate set-ups with a plethora of the best appliances. One thing in common, no matter the kitchen- the noise, chaos and the abuse, was the same.

His body temperature rose with the heat of the cooktop. He couldn't remember the last time he'd been in a kitchen and hadn't been half-tanked. Drinking and cooking went together, there wasn't one without the other, well not for a long-time anyway. It was all innocent fun at first, a drink to get through the busy service. Then a glass of something stronger to deal with the pressure. But the pressure had kept building until he was drinking an entire bottle off the top shelf each night.

But he was here now. In the modest kitchen of his sister's house where the early morning light streamed in casting a yellow glow. This was a simple act of preparing food for Sybella. He didn't need the drink. Despite the reassurance, his hand trembled.

'You're awake,' Sybella said as she entered the kitchen. Caleb had his back to her, but he heard the hesitation in her voice. He couldn't blame the kid for being tentative.

He turned, brandishing the hot pan and flipping the pancake. He smiled at her as it flew into the air and landed squarely on her plate. She giggled. Grabbing the leftover ice-cream and strawberries he created a stack.

'I've never had ice-cream for breakfast before.'

'I know you usually have eggs but there isn't any. I'll get some groceries today and you can have them tomorrow.'

'This is better,' she said and dove in.

'Wait!' He extracted his phone and captured a shot of the dish.

'What are you doing?' Sybella asked as he examined the photo.

Caleb paused. What the hell was he doing? Old habits he guessed. 'In the restaurant we'd take images of our dishes and I'd share them to social media. It's good marketing,' he shrugged.

Sybella asked exactly what he was thinking. 'But you aren't in the restaurant now, what will you do with that one?'

'Dunno, it was silly,' and he put his phone away.

'This is so good,' she mumbled through a mouthful. 'Are you having any?'

'I don't eat breakfast.'

'What? Mummy says you must eat breakfast each day.'

'Your mummy was very smart and yes, you should eat breakfast.'

'Why don't you then?'

The kid was giving him the Spanish inquisition. 'I always worked late at the restaurant, and I'd eat after we'd closed. I'd sleep late the next day and only have coffee until I was back in the restaurant and then I'd prepare myself a meal before work.'

That seemed to satisfy her, and she focused on her food until she'd cleaned the plate.

'Holy moly, for a little squirt you sure can eat!' he exclaimed as she licked her lips.

'I'm glad you enjoyed it.' He patted her on the head and she looked at him weirdly. Yeah, okay, she wasn't a dog. Lesson number three. He wouldn't do that again. 'What happens now?'

'Well,' she said, 'I have to get dressed and brush my teeth and pack my bag for school.'

'Okay, you get to it, and I'll clean up here.'

He was wiping his hands from the washing up when Sybella appeared back in the kitchen, bag on her back, dressed and ready. Her school dress was crumpled but he'd deal with that issue tomorrow, he couldn't become super dad in one morning, could he?

Opening the door, they almost tripped over a bright red ceramic dish sitting on the *'welcome'* mat.

'What's that?' Sybella asked.

'It's a casserole dish.' He reached down to collect it. Lifting off the lid, Caleb closed his eyes and inhaled. 'I'd say that's beef stroganoff.'

Sybella leaned in too, screwed up her nose before skipping ahead towards the gate. Hoisting the dish onto his hip, Caleb headed out too.

At school he headed straight for *Bight Right Inn*. 'Oh, thank goodness,' Kathleen exclaimed as she rushed over. 'We thought you weren't coming.' She bent over at her hips and caught her breath dramatically.

'What's that?' she asked after recovering.

His hesitation was only a flicker. 'Today's special, beef stroganoff.' Her eyes widened and she whispered, 'fancy.'

Caleb hated being in the school canteen, their food was embarrassing. Sure, it fitted into their made-up categories, but they could do better. Perhaps he was a Jamie Oliver in the making? He squashed that thought pretty quickly as he slathered extra avocado on the multigrain bread roll. Who was he to care anyway?

Bridie rushed in and his breath hitched. 'I'm ready to help,' she said and faltered. Again, she was resplendent in pink. He didn't realise he liked the colour so much. But while the colour popped, her sunken eyes were streaked red and she looked haggard. 'It looks like you're all organised,' she muttered, her smile off-kilter and less beaming than yesterday. Her legs still looked damn fine in her blue skinny jeans, though.

'I'm impressed. This place usually looks like a bomb has hit it during prep. What's your secret?'

He shrugged. 'No secret. A good chef cleans his own mess.'

Bridie opened the fridge. 'Wow! These look amazing.' She held up a salad roll and one of the fruit cups. 'What's this?' she pointed to the row of dishes on the bench.

Caleb bit his tongue. Anyone else and he would have snarled. For Bridie, he softened his tone. 'Beef stroganoff served on a bed of rice in individual cups.'

Bridie placed her arms across her chest. 'What can I do?' Her voice was softer too, almost a whisper.

He stood in front of her, so close he smelled berries mixed in with a hint of vanilla. 'It's all done. Go home and help your dad, or,' he realised he didn't know what she did, 'go get a coffee.'

Bridie glanced at Kathleen. 'I could serve at first break?'

'Sarah and Mabel are both here, so we're good today.' Bridie nodded. Once more, out of character, he wanted to rescue her, and he wasn't a rescuer.

She spoke first. 'You look better today.' They shared an unspoken exchange before she reached for her bag.

'I'll see you at the Bastille Day committee meeting tonight.'

She'd left before the words registered. WTF?

4

B ridie brushed past the people milling in the entry to the community hall. What the heck? Had she got the night wrong? No, she might be tired but was super organised and never messed up the details. Except, tonight the hall buzzed with activity. In amongst the fifty or so people present was a group of wives from surrounding farms. They stood in a huddle holding flutes and sipping sparkling wine. Wine? They never drank at meetings. There was also a selection of nibbles on a long side table.

She must have the wrong night.

Bridie searched for familiar faces and spied a few members of the local council, including Jacqueline, of course. Then there was Yvette, the bakery owner, Geoff, the editor of the local paper and every woman resident of Bellethorpe.

Something was up.

Bridie saw local schoolteacher and her dearest friend, Maggie and dashed towards her. 'Hey, what's up? Why is half the town here?' Maggie was also the secretary for the committee.

Before she could answer a hush came over the assembled group.

Bridie watched Caleb enter the hall. Maggie focused on the stranger along with every woman in the room. Bridie even heard their collective intake of breath. She had to admit she held her breath, too.

Okay, now everything made sense.

Tonight, Caleb's hair was still wet from the shower and hung in tight curls around his scalp. He wore a tight, plain black t-shirt with matching jeans and a shiny silver belt buckle. The right sleeve of his tee slid up to reveal the entirety of his patterned arm. It would not have surprised her if he'd ripped a motorcycle helmet off his head and dragged on a cigarette, such was his look. Except he appeared bright-eyed and rested but a scattering of dark stubble still lined his chin.

The man had to be trouble. Did that explain the butterflies swirling in her tummy at the sight of him?

Unfortunately, every woman in the room seemed to be experiencing a similar Caleb Stirling effect. A flare of irritation shot through her. She'd met him and spoken to him, helped him, and hadn't simply gazed upon him like a teen at a rock concert.

Word had clearly spread about the newcomer to town.

The more confident ladies of the group wasted no time gravitating to his side, pawing him with their talons, offering him drinks and food, while flashing their sickly smiles.

Bridie directed Maggie to collect extra chairs for the crowd and called the meeting to order. She was the President, after all.

'I am so excited to see everyone demonstrating such enthusiasm for the annual Bastille Day Festival. Thank you so much for attending. Lots of hands make light work, someone famous once said.' She smiled too broadly and paused for effect, wanting to drag out the moment. But she couldn't do it. 'This year, I'm pleased to advise Caleb Stirling,' she pointed which was quite silly because everyone clearly knew who he was, 'has volunteered to help.' Every head turned in his direction. 'Caleb, do you have a menu plan for the day?' she asked.

'Menu plan? Uh, no. Not yet. I don't know much about the festival or the requirements. Why are you celebrating the French national day – are you people French?'

For such a damn good-looking man he could be difficult. Or perhaps broody was more appropriate, or maybe sullen. She couldn't work out if he was deliberately rude or simply obstinate. Bridie plastered a grin to her face. 'Maggie, can you read out what food was available last year including the menu for the evening sit-down-dinner?' As Maggie flicked through her notebook of minutes, Bridie continued. 'No, we aren't French, Caleb, although sometimes we'd like to be.' A few people tittered. 'To explain, after the first world war, this area welcomed and resettled returned servicemen. Settlements were established around this region and the soldiers were given the privilege of naming them. They chose some of the battle fields as a mark of respect for their fellow men who didn't survive. You might be familiar with Amiens, Passchendaele, Bapaume, Messines or perhaps Fleurbaix, or Pozieres.' She rattled them off in her perfect French accent. 'The towns were connected by a railway line built in 1919. That created jobs as well as many other industries such as orchards, farming and even a mine at one time. The railway operated for over fifty years before closing around 1974.'

The room was dead silent. The locals knew this history, of course, but didn't often talk about it. Bridie continued, 'Many descendants reside in those towns today and as a testament to the past, to the soldiers and the way they forged new lives and for those of us prospering here now and proud of the region and its history, an annual festival is held. People feel an affinity and connection to France. And what better way to celebrate than with French food and culture. It's become a long-held tradition and one that we love. It adds a bit of flair and fun to our community.'

Caleb nodded in a solemn fashion. Bridie couldn't read whether that meant he thought they were all completely daft (and that wouldn't surprise her) or he accepted and respected the past and the way it's always been done.

'Last year Chef Armstrong had stalls with frog's legs and snails, stuffed mushrooms and French fries,' Maggie smiled but no one else joined in, 'and for the main meal he prepared caviar, a duck dish with some fancy name I can't pronounce, and fish with cheese for dessert. That's very French,' Maggie offered.

'And did everyone enjoy the frog's legs?' Caleb asked the group.

Bridie jumped in. 'I'm not sure it was about enjoyment; it was an authentic French experience.'

'France is a country with some of the most delicious produce and dishes in the world. Their food can be both authentic and a sensory experience.'

A shiver raced up Bridie's spine. His delivery was deadpan and bordering on patronising, but his words were like honey. She looked around and everyone was captivated.

'Great. You know what you're doing. What are your ideas for this year then?'

'Food is about a moment, a sense of place and time. It should transport you, be sensual, an unforgettable experience. Orgasmic if you will.' All of the oxygen was sucked from the room. He spoke to her and only her, his gaze intense, direct and she was inexplicably drawn to his words, his passion, him. Without blinking he held her gaze; it was like he caressed her with those dark, intense eyes. If a freak tsunami suddenly hit Bellethorpe, Bridie didn't think she'd be able to pull herself away.

'I can help you with the menu,' wealthy, married, wine maker Sally said.

The moment was broken. An over-the-top gulf of disappointment hit her. Caleb had seen her, really seen her and she'd felt alive, her nerve endings tingling in a physical sensation that rolled over her body. She'd felt important, singled-out and she'd admit it, desired. No man had looked at her like that in a long time. It left a pit of longing in her belly for more. To be loved and cared for and…when it ended, she felt it more keenly than usual, that sense of loneliness she fought to keep at bay. She lived amongst a kind and loving community, was very involved, and everyone liked her, but no one looked at her like that.

Maggie called an end to the meeting and confirmed arrangements for the next catch-up. Geoff reluctantly agreed to run a piece in *The Bellethorpe Times* and quizzed Maggie on the details. Bridie heard the conversations but did not join in.

Caleb had brushed off Sally and spoke with Yvette, one of the oldest members of their community and the long-term owner of the bakery. The bakehouse had been a fixture of the town forever and so had Yvette. Bridie became present once more as she watched their exchange. Of course, Yvette was eighty and little competition. *Competi-*

tion? She must be losing her marbles. But more likely it was the first spark of hope she'd felt in a long time. Or perhaps excitement. Problem was Caleb Stirling was a drop-dead gorgeous chef suddenly the father to a five-year-old and he lived in Sydney. Plus, he was a drunk, and if there was one thing she couldn't tolerate it was an alcoholic.

5

Caleb entered the cool confines of the tuckshop with a sense of relief. Arriving each morning meant he'd survived another day. The commitment he'd reluctantly given the school canteen had him waking up each day with somewhere to go and something to do. Dare he say it had saved him? Nah, it was too soon for that.

'Good morning, ladies!' he sang out as he entered, noting with pride the time; he was getting earlier each day. He wouldn't admit though, that he'd grown fond of the old, basic kitchen with its bare produce on the skimpy school budget. Plus, he enjoyed the low-pressure environment and easy food prep. No unhappy customers was an added bonus. He'd even adjusted to Kathleen's easy humour and ready smile.

Today the air was still and the mood quiet, none of the usual rushing and easy chatter. Kathleen stood with a woman he hadn't met before, their faces glued to a phone, squinting to catch whatever the image was on the small screen.

The phone lowered and the two of them did a double-take, their eyes shooting between him and the phone. Kathleen's mouth dropped open.

His gut spasmed.

With surprising agility, Kathleen was beside him in an instant and the phone thrust into his face, so close, the image blurred. 'Is this you?' she asked.

His body stiffened. Bracing himself, he stared at the image that had haunted him these last few weeks: him, intoxicated, looking ragged after late service. Not his best moment but the one that had gone viral.

Kathleen in her usual bulldog fashion didn't wait for a reply. 'Did you poison all those people?'

Caleb held in his large, deep sigh. 'I didn't poison anyone…'

'Food poisoning, same thing, right?' she gazed up at him with large round eyes. The other woman came and stood next to her.

'It was an accident, a mistake. A stuff-up. I didn't know the prawns were off. It was completely my fault…'

Kathleen was doing that dancing on her toes thing again. She made a habit of that when she was excited or anxious. Which was she? Excited at revealing the scandal? Everyone else seemed to enjoy it.

'But you fed those bad prawns to a famous girl band and they were hospitalised.' The corners of her lips turned up in the hint of a smile.

'Oh boy,' the other woman said eloquently.

'Yes, that's one way to describe it. But not only did they get sick from the food I served, they posted on social media about it and they have a lot of followers.'

The other woman put her hands on her hips. 'How do we know you're not going to poison us, too?'

'Oh, this is Ruby,' and Kathleen nodded in her direction before addressing the woman. 'He's not going to make us sick, Ruby.'

Dear old Kathleen was sticking up for him! She continued, 'He's not doing any real cooking, only making salad rolls and heating up stuff. He can hardly go wrong with that, right?'

Okay, not defending him.

'Right?' she turned to him for reassurance.

'I have been a chef for over twenty years, and this is the one and only time I've stuffed up and the whole world learned about it. My career is ruined, and no one will ever come back to my restaurant.' His words were calm but cut like steel. But he wouldn't, couldn't, talk about it.

'Let's get on with the prep. The children will be hungry at first break. Ruby can you please wash the lettuce and Kathleen, you cut the fruit and I'll attend to today's special, mac and cheese.'

His words hung in the air. That involved cooking. Would they object and throw him out of the kitchen? Kathleen placed her pale, pudgy hand on his arm, covering the beak of the falcon and said, 'The kids will love that.'

His mind was a jumbled mess as he stirred the cheesy pasta. A tremble commenced in his arm and was like a shock wave causing his hand to shake. Since being in the school kitchen, he'd controlled his cravings. It was not easy, and today, it was suddenly unbearable.

He gripped his hands together to ease the shake. Did he really think he could hide away in the country, and no one would know who he was or what he'd done?

*　*　*

CALEB DIDN'T KNOW WHERE TO GO OR WHAT TO DO. ON ROTE, HE HEADED back to the house where on the step sat three casserole dishes. Pressure pounded in his ears as the fury spiralled through him. With one foot he kicked those dishes. They crashed into each other, and he struck again. One smashed against the brick step and shattered. Grey, lumpy mince spread across the red concrete, mixed in with white mashed potato. One last boot and peas flew through the air landing in the garden. Over-cooked pasta congealed in a pool on the grass. He fought down his own urge to vomit.

Caleb couldn't sit alone in that house filled with memories of his sister and reminders of the shit job he was doing raising his niece.

So, he walked.

His sister's house was located on the high side of town, in a quiet street not far from the main drag, over a traffic bridge and flowing stream. Parkland surrounded one side and people traversed bike tracks. A building in the centre of the greenery had a large white 'I' identifying the tourist Information Centre. Surrounding it were well-tended garden beds overflowing with flowers in an explosion of colour.

The wind barrelled into him as he walked across the bridge, like ice against his cheeks. He pulled up his collar and dug his head into his chest and strode forward.

He glanced up as he passed the French Kiss bakery where Yvette wiped down the counter. After that, he passed a bank, a pharmacy, a clothing boutique with white plastic mannequins in its window. The traditional post office had an elaborate clock tower soaring above the low-set buildings. Then there was the *Koffee Shoppe* – he didn't have the energy to cringe at the name. He came to a roundabout and in the middle sat a large bronze bell hanging from a crossbeam.

Caleb reached the pub on the corner and craned his neck skywards at the two-story structure and read a timber sign advertising *The Belle*. Without hesitating, he entered through the double-barrel doors. Inside was quiet for the middle of the day but a roaring fire enveloped him with its warmth. The publican nodded and served him with no fuss. He was on his third pint before the door swung open once more.

Caleb didn't look up; he didn't care who it was, the voices washed over him. A female talked to the barman about wine deliveries. He tuned out and sipped his beer.

'I knew I recognised you the other night.' A shadow fell across the bar. A figure stood too close, strong perfume circling. 'Not only because you're hard to miss, but your face was familiar. Last time I was in Sydney I had dinner at Lavapond. It was the best meal I've ever had.' He looked up then, eyes flashing.

Sally.

He remembered her name.

She placed her hand on his thigh under the rim of the bar. 'Lucky you didn't poison me,' she purred and caressed his leg. 'I'd love you to cook for me again sometime.'

A gush of cold air filled the room with the opening of the door again. The fire in the grate flickered. 'It is him, isn't it?' The voice was shrill. The new woman rushed over, and Sally removed her hand. This woman searched in her over-sized handbag and extracted her phone. 'Can I please have a selfie?' She asked but the phone was already out and the camera function ready. 'Sally you be in it, too.'

The two women stood on either side of him and captured the image. 'I can't believe you're in our little town. Running away from the bright lights of the city, are you? I wouldn't worry about that little mishap, people will forget real soon.' The woman rattled on while photoshopping or whatever she was doing to the photograph, uploading it and sending it viral. Whatever. As fast as they'd arrived, they disappeared. Sally gave him a loaded look as she departed backwards.

Caleb downed the rest of his beer, nodded to the publican and left. He was grateful men weren't big on speaking. Luke simply saluted farewell. At least someone didn't care about him.

Next to *The Belle* was an old-fashioned sort of bottlo, meant to be a drive-through. He bought himself the most expensive, top-shelf vodka. Hey, if he was a celebrity, he may as well act like one. He gripped the neck of the bottle wrapped in brown paper.

* * *

'DID YOU ENJOY FRENCH CLASS?' BRIDIE ASKED SYBELLA.

'Oui, merci,' she replied with perfect intonation.

Bridie smiled. 'That's wonderful. Would you like to speak fluent French one day?'

The child smiled and nodded, and they exchanged a few more French words.

Caleb listened as he approached from behind. 'Hey, Bridie.' His voice sounded weird. Bridie turned to greet him, but Sybella rushed forwards and cuddled him tight around his legs before gazing up with her tiny brown eyes. His heart squeezed in his chest. He was all this kid had and she was so easy to please. Lesson number four. The kid smiled her toothy grin, and he wasn't sure if it was adoration or thanks. He gave thanks that he hadn't forgotten her today.

'Hi, Caleb. I wasn't sure if you'd be here, so I thought I'd take Sybella home for you. I also have dinner, save you having to cook.'

Caleb hid the paper bag behind his back and stared at the red casserole dish. There must have been a sale on the corning ware range at some stage. It had become his most loathed object. 'What is it?' he asked.

'Fish curry.'

Something different. Prepared by Bridie. For him.

A millisecond pause.

'Ah, brilliant… I love fish.' he said.

'Me, too,' squealed Sybella.

'Your timing is perfect,' he added. The sadness usually present in her eyes lifted and was replaced by a sparkle. He felt a lurch of excitement within.

'You'll have to eat with us, Bridie. It's only fair. Otherwise, you'll have to go home and prepare another meal and that's too much.'

Her facial features dropped a little then. Did she not want to eat with them?

'Well,' she said, taking in the two of them, 'that would be lovely.' She hovered, unsure.

'Are you hungry, Sybella?' he asked. She nodded and he continued, 'I skipped lunch and am starving. Let's head home now and we can eat afternoon tea after dinner.'

'That's very silly,' Sybella giggled.

'Yes, but I am very silly,' he replied. The kid just didn't know how much.

'Unless of course, you need to be somewhere else, Bridie. What are you doing here anyway? Shouldn't you be working in the orchard?'

'I run French classes a couple of times a week at the school, and I had a lesson this afternoon.' Bridie and Sybella broke into some French to prove the point.

'You speak French too? You didn't mention that the other night?'

'It's my father's property.' She paused and Caleb waited for more. 'But, yes, I'm a book translator.' The sparkle in her eyes grew brighter.

'Wow, that's impressive. In little old Bellethorpe you sit at home and write books in French. That's fantastic, I can hardly read English,' he joked.

Bridie transformed in front of him, soaking up his praise. Did no one ever compliment the woman?

'When do you possibly find the time? You're always here at school or at a meeting or helping someone out?' Caleb shook his head.

'Yeah, it's a bit tricky. Someone always needs a hand.'

'Do they? Or are they used to you doing everything?'

Her reply was too quick, and he realised he'd hit a sore spot. 'I don't do everything, it's a community effort.' She walked away without further comment.

Caleb followed behind with Sybella holding his hand. A few mothers blocked their path and snapped shots of him with their phone. Caleb glanced at Bridie and heard her muttering, *'What on earth,'* as the women retreated.

'A newcomer to town is always interesting,' she said and kept walking.

She didn't know. Could she be the only person in town who didn't?

Bridie reached the house first. She stopped and glanced at the path and across the yard and scorched him with a look. 'Didn't feel like shepherd's pie tonight?'

'I prefer fish,' he was quick and responded with like lack of emotion. Without turning her gaze back upon him, she said, 'Someone worked hard on those meals specially for you. Let's clean it up before they see.'

'Eww, that's gross,' Sybella tip-toed through the debris avoiding stepping into the mess. She raced inside once past the worst of it.

'I'm sorry,' he reached for Bridie's arm, working hard to conceal the bag. A swelling of emotion boiled up inside of him. 'I forgot myself. I'll clean it up. You go in and keep Sybella company and heat up the dinner,' his voice cracked without his consent.

Bridie's face was a patchwork of concern and that angst, that care, that concern, was for him. It only took him 700 kilometres to find someone who cared. Caleb slouched his shoulders and his lips trembled, holding back the tears. But he couldn't and the dam broke. It was the first time he'd cried, and the relief was enormous. The tears started silent and fat and trickled down his cheeks but when her arms encircled him, it was like permission, and he lost his control. Her grip was firm and close providing reassurance everything would be okay. Bridie offered comfort, relief from the pain he'd held inside, and those tears turned into ugly heaving sobs that racked his chest. Gasping for air, he clutched her tighter, and hung on.

6

'You know I don't care about your reputation or what people say or even if you're a drunk, but as Mayor of this town I'm responsible for my citizens.'

Jacqueline Kennedy stood at the head of the couch with her hands on her hips and glared down at him, as usual, with absolute disregard for his privacy.

Bloody woman. Couldn't she leave him the hell alone? He stretched out his legs, but one foot bumped the empty vodka bottle and it hit the rug with a soft thud. He expected a reprimand and braced, ready.

He was on the couch, again. Hungover, again. Damnit, but that wasn't the swear word he wanted to curse. His temples throbbed in unison and his throat was as dry as a desert. He wasn't surviving today. And Jacqueline blabbered on.

Caleb glanced at his watch. Shit. The room was too bright, Jacqueline's voice like a jackhammer. He was late for tuckshop and Sybella late for school.

'You're helping at school, and we've lined you up for the festival. People are relying upon you. This,' and she swung her phone around and Caleb saw she was on his Instagram page, 'cannot adversely affect the local community. We aren't a haven for people to run away and hide from their problems.'

'I'm here because my sister is dead.' He sat up.

That made her pause. Lips tight set, she glanced at the phone. 'You've got quite a following and at the moment you're being trolled. People are cruel.'

He ran his hands through his hair.

When he didn't say anything further, she kicked his shoe, her tone softer and said, 'You're a mess. Tidy yourself up,' Jacqueline pulled away the crochet rug he'd used as a blanket and folded it into a neat square.

Then Bridie barrelled in, making the tiny room even smaller. She gave a tentative wave. 'Sorry to interrupt.'

'Did you know about this?' Jacqueline shoved the phone in her face.

Bridie frowned. 'His Instagram feed? Boy you have a lot of followers.'

'No, not that,' and Jacqueline snatched the phone away and swiped at the screen. 'This.'

Caleb hung his head in his hands as Bridie took the phone and read.

'Putting aside the personal toll,' Jacqueline said and arched one eyebrow, 'this could be a marketing and PR nightmare. What are we going to do about it?'

As if she hadn't just read the damning article about him and his restaurant, Bridie lifted her handbag higher on her shoulder and smoothed her hands down the front of her white jeans. 'Well, first things first. Sybella is due at school. I have her clean and ironed uniform,' she held it up. 'And Caleb is due at the tuckshop. Caleb, you have a shower and I'll put the kettle on. Jacqueline can help.'

Entering the kitchen moments later, the two women sat at the table with Sybella who was eating a bowl of cereal. 'She likes eggs for breakfast,' he said and kissed the top of her head. The child offered him a sly smile.

'We could do a social media response or a series of posts about

Caleb's life here in Bellethorpe, sort of like a counter-attack?' Bridie was saying.

'Yeah, that's a good idea, but our older residents aren't on Facebook or TikTok or whatever and won't see it. We need something that covers all angles, something to inform the locals that everything is under control,' Jacqueline replied.

'I'm not responding to that vitriol. That feeds into these people. The moment I post anything, there'll be a thousand negative comments.' His voice rose and Sybella sat up straighter. He softened his stiff stance as he paced the kitchen.

'Okay, okay,' Jacqueline held up her palm. 'It's more important to address it locally for the moment anyway.'

'I know,' Bridie started, 'we'll get Geoff to run a piece in *The Times*, an expose: Sydney chef arrives in town to care for orphaned niece, helps at the tuckshop and agrees to cook for the festival.'

'Hang on,' his hands gripped the top of the chair in front of him. 'Why do you want to help me?'

Simultaneously they replied, 'Because we care,' and 'Because the town cares.'

Jacqueline looked at Bridie and Bridie looked at Jacqueline and both turned to face Caleb. Sybella pushed her bowl away.

'And we don't want people to become sick,' Jacqueline added.

'You all finished? Bridie asked and Sybella nodded. 'Go and get dressed and brush your teeth and we'll get you to school.' The little girl rushed away.

'I'll talk to Geoff today,' Bridie said as she cleared the table. Jacqueline nodded.

'No more secrets,' Jacqueline said and patted Caleb's arm. 'Let us help you for goodness sake, that's what this town is good at.'

Jacqueline left and Caleb went over to Bridie who stood at the sink rinsing the cups. 'Bridie,' his voice hitched, and he moved to stand behind her, 'leave the dishes. I can do them.' Caleb remembered the feel of her arms around him last night while he cried like a baby, her kindness and hushed words of assurance. Embarrassment mixed in with desire.

He stood parallel to her back, so close, warmth radiated off her body and he heard her breaths. He reached for one hand and placed it by her side. His fingers circled around her wet pinkie finger, generating only the slightest of touches. Bridie did a sharp intake of breath, lowered her head. Blood coursed through his veins at the reaction to him and at their closeness. He imagined moving her luscious locks out of the way of her pale cream neck and trailing feathery light kisses down the skin until she shivered.

'Uncle Caleb, I'm ready,' came a sweet little girl voice. He stepped back, dropped Bridie's fingers, his heart hammering too fast.

Bridie wiped her hands and avoided his gaze. 'I'll be off too. Have a lovely day at school, honey. Au revoir,' and Sybella beamed. When Bridie finally glanced up, she nibbled her bottom lip and a flush of pink tinged her cheeks, matching her pink shirt. He fought to control his groan as she turned and departed.

'Uncle Caleb?'

'Hmm.'

'I know a way to get everyone to like you.'

'You do?'

Sybella nodded and gestured for him to come close, and he leaned over, and she whispered in his ear.

'You think?' he asked, and she nodded again. 'Can we make a plan this afternoon?'

'Yes,' she agreed, then said, 'I think you're a wonderful cook,' and she kissed him on the cheek.

* * *

'Yes, Geoff, I know. Yes, it's a busy time of year, oh, okay, the boating and trailer show. Does it have to be covered in this week's edition? No, I didn't realise. But this is great material for the paper. The whole town is talking about him and we can set the record straight.' Bridie scribbled notes while holding the phone between her ear and neck.

'Okay, when does your new cadet arrive? Soon, yep, that's great but not soon enough. It'd be beneficial to run this piece now.' She sipped her coffee, but movement caught her attention outside her study window. Her father was in the field. The phone slipped and landed with a clunk onto the desk. She grappled to pick it up and apologise but Geoff talked on unaware. Listening, she watched her father bend over and pick a bright red berry and pop it straight into his mouth. He paused, savoured the flavour. Her spirits soared as he moved along the line of plants and lifted individual leaves with loving care and attention. He picked as he went and placed the berries into the cane basket he carried and tugged on a few troublesome weeds along the way. At the end of the row, he retrieved the hose and pulled it off the reel and watered the runners closest to him.

Please let him keep going; pick today's berries and then at least, her only task would be packaging and delivery. She could manage that. Picking took the longest.

Not for the first time her mind turned to their previously thriving patch that was so large it required seasonal pickers. They could still do with the help now, but economic return on their dwindling orchard didn't warrant the expense.

Geoff said something and her mind tuned back into the conversation. 'Okay, no worries, Geoff. I understand we're all doing the best we can. Forget I asked, take care.'

Her father disappeared from her line of vision. She tapped her laptop awake and searched *Caleb Stirling chef Sydney* and her screen filled with results. The guy was a serious celebrity. Heaps of restaurant reviews, some glitzy party shots and loads of food images. Bridie stopped reading to gaze at him: him in his kitchen garb, in fancy suits with slicked back hair and surrounded by gorgeous people. Her body warmed.

She kept reading:

Major mistake and career ruined;

Doors shut on famous Lavapond;

Band girl, Powder Puffs hospitalised with food poisoning;

Chef under investigation.

Ouch. The media had savaged him and his restaurant after the incident. Fuelled by the Powder Puffs who were the unfortunate recipients of the bad prawns. Her stomach churned at the gross detail and photos the quintet posted. Too much info! And despite Caleb's massive following and staunch supporters, the girl band generated greater negative commentary.

Shit. No one liked to have a lovely evening at a renowned restaurant end badly with off food. Every chef's worst nightmare she imagined. As she trolled through the comments on both social media and in the news, her coffee roiled in her stomach.

But then, she was hit with a new wave of enthusiasm. She, Bridie Finch would turn this around. Starting with their own small community.

7

———

You know there are rules about what food is served in the tuckshop?'

'Really?' Sybella responded.

'Uh, huh. You're supposed to eat, I can't quite remember, foods in the green category first and then purple foods sometimes and never the pink because they are evil,' Caleb said.

'Sounds weird. Pink food?'

'Well, the colours might be wrong, but the concept is right. Healthy foods are best and others in moderation.'

'Sounds 'bout right. I can work with that,' Sybella pulled a serious, concentrating face.

'I think this is the most marvellous idea you've ever had,' he told her.

'You don't know any of my other ideas!' Sybella giggled.

They sat together at the small, round table in the kitchen. Sybella drank a glass of milk and ate chocolate chip cookies. 'Can we sell these?' Caleb asked and bit into a biscuit.

'We should because they're so yummy,' Sybella agreed and chomped.

'Ah, but that's the problem. We need a menu filled with delicious but nutritious food.'

'What's nutritious mean?' she asked. Sometimes when Sybella spoke she had the slightest lisp.

Caleb explained.

Sybella said both teachers and students loved his new food at the tuckshop. Mrs Bingham only heated up frozen sausage rolls and pizza and made stale white-bread sandwiches. But now, it was fabulous she said.

Okay, he'd completely bombed in the five-star restaurant stakes but succeeded in the school canteen. At the moment, he'd take the praise.

Sybella said *everyone* would love him if he kept up his stellar performance (his words) because they already thought he was a complete dish (her teacher's words). And everyone would benefit because the kids were well-fed. And be one less job for someone else.

Lesson number five: the kid was smart. But he wasn't sure the convenor of the *Bite Right Inn* would agree with her summation.

'Okay, what should be on the menu?'

She shouted out some of her most-loved foods.

'Can you write a list?'

'I'm just learning my letters, Uncle Caleb, I'm only in prep you know.'

'Give it a go,' he encouraged.

It took a long time but eventually she produced a list, saying each item out loud as she wrote. He assisted with spelling.

'Okay. I love your ideas. But I'll need help because that's a lot of cooking. What should we make for tomorrow?'

Sybella's tongue poked out as she thought but then she shrugged.

'What's your favourite meal?'

'I love lasagne. It was mummy's favourite.'

'Did mummy make it for you?' he said and lifted a strand of hair out of her eyes.

'No!' she said and giggled. 'Mummy bought it and we heated it up in the microwave.'

'That sounds like your mummy.' He smiled but his heart was

breaking inside. 'I miss her.' Did kids talk about their dead parents? He had no idea.

'Me too,' and her head bowed.

'Will you help me make mummy's favourite meal tonight?'

'Yes! Can you teach me how to make it?' she bounced up and down in her chair.

'Yes, and we'll make extra and that will be for school tomorrow.' Caleb took the sheet of paper and they worked out the menu for the remainder of the week.

'My friends are gonna love this,' she grinned.

They prepared their ingredients for the lasagne. Caleb pulled over a chair and placed it at the bench for Sybella. His stomach churned and the gas ignition was like a light, setting fire to his agitation. God damnit! The room spun and he held his fist tight, resisting pounding it on the counter. No, he wasn't anxious about cooking, was he? No, he needed a drink, that's all. Cooking and drinking went together but that was normal, right? He'd been drinking the night of the disaster, but that wasn't him, that was the prawns. A niggling voice badgered him - could Caleb Stirling cook without having a bottle of his favourite drop in him? Of course, he could. He wasn't in that kitchen now. There was no pressure here. Maybe he could have one glass? But he couldn't, not in front of the kid. Even he knew that wasn't right. He'd have to soldier on, cope with the sweat gathering on his brow and his shaking hands. It'd all be fine.

'I love cooking,' Sybella said as the large dishes slid into the oven. 'I want to be a good cook like you.'

He ruffled her hair, radiating a sense of entitlement. He knew he could do it. 'I should have been here to teach your mum how to cook. I remember she used to make a pretty mean chocolate brownie.'

'Yeah, yum, she did. But, Uncle Caleb,' her head turned down and her face sullen, 'it was from a box.'

'No!' He feigned shock and horror, lightness returning. 'I'll show you how to make brownies with gooey caramel and extra chunky choc bits,' he promised. Happy, she nodded.

'You know the worst part about cooking?' he asked. Sybella shook her head. 'Cleaning up! But it's always best to get straight onto it. A good chef never leaves a messy kitchen.'

'Okay,' she agreed.

'I also have to plan some food for the French festival. Can you help me?'

'Oh, yes! Is that the festival with rides and music and animals?'

'I'm not sure. That sounds like a fair. This is to celebrate the French National Day and I'm to prepare French food.'

Sybella took a moment to ponder that information, but the oven timer chimed, and they extracted the bubbling dishes from the oven.

'Uncle Caleb can I take some photos?'

'Of course, do you know how to use my phone?'

With his back turned, Caleb continued washing up.

With a cheeky grin filling her cheeks, Sybella flicked her fingers across the screen of the phone until she found his Instagram page.

* * *

'WHAT DO YOU THINK?' HER BREATH CAME OUT AS VAPOR.

Bridie stood at Caleb's front door and handed over the newspaper. The traipse through the frosty grass had left her feet numb. She tucked her arms inside her pink puffer jacket and wriggled her toes in her boots but never took her eyes off him. He read with his head bowed.

He took so long she stomped her feet as the chill set into her bones.

'Sorry, come in out of the cold,' he said and moved aside.

Caleb once again looked like he'd just rolled out of bed. Bridie swallowed. He wore a white stretch t-shirt with denim wash jeans and bare feet but still hadn't commented on the paper.

The thrill of turning up with the paper was disappearing fast. She'd stayed up late to finish that piece for the early edition instead of focusing on her own neglected manuscript.

Renowned chef leaves the bright lights of Sydney to care for his orphaned niece and pitch in to assist a local community.

It was front page; she and Geoff had argued about that. The boating and caravan show was a good sponsor for the local rag, but in the end she'd won.

It had taken hours to trawl the internet and gather the information she needed. It hadn't been a chore. She'd devoured every morsel about the life of Caleb Stirling; the bits that were open for public fodder anyway; then she'd agonized over each word, description, sentence.

'You wrote this?' Finally, he spoke!

'Yes.'

'It makes me sound so good.'

All her defences tumbled down. 'Caleb, that's because you are. Can't you see? Sybella adores you and the community is all aflutter about the hot chef in the school kitchen producing the best food they've had for years.'

'Do you think I'm hot?'

Heat rose up her neck and her cheeks burned; she wasn't cold anymore. Caleb grinned and she couldn't form a reply. He returned to the paper anyway.

'Do you think it'll work? People will trust me?' His voice always sounded like he'd had a rough night, either that or smoked a packet of cigarettes. Today it tremored with hope.

'People already do, but for those few who mightn't, their doubts will disappear. They'll see you for the man you are. For the man that made a mistake and paid a huge price. For the man that is trying to redeem himself and get on with life. Who has chosen to come to our small town and care for his niece, the only relative she has and not only that, pitched in and helped where needed. What's not to love?' Her voice caught on those last words.

Of course, she didn't express her greatest fear: that he was the same as her father. She hoped he wasn't.

Their gazes locked, his intense and searching, trying to read her eyes, test her sincerity. She licked her lips, her breath not quite reaching her lungs. His gaze was tender, soft and caressed her skin. The pit of her stomach tingled.

He couldn't be a drunk, could he?

'Uncle Caleb.' The shout came from within the house.

'Have a cuppa,' he said but his throat didn't quite work and he had to clear his voice first.

She shook her head. Bridie needed to get the hell out of there and get a grip. 'Heaps to do. Remember there's a committee meeting tonight. Have you done the menu?'

'Argh, no, another one? You sure do meet a lot. I'll skip this one…'

'No way,' she said with a smirk. 'It's getting to the pointy end, and we need details.'

He shook his head.

'I'll do you a deal. Come to the meeting and afterwards we'll go to the local French place in the next town. You can get ideas.'

Quick as a whip he replied, 'I don't need ideas.' Another pause before their eyes connected again. 'But to say thank you for helping me when you don't have to,' he held up the paper, 'I'll attend the meeting and have dinner with you.'

Her heart was galloping out of her chest. *Shit.* Had she just asked Caleb out and he'd said yes? Nerves were already dancing in her tummy.

'See you tonight,' she said and broke their gaze.

* * *

'THE TOWN STILL CAN'T GET ENOUGH OF THIS GUY,' MAGGIE WHISPERED, standing beside her in the hall.

'Déjà vu, huh,' Bridie said by way of intelligent reply. Her friend looked at her quizzically. 'Have you been bitten, too, hun?'

'Don't be ridiculous,' Bridie scoffed but Maggie laughed.

'Well, just saying that I wouldn't mind biting that cherry, too,' and like everyone else in the hall, she turned to watch Caleb saunter into the room. Perhaps if the guy walked normally and didn't own the room when he entered, he'd draw less attention? Perhaps if he wasn't so damn cow-boy good looking with his tight jeans and messy hair, then the town wouldn't be so interested in him? Bridie couldn't tear her eyes away either.

On the positive side it had the town's people turning up.

They reached the item on the agenda about catering for the festival. All eyes turned to Caleb, like a king upon his throne, his subjects waited for him to speak. And in true Caleb style, he didn't offer what they sought.

'The menu, Caleb. Everyone wants to hear what you've planned,' it was Jacqueline who eventually spoke. He remained silent, his features not giving anything away. 'And it needs to be approved.'

Caleb stood and stared them down from his full height. Anger flashed in his eyes and his fists balled. It was the first time she'd witnessed his head chef persona where the critics said he was a hard arse in his own kitchen and there was only one boss, him.

She willed him to sit down and not wreck their hard work so far in repairing his image. Seconds passed and she detected him calming, his hands loosened and fell to his sides. 'No one said anything about approving the menu. If you want me to cook for your festival, I'm happy to. I'll stick to the brief and you'll have your French food. That's it.'

'I'll help him,' a voice sang out from the second row.

Evelyn. *Shit.*

Having relocated to Bellethorpe five years ago, she was still considered a newbie. Her Hollywood, old-style glamour still caused heads to turn. Tonight, she wore a vibrant green dress with her long blonde hair pulled back off her face. She matched him in the sauntering stakes as she cat-walked towards him. Bridie watched Caleb instead. His eyes narrowed as they raked from Evelyn's toes to her head.

'Oh, that would be fabulous, Evelyn, thank you,' Jacqueline replied. What, no!

'I work alone,' Caleb replied. Yes!

Evelyn stared up at him from her diminutive five-foot stance. Height did not intimidate her. Hands on hips, she said, 'Before relocating to Bellethorpe I worked at an exclusive hotel specialising in French food. I know a thing or two.'

'Wonderful,' Jacqueline commented. 'We'll set up a time for you two to chat,' she continued.

The door opened and Ruthie, Caleb's sixteen-year-old neighbour entered. 'Caleb?' her voice shook. 'Sybella is sick.'

'What?' Bridie stood.

'She's vomited a few times now. You need to come home.'

Caleb grabbed his jacket hanging off the chair and shrugged it on.

'I'm coming with you,' Bridie said. 'Jacqueline, you take over as chair and cover the last few items,' she blustered as she rushed out the door.

Caleb turned and said with a parting jab to the group assembled, 'I work alone.'

* * *

FAR OUT! WAS IT HIS LASAGNE? IT HAD TO BE. HE PAID SPECIAL ATTENTION to how he felt, but his tummy didn't rumble, he was okay. But he was also famous for his cast-iron will. It wasn't his stomach, though, it was the ache shooting through his chest that made him ill. He and Sybella had been the only ones to eat the dish. Conscious of Bridie following, Caleb walked fast ignoring the chill.

'Hey, sweetie,' he said as he reached her bedside. Her forehead was on fire and clammy. 'How are you feeling?'

'I'm okay, just feel a bit sick in the stomach.'

'I'm so sorry,' he said as she retched into a bowl again.

Bridie came in with a wet washer and held it to her forehead and placed a glass of water to her lips forcing her to drink. 'You know what's great? There are special ice blocks for kids when they are sick. I'll pop out to the chemist and get some.'

Sybella gave Bridie a thumbs up, but her eyes were shut before her hand landed back to the bed.

Caleb followed her out. 'I'm sorry about dinner. I would have liked to try that place.'

'That's okay, we'll go another time. You're needed here.'

He placed his hand on her arm, wanting, needing to say more but he didn't know how to express what he was feeling. 'Thanks,' was all he managed.

Shutting the door on Bridie, Caleb strode to the kitchen. He collected the dish of beef lasagne from the fridge and shoved it towards the bin. The solid mass didn't move, and he rammed it again. The dish jammed against the edge of the plastic tub and spilled over. With two hands Caleb thrust the whole thing in and pushed hard for good measure, cracking the bin and causing the dish to shatter to the ground and scattering the contents across the floor.

8

———————

'How are you feeling?' Caleb smoothed the hair off Sybella's brow. It wasn't clammy today.

'Much better,' Sybella replied and sat up in bed. The colour had returned to her cheeks and her eyes were sparkling once more. 'But, but, tell me,' she said, 'what did everyone think of the lasagne? Did they love it?'

Caleb didn't blink. 'I don't know, no one said,' and he turned his eyes away, suddenly very interested in the contents of her bedroom.

'What!' she exclaimed, 'I'll ask them tomorrow. I bet it was the best they'd ever had.'

Caleb kept his gaze diverted. He wasn't so sure the kids loved the frozen version he'd purchased from the local co-op this morning en route to school, but hey, who knew? It was much better than the alternative and that was poisoning the entire school community with his efforts.

'That vomiting was gross. Uncle Caleb, can wild berries make you sick?'

'Why do you ask?'

'Yesterday yukky Joshua Thomas dared me to eat a bunch of berries we found growing at the edge of the playground. He called me a baby when I said I wouldn't. I'm no baby so I ate them.'

She had his attention now. 'Did anyone else eat them?'

Sybella sat up taller. 'No one else was brave enough.'

He gripped Sybella's spare pillow tight to his chest. Was it possible his cooking wasn't responsible? A flicker of hope flared…but surely a few berries wouldn't make her vomit all night? But he guessed, she was tiny, a little waif of a thing. Doubt crept in. She'd eaten the dish he'd prepared only hours later; but he'd cooked the beef extra-long. If he'd had a drink, would it have been different? Too much coincidence…

Sybella touched him on the arm when he took too long to reply. 'Well, they could, I guess. It depends. How about next time you don't take the risk and call him a baby back for being an idiot?'

She giggled. 'Yeah, okay. It's not worth that gross sick. Next time I'll be braver and say no.'

Caleb didn't know what to do with that information. Berries or lasagne? A freak accident or his cooking? It was easier to think the worst. And no one was sick at school yesterday, so disaster diverted.

'As you're feeling better, I'm thinking we visit Bridie at her farm. What do you say we make berries and Greek yoghurt tomorrow for tuckshop? We can cut up the strawberries and place them in a plastic cup and top it with yoghurt and granola? Sound good?'

'Yummy, yes, except we need to use a recyclable paper cup, okay?'

'Okay,' he agreed.

He'd rarely used his car since arriving in Bellethorpe. It had taken an eternity to drive from Sydney but since then, he'd only walked the small distances in town. Except the *Finch Berry Farm* wasn't walkable but only a short drive away.

Dark clouds bruised the sky and turned the world a grey pallor; a gust of wind buffeted the car door as he opened it. Caleb hadn't bothered with a warm jacket but checked Sybella was wearing one. It was blue with stars on it.

'There's lots of fruit in this town, isn't there?' he commented as they passed *Appletree Orchard* with a large red golden delicious sitting atop a high pole. Then they passed a few wineries, that was more his style.

He could taste the crisp dry white liquid as they passed Carrington Estate Wines and then next, Cockatoo Ridge Winery.

Less than five minutes from the CBD of Bellethorpe, the rain bucketed down in large, fat drops and even in the car the temperature dipped to freezing. Whether it was the ominous weather or being out of the township, but it felt like they were miles from civilisation and that sensation on his first day of entering a horror movie returned. If it wasn't for the scattering of low-set fibro farmhouses and long stretches of fields with a variety of produce, he might be on a highway to hell. Times like this he wasn't sure he'd ever get used to the country.

The flash of a bright red sign became obvious through the weather. Green letters advertised Finch Berry Farm and sure enough, next to it was a grand red strawberry so life-like it even had the pips and a bushy green top.

Turning where the arrow indicated, they entered a long drive lined with tall, majestic eucalypt trees adjacent to fields of yellow grass. As they moved closer, paddocks filled with lines of berries surrounding a home set in the middle. 'She has a shop here, too,' he addressed Sybella as they pulled into a designated parking area.

'Yeah. It's only open on weekends, I think. Not sure. You can do a tour, too and once they had a train, you know for kids. You're too big.' She undid her buckle. 'We're gonna get soaked.'

Caleb wiped the frosted glass interior and searched outside for any form of shelter. 'Hey, what's that over there?' he pointed and Sybella raised in her seat to get a better look.

A blob of pink bounced up and down in frantic movements. 'That's Bridie. What the heck is she doing out there?' his voice became a whisper as a crack of thunder boomed across the sky. 'You wait here,' he commanded Sybella, and he raced out of the car.

The rain belted down in heavy sheets, blinding him. His shoes sank into the softening ground, and he was saturated through to the skin in seconds. Reaching her side, he shouted, 'Bridie, what are you doing?' With jerky and fast movements, Bridie kept searching for berries and shoving them into the basket at her feet. 'Bridie!' he said and touched her arm that flung back in fright, the berry she held, flying through the air.

'What are you doing? Stop,' he gripped her arm.

Bridie paused and looked straight through him, her gaze faraway. 'I have to save the berries. It's going to hail,' her voice cracked, and she started franticly picking again.

Caleb checked out the sky. The far horizon was a steely grey but everywhere else was a freakish Armageddon green as if hell was coming for them. He lowered his gaze to the rows of plants. There were masses of red berries. The two of them alone were not going to save this row, let alone this field. 'Where's your dad?' he yelled over the din.

Bridie didn't reply but kept working. Caleb didn't know what to do: it was madness to stand here in the pummelling ice-like rain and pick strawberries, but he couldn't leave her alone.

Sybella arrived with spare containers. 'Here use these,' she said. He looked at her with incredulity before she said further, 'I've picked plenty of strawberries before.' Curly strands of hair flattened against her face and Caleb's heart couldn't help but swell. He bent over and yanked every berry he could see but before his bucket was even half-full, hard shards of ice hit him.

'Sybella,' he pulled at her arm, 'run and get under cover,' the little girl hesitated until a golf-ball of ice hit her on the head and she gulped.

'Bridie, Bridie, you have to stop, you'll get hurt.' He trailed behind her while she moved along the line with incredible speed. She filled two buckets and stepped, toppling a third.

'No,' she sobbed and bent to her knees collecting fruit from the ground where they'd scattered. Their hands clashed as they rushed. Once full, he held it close to his chest and their eyes connected. He shook his head, and she did too. He grasped her arm and tried to drag her away, but she stood rock-solid. Putting the container down, he tried again. She was like a stubborn donkey, locking her legs and refusing to move. Caleb was stronger though and eventually she gave way and he propelled her along. Under the awning of the old shop, she begged him. 'Please save what we've picked.' He nodded and braced himself for the barrage of rain and hail as he ran the few hundred metres back to the field, shoved every loose berry he could see into his bucket and his pockets until they bulged. He ignored the ones that fell as he ran.

He paused under the shelter but saw an open shed. He gestured for Sybella to move indoors. Bridie was frozen to the spot, so he settled Sybella into a blanket and raced back outside. Bridie was on her knees and sobbing. He grasped her under the arms, but she fought back with surprising veracity.

'No! Leave me alone!' She buried her head in her hands. Caleb looked left and right. Where was her father? The farmer? Wasn't he worried about his crops?

'Where's your dad?'

Her eyes flew open, and anger flashed through them, turning them a violent dark green, like the sky. He'd never seen that look before. It was hostile. Through gritted teeth she said, 'He's inside sleeping off his hangover.' Caleb took a moment to process the words.

'Should I go and get him?'

He watched her rage seep away; her shoulders slump and the fight leave her body. 'He's like you, a drunk.' There was no mistaking the words, they were loud and clear and said without the vitriol of moments before. Caleb took one step back, shock reverberating through him.

'He deals with life's problems through the bottle too. Then can't get up the next day.' Caleb reeled from the word drunk, but Bridie continued. 'Yesterday was a better day. He was awake and picked fruit in the orchard. I saw him,' a sob broke through her words. 'I was so relieved because it meant I didn't have to do any picking. But I'm stupid. I don't know what I was thinking. I should have checked but I didn't. He probably picked less than a bucket, perhaps ate the rest. Now, look,' her voice rose again, and she pointed towards the fields, 'if I'd checked I could have picked yesterday's crop and there'd be less damage today. The berries will not survive the hail. They'll be bruised, maybe good for smoothies is about all.' Her whole body shuddered.

Without thinking Caleb pulled her towards him, his arms encircling her frame easily, but she was a dead-weight. She shook and he held her tighter as her chest heaved, sobs escaping but eventually receding to small hiccups. Resting his chin on top of her head, he smelled the scent of her hair, it was all citrus and fruit and clean. Her plump breasts rested against his chest, the shape of her hips and limbs moulded to him; she was all woman and he fought against the bolt of pleasure that shot through him. His body reacted with lust; his heart cracked at her despair, but his head recalled her harsh words. Is that what she thought?

'Let's go into the shed, Sybella's there.' Bridie pulled away, wiped her eyes and nodded.

Inside he placed her onto a barrel with an old blanket around her shoulders. Sybella offered a broad smile thinking the whole thing was a lark.

Drunk.

'Do you want me to go and pick some more?'

Bridie shook her head while tears rolled down her cheeks, visible now they didn't mix with raindrops. 'There's no point.' This woman who he'd only recently met, had been a constant ray of sunshine on his gloomiest of days, lent a hand to anyone who needed it and seemed to be the lifeblood of this community. Now she sat before him, completely desolate. Broken. He understood those feelings. But she'd been the one to help him, even when he thought he wasn't worth it.

Caleb Stirling wasn't used to helping others. He looked around him for inspiration. In the shed there were trays of picked strawberries and long benches with containers and water taps and other paraphernalia. He'd been in plenty of fruit and veg plantations and this looked like where they packaged up their produce.

'Sybella, do you want to help me prepare punnets of strawberries?'

Her eyebrows fused together. 'What do ya mean?'

'See these?' He held up some plastic tubs, 'we have to sort the berries into these for transporting to the shops.'

'Oh yeah,' she said, 'these are the ones we can take to the tuck-shop.' He wasn't so sure about that anymore, he sensed Bridie needed these berries. Nonetheless, the little girl jumped up, ready.

Bridie shivered.

'I'll make Bridie a cup of tea first. Bridie?' he questioned.

Bridie watched them, her face pale and streaked with tears and dirt. Her damp clothes sticking to her.

'No, let me make the tea and then I'll help,' she strode over near him, 'thank you,' she said and stood so close their bodies touched. 'I'm sorry about what I said, I didn't mean it.'

Drunk.

He stared at her hard. He wasn't offended, shocked was all. Shocked she might be right. Shocked that he'd been so stupid and more appalled that she might be alone out on this farm managing everything while practically running the town. He turned his head to Sybella who was humming as she took close-up photographs of the berries before placing individual strawberries into the container.

It wasn't a discussion for now.

9

Caleb stood, stretched out his back and rubbed his aching muscles. It was early, too early and he wasn't a morning person. But the day dawning around him with its muted palette of colour was spectacular, except it was freezing. The sun hadn't yet reached the tips of the trees, nor did it provide any warmth. Caleb blew on his fingers to warm them up. Manual labour was not his strength, he cooked the food, didn't pick it.

Jacqueline worked beside him, along with a small but worthy crew prepared for the back-breaking work. He'd rung the mayor knowing she'd have both the people power and the persuasion to gather an assembled group to help.

'You've done a good thing here,' she said and rubbed her own arms to get the blood flowing.

'How did everyone not know that Bridie manages this place alone?'

For once, Jacqueline was speechless and her response slow. 'She's so capable, no one suspected.' He'd confided in her on the basis she didn't blab. Wasn't gossip rife in small towns? He hadn't known Bridie long, but it was easy to work out she didn't want her dirty laundry aired, otherwise people would know of her plight. So, on the basis her dad was laid up, and because of the freak storm yesterday, help was needed to pick the decimated strawberries. And like he knew she would, Jacqueline had shone, and the arrangements were made before the moon was out in the night sky.

'Are we throwing these?' Jacqueline asked and pointed to the buckets of bruised berries.

'No. Give them to me, I have an idea.' The mayor studied him but simply nodded.

Caleb glanced once more towards the house. He hadn't advised Bridie they were coming, hadn't spoken to her after yesterday. Given she hadn't run through the field and demanded to know what was going on, and refusing their help, he guessed she wasn't in a good place today. He hoped she was fast asleep.

* * *

At home hours later, he sat in the kitchen with Sybella, his laptop in front of them. 'You know 'bout the web, right?'

'Yeah, duh,' she replied.

'Right. Okay, search French strawberry treats or something like that.' Sybella stuck out her tongue in her signature move and typed with one finger.

'Wow,' she said, 'yum, yum. There's heaps of options.' He scuttled closer beside her.

'Remember the festival?' Sybella nodded and he continued. 'Okay, what we're gonna do is make strawberry desserts with berries from Bridie's farm and sell them at the festival. She gets the proceeds and the credit. Like those pink macarons, everyone will love them, right?'

Sybella nodded enthusiastically but said with a straight face, 'I think we need to practise and make these right now,' and she pointed to the screen. Caleb shot his look between the computer and her and after a few agonising seconds, smiled and agreed.

'And make extra for tuckshop,' she said as they were half-way through making the strawberry mousse, 'because this is tasty and it's made from fruit, so it's healthy.'

Caleb put his finger in the bowl and licked it. 'Absolutely, this is damn good.'

Sybella hugged him around the waist, her eyes wide and round. 'Bridie is going to love them!'

* * *

CALEB TUCKED HIS CHIN INTO HIS CHEST AND WALKED DOWN HIGH STREET. How did the locals manage these weather conditions? It wasn't just cold, Sydney was cold in winter, this was arctic. Wasn't Queensland the sunshine state? The lake he passed wasn't solid yet but displaying a thin sheet of ice and any visible blade of grass was unyielding with frost.

End of July now and he'd been in town three weeks.

Tucking his head almost out of sight was useful, though. He could hide from people (and thereby ignore them) particularly with his cap on his head, and his bare neck wasn't exposed to the weather. Perhaps he needed to invest in a scarf? But buying winter clothes would acknowledge he was hanging around. Was he?

John the greengrocer was setting up his footpath stalls as Caleb passed. Large and healthy oranges and carrots the centre of his display. 'Well done, mate, can't thank you enough. I've got a littl'un at the school and he's coming home everyday raving about tuckshop. You've sure made a difference. First, challenge healthy food for these kids, and then next conquer their addiction to computer games. You can't help with that, can you?' he joked but didn't wait for an answer.

Outside the next shop, *Pretty Petals Flowers & Gifts*, the owner, a woman he hadn't met before, rushed out from behind the counter wearing a bright purple apron and holding a bunch of yellow flowers. He had no idea what they were, but the scent was distinct jasmine, like he'd use in cooking. The fragrance conjured up memories and he batted them away, desperate to stay in the here and now. 'Oh, Caleb. I saw the article. Well done to you, thanks so much for helping our community. We can't thank you enough. And the festival, too. We need more newcomers like you,' she said before galloping like a gazelle back inside the shop, taking the delicious smell with her.

Shortly along the road he came to the *Koffee Shoppe*. These country people were showing him such gratitude, he'd forgive the cliché and kitsch name and see if they delivered on their promise of 'the best coffee in town.' He pushed open the door and a bell trilled. The place was buzzing, that was a great sign. But it was also tourist season with city-slickers in town for the roasting fires and winery tours. In the queue, women with prams smiled in his direction, and the kids running around high-fived him. A couple of old-timers sitting at the table in the front window came over and slapped him on the back. No words, just a nod of the head.

It had to be the article. Was Bridie right? Had the locals accepted him? His gut twisted. He didn't want to help in the tuckshop or be on the festival committee; he'd been bullied into both positions and never talked his way out of them. The persuasiveness of the town and its people had done him over. He'd only ever acquiesced with the view to getting out of both as quickly as possible. But he hadn't acted on it, that spoke volumes, right? And if he pulled out now, who would feed the kids and make sure the festival wasn't a flop?

Plus, Sybella had been so proud of him. That smart little beggar had known how to earn the hearts of the community. At the top of the queue, the barista smiled extra brightly, and he placed his order with his chest thrust out and shoulders back, standing tall. He ignored that it was a bean he wasn't familiar with. It might be local produce and the best he'd ever had.

His phone buzzed in his pocket, and he extracted it. His business partner, Marco, again. Feeling better than he had in weeks, he reckoned he could manage a chat.

Marco was momentarily speechless. Said he'd been ready to leave another lengthy voicemail message that would be ignored. Caleb winced. If he owed anyone something it was Marco, who'd believed in him and his restaurant vision and had invested his hard-earned money. His friend deserved better.

'What? How do you know where I am?' Caleb spluttered. At Marco's next words, the colour drained from his face like a visceral sensation. 'No, no…' he muttered. Forgetting his coffee, he rushed outside and scanned the street for a newsagent. Spotting it across the road, he bolted, holding up his hand and apologising to the cars he jay-walked in front of. Inside the tiny shop he held the phone to one ear and searched the pile of papers, disregarding the local rag and reaching for the national bulletin. It was at the back, a thick pile sitting by itself. Perhaps no one read *The Australian* in Bellethorpe? Marco nattered in his ear, but Caleb focused on the front page. A photo of his beloved Lavapond with its door bolted shut. It looked desolate and empty. He could handle that of course, but below in the corner, was a photo of him taken years back, looking young and fresh wearing his stripy kitchen gear and chef hat. Rifling through his pockets he searched for change and handed over a bunch of coins to the young girl at the counter. Outside the barista handed him his take-away coffee. She'd chased him across the street to deliver his coffee? Befuddled, he managed a thanks and strode back towards the park. He plonked himself on the closest park bench and placed the paper beside him, took his first sip of coffee. Yep, as he suspected, it was rubbish.

'Mate, it's not as simple as hiding away. I confess it's been convenient but I'm here for Sybella. She needs me, I'm her guardian now and my top priority.' He sipped the drink again as Marco replied and grimaced as the burnt flavour slipped down his throat.

'It's not quite that straightforward. I don't know whether I can uproot her and return to Sydney. You think I need to reopen? Seriously? No one will turn up…' They argued back and forth, and he kept drinking, at least the flavour kept his mind off the unpleasant conversation. 'Listen, okay, I promise not to ignore you anymore, but I need some time to mull things over.'

One thing he couldn't share with his oldest friend, didn't know how to express, was his feelings about being back in a kitchen. Despite the freezing conditions, sweat droplets formed on his brow, his arms became moist and the coffee roiled in his stomach. It was one thing to cook at home…

Caleb picked up the paper. It was savage and in stark contrast to the words written about him by Bridie. If she'd been kind, this male journalist was out for his jugular.

Fled with his tail between his legs from embarrassment and not heard from again

Resurfaces in dingy old Qld town, hiding perhaps?

What was once our most successful chef is now our most hated

How can anyone ever trust his cooking again?

And that wasn't the worst of it…. Caleb screwed the paper up into a ball before hurtling it and his paper cup across the green space.

* * *

BRIDIE SAW CALEB AND WANTED TO SCREAM, STOMP HER FEET, PUMMEL HER fists against his chest; wanted to release her frustration and anger. At him, at her father, at people who drank too much, hell, people who drank at all.

But she didn't do any of those things.

She watched him in the kitchen. He stood in front of the free-standing cooktop and oven, muttering to himself before he seemed to lose his balance, lean to the left, connect with the wall with a heavy thud and right himself. Caleb took one step forward, paused and then stepped back, only to repeat the movement. Eventually he turned the knob and ignited the gas on one of the plates. He leaned down close and listened to it crackle awake. Bridie swore she saw his bare arms erupt in tiny, charged bumps. Still chatting to himself, he reached across to the bench where various tiny dishes were lined up. He threw into the pan what appeared to be onion and then a dash of olive oil.

There was no mistaking it, Caleb Stirling was drunk. And if there was any doubt, which there wasn't, the sweet sickly smell permeating the room was a dead giveaway. It was like a bottle of wine had been spilled over the lino floor and left to mutate. Not to mention the three or so bottles lined up in a row near the recycling bin. Not in it, mind you.

At least he liked to mix it up.

As he reached for another dish, he caught a glimpse of her, and he turned.

'Shit, Bridie, you can't scare people like that!' His words were steady; some people really could hold their alcohol.

'I'm sorry. I came to check if you're all right. I saw the paper.'

'Your plan didn't work, did it? The locals of this town might believe your glowing character reference of me, but the city folk aren't fooled so easily. They know the truth.'

'There's nothing about truth in that article. That's to mare your reputation and pick on you. They should be ashamed of themselves.'

Caleb broke out laughing, but it didn't have the resonance of a good old belly chuckle, it was hollow, and had an evil cadence to it. Bridie cringed.

'Yes, those naughty little journalists calling me names and ruining my career,' his arms gesticulated wildly, and his voice rose higher as his agitation increased. 'You know what, Bridie Finch, they didn't ruin my career, I did. One of the top chefs in Sydney and I served up bad prawns, rookie mistake. And I just happened to serve them to celebrities who now want my guts for garters. Everything they said is true.'

In response to his rising voice, she spoke softer, quieter. 'You're allowed to make a mistake. You're only human.'

'Making a mistake is letting your kid's birthday cake flop or the roast chicken burn on a Sunday afternoon. Not when you lose your entire business and all that you've worked for. That's not a mistake, that's a fucking disaster.' His body softened but too much because he had to grip the chair in front of him to stay up right. The pan sizzled behind him, and he turned his head slightly as if to acknowledge it but didn't move.

Bridie went over to the cooker and turned off the gas.

Roughly, he shoved her hand away. 'I don't need help in my kitchen. I don't need your help at all. No one does. You said it. You were right. I am a drunk, just like your father. I don't deserve your help, hell, I don't want your help and he picked up the ceramic dishes and smashed them one by one onto the ground.

Hearing the ruckus, Sybella entered the room, silent tears rolling down her face. Bridie drew the little girl into her side and held tight. Caleb collapsed to the ground amongst the shards of sharp glass and china.

Her instinct to help was overwhelming. She placed Sybella gently into a chair and moved towards him, placed her hand on his shoulder. He shrugged it off as if her touch repulsed him. 'Leave me alone!' he screamed, and Bridie jumped back in fright.

The curly hair that she adored, flopped across his forehead but he shot her a cold look, gone in an instant and replaced by regret. The edges of his eyes softened, the creases deepening and his lips down-turned. He didn't mean it.

With every fibre of her being she wanted to stay, to comfort and reassure him. Make him chicken soup and clean up the mess and tuck him into bed and say everything will be all right. But a heaviness weighed down upon her, turning her body to lead. It was defeat and she felt it deep within her heart.

Caleb was an adult and intoxicated and responsible for the care of a little frightened girl.

Bridie whispered to Sybella and suggested she get her night things and they'd have a sleepover and when they came back in the morning, Uncle Caleb would be feeling much better.

But would he?

Caleb saw Sybella at the school gate and his feet broke into a run without his brain telling them to. The cold air cut through him like ice, and he struggled to breathe. He'd run over hot coals if he had to; nothing else mattered but her.

She wore a pressed school pinafore with two pigtails, her pink unicorn bag on her back. Seeing him, she bolted too, and they met halfway. He folded her into his body, and she snuggled in willingly.

When she unravelled herself, tears pooled in her eyes. 'You won't leave me too, will you? Like mummy?'

He knelt down to her level and held her in place with his large hands on her arms. 'I'm not going anywhere, you hear?'

She grinned and swiped roughly at her tears. He encircled his large hand around her small one and they walked towards her classroom, swinging their arms as they went. Bridie stood by the gate. As they ambled closer, she turned and marched away. Caleb's hand was mid-air in a wave, but she didn't see.

Relief swam through him and he gripped Sybella's hand tighter. His bloody temples throbbed though, so hard it thrummed in his chest. He was right worn out. He'd had many a bender before, long nights in the kitchen and drinking too much to deal with the pressure. He rarely drank outside of work, but that wasn't saying much, he was always working. Most times, a good sleep and he'd be up and at 'em doing it again the next day. But working wasn't emotional. The kitchen was his domain, he was king.

Last night was different. When he'd realised Sybella was gone, his heart had torn open, and he'd sobered, fast. Yes, his life had gone to shit but the kid had lost her mother, she was all he had. Caleb didn't know why he was so slow on the uptake. Stupid.

Forgiven, the orange orb sun in the sky brightened, his footsteps became lighter and his own problems were put in perspective. Everything had hinged on her. If she'd rejected him as a useless surrogate parent, he didn't know what he would have done. His new world, the one he was forming, would have crumbled.

At her classroom she asked him if he had stuck to their planned menu for lunch today.

'For sure,' he replied. In the early hours of the morning that was his only focus and he was now prepped and ready to serve up another tuckshop special. Sybella offered a thumbs up which was a lot more than he deserved. Caleb embraced her again and watched her place her bag on the rack and extract her drink bottle before greeting her classmates. He stood longer than necessary and soon she shooed him away, embarrassed.

Familiar with the narrow corridors of the school after almost a month in town, Caleb headed towards *Bite Right Inn*. He could even say the name now without flinching. Except unlike other mornings there was a flurry of activity as he approached. Extra bodies filled the kitchen and bowls, and utensils and food covered the benches.

'Ah, you must be Caleb.' A giant of a woman approached him, and his first unkind thought was of the Trunchbull from the Roald Dahl tale of Matilda he'd read as a child. Might have been the last book he'd read. But she didn't have either a mole on her cheek nor her hair pulled back into a bun. But she was rather severe looking and serious, one hand to her hip.

'I'm back. Thank you for filling in for me at such short notice, but I've got it from here.'

The words echoed in his head.

Over the woman's shoulder, Kathleen shot him a sympathetic look, but what did it mean? Was Kathleen sorry he was being ousted or feeling sorry for herself back under the reign of Mrs Bingham?

The convenor moved her hand to the bench blocking his entry to the kitchen. He wanted to continue helping but he wouldn't fight her for it.

'Right then. I'm glad you're feeling better, Polly.' Her left eye twitched at the mention of her first name. 'I'll be off then.'

Shit. All those pieces that had fitted back together so perfectly after seeing Sybella felt loose and shifting in his chest now. The throb in his temple worsened.

* * *

Her father wasn't in the armchair when Bridie returned home. How ironic; she'd already imagined making him endless cups of tea, pumpkin scones and even taking off his boots and socks. One sole ray of sun streamed through a gap in the curtains and landed on the chair, colouring the old fabric in the most gorgeous orange glow.

For a brief moment, she imagined sinking into the soft cushions of the chair and letting the golden rays caress her skin. Ha! The stuff of fantasies. It took her less than thirty seconds to dismiss the idea as preposterous. What a self-indulgent thing to do in the middle of the morning. Instead, she put the kettle on and craned her neck around the window frame to catch a glimpse of her father. There weren't any berries to pick so what was he up to? The house was as quiet as a church and after a few moments, she heard the tinkle and crash of tools in the shed. Bridie reached for another cup and tea bag. Despite the stream of sun into the front room, the kitchen was cold. She'd make him a warm tea because the shed was usually freezing, too.

Bridie listened to the kettle bubble and slid her gaze around the kitchen searching for crumbs, dirty dishes, anything, to still her twitchy fingers. Is what Caleb said true? Did people not need her help? He might not want her help, but everyone else did, didn't they? Her father would be starving and wearing filthy clothes without her. Hell, he'd have choked on his own vomit by now. The primary school would be in a right pickle if she didn't take their weekly French classes. There was no budget for languages, nor culture; she provided that for free. And then the committees – the business chamber would not have a secretary, the creche wouldn't have a supply fill-in, the agricultural society wouldn't have any crafts for the charity foundations they supported, and God forbid, the French festival would not be a thing. And in times of illness, she weaned this town back to health with her chicken soups and hot drinks.

The kettle sang, its whistle piercing the air. Huh, she was most definitely needed in Bellethorpe, in fact, she wasn't sure how they'd survive without her.

Damn, Caleb. Bridie filled the cups and let them steep, gazed out the window. Why then did she feel so discombobulated this morning when she didn't have an urgent task to attend to? For sure, she could find one, but as if to prove to herself, she didn't. Her life was full, it was. But she was an essential service. Yes, that was right. Essential. What did Caleb think Sybella would have done last night without her?

She rescued the tea, shrugged her coat back on and headed outside. Her father was head-bent in the tractor. Today was a good day and she was grateful for that. He smiled enough for his cheeks to crease with lines and accepted the cup. 'Almost got her,' he said. Her smile faded, that old clunker hadn't worked for years. Was he losing his memory too?

On the short walk back to the house she reminded herself that today was a workday for her. Yes, she accepted that the French manuscript usually came second trump to urgent community tasks, but not today. Rinsing her used cup in the sink she noticed a chipped nail on her left pinkie finger. 'Damnit, when did that happen?' she cursed. But it didn't matter, did it? She had plenty of time and she resiled to redo both her fingers and toes before tackling the manuscript.

Her phone beeped and she flicked the screen with one finger to see the beginning of a message. Huh! She should shove that phone in Caleb's face and prove that she was indispensable. Rudy from the next farm had a fence down and needed her to keep an eye out for his missing sheep. Well, at least she didn't have any berries for them to munch on and ruin.

Bridie stayed focused on her task until her nails shone with pale pink polish. The colour buoyed her mood immediately. Clean, neat nails could do a lot for your disposition, she agreed.

Taking care not to smudge her handiwork, she sat at her desk ready for a full day of translating. Getting lost in the French conjunctions was exactly what she needed. Her mind was already returning to the last point in the story when her attention was drawn to a sticky note stuck to her computer lid. A reminder – *flyers* she had written in bright pink swirly writing. Oh yes, of course. She reached over to the four trays piled high at the edge of her desk and extracted the first sheaf of paper. It was a draft brochure advertising the French festival. Bridie collected a pen and poised to write suggestions for improvement. The nib was touching the paper, but she stopped. The brochure was beautiful – all the reds and whites and blues, a kaleidoscope of fireworks, and images of delicious French food. Well, that made her think of Caleb, damnit. Did it matter if the centre was slightly off or the words a tad too small? She was pretty darn sure if she put it to the committee, they'd adore it and approve it without a second thought. Why was she always so finicky? It was hard to admit but she did desire things being perfect, but they were her perfect. It appeared she had high standards. Perhaps good enough was okay. She replaced the lid on the pen and put the flyer to the side. Plus, it meant she could devote herself to the manuscript and be swept back into the beautiful Alps of the south-east coast of France.

But before she'd turned the first page, another message arrived, from Sue this time, needing a donation of cakes for a celebration this weekend. Bridie'd whip those up later but then she noticed social media notifications and flicked open the app. The farm had a feed and she used to manage it meticulously and post every day. Now it didn't seem worth it. No point driving tourists if you didn't have the produce to sell.

It opened at the last page she'd searched. Caleb. There were new posts to his feed. Food dishes of a lasagne and some sort of stew and strawberries. Oh, her farm. Against her wishes, her chest flooded with warmth at the sight of bunches of bright red berries. In the corner, only the slightest edge of a bruise was obvious. The shots were after the storm. She slumped back into the chair. There were comments and she couldn't avoid checking. Poor Caleb, he was trying to do the right thing and get his life back to some semblance of normal with the images, but the comments varied. Vicious trolls couldn't help themselves, but others were kinder. She touched the heart and clicked open the feed. *'Thanks so much for visiting Finch Berry Farm, come again soon'* and she used the strawberry emoji, three times. She flicked onto one of her favourite images of Caleb and gazed at it, a flood of emotions spiralling through her, none of which made sense. She remembered the feel of his arms around her, the care at which he held her, gentle yet firm, she had felt safe and cared for. What would his lips feel like against hers? Would they be soft, how would taste? He was right though; she cared for everyone else, but no one cared for her. Her father hardly remembered her existence. No, she was being ridiculous. The entire town cared for each other, and she was one of them.

The phone rang, shocking her back into the present. 'Oh, hi Maggie. Oh, poor thing. Of course, I can, I'll come straight away. Tell Rose not to worry I'll look after Nash until she finishes work. Of course. See you soon.'

With nails dry now, Bridie tidied the pages of the book into a neat pile. She'd tackle that tonight after dinner, maybe pull an all-nighter to finish. Then she could send it away and be ready her next assignment. She retrieved her medical kit with every conceivable item a sick child might require and rushed out the door.

* * *

CALEB HADN'T NOTICED THE TEMPERATURE IN THE KITCHEN DIP, BUT WHEN he answered the door, snow flurries fell from the sky and melted upon hitting the earth. Shoving his hands under his armpits for warmth, he registered the couple in front of him.

He'd been deep in soapy suds scrubbing a pan when a knock landed to the front door. He'd startled, certain he'd heard wrong. No one in this town knocked, they only barged in with no regard for his privacy. But there was another rap. Quickly, he checked the oven; the tarts and pies he'd spent the entire morning baking, were not yet ready. Baking was safe; baking wasn't cooking. Well, that's what he kept telling himself anyway. And given it wasn't cooking, he was sober, too. Did he crave a drink? Hell, yes, but he'd resisted. Another triumph, he'd proven to himself again it was possible.

'Mum. Dad?' It couldn't be.

'Something smells delicious,' his father said.

Perhaps he was drunk. There was no way his parents could be standing at his door in Bellethorpe, Queensland, Australia. Caleb hadn't seen them since he was fourteen years old, since the day they left.

It had been a day of reckoning. His parents announced they were moving to the Philippines to be missionaries; to save the world one person at a time. They'd always been God-fearing folk and attendance at church on Sundays had been compulsory during his childhood. Caleb hadn't minded, the supper afterwards was great. As a kid, he was easy to please. Until he wasn't. Until there were better things to do with his Sunday and as he grew, he no longer shared the philosophies of his strict and over-bearing parents. The division had been forming for some time before their declaration. Before they'd chosen to care for people that weren't their family. Before they'd abandoned their children and fled the country.

Abagail was only eighteen, slices of her leftover birthday cake still in the fridge. Maybe they thought having one child obtain adulthood was enough? He wasn't sure. What he did know though, is that they hadn't bothered with him over the years, and he had returned the favour.

Not like his sister though; she dedicated her young adult life to him; him who'd repaid her by not only by going off the rails, but out of control until he couldn't stand the hurt he caused any longer and he took off at sixteen and travelled the world. No high school leaving certificate, unskilled with a mouth to match. In those days it was a matter of doing whatever work he found.

But he would never regret those stacks of dishes out the back of shabby take-aways and restaurants because those places had formed his passion, his passion for food. And once he found it, he never looked back, only forwards. He'd climbed that hierarchy however he could.

There was no regretting his journey; it had made him strong, disciplined and once mature, he realised the pain he'd caused his sister. Upon his return to Australia, only those few short years ago after working in the best restaurants of London, he'd reconnected with her and seen her as often as possible. Now she was dead; but Sybella was here and she needed him.

Did his parents even know he was a chef? His father mentioned the smell…but yes, of course, his sister had kept in contact, as daughters did, he guessed, perhaps out of loyalty.

'Mum, Dad?' he repeated needing recognition it was actually them.

'May we come in?' his mother spoke.

'What are you doing here?'

'We've come for Sybella, of course.'

11

T he earth titled beneath his feet. 'What the...' but he stopped. Not that it mattered, he could swear in front of his parents, couldn't he? He was an adult and an adult who swore. It was that niggling old thing called respect. He'd honour that niggle, but he wasn't convinced they deserved any respect.

'I'm Sybella's legal guardian. Those were Abagail's wishes.'

A ripple of laughter trickled out of his mother. His father's mouth spread into a thin-lipped smile but he didn't join in the chuckle. It was condescending and patronising and anger swirled in his gut. Without waiting for the invitation that wasn't coming, they moved past him and into the house and, placed their simple, small two suitcases in the living area.

'Where is she?'

In an exaggerated move, he checked his wrist, but he wasn't wearing a watch. 'She's at school.'

'Of course,' his father nodded.

'Let's have a cup of tea, then,' his mother said and walked into the kitchen.

Caleb remained silent as his father seated himself at the table and his mother put the kettle on to boil and wiped down his kitchen benches covered in flour. He watched them in a daze, as if the scene was playing out in front of him but he wasn't part of it. He sure wished he wasn't, this was a nightmare.

'Have you even met Sybella?' he asked. They both shook their heads. 'When was the last time you saw Abagail?'

'Oh, let's see. Before Sybella was born, I think about ten years ago.'

Ten years?

'And why are you here now after all this time?' Nothing made sense. These people who called themselves parents hadn't seen their children for years and now surfaced without warning and wanted to turn their lives upside down? His anger simmered below the surface, ready to explode, like mini darts from the pores of his skin, but he wouldn't give them the satisfaction of seeing him lose control. He ground his teeth together and curled his fingers in and out.

His mother delivered three cups of tea and sat at the table like they were having a civilised afternoon catch up. Somehow, he didn't think the tea would cut it. It was her who spoke first.

'Sybella is a child born of sin, a bastard, born without the support and love of married parents and not aware of God's love. She needs to learn the scriptures and lessons of the Bible to be welcome into God's arms and not repeat the sins of her mother.'

Caleb took a sip of tea that scolded his throat on the way down. It was exactly the jolt he needed to prevent the vitriol spewing from his mouth. He willed himself to stay calm, but it was bloody hard.

His mother wasn't finished. 'We're much more established now. Our accommodation is clean and comfortable. We have running water and our own bathroom. Unlike years ago, we were not equipped to keep a family in the Philippines. It was too remote but now we're in a proper town with a school and church, shops and other families.'

Ah, there it was. So, they did hold a semblance of guilt. It pleased him. No doubt, God forgave them for the sin of abandoning their children. He chanced a look at his father who sipped his tea unperturbed by his wife's harsh words.

'You've been baking,' he gestured to the oven. 'Abagail said you were a cook.'

That made him sound like someone out the back of the local chippie, or *gulp,* in the school tuckshop.

'Any chance we can have a slice with our cuppa?'

'No. They're for a festival in town next week.'

His father nodded, disappointed, searching the kitchen for another source of snack.

'Abagail was your daughter and a grown woman and a wonderful person and mother. At the age of eighteen you left her to raise a teenager when it was not her responsibility and she did a great job.' His mother went to interrupt, but he held up his palm. 'She did a fantastic job; it was me who stuffed up and made her life difficult. She moved to this town and made a life for herself and her daughter and was an important member of this community. She died of breast cancer, and you didn't return for her funeral or send flowers or make an appearance for your granddaughter then. It was the people of this town that supported her during her illness and cared for her daughter until I arrived. They are now supporting me. You've done nothing.'

His mother shifted in her seat, shuffled her feet. Caleb imagined the defences forming: it was God's will they had to help other people; they were chosen; the plight of others could not be ignored. He'd heard them all before and he wouldn't listen again today. Thankfully his father said nothing but looked to his mother for guidance. 'We have a right to know our granddaughter,' she said.

'Yes. But not to right any wrongs you say her mother committed or to convince an innocent child she entered the world in sin. That's, that's despicable.' He paused. 'Your job is to love her as grandparents dote upon a grandchild, nothing more, nothing less. If you can't do that, you need to leave.'

His skin rippled with tension and with the oven set to hot, the room was oppressive and starved of oxygen.

'We are entitled to see the child.'

'Yes, Father, you are.'

'We'll let her decide.'

'Decide what?' he asked his mother.

'Whom she'd like to live with.'

'She's five!' he exclaimed, and his father jumped.

The oven timer went off. Beep. Beep. Beep, breaking the tension. Caleb rose, removed the three dishes from the oven and placed them onto the bench. The aroma of baked strawberry blanketed the kitchen, a sugary vanilla heaven. He heard his father inhale heavily.

With his back still to them and holding the benchtop for support, he said, 'I'll collect Sybella from school and bring her home. I'll tell her you're here and that you wish to meet her. I'll relocate to the pub temporarily and you can stay here and spend time together, get to know her.' He turned to face them. 'Do not brainwash her with your God-fearing ways. If you do, you'll no longer be welcome.'

* * *

'CALEB, WHY ARE YOU STAYING AT *THE BELLE*?'

Jacqueline entered the community hall for the last festival committee meeting. Twenty or so people gathered, much less than his previous presence had garnered. Had his charm worn off? Bridie ignored him, but at Jacqueline's words, she paused with her cup under the urn, mid-stream. Her head tilted towards them waiting for the answer.

Caleb set out the pink macarons on the white plate. It had dramatic effect and he liked it.

'Did you make these?' Jacqueline swiped one, ruining his artistic display of the French biscuits.

He swatted at her hand, and she laughed but still took a bite. 'Oh my, these are divine. Where's Yvette?' The mayor spun on her feet and locating Yvette sang out that she simply had to try them.

'They are for everyone, hold your horses. It's a taste test. If everyone approves,' he emphasised the word, 'I'll make them next week.'

'Okay, good distraction. But what's up?' she persisted.

Caleb shrugged. But that was for show, it didn't sum up the situation at all. 'My parents are in town.' He let that hang.

'Your parents?' Jacqueline sounded as incredulous as he felt.

'Uh, huh.' Bridie had poured her tea and stood next to them, listening.

'What do they want?'

Caleb told her.

'No,' Jacqueline tugged Bridie in closer almost sloshing her hot tea. 'They can't.'

Caleb wasn't sure what they knew of Abagail's history but gauging by the reaction, his sister must have shared.

He fingered the plate of macarons. 'They are staying at the house and getting to know Sybella. Hopefully, after a short period of time they'll return to their work in the Philippines. I can't image they'll want to be absent for long.'

Jacqueline grasped his upper arm and stared at him straight, their faces only inches apart. 'Caleb, we're here for you. Anything you need, please sing out. We don't want to lose you or Sybella, you're part of our community now.'

Caleb couldn't bear the intensity of her gaze, or her words and he turned away. He couldn't look at Bridie either.

Maggie called the meeting to order, and they sat in a tight circle tonight. Jacqueline insisted they start with the macarons which were devoured in silence. Bridie chewed hers slowly.

'Would you like me to make them for the festival? I think we should have a special macaron stall.'

There was a unanimous vote in favour. 'Can you make a variety of colours?' they asked.

'Yeah, I can,' he replied but he wouldn't let on at this stage he was only making one flavour - strawberry. He'd make up an excuse on the day for the lack of chocolate and coffee biscuits.

'I have drafted what I'd like to be the menu,' he held up a piece of paper. 'Shall we go through that now?'

Caleb addressed the gathered group, but his gaze landed on Bridie. As she watched him, he saw a contemplative flicker in the shadow of her eyes. They hadn't spoken in days. Was she feeling the absence as keenly as he was? He missed her, and dare he say, her help. What he'd always considered interference, he now realised was significant, but subtle events that made each and every day brighter. But, mostly, he'd missed her company. While she hadn't spoken to him tonight, he'd felt her scrutiny. Each time he looked up, she'd be peering in his direction, and quickly glance away with a flush of heat colouring her cheeks. Did she miss him too? He hadn't realised what a large part of his life she had become. Or perhaps when something is readily available you take it for granted?

He'd make amends tonight after the meeting.

Gosh, he was either surrounded by simple folk in this town or these people were the nicest he'd ever met. Each item he read out was greeted with oohs and aahs and compliments. It was one sure way to feed his ego—that badly needed feeding. Finally, Bridie spoke. 'I think that is the best menu suggestion the festival has ever had.' She smiled, warm and genuine and his entire body fizzled in the glow.

'The decision of the committee is unanimous. It sounds wonderful, Caleb, and we cannot thank you enough for contributing this year. You may become our annual French chef.'

The words were kind but cut through him. Would he be here next year? If his parents took Sybella he'd have to head back to the city and that thought made him sick. It had only been a few short weeks, but it didn't feel like his life was there anymore; and certainly, with his career in tatters there was nothing left for him.

'I know we are the festival committee,' said a fellow seated at the back. Caleb judged him immediately as a farmer with his faded and torn jeans, check shirt and hard-wearing boots covered in dust. But he didn't like to stereotype people. 'But,' the man continued, 'can we please pass a motion that Caleb be reinstated to the school canteen. The kids loved his food, they ate it, it was healthy and delicious, and no offence intended, but so much better than anything the wonderful Polly makes, even though I acknowledge she's been single-handedly holding the reigns for years with little assistance. My little Sam is now refusing to eat tuckshop since Caleb stopped cooking.'

There was a cluster of clapping from the group and Bridie wore a grin that spanned her entire beautiful face. Caleb held up his hands for silence and was glad when it took a few minutes for quiet to descend. The swelling in his chest prevented him from speaking immediately. He was chuffed but that wasn't where he belonged. 'I am very happy to set a menu and take people through its preparation. But the tuck-shop is not for me long-term.' The problem was, he didn't actually know what was, nonetheless he continued. 'I can advise Polly if she's open to it, if not, someone else with a passion for healthy food should take over. But I'm happy to be like a consultant, I guess.'

'I'll talk to Polly and raise the issue at the next P&C meeting,' Jacqueline agreed. 'Any other issues for resolution regarding the festival?' she asked. 'It's next Saturday!' she reminded everyone.

Bridie ran through the last of the arrangements – stages, entertainment, animals, rides. Caleb sat back and listened, glad not to be involved. Thankfully under Bridie's guidance, everything was well under control.

The door creaked open, and all heads turned in that direction. Caleb watched his mother enter. His heart accelerated and nerves gripped his middle like a vice. 'Heather?' he refused to address her as 'Mum'.

'Hello, everybody. I'm sorry to interrupt. Sybella is going to sleep and wants Caleb to say goodnight.'

He slumped back, relieved. Is this what parenting was? A gambit of emotions that sped through your body so fast you couldn't catch them. At the sight of his mother, he'd feared the worst. Now his insides turned to mush. Instinctively, he tilted his head and turned towards Bridie. Her smile was uncertain and small, but it was there, and it was for him. Sybella had to come first, and he'd go to her now, but he thought he and Bridie might just be all right.

'What are you doing, love?'

The chill of the early morning dawn held her in its embrace, and she shivered, right down to her core. Bridie tugged the pink beanie down to cover her ears and moved her hands in the fingerless gloves trying to retain some warmth. The sun didn't yet cover the fields in its golden glow and the frost hadn't yet melted on the blades of grass.

'Picking, Dad.' His grin infectious as she smiled back.

'It's Sunday, you should be in the shop. This is my job.'

Pausing a moment too long, he knelt down to her bent position at the height of the strawberry plants and placed his rough and thick-fingered hand on hers, stilling its movements.

'I'm so sorry for being useless. It's hard during July, I almost can't bear it. I lose myself because the pain is too great, the sadness overwhelms me and the only thing that helps is the drink. Forgive me, let me get through this time of year and I'll be right again.'

Bridie's throat constricted. She wished it was only the month. She seethed with mounting rage that her father had dropped the bundle and she'd been left to pick up the pieces, yet again. Bridie was adept at keeping her feelings locked tightly inside of her. How could she hurtle angry words at him, anyway? Who was she to understand grief and how it affected people? Her father felt the loss of their mother and brother from the tragic car accident years ago more keenly in July, the month of their death. Bridie's pain surfaced on a daily basis, but she didn't have the luxury of letting people down. And she didn't want her father to feel bad about his behaviour when anguish gripped him so heavily. Nonetheless words of forgiveness didn't slip off her tongue, nor reassurances.

'It's only early, let's work together for a while and then I'll head to the shop. You'll be due a cuppa by then, too.'

He removed his hand and the moment of tenderness between them disappeared. Her father skipped over a row and commenced picking. They worked in companionable silence until Bridie spoke. 'Dad,' she was nervous, new ideas had never been his thing. 'I saw on the internet that some strawberry farms are running 'pick-your-own' weekends and school holidays. They open up their patch for an entrance fee and people pick their own berries and take them home. You know, it's like a set fee per punnet. I was thinking we could do something like that. Everyone loves pretending they're farmers for a day and then,' she paused, 'given we don't have any help, that would help reduce some of the workload of picking.'

Her father had his head down and kept picking. It was quite methodical work once you got in the zone. You had to pay attention, though, because those delicious looking berries were deceptive, they required a tug before releasing from the bush.

'Now that's a novel idea. Would never have thought of it myself. If it works, we might be able to get the back field operational.'

The sun was an orange ball risen high in the sky now. Bridie wished it let out some love in the way of warmth, but she still shivered. She wasn't cold, though, not anymore, her father continued to pick and today he was open to her new idea. Mulling over her disbelief, she heard a car rumble down the drive. Could this day get any better? 'Better get back up to the shed,' she said and stood, stretching out her back. 'Come up for a cuppa when you're ready.'

'Don't worry about packaging these, love, I'll do that. You must have a story to finish, you attend to that during the quiet spells in the shop.'

Bridie almost danced across the field towards the house and shop. Let's hope their visitors bought out all their home-made jams and strawberry ice-creams.

* * *

'PLEASE UNCLE CALEB, CAN I HAVE THE DAY OFF SCHOOL AND HELP YOU?' Those tiny almond eyes bored into him, pleading. He'd told his folks they needed to clear out for the day. Tomorrow was the festival and he had stacks to do and needed the kitchen.

His mother was quick. 'We'll take Sybella and go for a day trip, visit fellow parishioners in nearby towns.' Caleb caught Sybella roll her eyes.

They'd survived the week, so far. His parents were manically trying to convince their granddaughter what a life they could provide in an exotic foreign land, away from her friends, her school, the community and any close proximity to the memory of her mother. They needed to up their campaign, but Caleb wasn't going to help them. What had caused him such angst, now didn't matter. That kid was stubborn, perhaps she'd inherited that streak from him, because she wasn't having a bar of it. It made him enormously proud, but also relieved. Any battle he thought might have occurred over trying to convince her to stay, was unlikely now, unless his parents refused to accept her emphatic no.

Caleb prevaricated. Sybella had been a fabulous trooper, enduring many days with her grandparents. What would be one more? And he was going to be flat out. But he couldn't do it to the nipper, and he agreed to let her help. She squealed and jumped up and down on the spot while his parents looked forlorn.

He'd been baking for hours and had already produced 200 strawberry macarons. His father gazed at them longingly decorating the bench. Caleb pulled out his tart bases and let them warm to room temperature. He'd prepared the crepe ingredients and hoped the stall he'd arranged would be prepped and ready to go tomorrow without any hassle. The committee assured him there was plenty of willing helpers, too many in fact. Hopefully that meant Bridie wasn't doing everything.

The front door clicked shut and his shoulders relaxed. Sybella was beside him in an instant and he lowered himself to give her a big hug. Just the two of them again; it felt right. 'Okay, my assistant, you need to wash your hands and put on an apron. Then we're going to bake the strawberry cakes.' He fussed at the bench moving unnecessary ingredients and other items out of the way.

'How many?' she asked.

'I think we need at least ten.'

'Wow, that's a lot of cake.'

'Sure is,' his mind swirled with tasks. 'While they cool, we'll prep the ingredients for the baguettes, but they'll be prepared fresh in the morning. I have bakers delivering the French sticks before the sun will even be thinking about rising.'

'The food is going to be so good! Everyone is going to love you Uncle Caleb,' and she beamed up at him with one of those smiles that melted his insides and left him a gloopy mess.

'And you too, kiddo, my helper extraordinaire.'

They worked tirelessly. 'What are you doing with all those photos?' he asked her as she'd whipped out his phone once more capturing cooling cake slabs and tart bases while he sliced chicken and whipped cream.

She shrugged and he forgot about it.

'I'm tired Uncle Caleb,' she said mid-afternoon and collapsed into the kitchen chair.

'I need to sort out some serving platters and plates. Let's pop these into the fridge to set and we'll find Bridie. She'll know where I can source some.' Sybella nodded, head supported by her hand. 'Tell you what, can you please taste test this one?' and he slid a fresh, small, strawberry tart across the table. Her eyes popped open as wide as saucers; her energy immediately invigorated.

Sybella rubbed her tummy as they left the house, still singing the praises of the tart. 'That was the best thing I've ever eaten.'

Caleb laughed. 'That's the finest praise I've ever received,' he said, wiping the crumbs away from the corners of her mouth, the only evidence of the treat she'd devoured.

The festival was in the local showground, only metres from their home. 'Sybella, is it always this cold here in winter? This town is freezing!' Caleb said as they walked. Whenever he'd left the house recently, it felt like the South Pole. The little girl giggled, 'Yeah, I guess. We get snow sometimes and we can ski and skate!' The temperature must be below freezing so he believed the snow bit, but enough to ski? That he would have to see for himself.

To make matters worse, the sun slid behind a cloud and the world grew dim. He shuffled faster as a thunderclap rumbled the sky and forced the clouds overhead to rush past. A slight breeze picked up and the familiar fresh scent of rain permeated the air.

'Oh, no, not rain,' Sybella moaned but they'd reached the grounds. It was a hive of activity, people bustling to and fro, carrying tents and chairs and tables. Various marquees were set up forming a white tent wonderland. They wandered past signs indicating ticket sales, drinks, a bar and walked through tables and chairs scattered across an expanse of lawn. He spotted Bridie; she was hard to miss; a burst of pink in amongst the bleakness of the day. Her hair was pulled back into a ponytail with random curly strands framing her face, the bubble jacket was patterned with strawberries. She was a living, walking berry.

An unexpected wind gust swept the red check tablecloths into the air, and Bridie scrambled to chase after them. Rushing over, Caleb managed to save a couple. 'Do you have something to secure these with?' he asked. Bridie paused at the sound of his voice and turned, smiling but her body was ramrod straight. Caleb detected the strain around her eyes and mouth.

She stared at him for a moment too long. Was she happy to see him? 'Oh, thank you Caleb, Sybella, yes I do. Hang tight. I have a bunch of lantern lights for each table.' She disappeared for a second and then produced a box. Working together they placed the lights on each table.

'These look beautiful,' he said.

She gave him that contemplative look again as if she considered everything he said. 'The white marquees mixed in with the red and blue will look incredible,' he continued.

'Thank you,' she replied, her voice tentative. 'Would you like me to show you around so you're familiar for tomorrow?'

Before he could respond, someone yelled a question at Bridie, and she became distracted answering. When she'd finished, he said, 'Yeah, that would be great, thanks. I'm wondering if you have serving platters for the sweet food?'

'Oh, yes, of course. I've hired everything. You'll have more than you need. C'mon, Sybella,' and she grasped the girl's hand and they traipsed across the grass. He fought against his need to walk with them, to clasp her other hand, hold it close, warm up her fingers, be near her.

They arrived at the kitchen specially made for a chef and industrial in its fit out and size. 'It's all yours,' Bridie said.

Caleb scanned the space, feeling a little bit like he was floating. His heart beat faster than it should, and his palms became clammy. All of a sudden, he was back in the kitchen at Lavapond. There was the noise of guests eating, drinking and talking, the clash of cutlery, the yelling of abuse and he felt the heat from the cooktop; it was all too real.

How can anyone ever trust his cooking again?

He flinched.

'So, what do you think?'

He heard the words, but they didn't register.

'Caleb?'

Sybella kicked him in the shin.

'Oh, ah, it looks as if it has everything I need. And clean, too.' Bridie stared, wanting more, but his lips were stuck together. Letting it go, she went to one of the open cupboards and extracted a handful of serving platters. 'This is where they're stored; take as many as you need. Probably best to bring the food over and we serve from here tomorrow?'

'How many people are expected for dinner again?' he asked as if she hadn't spoken.

Bridie paused, hand to chin in contemplation. 'Uh, let me see. I think we've booked for around one hundred.'

One hundred? The sting of bile rose in his throat. He swallowed and tasted the bitterness and sharp tang.

A man opened the flap of the tent and dashed inside. 'Oh, thank goodness I found you, Bridie. We're having a disagreement over whether the jukebox should be placed to the left or right of the stage. Can you please come and sort it out?' Bridie nodded and turned back to face them, pausing.

'You go, you're busy. We'll see you tomorrow,' he managed.

Bridie's lips parted as if she wanted to say something, but then she closed her mouth and left.

When she was almost out of sight, Sybella screeched, 'Bridie, the tarts are the best, you'll love them!'

'I'm sure I will,' she said and waved with a weak smile.

13

The crack of the lid on the soda bottle and the eruption of the fizz had him salivating. Back at *The Belle* that night, Caleb's hand shook as he held the glass and poured. The clear liquids mixed, and the ice popped. A squeeze of lemon and he took one sip, and the strong hit calmed him immediately. Then he downed the rest in one gulp.

The self-recrimination started immediately: *he'd just have the one drink to calm his nerves; to get on with preparation; to ensure he was in the right frame of mind.* Blah. Blah. Blah. It was bullshit and he was man enough to admit it. He poured the next shot before his brain caught up. It was gone in seconds too. It was like a drug - intense, immediate relief until he returned to a state of normal. Caleb needed to recalibrate his normal. But, damnit, he'd do that tomorrow.

In his dingy hotel room, rain drops splattered the tin roof and only served to remind him of where he was, and why. Anger made the blood run faster through his veins. He was in town because his sister died, but the uncanny timing could not be denied. It was funny how his major life stuff-up thwarted the death of his sister. Bellethorpe was unequivocally linked to his career failure as he'd tripped over his own feet rushing into town to hide and recover.

And now, his parents had complicated matters. He wasn't at home with Sybella, instead, he was at the pub, again. Alone, with his demons.

Another drink and his mind turned in a different direction: the berating started. *What a baby! Just get on and do what you need to do.* The chance of poisoning more people with his cooking was practically near impossible. He guessed it was the 'practically' part that had him frazzled. He was a bloody good chef. One mistake did not negate the years of hard work and success.

How can anyone ever trust his cooking again?

So, yeah, he'd have these few drinks to calm his frenetic mind, and tomorrow he would make the best bloody French feast this town had ever seen.

* * *

BRIDIE LAY IN BED LISTENING TO THE RAIN PUMMEL THE EARTH, IMAGINED the rain puddles deepening, the mud collecting and everything damp to the touch. Today of all days, on their annual Bastille Day Festival, the sky had to open up. If only she could control the weather too.

The drops on the roof eased and she rolled out of bed having hardly slept. She searched her dimly lit room for her wellies, at least they were pink. She'd need them today, even if the weather cleared, the ground would be soggy for hours. A craving for a warm cuppa was irrepressible and would clear her foggy mind. Cradling the mug, she headed outside. The sky was a grey blanket crowded with heavy, dirty clouds. She spied a triangle of light behind the hiding sun and hope sparked. It might clear. The best part of the day was towards the afternoon anyway when people relaxed with drinks and music. She breathed in and out, it would be okay.

Stall holders were setting up as she arrived at the showgrounds. Bridie released a sigh of relief at the sight of the marquees still standing and nothing damaged or blown away.

She was hanging the tablecloths out to dry when she heard her name and saw Sybella racing across the field. 'Bridie! I can't find Caleb. Can you help me?'

'Of course, let's check the pub.'

Sybella knocked on the door with her little knuckles barely raising a sound. Bridie pounded, waited, turned the knob. It was open. 'Caleb, knock, knock,' she made her voice light, but she was frightened of what they'd find. Sybella had no such inhibitions and raced into the room and onto the bed where a figure lay.

'Uncle Caleb,' she hollered and thumped his arms and back. 'Wake up! How could you sleep in today?'

Bridie stood back but heard a groan as the body rolled over. Sybella whacked his chest. 'Uncle Caleb,' she drew out the words and her voice cracked as if the five-year-old realised this might not be a funny joke.

'No. No. No,' she whispered but couldn't bear to look at him. Her chest felt like someone stomped on it and she grappled to breathe and bent over trying to quell her rising fear.

She'd known. Who was she kidding? She wanted to believe, did suspend belief for a while, but more importantly, trusted him to do his job. That was why she outsourced. Bridie Finch wasn't a chef, thank God, otherwise she'd be responsible for the food as well as everything else. Deep down, she'd known she couldn't rely upon him. He was a quick smile and kind word but at crunch time he couldn't deliver. It didn't matter how many times she defended him; Caleb Stirling was a drunk. Maybe she needed to ply him with more alcohol, and he'd perform today, enough to get him through anyways.

Now she really was going crazy. Bridie stood up tall, her breathing coming easier. She pushed the disappointment away, but it was replaced by overwhelming, crushing defeat. Fatigue washed over her; from lack of sleep, from weeks of preparations, from keeping every-thing going, for being responsible. Her shoulders sagged with the heavy weight. Bridie wanted to curl up in that bed and hide from the world too.

But that's not what she did, was it?

At the lack of response from Caleb, Sybella cried. 'Bridie, he's not dead, is he?' That snapped her quick-smart out of her stupor. The poor kid.

'Sweetie,' she touched Sybella on the shoulders, 'he isn't dead, I promise,' and she guided the girl back to the edge of the bed. Meanwhile her gaze scanned the room for the culprits; they lay in a jumble off to the side. Gin was his choice this time and there were two empty bottles. That was why there was no smell. She'd learned a lot over the years from her over-indulging father.

Bridie zoned in to do what she did best, care for others, ensure they were okay and get on with things, by herself if she had to.

'Caleb,' she yelled and shook his shoulders. He roused, his face creased from a deep sleep and his hair tousled. She refused to listen to her erratic heartbeat, that was adrenalin, right? His bare arms lay outside the bed linen to reveal the top of his chest where a sprig of hair sat at the nape of his neck. A groan escaped as his eyes flicked open, she presumed the pathetic daylight creeping into the room made his temples throb. Good.

'Sybella, honey, can you run downstairs to Luke the barman and ask for a bottle of water and some aspirin, please?' She nodded and backstepped off the bed, her eyes peeled to Caleb.

After she'd left the room, Bridie leaned over, pulled the sheets up to cover his bare chest and unleashed her anger. 'How could you be so irresponsible? The festival is today, today Caleb!' Her intonation rose at each word.

His head lifted, and he rose onto his elbows with effort. Dazed, he glanced around the room, taking in the dingy setting and peered out the window. 'Shit, Bridie, I can't do it. I can't cook for all those people. What if I do it again?' and he fell back against the bed and covered his eyes with a pillow.

'You're a fool,' she said and ripped the pillow off his head. 'What do you think you've been doing? What do you call the food you've prepared for the tuckshop, for others, that you've fed Sybella every night? Is that not cooking?' she mocked him.

'That's different,' he pouted.

'No, it's not. You haven't killed anyone that I'm aware of. For God's sake, get over yourself,' and Caleb reached for the pillow again, but it was out of reach, and he pulled the sheet over his head instead. 'For once, Caleb Stirling, this isn't about you. This isn't about your career, or your fancy restaurant or how good a chef you are. This about community. A tight-knit group of kind people that celebrate together once a year. Do you think they care how you made the cakes? Or what you serve for dinner? They aren't five-star clientele but good-hard working folk. And you know what, they deserve better.'

Caleb remained silent.

'Argh!' Bridie collected the bottles and threw them in the trash with a loud clunk that emitted a further unpleasant sound from Caleb. Bridie stood with her hands on her head, feeling in that instant as if she might explode. Rage rolled through her once more. What on earth was she going to do?

Sybella returned and Bridie shoved those drugs into Caleb's palm rougher than necessary, but he didn't move. This was no time for nonsense. She lifted an unwilling Caleb to a sitting position. 'Drink this,' she said and forced the water to his lips. He took a tiny sip. 'No, all of it.' Her handbag left at the festival had her emergency kit, that'd sort him out, not that he deserved it. Today, she was pleased she couldn't offer him all the tonics in the world. If he was going to be so stupid, let him pay the price.

Once the bottle was empty, she lowered him down to the bed and tucked him in. Sybella watched on.

'Hey there,' she said and slid her hand across Sybella's silky hair. 'Uncle Caleb needs to sleep for a while, so we'll leave him be. Is all the food that you prepared at your house?'

The girl nodded. 'I helped yesterday; I know where it is. He told me about the French sandwiches too, so I know how to prepare them.'

Bridie flashed a tight, tentative smile. 'Ah, that's great. We'll be a team. First thing we'll transport the food and make the baguettes. Remember the long, narrow French bread is called a baguette,' her voice returned to its normal timbre.

At the house, Caleb's parents asked a million questions. Bridie was livid for sure, but she wouldn't make matters worse with his parents. She avoided the answer they most wanted – where was Caleb? Side-stepping beautifully, she placed a stack of boxes into Ian's arms. He spluttered and reverted to Heather for guidance, but she was similarly armed. 'Can you please help by carrying these across to the show-grounds? I can take it from there,' and she offered her warmest smile.

It took a few trips but everything they needed was where it should be. Bridie didn't want to admit but the sweets looked amazing. There was an assortment of tarts, cakes and macarons. Oh shit, she realised she'd forgotten to bring the punnets of strawberries. Man, she hoped her father was awake this morning. He'd promised to attend the fair, so she might be in luck.

Sybella placed the treats onto plates for display. Bridie did a double take. Every sweet was strawberry. 'Sybella,' she asked sidling up to the girl, 'are there any other cakes?'

The girl shook her head and her lips dropped. 'Don't you like these ones?'

'No, sweetie, I love them. I notice they're all strawberry...' her voice dropped, uncertain what that meant.

Sybella beamed. 'Yes,' she cried, 'yes, Uncle Caleb saved your bruised berries and made all of these, for you and your farm,' and she looked left and right searching for something. 'Oh, he wanted a sign too, but I can't see it.' She turned back to Bridie. 'You know a sign advertising *Finch Berry Farm*, so everyone knows where the berries come from.'

Hundreds of thoughts slammed into each other in her head, but none made coherent sense. For once, she was speechless.

Joel, running the drink stall, approached and sought help. 'Sybella, keep going and I'll be back in a tick.'

In record time Bridie put out spot fires: missing tables, location of equipment, introductions, checking playlists and pricing of produce. Racing back to Sybella, she noticed the clouds had cleared, the sun was dull, but present in a pale blue sky and it hadn't rained in hours. It wasn't freezing, either. There were millions of other tasks, but instead, she pulled up a chair once she reached Sybella and they made baguettes.

A miracle occurred over the next hour. Everyone left her alone, there were no questions to answer or decisions to make. People coped. On their own. One part of her experienced a pang of sadness, she liked being needed. She knew what the locals called her – the do-gooder, bleeding heart or good Samaritan. But she genuinely enjoyed helping people. It gave her purpose. But somewhere along the way, she'd become the only responsible person in town. Want something done? Give it to Bridie.

The other part of her was relieved that she'd enjoyed a break. What a treat! Bridie looked around the field. There were people rushing but they were happy and smiling and helping, having a great time. Reality check – if she wasn't here, the day would proceed with success. It was a team effort. *Ouch.*

Even though the celebrations were in full swing, she wasn't inclined to move. Sybella gave her a cold lemonade and she pecked at the leftovers from their sandwich prep. Man, that duck was good! Caleb the man who said he couldn't, could sure as hell make a great French roll.

'Oh, love, there you are. Where should I put these?' her father approached with boxes of their punnets.

'Dad, thank you,' and she wrapped him in an embrace. She'd forgotten to ring him, and he'd remembered. 'That's okay, love. I saw a spare gazebo over yonder, should I go and set up and see if we can flog a few?'

She laughed and it released the tension that had been bunching in her belly, hell, for years. Usually, she'd insist he relax and enjoy himself and she'd take over and simultaneously run three stalls at once. Something hard and sharp shifted within her. She could not do everything and why did she think she ever could? 'That would be fabulous. Thank you,' and she tossed him a money bag and off he trotted.

Sitting on a picnic blanket and listening to the band play, she helped herself to a flute of icy cold French champagne. Bridie sipped the cool liquid; it felt momentous because she never drank. Would this lead to trouble? No because the rain had cleared and left them with a sparkling, bright clear winter's day. It was idyllic.

'Bridie, can you please come and help me?' Sybella held her hands in front and swung them side to side appearing unable to contain her excitement.

'Sure,' she said, and the little girl swept her along.

14

———————

'Y'ou're a drunk! And not a fit carer of a five-year-old,' his father said.

'We read about what you did in the newspaper. Abagail said you were a fine cook, but a good chef doesn't make his customers sick,' his mother said. 'And look at you,' she spat, 'you're dishevelled like a common hobo. You stink of alcohol and look like you haven't slept in days...' she closed her eyes and prayed but he zoned out from the words.

Caleb held a pan in his hand and gripped it so tight his knuckles turned white. 'I don't care what you think of me. You aren't taking her!' He slammed that pan down onto the steel make-shift bench where it didn't make nearly as much clatter as he'd hoped. It hurt his head, though.

'Now, if you'll excuse me, I have dinner to prepare,' and he turned his back on them.

'Son, if we leave now, we won't be back and that child will never be accepted by God,' his father said to his back. Caleb did not reply.

Light penetrated the tent as Sybella entered with Bridie. He glanced up to catch her expression. Astonishment. Caleb raked his hand through his hair. He didn't doubt his mother's sentiments, he must look like shit. But after the water had soaked up the alcohol and the drugs had kicked in, he'd got moving. There wasn't time for making himself respectable. He had a festival to save.

Seeing Bridie made him remember the gut-wrenching disappointment he'd caused. The look on her face when she'd seen him this morning would be forever etched in his mind; his guts churned as he recalled her reaction. That was all it took.

Bridie leaned down close to Sybella and whispered in her ear before the girl raced away. 'What can I get you?' she asked as she stood close to him.

'Are you making me a drink?'

Bridie spluttered, 'No! I'm offering my help or water or Panadol or anything else you might need.'

He cracked a grin. 'Well, I was thinking that one wee dram might warm me up enough to get through dinner.'

She twirled on the spot real fast, her face a mural of emotion. Her eyes searched his, darting left and right. 'I'm kidding!' he surrendered.

'Oh boy, I actually thought you were serious,' and she blew out a breath. It was sweet like the champagne she still carried.

'Do you feel all right?' she asked, hesitating, like she was scared of the answer.

'No. I'm smashed, but my head is now only a dull ache, so for that I'm grateful.'

'Can you do it?' she asked quieter again.

'It was you, Bridie Finch who told me I can. Are you having doubts?'

'Me, no.' She shook her head too forcefully. 'I think you're a brilliant cook.'

The words dried up in his mouth and he couldn't speak. He cleared his throat. 'I hope you have good public liability insurance,' he said deadpan.

'That's not funny.'

He turned to her then, stared into those crystal-clear eyes he loved. The eyes that always looked at him with such concern and care. They were clouded now, filled with uncertainty. He'd caused that. 'Bridie, I'm scared. Scared I'm going to get it wrong. Scared people will get ill.

That they'll hate it. No,' he paused, 'they won't hate it. If I get it right, it'll be the best French dinner this festival has ever had.'

She reached out and placed her hands on his hips. His breath hitched. 'Can you please harness that confidence and believe in yourself. The beef is fresh, direct from a farm that I sourced myself. The chicken the same. This isn't seafood. This is good quality Australian farm-grown produce. You cannot go wrong.' Her breath brushed his cheek, and his knees went a little weak. 'I'm sorry for what I said earlier, I believe in you.'

'Please don't apologise. I stuffed-up. But I'm going to make it up to you with this dinner. Okay?'

'Don't do it for me, Caleb prove it to yourself.'

Their bodies touched. Her chest heaved and his mouth went drier, if that was possible. Her stare contained longing and he matched her desire.

'I'm back!' Sybella came to stand between them.

His heart jolted. 'Hey, jitterbug.'

'Thank you, sweetie. Okay, Caleb. Take these.' Bridie punched out two strong painkillers and handed them over with more bottles of water. Then she mixed a Berocca and forced him to drink while the bubbles still fizzed.

'Now I'll be needing the toilet,' he groaned and Sybella laughed. 'Can always rely on you to laugh, hey,' he brushed his fingers over her cheek, and she asked him to lift her onto the bench.

'Uncle Caleb, do you think mummy would have liked the festival?'

The world around him stopped. 'She would have loved this festival, right? She wouldn't have had to do any cooking and there's music and dancing and games and rides. She would have taken you on the rides and…'

'Do you want to go on the rides with me?' Bridie interrupted.

Sybella declined. 'I want to stay here and help. I want to be a good cook.'

'Okay, Sybella, sweetie, I'd love your help. We have a lot of work to do, though, are you sure? You could be out having fun.'

'Yes, I want to help.'

'Okay, you help but Bridie has to go.'

'What? No, I'll help too.'

'No, I insist, you must go and reward yourself with the spoils of your hard work.' Together big and little hands gently pushed her out of the tent.

'Okay, kiddo, let's do this.'

* * *

CALEB STOOD IN THE SHADOWS WATCHING THE CROWD. IT WAS A SCENE OF pure joy: laughter, happy screams, people milling on picnic blankets and couples strolling hand in hand. In the dinner marquee guests finished off the last course. French cheeses were always something to linger over.

He was no festival connoisseur, but he gauged the event a huge success.

His head no longer throbbed, but his arms and legs ached, and his eyes were like saw-dust. In usual circumstances he'd pour another long-deserved drink after a frantic night in the kitchen. He realised with dawning clarity, that his behaviour had to change. Alcohol was to be enjoyed and fine wine an indulgence, not a coping mechanism to get through, get on and ultimately get out. He was a chef for goodness sake, he understood appreciating quality. Alcohol needed to be treated the same way.

And tonight, he'd cooked for one hundred people without a drop of alcohol in his system, well, none that wasn't left-over anyways. Triumphant! The first step in the right direction.

'Caleb, thank you, that was incredible,' Yvette patted him on the arm. 'The best meal I've had in a long time and certainly the best French festival.'

'That was awesome, man,' another bloke slapped him on the back as he exited the tent.

'Caleb,' Jacqueline paused for effect, touched him on the arm, 'that was amazing. You're an incredible chef, those flavours, the presentation, it was all sublime. In case you're unsure, you have a place in this town, you've earned it. I hope you'll stay.' That made his heart twist in his chest.

A procession of people left the marquee and each congratulated him. Could he accept that he might be back? That he'd overcome his disaster, his fear?

There was a heavier slap to his back and a hand gripping his.

'Good to see you.'

'Marco, you're here.'

'Had to come and check out where you've been hiding.' Caleb went to interrupt but Marco stopped him. 'No, it's okay. I understand. This place has potential, especially with this weird French thing it's got going on. There're a few vacant spots in town. Want to try something different?'

'Are you serious? You're happy to take another risk on me?'

'Of course. You're one of Australia's best chefs. We have some stuff to sort out with Lavapond before we can start a new venture, but yes, I say we do it. You will draw the crowds no matter where the restaurant is.'

'Mate, I won't let you down.'

'You never have,' and he walked away, 'oh and well done with your Insta feed and those pics, people love them, keep it up!'

What? He snatched out his phone and caught a glimpse of an endless feed of food pics, but Bridie approached.

'You did it.' She glowed in the moon-lit sky.

'You don't ever drink. You had some champagne today?'

'No, I don't usually drink. My father deals with life by drowning himself to the point he can't wake up the next day, and sometimes worse. I've detested drinking ever since, seen it as a sign of weakness, blamed it for making people behave badly, but it wasn't the drink, it was them. My father struggles and will probably always struggle, with or without alcohol. He has good and bad days. Like everyone else, I've indulged him and picked up the slack too often.'

'I'm so sorry about this morning. I'm not like your dad, I only ever used to drink in the kitchen, and it was a habit, not an addiction. Busy service, pressure, everyone did it. I realise it's a mistake and I promise to stop doing that.'

'For me?' her voice quavered.

'Yes, for you. I don't want to do anything that makes you uncomfortable.'

'Thank you,' she bowed her head before gazing into the distance. 'But I have to thank you too. You've made me realise that I'm not the one running this town, I am not the sole person responsible for the tuckshop, minding sick children, making cakes and running a farm and trying to translate books. I've always been alone and it's nice to be needed but it's become a bit out of hand.'

'A bit?' he joked. 'You won't have time to help others anyway because I need you. Sybella needs you.' He moved closer so his breath fanned her face, placed one hand to her cheek and let the other wind through her hair that flowed around her shoulders. Her eyelashes fluttered and she inched closer, their bodies warm. His head was pounding for a different reason as he massaged her cheek with his thumb and shivers of delight bolted through his body. He swept her hair to the side and planted a kiss to the soft skin of her neck. She leaned her head back in response and he trailed a row of kisses from her collar bone to her jaw. Their lips met and lust engulfed him, desire rocking through him. Caleb wanted more and he pressed harder and tasted all of her, smothering her with his kisses. She quivered under his touch, and he moved back to let them both catch their breath, but Bridie found his lips once more, her arms surrounding his back until his body burned.

A crack blasted above their heads and the sky erupted in a kaleidoscope of colour. Bursts of fireworks in spirals of red, white and blue filled the sky, trails of smoke billowing after each explosion. Caleb lowered his gaze and saw the lights reflected and dancing in Bridie's expression.

'Fireworks!' Came a shriek and little hands clasped around their joined legs. Caleb lifted Sybella up to join in their embrace and the three of them cuddled, enjoying the best French festival Bellethorpe had ever seen.

THE END

MEGGIE & MAX

SUSAN MACKIE

He's the new Vet with something to hide.
She's got a wedding to organise.

Meggie
& Max

Susan Mackie

For Marion (Mum)

*and all the wonderful folk who keep
small town communities
alive and thriving.*

Susan Mackie

1

———————

'We're here Sis. Barrington Homestead.'

Meggie opened her eyes, stretched, then grinned at her brother before turning to look through the windscreen. The car was still, although she could hear the engine running. Angus had stopped at the start of a long driveway, lined with poplar trees. The setting sun created a golden glow through the tall trees, and with a glimpse of the homestead in the distance she subconsciously ran her fingers through her thick, dark hair.

'Are you ready for this?' Angus winked before putting the car in gear. 'You'll love Rose, don't worry. It's wee Charlie that might test you.' His eyes crinkled at the corners. Meggie hadn't seen Angus for four years, but she loved how happy and settled he was, with his fiancée, Rose and their small son.

The paddocks on either side of the driveway were green and lush. They'd had good rain over the summer. The homestead was now fully in view. She'd seen pictures of course, but the dignified lines of the old home took her breath away. She saw Rose run lightly down the steps, waving as they pulled in. They'd spoken many times in the last few years and Meggie hoped the easy warmth they'd shared on the phone and in video catch-ups translated into real life. She could use a friend. A sister.

Rose was at the car door before they'd fully stopped, yanking it open as Meggie unfastened her seatbelt. Stepping out, Meggie was eye to eye with Rose for the briefest moment, before she was pulled into a tight embrace, Rose's cheek against her own. Meggie drew her breath in, then hugged her soon-to-be-sister-in-law back with the same degree of fierce, generous warmth. They took half a step back, still holding each other, then Rose pulled her in for another quick, tight, squeeze saying quietly, 'Oh Meggie, we're so happy you've come home. Welcome to Barrington.'

Meggie laughed, as Angus stepped between them, an arm around each of their shoulders. 'Now don't think for a moment that you girls can gang up on me. I've got little Charlie and Woof on my team, so that's three against two.'

Cattle dog Woof, hearing his name, promptly joined them, sitting at Rose's feet, his tail wagging madly against their legs. Meggie knelt down, patting the dog while she composed herself. They'd said she was welcome. Had been telling her so for months. And to stay as long as she liked. But she hadn't been sure if she'd *feel* welcome, she'd been overseas for years. But this was a good start. It was as if Rose knew exactly what she needed, in that moment. And Angus. Well Angus had always looked out for her. They'd been close growing up and she knew he'd welcome her. But he was getting married, and she wouldn't blame him if having her here would be complicated.

'Take Meggie in, show her the house. I'll bring the bags.' Angus opened the back of the red Jeep, hauling out two large suitcases. Meggie hadn't told them she wasn't returning to California. She was keeping that to herself a bit longer.

'Let me help you Gus. They're heavy. I almost exceeded the weight limit with those. But I do have some wine for you from the Napa Valley, so be gentle.' Meggie stepped toward him, but paused as Rose snorted, then laughed loudly.

'Gus? Really? Gus? Is that your nickname? Why do I not know this?' Still laughing, Rose was now bent over, holding her stomach. 'Wait until I tell the local lads this one. Oh, that's priceless.'

Meggie giggled too. It was her private name for Angus. Only their grandfather and Meggie had ever used it. One or two had tried at High School and been sorry afterwards, Angus hadn't taken their teasing lightly.

'Rose, where's Charlie? It's too late for nap time.' Angus changed the subject, then chuckled as Rose paled before racing up the stairs into the homestead without a word. Turning to Meggie, he said, 'Honestly, we can't leave him unsupervised for a moment. And well, if he's quiet, that's all the more worrying.' Meggie chuckled inwardly at the delight and pride on her big brother's face. Whatever little Charlie was up to would probably be fine by him. Meggie followed him up the stairs to the veranda, as Rose returned, flushed, holding two and a half-year-old Charlie on her hip. He had crumbs around his mouth, and something firmly gripped in his pudgy right hand.

'He was in the laundry.' Rose shook her head at Charlie who leaned back in her arms, his eyes focussed on the dog. 'Woof. Good Woof.'

'And is that dry dog food in his little hand there?' Angus shook his head in mock disgust, turning to Meggie. 'He likes sharing his food with Woof ....'

'Is that okay?' Meggie hesitated for a moment. 'That he's eating dog food?' She looked from Rose to Angus.

'Um. He's eaten worse. We have stories.' Rose shook her head, then beckoned Meggie. 'Come in, we'll show you the house. And you have the whole bed and breakfast section to yourself.' Rose lowered her voice. 'Charlie hasn't worked out how to get that door open yet, so you'll be safe.'

Meggie grinned, following them into the house. She stopped for a moment in the grand hallway. It's polished floors gleamed, a lovely warm contrast to the cream timber walls and white pressed metal ceiling. 'Welcome to Barrington Homestead.' Angus and Rose spoke together, little Charlie was now wriggling to get down. Meggie turned around, taking it all in. Yes, she did feel welcome.

Meggie looked at her brother and Rose. 'Thank you.' She said it quietly, but hoped it conveyed how grateful she was to be here, to be welcomed without question.

2

___

Max glanced at his watch. Almost an hour early. Good, he can stretch his legs and have a look at the town before his interview. Not an interview exactly, a meeting. He'd already committed to the Locum position at Barrington Vet Clinic for the full three months.

He'd been here before. Two winters ago a late cold snap had dropped several inches of snow in the Barrington Tops overnight. They'd followed a steady stream of vehicles from Newcastle to Barrington. So many happy families. They'd built a snowman, had a snowball fight and roasted marshmallows over a fire in a large drum while the children ran around, jumping in snowdrifts and making friends with strangers. It had been a really happy day.

Turning, he looked at Tommy, who was gazing around with interest at the locals coming and going.

'Ready mate?' Max pointed to a café on the other side of the road. 'We've got time for a milkshake if you're thirsty.'

Tommy didn't hesitate, undoing his seatbelt as he spoke. 'Okay. And maybe some cake?'

Max laughed, reached over and ruffled his son's hair. 'Is there ever a moment when you're not hungry?'

Pausing, Tommy seemed to consider his words. He grinned at his father. 'Nup. Always hungry. Unless its green stuff. Not so hungry for green stuff. Ever.'

Max laughed out loud, and Tommy joined in. It felt good. Natural. They couldn't grieve forever. Laughing was therapeutic. He'd read that somewhere. Noting the way Tommy's face lit up, Max knew they needed to laugh more. And to let Tommy know it's okay to be happy.

They walked across the road, busy for a small town on Friday afternoon. Max resisted the urge to hold Tommy's hand. His son had mentioned recently that eight-year-olds don't need their hands held.

Tommy bounced straight up to the counter, peering at the arrangement of cakes and slices. Standing behind him, Max smiled at the woman cleaning the coffee machine.

'Afternoon. Is it too late to get a milkshake and a coffee? We can choose something from the drinks cabinet if you're already cleaning up for the day.' He wanted to start off on the right note in this town. Although he'd almost kill for a coffee right now.

'No problem at all. What would you like?'

Her smile was warm, and he nodded, pleased. Something loosened a little in his chest. He turned to Tommy. 'Come and order son. Tell the lady what you'd like.'

Tommy grinned at his father before turning to the woman. 'A chocolate milkshake. And a piece of apple pie please.' Max was about to speak when Tommy continued. 'And Dad will have a large double shot Americano. With a lid please.'

'I like a customer who knows what he wants. I'll get that started straight away. Why don't you take a seat and I'll bring it out in a moment. Would you like cream or ice cream with your apple pie?' The woman was warm and friendly. And obviously used to children.

'Both please. And two spoons.' Tommy looked earnestly at the lady. 'I'm trying to fatten Dad up a bit.'

Max snort-laughed and nudged Tommy with his elbow. Seeing Tommy relaxed and making jokes almost choked him up.

'Two spoons it is then.' She was chuckling too and somehow it felt like this little town had just made them welcome.

They sat at a table on the pavement. Max could see the sign for the

Vet clinic further down the street. So the café would be his local for the next three months. Good. Tommy was reading shop signs, asking questions and generally being more communicative than he had in months. Max relaxed.

'Well I see you've picked out the best table for people watching. Here's your milkshake.' She leaned toward Tommy as she placed it on the table. 'There's an extra shot of chocolate in it, you let me know if it's okay, won't you.' Tommy said yes quickly, half-standing to reach the straw with his mouth, taking such a big sip his cheeks were sucked in.

Smiling broadly, she placed the coffee in front of Max, and set the large slice of pie between them, with two spoons and forks. 'I'm Debbie by the way.'

Tommy swallowed. 'I'm Tommy. Best. Milkshake. Ever.' He picked up a spoon, then remembered his manners. 'Thank you Debbie. This is my dad, Max.'

Max held out his hand, taking Debbie's slender one in his. 'Nice to meet you Debbie. It seems your milkshake has the Tommy Masters tick of approval.' He watched as Tommy nodded his head enthusiastically, a bite of apple pie already in his mouth.

'Well that's good news. Let me know if the pie gets the Tommy Masters tick too. Our baker, Cathy, will want to know.'

Tommy was nodding and chewing but pushed the plate closer to Max. Picking up a spoon, Max took a large bite, closing his eyes for a moment as the pastry melted in his mouth and the fresh apple and cinnamon taste hit the back of his tongue. His eyes widened. He realised, as he did, that he hadn't been tasting food for months. Oh, he'd been eating. But not enjoying. Not tasting. The pie was good, really good. He looked up at Debbie. 'Best. Pie. Ever.' She laughed and returned to the kitchen. Max watched her. She thought he was being polite but damn it, he meant it.

3

____

Meggie stretched and rolled onto her back. She'd slept well. Angus had insisted she have dinner with them and stay up, only letting her go to bed when they did, to overcome jetlag. He was right, she'd slept right through the night and felt rested. She picked up her phone. Almost seven, she was sure Angus would be up. He'd said last night he'd feed the horses and check the cattle before he went to the clinic.

Dressed in shorts and a tank top with her long dark hair in a high ponytail, already feeling the warmth of the Australian summer, Meggie walked from her quarters to the door of the main house. She didn't want to wake Rose and Charlie, so she opened the door softly. Stepping into the hallway she could smell something cooking. Toast? Walking quietly along to the kitchen she paused. Rose was speaking to someone.

'And you're going to eat your eggs with the spoon. Not your fingers. The spoon. See, like this.' Meggie stepped into the room. Rose had a tea towel over her shoulder and a splatter of something, vegemite perhaps, on her tee shirt. Her face was flushed and ponytail lop-sided. Charlie was perched in his high-chair, a Sippy cup in front of him and what looked like scrambled eggs and pieces of sausage. He had vegemite all over his cheek and the child-size fork firmly clutched in his chubby hand.

'Morning Rose, Charlie.' Meggie kissed her nephew on the top of his head, then patted his ginger hair, before walking across to Rose.

'Morning Meggie. Did you sleep okay?' Rose picked up the electric jug. 'Tea? I usually get a coffee from Deb's when I go into town.'

'Best sleep I've had in ages. I'll pour myself a glass of water, thanks Rose. Coffee in town sounds perfect.' Meggie glanced out the window. 'It's going to be warm, I've got to get used to the heat again.' She watched as Rose wiped Charlie's hands and face with a damp cloth, then lifted him out of the high-chair. He ran to a large mat in the living area covered with wooden blocks and farm animals and promptly sat down, absorbed in a game of his own making.

Rose pulled up a stool to the kitchen bench, patting the one next to her for Meggie. 'We are so pleased to have you home. Thank you for making the trip.' Rose took a sip of her tea. 'Your Mum will be here in a few weeks for the wedding, I'm sure she can't wait to see you.'

'I'm happy to be home Rose. I think I've been away long enough.' Meggie glanced outside, she could see Angus striding toward the house, Woof trotting beside him. Looking back at Rose she added softly, 'I'm not sure I want to go back, Rose. I think my time there is over.'

If Rose was surprised, she didn't show it. 'Help me get this wedding organised and done, and then think about what you want to do next.' She stood as Angus walked in. He kissed Rose full on the mouth, then grinned at his sister, giving her a wink.

'Megs. Sleep okay?' He picked Charlie up, settling him on his hip. 'What have you been up to Charlie?'

'Great sleep, thanks Gus.' She sat back as Angus bustled around the kitchen, his son still in his arms while he fixed himself a bowl of cereal. Setting Charlie back on the floor, Angus leant over his bowl, spoon in hand. Charlie wandered back to his blocks.

Loving the way Rose and Angus responded to each other, chatting about their horses and cattle, their plans for the day, was relaxing for Meggie. Her tourism job had been hyper busy, dealing with events, demanding clients, temperamental chefs, overwrought brides and more recently a disintegrating relationship with her boss. Whatever she did next, she knew it would never be as stressful as her work in Napa Valley.

Meggie and Rose cleaned up the breakfast dishes while Angus went to shower before going into town to open the Vet Clinic.

'He's got a meeting this afternoon with a Locum Vet. If all goes well he'll start next week, staying for three months while we prepare for the wedding and have a brief honeymoon after.' Rose paused, glancing at Charlie, still playing on the floor. 'Angus works such long hours and does a lot of travelling around the district. I've asked him to consider an employee, maybe a future partner in the practice, so he can be home a bit more.'

'So this Locum will stay longer if it works out?' Meggie was curious.

'I don't think Angus has discussed the possibility of ongoing work. He wants to see how the fellow, Max, is with the locals. He's had considerably more small animal experience than large, coming from Newcastle, but has indicated a keen interest in equine health.' Rose let the water out of the sink, leaned her back against it, her expression unsure.

'There's more. Angus wants another baby. Before Charlie gets too much older.' She frowned slightly as she looked at Charlie, now stacking wooden blocks up into a tall, wobbly tower.

'And you don't?' Meggie wasn't sure if she should ask, but Rose had started the conversation.

'I do. Really I do. But Charlie is a handful and I've asked Angus to consider changing the way he works, to be home more.' A flush had crept up Rose's neck and Meggie reached out, touching her shoulder for a moment.

'What is it Rose? What's holding you back?'

Rose sighed. 'I've always been a strong, independent woman. Thought I could do anything I set my mind to. But having Charlie. Well. He's flipped some sort of a switch in me. I'm softer somehow.' She grinned sheepishly at Meggie. 'That's not a bad thing. But it's also made me a bit, I don't know, clingy. It's not the right word, but when Angus works long hours I resent it. I feel like I'm raising Charlie on my own at times. I'd like him home more. Running the farm together. Taking Charlie outside to do farmer-stuff when he can.' Rose took a deep breath. 'If we can get someone to handle the Vet Clinic in town most days, Angus could almost run the large animal work from here. He'd still have to go out to farms…' She trailed off, looking up.

Meggie turned to see Angus striding towards them in a clean shirt and jeans, his hair damp from the shower.

'What are your plans today Megs? Want to come into town and have a look around?' Angus wrapped his arm around her shoulders, giving her a brotherly squeeze. 'It'll be a bit slower than you're used to, but it's a great little town. What do you say? Want to ride in with me?'

Meggie nudged him with her elbow, dislodging his arm. 'I've already got a check-out-Barrington date, Gus. I'm riding in with Rose and Charlie.'

'Oh, I see how it is. The girls *are* ganging up on me.' Angus grinned at both women.

'There's coffee involved. Rose promised coffee.' Meggie laughed at his expression. 'Go Angus. I'll drop into the Clinic later, I'd love to see it.'

Angus kissed Rose and turned toward the door. Suddenly Charlie let out a wail, getting to his feet he ran toward Angus, arms in the air, knocking his tower of blocks flying as he went.

'Daddeeee, daddeee!' Rose scooped him up into her arms, but he wriggled, arms still out, trying to get to his father. Angus tousled Charlie's hair. 'Gotta go buddy, be good for Mummy and Meggie.'

Mouthing 'sorry' to Rose, Angus shot out the door. Rose patted Charlie's small back, now sobbing against her shoulder as if his heart would break. 'Daddeee! Want Daddee!'

Rose rocked back and forth, making soothing noises. Meggie picked up Charlie's Sippy cup, holding it out to him. He looked at her suspiciously before taking the cup in his hands, sipping in between sobs. It was a full five minutes before his tears subsided and Rose could set him back down with his toys.

Meggie raised her eyebrows at Rose. 'And this happens, how often?'

'Every day. Every bloody day.' Rose looked fondly at Charlie. 'He's often in bed when Angus gets home. Especially if he's been in the clinic most of the day, then gets a call out to a property. Sometimes he's gone in the morning before Charlie wakes up. This is what I mean. He needs Angus to be here a bit more. We both do.' She sighed.

'Oh Rose, I totally see what you mean. Let's hope this guy, Max, works out. Maybe he's the answer.' Meggie grinned cheekily at Rose. 'But you know what would help in the meantime?'

Rose laughed. 'What Meggie? What would help?'

'Coffee. It's morning, so coffee would help.' Meggie giggled. 'But around four o'clock this afternoon, wine will be the answer!'

Rose laughed and threw her arms around Meggie. 'I love you! Give me ten minutes and we'll head into town. My friend Deb owns the best coffee shop.'

4

———————

Max hesitated at the door to the clinic. He looked down at Tommy. 'Ready mate?'

Tommy grinned at his father. 'I'll be so polite and quiet, you won't recognise me Dad.'

Max chuckled and shook his head. 'You're a good kid Tommy. Just be yourself.' Hiding his own nervousness, he pushed open the door and a little bell tinkled. Stepping inside, he closed the door. Max looked around the clinic waiting room, it was empty. He looked toward the reception counter. Unattended. He cleared his throat loudly.

A door beyond reception opened and a tall man stepped out, striding toward them. He had a friendly smile and looked from Max to Tommy and back to Max. His face showed nothing more than pleased curiosity.

'Angus Hamilton. You must be Max.' He held his hand out, shaking Max's hand firmly. Then he looked at Tommy, with an eyebrow raised. 'And you must be Max's assistant.'

Before Max could speak, Tommy held his small hand out to shake with Angus. 'I'm Tommy. I'm going to be a vet too when I grow up, like Dad.'

'Excellent.' Angus grinned at Max. 'Two for the price of one.' He paused for a moment. 'This is the waiting room, and reception is over there. Melanie is our full-time receptionist and Vet Nurse, but we close at three on weekdays unless there's an emergency. I attend to the large animal work in the afternoons.' Angus turned the sign on the front door to 'closed.'

Max looked around. The waiting room and reception area was clean and more modern than he expected. He nodded to Angus before turning to speak to Tommy. 'You can wait here Tommy, while I see the rest of the clinic with Angus.' Tommy slid his backpack off and sat in the nearest chair.

'Well Max, if Tommy is going to be here with you for the three months, he should come on the tour too.' Angus looked questioningly at Max.

Taking a breath, Max chided himself for not explaining his situation to Angus before he came. He badly wanted this to work out. He and Tommy need the change, the shift from their usual routines.

Quite firmly, but quietly, Max responded. 'He will be with me Mr Hamilton.' He paused as he watched Tommy stand up, not bothering to hide his eagerness. 'It's just the two of us. Now.'

Angus said okay, not asking for an explanation and Max felt relief wash over him. They followed Angus through to the surgery and operating theatre, then out through a back door to a newer building, a small animal hospital. There were two dogs in residence, one bandaged around his front leg, sitting quietly and another sleeping in an enclosure.

'What happened to these dogs Mr Hamilton?' Tommy knelt in front of the sleeping dog, who opened an eye and wagged his tail slowly.

'Call me Angus, Tommy.' Angus crouched down beside the boy, opening the door of the enclosure. He reached in and gave the dog a gentle pat. 'Shadow was bitten by a snake yesterday. A king brown. He's had anti-venom, but it took a while to work. We're keeping him under observation for another night.' He turned to the other dog. 'This one fell off the back of a tractor. Broke his leg. He'll go home tomorrow too.'

Standing up, Angus turned to Max. 'There are days when we don't have any animals overnight, but sometimes there are several. As I mentioned on the phone, there is a flat attached, I sleep in here when I have an animal that needs intensive care. But its available for you, and Tommy, as part of our arrangement. I'll take you through to it.' Angus opened a plastic container, offering it to Tommy. 'You can give the dogs a bit of dry food each if you like.'

Tommy took a handful, tipped half into his lap then reached out to Shadow, holding the rest of the food in his open hand. Shadow gently nibbled the food, then licked Tommy's hand thoroughly. Tommy crooned gently to the dog, giving him a pat before turning to the next one.

Angus stepped away and Max followed. Tommy was happily patting the dogs, speaking softly to them while they ate.

Max looked Angus in the eye. 'I didn't mention Tommy. I, we, really need the change. He's a good kid, he's used to animals and he's good at keeping himself busy when I'm working.' Max exhaled, waiting for Angus to respond.

'It's all good Max. I can see Tommy is a great kid. I have no problem at all.' Angus eye-balled Max. They were a similar height. 'I can talk to you about school options too. Melanie's daughter starts Grade Four at Barrington when school returns in a couple of weeks. What year is Tommy in?'

Max's relief was palpable, he was sure Angus was aware of it too. 'He's going into Grade Four too. Should be Grade Three, he's eight, but he started early. Needed the stimulation.' He knew his pride was showing, but Tommy was bright. It was great to see him so happy and relaxed today, but perhaps he was simply reflecting Max's own mood.

With the dogs settled, Angus took Max and Tommy through to the apartment. It was little more than an oversize motel room, but had a kitchenette, bathroom, lounge area with television on the wall and a large bed. Tommy had been sleeping with Max for months, so it would do. For now. If the job turned into something more permanent, Max would rent a bigger place.

The men chatted about the work, the patients, the schedule and ended the meeting with a handshake.

'Are you driving back to Newcastle today Max?' Angus walked out through the front door with them, locking it as he went.

Max looked at his watch. 'Yes, we'll get back before dark if we go now. We've got a bit to organise so I'm ready to start on Monday next. Is it okay if we arrive next Saturday, to settle in?'

'Sure. Give me a call when you're close, I'll meet you here.' Angus shook hands again with Max, then Tommy. Max was proud of the way his boy looked up at Angus as they shook hands.

'I'll get the paperwork to you by email on Monday. Any questions, give me a call on the mobile. Any tricky questions and you might be better to call Melanie on the main phone, she's got all the admin information.' Angus grinned.

Ten minutes later they were driving out of town, heading to Newcastle.

'It went well, didn't it Dad?' Tommy was still in a state of happy excitement.

Max glanced at Tommy. 'It did mate. It went really well. I like Angus Hamilton, and I think his Vet practice is thriving. I'm going to do such a great job, that at the end of three months he'll want to keep me. Keep us.'

'You're a great Vet Dad. The best. Of course he'll want us to stay.'

Max turned the radio up, it was the local station playing country music. They sang along with Kasey Chambers' *Am I not Pretty Enough*, laughing loudly at each other. As he drove, the tightness in his chest loosened another notch.

5

———————

A week in Barrington and Meggie already knew a bunch of locals by name. She'd driven into town in Rose's bright red Jeep, with a list of jobs to do and groceries to fetch. With only six weeks to the wedding, Meggie was employing all her event management skills.

Sipping on her second chai latte, Meggie scrolled through the spreadsheet on her iPad. Rose and Angus were getting married at Barrington Homestead with a core group of family and friends in attendance, so it wasn't a big wedding. She'd convinced them to get a marquee for the backyard for the dinner and dancing, leaving the homestead kitchen for the caterers and the wide verandas for pre-dinner drinks and canapes. The ceremony would be simple, conducted by a civil celebrant near the front steps. It was perfect, really. Meggie sighed. It was *her* perfect wedding, and she wondered, for a moment, if she had pushed her wedding concept a little too hard. But Rose had been happy to leave it to Meggie.

'Hey Meggie, how are the plans coming along?' Debbie slid into the seat across from her, a coffee in her hand.

'I was thinking how simple and easy this one is. I'm so used to big. Not just big. Huge. Monstrous weddings in Napa.' Meggie made a face at Debbie. 'And not only the weddings. The brides. Monsters, all of them!'

'Ha! I've heard stories about bridezillas. But you won't get that here. Not with Rose.' Debbie sipped her coffee, then screwed up her nose, making Meggie smile. 'Rose isn't a girlie girl. Her only real wish is to be married at the homestead, with as little fuss as possible.'

'There will be fuss.' Meggie's eyes twinkled. 'Not much, but enough. I want this to be beautiful and memorable. For Rose, Angus and all of us on the day. But I understand her wish for simplicity, so that's what we'll have. Simple elegance. Maybe a little bit traditional too, in keeping with the setting.'

'Oooh, sounds like you have some surprises up your sleeve Meggie. Let me know if you need a hand.' Debbie finished her coffee and glanced at the counter. The mid-morning rush was beginning.

'We still need to sort out your matron-of-honour outfit Debbie. The bridal store in Newcastle is sending the wedding gown up next week. We'll have a fitting and consider a style that works with it for you.' Meggie started to rise. 'I've got some ideas. We'll talk.'

'Sure. Let me know when. My mother-in-law said she'd have little Charlie for an afternoon, she's watching Woz anyway, so we can sort the dress out.' Debbie turned.

'Woz?' Meggie was laughing. 'I'd forgotten how much we shorten names here. What's your little boy's name?'

'Warwick. But he'll get Woz once he starts school. We're getting him used to it.' Debbie grinned, then sped toward the counter where a small group were waiting.

Laughing to herself, Meggie packed her iPad and notebook into her satchel. She'd only met Debbie a week ago and could see how close she was to Rose. Both confident, generous women, they had immediately pulled Meggie into their circle, including her without forethought. Walking toward the Vet Clinic, Meggie looked up and down the street. She liked this little town. While she knew she'd get a job in the city with her qualifications and experience, she wondered if she could find a job here, in Barrington.

Accommodation was also on Meggie's mind. Most of the wedding guests were local, so that wasn't her problem. Meggie and Angus's mum Helen and new partner Barry were arriving in two weeks, staying through the wedding and honeymoon. They were going to wrangle little Charlie for three weeks while Rose and Angus enjoyed their honeymoon. Meggie chuckled. While she knew they'd been frequent visitors to Barrington Homestead since Charlie was born, she wondered how they'd manage for a full three weeks. Charlie's adorable, but a handful. But they would need to stay at the house and the guest wing that Meggie was currently occupying was the logical place. There was a guest room in the main house, that Rose and Angus suggested she move into, but she had in mind something more permanent. Something of her own.

Pushing open the door of the Vet Clinic, Meggie glanced around. Only two patients waiting.

'Hi Meggie.' Melanie, the Vet Nurse, called out and gestured her to the reception area with a smile. 'Angus won't be long, only has a couple of patients, then we'll close for lunch for an hour.'

'Hi Melanie. Thank you.' Meggie was about to take a seat and wait for Angus, but she turned back to Melanie. 'You're a long-time local Melanie?'

'Sure am. Grew up here. Can I help with something?'

'Yes please. There's a few real estate agents in the main street, can you recommend who might best provide some advice? On accommodation.' Meggie nibbled her lip.

'If it's for wedding guests, you might be better speaking to the local tourism officer. I can give you Wendy's number.' Melanie picked up a pen and post-it note.

'Well. Not really for guests. Our mum and step-dad are coming for an extended stay, and I want to give them the guest suite at the homestead. I thought I might try and find something in town for myself.'

'Oh, of course. It's a pity the locum will be using the flat here at the clinic, which might have done for a couple of months. He arrives tomorrow.' Melanie, picked up a business card from her desk, handing it across to Meggie. 'Drop into Evans Real Estate, it's a few doors further down the street.' She pointed to the name on the card. 'Ben Evans, er junior, is my husband. He'll look after you. If he's not in, Harriet Russell will sort you out.'

'Your husband? Perfect, I'll go there right now. Can you tell Angus I'll come back at noon, maybe we can have lunch together?' Meggie thanked Melanie with a nod and moved toward the door.

'No problem, I'll let him know. Good luck.'

* * *

PUSHING OPEN THE DOOR OF EVANS REAL ESTATE, MEGGIE GLANCED IN. A blonde woman about her own age was speaking on the phone at a desk to one side. There was a beautiful sign on the wall behind her stating 'Barrington – A Place to Start Over.' The words resonated with Meggie. That's exactly what she hoped to do. Start over. The woman was welcoming and gestured towards a chair in front of her desk, so Meggie sat down.

Putting the phone down, the woman walked around the desk, hand out to shake Meggie's. 'Hi, I'm Harriet, thanks for coming in.' While shaking Meggie's hand, she looked up at her for a moment, then grinned broadly. 'You must be Meggie! I can see your likeness to Angus, and a bit to your mum too. Tall people, all of you!'

'Nice to meet you Harriet.' Meggie relaxed. 'This is a small town thing, isn't it? Where everyone knows everyone? I bet you're a generational local like Rose, Debbie and Melanie.'

'Ha, not so much! Actually, I moved here a bit more than a year ago from Sydney and I absolutely love it!' Harriet radiated warmth and Meggie felt drawn to her. 'But you're returning from quite a few years in California, if I have my facts right, so Barrington must seem really small after that.'

'It's different, of course. But in a good way. I already know a bunch of people and the café down the street makes my favourite coffee before I finish ordering and I've only been here a week!' Meggie knew she sounded excited, but she had such a good feeling about the place.

'Debbie has that place running so well, it's a real drawcard for the town. I don't know how she does it with a one-year-old, but she has a great team, and her mum and mother-in-law are local and help with little Warwick.'

'The coffee there is brilliant. Better than the States, actually.

Australians are much snobbier about their coffee than almost any other place I've been.' Meggie laughed out loud at the thought, 'good barista-made coffee in Australia has definitely become a *thing*, even in small towns.'

Chuckling with her, Harriet added, 'The coffee is good and you're right, we expect that now, even in small towns. And I'm so glad to finally meet you, Angus has been speaking of you a lot since you said you'd return for the wedding.'

'It's really nice to meet you too, Harriet.' Meggie pulled out the business card Melanie had given her. 'Melanie said her husband Ben owns the business. I'm actually looking for some real estate advice.'

'That's great. Ben's out with clients but perhaps I can help.' Harriet raised her eyebrows.

Meggie pointed at the sign on the wall. 'That's what I'm looking for. A place to start over.' She took a breath. 'I really haven't discussed it with Angus and Rose in any detail, but I've decided not to return to the United States. If I can find work and a place of my own, I think I'd like to stay here.'

6

'It's not big mate, but we'll be cosy here.' Max looked around the apartment. Their bags were in a pile on the floor, the space looked much smaller than he remembered. Taking another look at the kitchenette area, Max noted the fridge was little more than a bar fridge and the cooking appliances consisted of a microwave, toaster and kettle. He frowned. It was enough for breakfasts and lunches but perhaps an air fryer would help for some dinners. He'd left everything in their house in Newcastle, as he'd rented it out for the three months. He brightened. There was the café and a couple of pubs for dinners, they'd be fine. Tommy wasn't a fussy eater.

He smiled. Tommy was already setting up his gaming console. The television on the wall was at least a late model one. He'd also brought a big plastic tub of Lego, but Max knew that Tommy would prefer hanging out with him in the clinic before and after school to help look after patients in the animal hospital. The area was full of places to bushwalk, mountain bike and canoe and Max thought they'd have a crack at those on his days off.

Glancing at his watch, he ruffled Tommy's hair. 'Want to have lunch at the café? Then we can buy a few groceries.'

Tommy stood up quickly. 'Sure Dad, I'm starving.'

They went out through the back, rather than walk through the clinic, which was closed. Their car was parked at the rear, Angus had met them when they arrived and directed them to the rear entrance, where he'd walked through and given them the keys to the apartment and clinic. He'd invited them out to his home for dinner, but Max had politely declined, saying he wanted to get settled in. Angus had said they'd have plenty of opportunities during the coming weeks.

As they walked down a side lane back to the main street, Tommy was asking questions about school. He was starting on Monday and seemed curious rather than anxious. Max was relieved. He'd seen a big change in his son since their trip to Barrington the week before. He felt it too. A fresh start, a different environment. It was what they needed.

The café was quiet, lunch time almost over. Debbie, from last week wasn't there but the girl that served them was friendly and they didn't wait long for their sandwiches. Tommy's chatter stopped the moment the food arrived, and with eyebrows raised in amazement Max watched him devour his sandwich and milkshake. After months of moping and a lack of interest in food, it was heartening to see Tommy so animated. Max enjoyed his sandwich and coffee too and he knew the change in Tommy was a reflection of his own mood, returning slowly to a sense of normality.

They filled the rest of the weekend in setting themselves up in the apartment and exploring some of the walking trails close to town. They kicked a football around in the park on Sunday afternoon, and then took a walk around the Barrington School grounds, to familiarise Tommy before the next day.

'What do you think Tommy. It's a bit different from Newcastle Grammar.' There were only a few buildings, three of them classrooms and one a library and maybe admin space. Max had spoken to the Principal during the week, they were happy to have Tommy and would put him in a Year 3 & 4 composite class. Tommy had the requisite grey shorts, blue shirt and black shoes for day one and Max would buy a couple of the school sports tee shirts for other days.

'It's really small isn't it Dad? But it has a tennis court over there, and a footy oval.' Tommy pointed and Max noted how neat the sports fields were. In a small town like this there was likely a parent working bee for stuff like that. He'd check into it, put his name down to help out. He really wanted to get to know the people here, and the parents of Tommy's classmates would be a good start.

'It's small, but I've heard that small schools are better. Less kids in class, friendlier.' He glanced down at his son as they walked back to the car. 'Are you worried about it?'

'Nah. I'm not worried about it. But I'm hoping I'll make some friends.' Max opened the car door and waited while Tommy settled himself with the seatbelt on.

'You'll make friends Tommy. Some of the kids will be farm kids. You might be invited to their farms where they'll have dogs, cattle, horses and all sorts of chores to do.'

'That'd be cool. I'd really like to ride a horse.' He bounced in his seat. 'That would be the best. A new friend with a farm, and horses!'

Max chuckled to himself as they drove back to the clinic. Then he frowned. Tommy wouldn't be able to reciprocate with a sleepover, they only had one bed. If it seemed to be working out in the first few weeks, he'd look at renting something bigger. He glanced across at Tommy and a sob caught in his chest. The shape of his face, his delicate ear, so much like his mother. The sight caught him unawares, his fingers tightened on the steering wheel.

With some sort of weird sixth sense, Tommy knew. He spoke quietly. 'Are you thinking about Mum?'

Max let out the breath he didn't realise he was holding. He looked sadly at Tommy. 'Yep. I am. I think about her a lot. But Tommy?'

'Yes Dad?'

'Being here. In Barrington. It's better than being at home isn't it? A fresh start?' Max watched the emotions play across his son's face.

'I like it here Dad. We'll never forget Mum. But somehow, it's easier being here, away from our house. Away from everything. I think we can be happy here Dad.'

Max was barely able to speak. He swallowed, then grinned at Tommy. 'I think we can be happy here too. Of course we'll never forget Mum but thinking about her seems to hurt less here.'

Tommy wiped the back of his hand across his eyes. Seeing that small gesture nearly undid Max. 'I love you Dad.'

'Love you too, son.' They looked at each other then, as they pulled up at the back of the clinic. Both with tears in their eyes. Without warning Tommy laughed. The sound was infectious. Max found himself laughing too. 'What?' he said. But Tommy couldn't answer, he laughed even harder. They opened the car doors and Max found himself bent over at the waist, laughing. Really laughing. He didn't know why, but it felt good.

Tommy came around the car and threw his arms around Max, tears of laughter running down his face. 'We're turning into a couple of sooks Dad. We're in the country now. We need to man up!' This brought on another bout of laughter, and they walked inside, Max with his arm around Tommy's slight shoulders. The moment had been good for them. There was something about this little town, it was working its magic on them. Max felt lighter. Laughing was good, natural. And he didn't feel guilty about having a happy moment.

Meggie put her wine glass down. 'I'd forgotten how good Australian wine is. Everyone raves about Napa Valley vintages, but honestly, this is better than anything I tasted over there.' She picked up the bottle and looked at the label. 'Tyrrells. Semillon. Of course. One of the first dozen winemakers in Australia. Hunter Valley, established in the eighteen fifties.'

Rose snorted. 'Oh you know your wines. I just drink what I like, and this one goes perfectly with my Thai beef salad.'

Meggie grinned at Angus as he topped up their glasses. 'When I left you were purely a beer man Gus. Did Rose civilise your taste buds?'

'Thank you very much Megs. I was always civilised. Sophisticated even. But you were too young to notice.' He picked up his glass, little finger sticking out and took a delicate sip.

'Oh stop Angus!' Rose turned to Meggie, laughing. 'He had two quick beers when he came home, so he's happy to share a wine now. He's trying to impress you.'

Meggie sat back, watching Angus and Rose banter back and forth. Little Charlie was asleep and with the evening still warm they had decided on a late dinner. She wanted to tell them about giving up her suite and moving out before the wedding but hadn't found the right moment. She knew Rose was enjoying her company and as well as planning the wedding, Meggie had been able to look after Charlie most afternoons and Rose was getting some writing done. She was an accomplished author and Meggie admired her for it, although she had no idea how she found time most days.

'Did Max arrive today? Do you think he'll be keen to stay longer than three months?' Rose asked as she passed the salad to Angus.

Meggie watched as Angus served himself. She knew that look. Angus was thinking before he spoke. She glanced at Rose, and almost laughed. Rose knew that look too.

'He did arrive on time. They did.' Angus passed the salad back to Rose and chewed thoughtfully on a mouthful.

'They?' What do you mean *they*? I thought he was on his own? You didn't say anything about a partner. Wife?' Rose fired her questions off in quick succession and Meggie could see that Angus was drawing it out, but she was curious too.

'I know. He has a pet. A dog. Or a fish. Maybe a turtle.' Meggie giggled as she took a bite of salad. It was really good. Fresh. Crisp. A little spicy. It suited the wine perfectly.

'No. Not a pet. He has a Tommy.' Angus was enjoying this. Meggie glanced at Rose. She had her thinking face on.

Rose spoke up. 'I know. Boyfriend. Tommy is his boyfriend.'

Angus shook his head. 'Give in?'

Meggie elbowed him. 'We're not five! Tell us!'

'Tommy is his eight-year-old son.' Angus sipped his wine. Meggie and Rose looked at each in surprise.

'His son? Just the two of them? Did he even ask you about this? Where's the mother?' Rose was drumming the table with her fingertips.

'I knew. He brought Tommy with him last week. He's a nice kid, wants to be a vet too. He was really good with the two dogs in hospital.' Angus leaned forward. 'Honestly? He didn't tell me why. But I can see they've been through something. I think they're grieving. I also think he's taken this job to give them a fresh start, or a change of scenery at least. Perhaps somewhere the memories aren't as strong.'

'Oh. Oh that's sad.' Meggie and Rose looked at each other.

'Why didn't you invite them for dinner?' Rose now glared at Angus. 'I could have cooked something suitable for all of us.' Meggie agreed.

'I did. He declined. I don't think he's ready.' Angus reached for the wine and poured the last of it into the girls' glasses. 'He was wound up I think, waiting for questions. I didn't give him any and he relaxed.' He looked carefully at his wife and sister. 'So don't come in on Monday and interrogate him. He'll tell us when he's ready and I'll invite him for dinner again next week. Let them settle in. He has Tommy booked into school on Monday, so I'm hoping that's a sign he's thinking more long term. My gut feeling is he's a good Vet and I can already see he's a good dad.'

'The flat at the clinic isn't very big. It only has one bed and not much of a kitchen at all.' Rose began clearing the table.

Angus stood to help her. 'I know that Rose. But let them settle. I'm sure Max knows what he's doing.' She sighed, said yes.

Meggie stood, her moment to discuss her own situation seemed to have passed. She'd had a good talk with Harriet the day before and was going to look at a two bedroom rental on Monday. It was across the road from the Vet Clinic, the top floor of the Post Office. It used to be the residence for the Postmaster General, back in the day, but Australia Post had been renting it out, often to staff, for decades. While Meggie didn't need two bedrooms, it was loads cheaper than a one bedroom in the city. She'd also spoken to Harriet about buying a second-hand car. She said she knew of one that might be in the right price range.

Carrying the last dishes through to the kitchen, Rose was already washing up and Angus drying. Meggie said a quick thank you for dinner and goodnight and left them to it. Back in her room, she sat on the bed for a moment, not sure if she wanted to have a good cry, or long bath. She decided on the bath. Her decision to move on from her old life, old situation, was good. She'd find her way here. There were good people around her and the warmth she received from Angus and Rose cemented that decision. Having family around, and friends, was pure gold.

8

———————

re you ready mate? Your first day at Barrington School?'
Max unbuckled his seatbelt, they were parked with several
others in front of the school.

'Yep.' Tommy looked excited and nervous at the same time.

There were several parents milling around the front gate, some
with smaller children in oversize uniforms. One little girl was crying in
her father's arms and Max watched as an older child came from inside
the school grounds and spoke to them. After a few moments the father
put his child down, her tears had stopped, and she took the older girl's
hand and allowed herself to be led inside the schoolyard.

About to step out of the car, Max was startled by a tap on his
window. A cheerful-looking blonde woman was standing there.
Tommy was already scrambling out of the car on the other side, his
backpack slung over one shoulder.

Opening the door, Max stepped out. 'Hello.' Tommy came around
the car and stood beside him, looking curiously at the woman.

'You must be Max. And Tommy. I'm Melanie, from the clinic.
Angus told me to watch out for you today and I know everyone else
here, so it was easy to find you.' She looked toward the school gate.
'Tiff! Tiffany! Come and say hello.'

'Oh hi Melanie, nice to meet you.' Tommy was fidgeting, and Max knew it was a sign of nerves. Two girls, about Tommy's age, ran up. Both fair, one was petite and obviously Melanie's daughter. Her friend was taller, her hair blonde and curly.

'Tommy, this is my daughter Tiffany and her friend Billie. I think they are in your grade.' Melanie nudged her daughter forward a little.

The other girl, Billie, gestured to Tommy. 'Come on, we'll show you our classroom.' Tommy looked from Max to Billie and Tiffany. They were starting to turn toward the school gate. He hesitated. Billie stepped back, waiting. 'I started here last year, it's a great school. Much better than my old one in Sydney. Come on.' Tommy took a step toward the girls, then turned to Max. 'Seeya Dad. Have a good day.' Then he was running with the girls, into the school grounds.

Max let out a sigh, then turned back to Melanie. 'Thank you Melanie. The girls will break the ice for him.' He chuckled. 'But there might be a conversation tonight about girls as he hasn't been friends with any before. They're like a whole other species to Tommy.'

Melanie chuckled. 'I hear you, but it's a funny thing with small schools. They seem to generally all play together. They kinda have to, to make up teams for any sports and it translates back into the class-room.' They walked back to their cars together.

Melanie stopped for a moment. 'I'm sure you'll want to pick up Tommy today, and maybe all this week. But I was thinking that once he's settled, I can pick him up when I get Tiff and he can hang out with us some afternoons. Billie comes home with us sometimes too, but she lives on a farm further out and often gets the bus.'

Max looked away for a moment. Melanie's words brought a lump to his throat. He'd been worried about juggling Tommy and work in the afternoons, especially if he had to go out to a property. He'd expected to take him everywhere he went. To find some help, some support, on their first day really touched him. He looked back at Melanie. 'Thank you. Thank you very much. I'd really like that, and I hope we can return the favour and help out with Tiffany too.'

'Of course. That's how we operate here.' Melanie smiled over her shoulder as she walked to her car. 'See you in the clinic shortly.' Max waved and opened his car door.

'Oh Max?'

'Yes.'

'How do you like your coffee? I'm picking one up for all of us this morning. You know, a welcome to the business thing.'

Max grinned. 'I never say no to coffee. Americano please.'

Melanie gave a thumbs up and got into her car. Max waited while she backed out, then he pulled out and drove into the clinic. He sang along to the local radio station all the way.

* * *

THE MORNING PASSED QUICKLY. MAX WORKED ALONGSIDE ANGUS IN THE clinic, seeing to a variety of patients. This was where he felt most comfortable. Small animal clinic. While the patients and ailments were largely familiar, the clients were quite different. Polite, friendly, grateful. Sure, he had a lot of pleasant clients at the Newcastle practice, but there were also many who were rushed, ill-mannered, neurotic and difficult.

'That's it for the morning Max.' Angus stretched. 'We need to get some lunch then we're off to preg-test heifers out at Drum Murray's property. He has a mare in foal too, so we'll check her while we're there.'

'Great. You've really got a busy practice here Angus, I heard Melanie rescheduling some for tomorrow morning that we couldn't fit in.' Max washed up at the sink in the surgery. Their last patient, a cattle dog, had required stitches in her side after an incident with a barb-wire fence.

'I can see you're at home in the clinic already. No need for us to work together here all the time.' Angus chuckled. 'You hardly need supervision.' He moved over to the sink as Max finished, saying over his shoulder, 'I'd like to take you to a few of the properties where we do most of our big animal work, horses and cattle mainly. A few sheep, some goats and there's an alpaca farm too. Do you want to grab lunch together at the café? I've already got some ideas on how best to move forward.'

'Lunch would be great. Thanks Angus.' They walked out to reception together, Angus speaking briefly to Melanie before they left the clinic.

'Does Melanie take a lunch break?' Max noted he and Angus were a similar height and build, although Max knew he was a few years older.

'Mel likes to eat at her desk, that way she can finish at three to pick Tiff up from school.' Angus glanced at Max. 'She's a really good vet nurse, practically runs the business side for me too.' He hesitated. 'She will help out with Tommy. Pick him up and keep him after school. If you need it, that is.'

'She offered this morning, at school. Introduced Tommy to her daughter and a friend.' Max hesitated. 'I'm grateful.' Angus said 'good,' as if it was no big deal.

They sat at an outside table. Max glanced at the menu then at Angus. 'What's good? I'm starving. Must be the country air.'

'It's a burger for me. Chips and salad. Can't go wrong.' Angus hadn't even looked at the menu. Max stood. 'I'll order for us.' Before Angus could respond Max was at the counter chatting with Debbie.

He returned with cutlery and napkins. 'Debbie said you usually have an iced coffee at lunchtime, so I've ordered that too.'

'Thanks Max. You don't have to buy lunch for me.' Angus grinned. 'But it's gonna taste better 'cos I didn't pay.' He threw his head back and laughed and Max joined him.

'There is something I need to talk to you about Angus. Now might be a good time.' Max spoke quietly.

'Go ahead mate.' Angus focussed on Max, nodding encouragement.

'Tommy and me. We're on our own.' Max paused, looked down for a moment, then back at Angus. 'My wife, Liliana, was killed in a car accident almost a year ago.' He paused as their drinks were delivered to the table.

'Mate, you don't have to explain anything. I realised there was a reason you were here, and not because you have Tommy with you. A change, or a fresh start. It's all good with me. I'm already confident you can take care of the clinic while I'm away.'

'You're right. We need the change. So badly that I didn't tell you our situation, or about Tommy. I hoped you'd be okay with it.' Max took a sip of his drink, then looked Angus in the eye. 'Thank you.'

Their burgers came and they tucked in with gusto. 'And about Melanie. Nice lady. I'm hoping we can work together with the kids a bit, share the drop-offs and pick-ups. Afternoons especially when I'm away from the clinic.' Max grinned. 'Although Tommy would give his eye teeth to come out to the properties, especially equine work. He's horse-mad.'

'We've got horses. Well, Rose has. Bring him out next weekend, we'll have a barbecue. Rose can introduce him to her horses.' Angus put his cutlery down, he'd eaten about half of the burger. 'This calls for a more aggressive approach.' He picked the remains of the burger up in his hands and took a large bite. Max laughed. The relief he felt at finally telling Angus lightened his mood, his whole being.

9

———————

Meggie followed Harriet upstairs to the post office apartment. The wide staircase was made of solid timber and the treads were old and worn, although the exterior of the building was sandstone and as solid as the day it was built, around nineteen hundred. They came to a small landing, also timber, the boards old and gnarly, but polished and clean. Harriet opened the door to the apartment and Meggie stepped into an enormous open living room. It may have been two rooms at one stage, there was a decorative timber arch high in the centre of the room and large windows, not quite floor to ceiling, along the street-facing side.

The kitchen ran along the wall at one end of the big room and Harriet took Meggie through to a smaller area, now a butler's pantry that also enclosed a washer and dryer.

'So gorgeous! I'm really surprised it hasn't been used as holiday accommodation.' Meggie turned around in the small room. 'What would this little room have been used for, back in the day?'

'Probably a broom closet or cleaning room. There are back stairs right out there, down the exterior of the building into the laneway. Needed to meet fire emergency guidelines, but I'd say they used it for access to the backyard. They would have had a clothesline and kitchen garden out there. And an outside toilet and laundry.' Harriet walked back into the main living area.

'There are two bedrooms, they wrap around the other side of the building as the staircase really comes right up through the middle.' Meggie followed Harriet through another door. The bedrooms were large with good size windows, and a bathroom sat between them. The apartment was furnished, some of it a bit dated, but solid enough. Meggie was entranced. She had no idea she could rent something like this in Barrington.

'I'll take it! When can I move in, it's perfect for me!' Meggie almost skipped back to the kitchen. It had a big fridge and a gas stove. She clapped her hands. And while it was quite warm upstairs today, she could see a large reverse cycle air-conditioner in the living area.

'As soon as we get the lease signed. I'll email it to Australia Post, but they're usually pretty quick. Come back down, we'll go to my office, it's cooler there.'

Meggie followed Harriet out into the street, then across the road to her office.

'Cold drink Meggie? I have some diet soda out in the kitchen.' Harriet raised a questioning brow.

'Thank you, yes please. I'm still not used to the heat, although it's only been a week.'

While Harriet brought the drinks through, Meggie placed her passport and other identification on the desk. She looked across at Harriet. 'I don't have any current rental references. My accommodation in Napa was provided by the company.'

'Not to worry. You've got identification and you have family locally. I'll referee you myself.' Harriet set about handing the lease documents across, indicating where Meggie should sign.

'I've made it for six months, but I'm sure we can extend it if you need.'

'Great! I'm serious, I'd like to stay here.' Meggie looked up, her hand poised to initial the next page.

'I know you're serious. But I am curious about your plans. You have the wedding to organise, but after that?' Harriet seemed genuinely interested, so Meggie took a deep breath.

'Well. It's a small town, I realise that. But it's so beautiful. It could be a good place for weddings and events, you know wedding and engagement tourism.' Meggie sat back, watching Harriet's reaction. She wasn't disappointed, Harriet leaned forward.

'Brilliant Meggie, bloody brilliant! We need your skills here. But you're thinking too narrowly.'

Meggie laughed. She was pumped. She wanted to discuss this with Rose and Angus but wasn't sure of their reaction. 'Too narrowly? How?'

'Think bigger. Bigger events. Australia Day. A festival here, showcasing local food, art, music. Great for tourism. Then reproduce that a few times a year. A winter festival. So many come here from the city for the snow. While we don't get it down here, it's where everyone starts before heading up to Barrington Tops when there's a fall. Spring. You could do something around weddings. Like a fair.' Harriet drew a breath and sat back.

'Really? I love these ideas. Getting paid as a wedding organiser is one thing, but how does it work when putting something together for the town, the community?' Meggie's mind was racing, but she was mindful it would be a business too. 'Community events are great, but they don't pay the organiser very much.'

'Funding Meggie. Grant funding. Council funding for tourism and small business. State funding. We could put a proposal together for a few main events each year and take it to Council, then the State. Sponsors too.' Harriet waved her hand around the office. 'Evans Real Estate would sponsor and there'd be others. You'd be bringing opportunity to the area, showcasing it.'

'Wow! Thanks Harriet. Great ideas.' Meggie paused. 'But they're your ideas, why would you give them to me?'

'It's an opportunity that's too big for me, and while I have some of the skills, I'm lacking in areas that you have an abundance of. Think about it. I'm happy to give you the ideas. Take them. Run with them.' She paused. 'But I'd also be happy to talk collaboration. Partnership perhaps. But no pressure.' Harriet scooped the lease up. 'First things first. Let's get you moved in across the street. I think you'll be good to go by the end of the week. When does your mother arrive?'

'Next weekend, so that's perfect. And we have a wedding dress fitting this week and I'm yet to organise Debbie's matron-of-honour dress. So a bit to do.' Meggie stood up. 'I'll talk it through with Angus and Rose too. Can I get back to you on the business thing?'

'Of course. No rush. I can't see anyone else jumping into the marketplace. Wait until after the wedding if you'd rather.' Harriet walked around her desk, but Meggie could see she was excited too.

'No.' Meggie spoke firmly.

Harriet seemed taken aback. 'No what?'

'No I won't wait. I'll talk it through with Angus and Rose and I'll do some research. I'll let you know my thoughts by the end of the week.' Meggie spoke in a rush, then breathed out. 'I'm really excited! I'm really-bloody-excited! No waiting Harriet. I need to work out the details, business structure options and budgets. But I'm in!'

* * *

GLANCING AT HER WATCH, MEGGIE SAW IT WAS PAST LUNCHTIME AND wondered if Angus would have time for a chat. As she neared the Vet Clinic, she saw Angus walking toward her with another man. Max, the Locum Vet, she assumed. He was easily as tall as Angus and broader across the shoulders. She raised a hand in greeting as they neared her, now at the front door to the clinic.

'Hey Megs. Are you looking for me?' Angus looked pleased, then turned toward the other man. 'Max, this is my sister Meggie. Meggie. Max.'

Meggie looked up at him. 'Hi Max, nice to meet you.' He took her hand in his and she immediately noticed how big it was. She was a tall woman and secretly thought she had man-hands, but hers seemed almost delicate, and feminine, gripped in his giant paw. He mouthed a greeting, but she barely heard it, as she stared at their hands. Suddenly she realised he had relaxed his grip and her hand was still in his. Blushing, she drew it back quickly.

If Angus noticed, he didn't comment. Inwardly she thought that was more for Max's benefit than hers and it was likely he'd tease her later.

Meggie turned to Angus. 'I was wondering if you'd have time for lunch, but I can see you're on your way back from the café, so I guess that's a no.'

'Sorry Megs. We're heading out to do some preg-testing. Was there anything urgent you wanted to talk about?' As Angus spoke, Max nodded at Meggie, then entered the clinic, leaving her outside with Angus.

Shaking her head, Meggie answered. 'No. Not really. Well, yes, I want to talk to you. And Rose. But it's not urgent. I'll join you for dinner tonight, for a chat, if that's okay?'

'Of course. Work it out with Rose. I won't be late.' Angus reached for the door.

'Max. The new guy. How's he working out?' Meggie inclined her head toward the door.

'So far he's been great.' Angus pulled the door open. 'We'll chat tonight then, okay?'

10

———

Walking from the heat of the day into the clinic, Max put his right hand in his pocket. It had tingled in an unfamiliar way when he'd gripped Meggie's. He clenched it a couple of times, then spoke quietly to Melanie. 'Any messages?'

'No. It's been quiet. Drum Murray called to say he has the heifers yarded, so you can head out there when Angus is ready.' Melanie walked to the copy machine as she spoke, then turned back to Max. 'You might need to take two vehicles out there if you want to be on time for Tommy this afternoon. Or I can pick him up when I get Tiff and drop him back later.'

'Thanks Melanie. I'm not sure. It's his first day and it's hard to know if it's been a good one.' As Max spoke, Angus walked through to reception.

'Was Billie at school this morning?' Angus directed this to Melanie.

'Yes, of course! She and Tiff took Tommy into class together.' Melanie turned to Max. 'Billie is Drum Murray's daughter. She'll go home on the bus or perhaps Harriet is picking her up. That's Drum's fiancée. I'll give Harri a call.' She was already dialling before Max had time to really follow the conversation.

Angus nudged Max. 'Let the girls work it out. Tommy can come out there with Billie and watch us finish the testing. Do you think he'd like that?'

Max relaxed. His shoulders had been tense, but he could see how hard they were trying to ensure Tommy was included. When he thought about it, he knew no matter what sort of day Tommy had, he'd still rather come and do 'vet stuff' than homework. 'Thanks Melanie. If you can work it out with, Harri is it?' Melanie nodded. 'If you can work it out with Harri, then Tommy will be happy knowing he's coming to 'work,' so thank you, that's perfect.'

Leaving the clinic in the Vet vehicle, Angus pointed out a few landmarks on the way to the Murray property, including the river and places to kayak and swim. Max leaned forward in his seat to get a better look. So many outdoor activities in this region.

Angus interrupted his thoughts, 'Tommy will be in good hands with Harriet. She came here little more than a year ago, runs a business within the Evans Real Estate agency.' He pointed to a cottage set back from the road, lovely gardens in the front yard. 'That's Bellbird Cottage. Harriet owns it. She's also Drum Murray's nearest neighbour.' Angus paused for a moment. 'Drum's divorced, his little girl Billie is with him full time. Harri's been great for both of them.' He glanced at Max. 'I don't know the personal details of all my clients, and probably wouldn't fill you in if I did. But Drum's a mate, you'll like him.'

Max thought about Angus' words. He wanted to get along with clients, and he appreciated the extra information provided by Angus. If Drum was a mate, Max wanted to make sure he looked after him. And if Tommy settled at school, he was really keen to make this a permanent move. They could sell the Newcastle house. He brought himself back to the present as they pulled up at a large shed, and cattle yards. Max could see at a glance it was a good operation, and a big property.

Angus made quick introductions and they started working. While Max hadn't done a lot of cattle work, he'd done enough to keep them moving into the holding pen for the test. They had more than sixty to run through. Angus did the first thirty while Max and Drum moved the cattle in, then out after the test. Max took over for the second half and found it easy going. The cattle were used to being handled and the facilities modern, making their job quicker than he'd expected.

They only had a few left when a little red car pulled up by the fence. Max didn't have time to do more than acknowledge Tommy had stepped out of the car with a woman and the little girl he'd met that morning, Billie. From the corner of his eye he could see Tommy sitting on the top rail of the fence.

'That's it Max, last one's through!' Angus called out from the other side of the fence.

'Right.' Max started packing their equipment up, then walked out through the gate to stack it by the car. He found a tap on the side of the yards and turned it on, washing his hands and arms. Angus appeared beside him.

'Drum has a mare in foal, we're going to have a quick look at her before we go. The children have gone through to the stables with Drum.' Angus grinned. 'Your Tommy was practically jogging on the spot and Billie was giving him a lecture on being calm around the mare when they get there.' Max chuckled.

'Tommy's keen. And horse mad. But he knows to be calm around animals, so he'll be okay.'

They walked to the stables and Max marvelled at how comfortable he felt with Angus. And while he'd not spoken much to Drum, he could see the men were cut from the same cloth.

Inside the stable the mare was tethered in a large enclosure, her nose in a feedbag. Tommy came to stand quietly beside Max as they all looked at the mare for a moment.

'Hey Dad.' Max looked down. Tommy was grinning, his eyes shining, as he looked up at him.

Max ruffled his hair. 'Good day?'

'The best.' That was enough for Max, they could talk later. He stepped into the stall with Angus.

Billie and Tommy hung over the gate, watching. They didn't speak much, until Max heard Tommy ask her if she had a horse. 'Oh sure. Chippy and Lady are my favourites. Wanna come and see them?'

Max glanced up, checking with Drum.

'They're in the paddock right here, all good.' Drum turned to his daughter. 'You and Tommy can take a bit of hay out to the feed bin for the horses, but don't go inside their paddock, you've still got your uniforms on.'

The kids disappeared and Max and Angus got on with checking the mare. Satisfied she, and the foal she carried, were in good health, they stepped outside the pen.

'A nice type of horse Drum. What's her breeding? Stockhorse? A bit of Arabian blood?' Max inclined his head toward the mare.

'She is a beauty. I bought her from Rose Gordon, her grandfather bred her from his old stallion, Topper. You're right, stock horse-Arabian cross. Rose broke her in, but she hasn't been ridden much. The foal is by my stallion, Jack. She's for Harriet to ride once she's foaled.' Drum folded his arms across his chest. Max thought he looked pleased with himself.

'Do you have time to come up to the house for a cuppa or a cold one?' Drum led them outside. Max could see two horses eating from the feed bin, but no sign of Billie and Tommy.

'We'll come up Drum.' Angus nudged Max. 'That's where your son will be.'

Drum laughed. 'Billie and Harri baked a carrot cake last night. They wanted to welcome the new vet. Tommy is a bonus.'

'What about me?' Angus tried to look miffed, 'I'm the old vet and I don't get baked goods when I come here.' He shook his head. 'Well, not every time anyway.'

They walked to the homestead together, chatting generally about cattle, horses, dogs and the weather. Max relaxed, enjoying the easy conversation. If Tommy asked how his day was later he'd give the same answer. The best.

11

———————

Little Charlie was finally down for the night and Meggie, Rose and Angus had moved to the back veranda, relaxing in the slightly cooler evening air.

'How was Max today Angus?' Rose passed a platter of cheese and olives across to him. Meggie shot a quick look at Angus, keen to hear his response.

'Well now, Rosie my love.' He leaned back in his chair giving Meggie a knowing look. She frowned and shook her head. He had his teasing face on, and she wasn't in the mood. 'You might as well ask Megs here. She met him today.' Meggie let out a frustrated sigh. Brothers!

Rose narrowed her eyes at Angus then looked at Meggie. 'Did you Meggie? What do you think of him?'

Meggie glared at Angus, then answered Rose. 'I only met him for a moment, at the door to the clinic.'

'But you must have an impression, even from a brief meeting?' Rose may have been teasing too, Meggie wasn't sure.

Taking a sip of her wine, Meggie thought about what she could say to describe Max. A small smile played around her mouth as she looked at Rose. 'He's big.'

Rose snorted her wine, laughing. 'What? Big?' She looked at Angus for confirmation, but he gave nothing away. 'You mean, overweight big?'

'Just big. Tall. Maybe taller than Angus.' Meggie squinted at her brother, before turning back to Rose. 'But broader. Chest, shoulders. He's a giant.' Rose was laughing softly, leaning forward. Then Meggie remembered something. 'And big hands. Enormous hands.' She lifted her right hand up and waved it in front of Rose. 'Made my hand look small. Ladylike. Delicate even.'

Angus was chuckling now, and Rose threw her head back and laughed. 'Oh Meggie, what an impression he's made on you! I can't wait to meet this giant of yours.'

'He's not mine. He belongs to Angus.' Meggie lifted her glass to her lips. Darn. It was empty.

'Oh hold on girls. He's not mine. Don't make this weird now.' Angus shook his head, laughing, and lifted the wine bottle. 'Empty. Should we open another one?'

Meggie jumped in quickly. 'No. Not for me anyway. I actually want to talk to you guys about something.'

'I'll get some soda water for us Meggie. But can you wait a moment, I still want Angus to tell us about Max. About the vet stuff.' Rose walked back into the kitchen, returning with a jug of soda water and three glasses.

'He's good Rose. A good vet. He was great at the clinic today. Has a nice way with the patients and their owners. He had Margaret O'Brien practically purring, more than that old cat of hers, and you know she's always sharp with me.' Angus crossed his legs, comfortable in the wicker chair. 'But he was great out at Drum's with the heifers today too. Not over-confident, but as soon as we had the job started he was fine. When we checked the mare, Storm, it was obvious he knows equine health, that's for sure.' Rose had leaned forward. 'And before you ask, Storm is doing well, she'll foal in about a month, we think.'

Meggie was about to speak when Angus added more quietly. 'Max told me today that his wife died in a car accident almost a year ago. That's why he has Tommy here. They're looking for a fresh start. I'd say he's a bit older than me. Late thirties perhaps.'

'Ohhh!' Meggie and Rose spoke in unison. Meggie glanced at her hand, recalling how it looked inside Max's. It's good he'd told Angus about his situation and note to self; he's unlikely to be looking for romance. And neither is she. Not yet anyway.

'Now tell us about your stuff Megs. You've been busting to all evening.' Angus patted Meggie on the shoulder.

She took a breath and started, quickly blurting it all out. About not wanting to return to the States and hoping to stay permanently in Barrington, moving into the flat to give their mum and Barry the suite at the homestead, and about the conversation with Harriet Russell and the business concept. She drew a breath and looked at them.

Angus stood up, held his arms out. Meggie rose and walked into them. He held her tightly and she felt a sob rising in her throat. 'I couldn't be happier Megs. Make this your home. See you all the time. For Mum to be able to visit both of us, and our children.' He squeezed her tight. 'No pressure. But having you nearby is the best news.'

Rose moved next to him while he spoke and somehow Meggie found herself enclosed in her arms, both sobbing. 'Just. So. Happy. When my grandfather died I had no family. Now I have a husband and Charlie, parents in-law and a sister!' Meggie's cheek touched Rose's, their tears mingling. This was what she had missed in the States. Yes, she'd made friends. But Angus, her big brother. Nothing replaced him. And Rose. A sister? Yes. All she could think was, yes.

Meggie knew there was other stuff. Stuff she wanted to leave behind in Napa Valley. It wouldn't be easy. But having a secure home and her family, that would help.

12

———————

Tommy didn't say much on the way back to the clinic in the Vet car with Angus driving. Max knew he'd have plenty to say later. Watching Tommy say goodbye to Billie and Drum, and thank Harriet for afternoon tea, Max felt more than a little proud. Tommy had been friendly and polite, and he could see he had an affinity with Billie, racing off for another look at the horses while the adults drank their tea. But he had returned when he was called, with no fuss made.

Angus thanked Max for a good day's work when he dropped them at the back of the clinic, and Max felt he should be thanking Angus instead. But he waved as Angus backed out, then walked through to the apartment with Tommy.

'Take a shower mate, we'll walk across to the pub for a quick meal tonight.' Tommy said okay and headed to the bathroom. 'Any homework due tomorrow?'

'Nup. It was all easy stuff today. I sat with a boy called Fred Jennings. He comes to school on the bus, from further up in the mountains. He's got a lot of older brothers and they live on a big cattle farm.' Tommy paused, one hand poised to open the bathroom door. 'He was a bit of a show off and called me a city slicker at lunch time. I wanted to like him, but he was kinda rude to me in front of his brother in year six and then he teased Billie Murray.'

'Oh really? Did Billie get upset?' Max had liked the forthright little girl.

Tommy shook his head quickly. 'Not Billie. She told him she'd help with his reading if he went to the infants class to get a book he could manage. He went bright red, and she skipped away.' Tommy chuckled, then looked like he wanted to say more, so Max prompted him. 'And?'

'Nothing.' Tommy stepped into the bathroom and closed the door. Max frowned, he wondered if other kids had been cruel because he was new. He hoped Billie hadn't. Or Tiffany. That would be awkward.

Max ordered a steak and ginger beer, and Tommy had a kid-size schnitzel and a glass of lemonade. Max would have liked a real beer, it had been a busy, hot day, but he didn't want to get in the habit of having one every day. They didn't speak much while they ate but stayed after to finish their drinks.

'And was the afternoon okay at school, after Fred was rude?' Max's heart dropped as Tommy hung his head for a moment.

'I don't want to say.' This worried Max more.

'I think you should tell me Tommy, you always have before.' He didn't want to push too hard but needed to know if there was anything brewing at school he could circumvent.

Tommy looked across at him, slightly flushed. 'Billie was right, Fred's not a very good reader. He's almost a year older than me and doing the year three work, while I'm already on year four stuff.' He stopped, looking distressed for a moment. 'Fred tried to look at my maths, and I covered it with my elbow. He kicked my foot under the desk.'

Max considered his answer for a moment. 'Well Tommy, letting Fred copy your work wouldn't really help him learn, so you did the right thing. But you also know that you find a lot of schoolwork easier than others do, so you shouldn't tease him about it.'

'I didn't tease him. But Miss Bolitho saw him kick me and she moved me to another desk and now I'm sitting in a three, not a two.' Tommy had tears in his eyes.

'What's a three?'

'The desks are in twos and some threes. I'm at a three at the back now. It's for the kids doing the year four work.' He still seemed upset.

'Is that a problem? You already said it wasn't too hard for you.' Max was confused but needed to get to the source of Tommy's unease.

Tommy hung his head again and muttered something.

'Tell me, Tommy. What's bothering you? Don't you like who you're sitting with now?'

Tommy looked up, his eyes bright with unshed tears. 'That's just it Dad, I do like who I'm sitting with. Billie and Tiffany.' He wiped his eyes with his arm. 'But they're girls! I've never been friends with girls before!'

Relief washed over Max, but he tried not to let it show on his face. 'Well Tommy, I don't think it matters much. From what I saw of Billie this afternoon, she was happy to feed the horses and show you around the farm. It's not like she asked you to go to a doll's tea party, is it?'

'No. She's great. She knows about lots of farm stuff, especially horses and she even said she'd let me ride one of hers next time.' He shook his head slowly. 'I'd really like that, but I don't want to get teased about playing with girls, you know, at school.'

'Tiffany's mum already told me that the boys and girls at Barrington don't seem to care, and often play together. I don't think it's a problem Tommy, and you're sure to make friends with some boys too, although maybe not Fred.' He watched as Tommy digested this, then looked up, happier now.

'So it's alright then? That I'm friends with Billie and Tiffany?'

'It's better than alright. It's perfect. Billie's Dad is one of our best clients and Tiffany's mum is our Vet Nurse.' He reached across, ruffling his hair. 'Come on mate, we've got time to watch a bit of the tennis before you go to bed.' Tommy grinned then and finished his lemonade in one big gulp.

They strolled back to their flat, and Tommy was asleep before the tennis really got started. Max turned the television off and sat on the couch for a while, casually looking at real estate in the area on his iPad. He had a good feeling about it, but it was a bit soon to make anything permanent.

13

Meggie made some healthy snacks first thing in the morning, supervising Charlie while she worked. Debbie, Melanie and Harriet were coming at three for their first look at Rose's wedding dress, and Rose had laughed when Meggie asked about afternoon tea and said she wouldn't eat anything at all between now and the wedding if she wanted the dress to fit. It had arrived at the courier depot the night before and Rose rushed into town after breakfast to pick it up. Meggie hadn't seen it and was really curious, and when she asked Debbie if she knew the style she'd shaken her head. 'No, Rose hasn't given me any hints at all, although with her height and figure she can wear any style she chooses.'

In fact, Rose hadn't been keen to show anyone the dress, wanting to keep it a total surprise. But Meggie had gently advised they needed to see it to make sure they found a bridesmaid dress for Debbie that worked with it, and to ensure the simple decorations for the wedding fitted with her chosen style. She'd given in, then become quite excited and wanted Harriet and Melanie to see it too. Debbie's mother-in-law Jill was coming to pick up Charlie at lunch-time, keeping him for the afternoon.

The day flew by, Rose rushed home, carrying the large, well-wrapped clothing bag to her room. They had a light lunch after Charlie was picked up and spent some time running through Meggie's initial ideas, and budget, for the wedding. Meggie suggested an elegant white and rose gold theme, with pops of colour provided by roses from the garden, set around the marquee. Low vases on the tables and a few tall vases on plinths near the entrance and each side of the dance floor. She wouldn't introduce another colour until she saw the wedding dress, although she assumed it would be white. Rose still needed to choose a style and colour for Debbie.

'I love it Meggie, thank you.' Rose clapped her hands, 'you're brilliant at this. I wouldn't have known where to start but this is perfect. I hope you love the wedding dress, 'cos I think it fits with the theme too.'

Nodding happily, Meggie felt a small glow of pleasure. She wanted the day to be perfect for Angus and Rose and was thrilled to be involved.

Debbie, Harriet and Melanie arrived after three, with two bottles of French champagne. Debbie held one aloft as she rushed in. 'Girl time! I don't care that it's only for a couple of hours, I'm so excited to see your dress Rose.' She set the bottle down, reached up and hugged Rose tightly. Harriet and Melanie laughed as they entered.

'Jill has Charlie and Woz, does she have Tiffany too?' Meggie looked at the women as Rose asked the question.

'No, Tiffany and Tommy went home on the bus with Billie. Drum's giving them all a riding lesson. Melanie will pick up Tiff and Tommy when we're done here.' Harriet said this with a chuckle. 'I left some afternoon tea for them all, but I think Drum will have his hands full. Tommy's a beginner and Billie will want to help with his lesson.' The five women looked at each other and laughed.

'Now Rose, you need to get this dress on, we can't wait to see what you've chosen.' This was from Debbie, who then leaned toward Meggie, saying in a loud whisper, 'she didn't invite her best friend to go wedding shopping, so you know, she might just have white pants and a tee.' Meggie giggled, then quickly looked at Rose in case she was offended. But she was laughing with all of them.

'Oh come on. I dress up. Sometimes. When the occasion calls for it.'

Rose shook her head, wagging a finger at Debbie. 'You don't think I've got any style at all. But wait, you'll see.'

Debbie wagged a finger back at Rose. 'Rose darling. You are a stunning woman and would look good in a hessian bag. But I don't want you wearing one down the aisle.' They all giggled, and Meggie relaxed. These women genuinely care for each other, and she felt sure Rose had chosen something special, her excitement was palpable.

Head high, Rose pointed to the champagne glasses on the kitchen bench, along with the small platter of snacks Meggie had made earlier. 'Pour the bubbles girls, while I transform into a bride.' She turned toward the hallway.

Meggie called out, 'do you need a hand Rose, to get into it?'

Rose stopped, turned back to them. 'Probably. I will on the day. But today I want to surprise you all. Talk amongst yourselves please, I will return.'

Meggie poured the drinks and ensured the others had something to eat. The women included her in their conversation, and she relaxed. Her ears pricked up when Melanie mentioned Max.

'He's a good Vet, the clients and patients have taken to him. He said the clients are not always as easy to get on with in the city practice, always stressed and busy. Says he loves it here already. Tommy is a really nice kid and sits with Billie and Tiffany in class.'

'Is he divorced or separated? Is that why they're on their own?' Harriet asked quietly.

Melanie shook her head. 'His wife died in a car accident. He told Angus on the first day, but you know Angus, he didn't say a thing to me. Then Tiffany told me. Tommy told the girls when they asked where his Mum is.' She paused, 'apparently Billie told him her mum lives in England, and she never sees her either.' Melanie glanced at Harriet. 'Then she said she has Harriet now and she's a lot more fun.'

Harriet snort-laughed with a mouthful of champagne, then wiped a tear from her eye. 'Love that kid. Billie.'

Movement caught their attention. Rose walked toward them, and they gave a collective, 'ohh!' She wore a rose gold silk satin gown, with an off-the-shoulder low cut sweetheart neckline, fitted to the waist, then draped softly from her waist to the floor. She turned in a circle, the back dipped in a low cowl to almost her bottom cleavage, held together by a delicate criss-cross of matching chain.

Meggie felt tears spring to her eyes. Rose looked beautiful, the dress absolutely perfect for her. It clung to her in all the right places and had an old-Hollywood-glam look about it. Meggie squinted thoughtfully as the other women moved toward Rose, touching the fabric, exclaiming and clapping their hands, turning her around for another look at the back.

Rose looked over their heads, meeting Meggie's gaze. She looked unsure. 'What do *you* think Megs?' They all turned to Meggie. She stood, walked toward Rose, almost in tears. Rose had never called her Megs before, always Meggie. A wave of affection for her soon-to-be-sister-in-law washed over her and she touched Rose's face. 'Spectacular. Original. Stunning.' She was rewarded by a happy smile from Rose. 'This dress. It's perfect for you. It's totally old Hollywood glam. Seriously, movie star Rita Hayworth could have worn this to the Oscars. Wherever did you find it? The material, the style. It's nothing short of superb.'

Rose grinned at Debbie. 'The vintage bridal store in Sydney where we found Debbie's dress. I loved what Debbie wore to her wedding.' She turned to Meggie. 'It was a nineteen fifties tea-length gown. But when I tried them on they didn't suit. I'm too tall, the skirts too full. So the stylist took me into the nineteen forties room, where everything was satin and slinky. I tried on about ten, but this one, the colour I think, stood out for me.' She giggled. 'And the back is a little bit sexy. I feel like a siren or a sex goddess, in this dress.' She thrust her chest out a bit. 'It's even got a built-in pointy brassiere.' She looked again at Meggie. 'I was thinking Katherine Hepburn may have worn something like this, but Rita Hayworth is better, she had auburn hair too!' She laughed, pointing to her own thick hair, which she had pulled into a loose bun at her neck.

Meggie looked at Debbie, thick blonde hair and a few inches shorter than Rose. 'Stand next to Rose for a moment please Deb.' Debbie moved to Rose's side, they giggled at each other. Meggie moved between Harriet and Melanie, linking her arms through theirs, facing Rose and Debbie. 'I'm thinking navy blue for Deb, similar sweetheart neckline in front but not the low back, then pinched in at the waist like Rose's dress, but ending in a neat pencil skirt mid-calf. Nineteen forties peep-toe-pumps in navy. What do you think?'

'Yes!' They all spoke at once and Rose spun around happily. 'I can see that. I can really see that. I love it Meggie.' She turned around. 'I'd better get out of this dress now. I'm dying for a glass of champagne.'

'Wait.' Meggie was scrolling through her phone. 'Do you have any fixed ideas about what Angus should wear? And Jamie, as his best man?'

Rose nodded. 'Black tie, I thought.'

'Perfect. Black tie it is. We've moved from simple elegance to something a little more glam, but I can work with that.' Meggie and the others agreed, all chatting at once.

Rose took a step back, and spun in a full circle, until she was facing them again. She was radiant. 'I'm getting married girls, I'm really getting married!' They cheered. 'Megs, can you come and help me get out of this please, I'm terrified I'll step on the hem and tear it.'

Meggie followed Rose to her room. She gently undid the zip hidden in the side of the dress, then lifted it over her head. Rose turned to get dressed while Meggie carefully returned the gown to the clothing bag. Meggie lay the clothing bag across the bed and was about to leave, but Rose was dressed now. She stepped forward and hugged Meggie, saying quietly in her ear. 'I've always wanted a sister.'

Tears sprang to Meggie's eyes, her face beside Rose's. 'Me too, Rose, me too.' They stepped back, gazing happily at each other. Then Rose picked up the dress in its protective bag and thrust it at Meggie. 'Hang it in your room, I don't want Angus to have the slightest idea.' Meggie touched her hand gently and took the dress.

14

Two weeks in and Max had settled into a routine, with work and Tommy. He was handling most of the clinic work now, with Angus spending more time on his own farm. They were doing the large animal work together, but not every afternoon, so Max sat with Melanie some days to learn the patient filing system and accounts. He'd picked Tommy and Tiffany up from school several times, giving Melanie a chance to do her shopping and run errands. It was working well, and the kids were great. He wasn't comfortable taking Tiffany to the flat, it was so small, so he generally let them help him in the animal hospital and took them to Debbie's café for afternoon tea.

The highlight of Tommy's week was going home on the bus with Billie and Tiffany, where Drum Murray gave him a riding lesson. Max had driven out after work with Melanie to pick them up and had been impressed at how confident Tommy was on the part-Arab pony called Chippy. Billie was on a larger horse called Lady, and Max knew in an instant she'd been riding for years. Tiffany said she usually rode Chippy, but she seemed happy to let Tommy have a turn.

'I've been at Rose and Angus's this afternoon, you know, wedding dress stuff.' Melanie chatted as they drove out to the Murray farm. Max nodded. That's why he'd been hired. The wedding was only a few weeks away, then Angus and Rose would be away for their honeymoon. 'Rose would like you and Tommy to go out to their place for dinner on Saturday night. It'll be us, you met my husband Ben the other day, Drum, Harriet and Billie, and Debbie from the café with her husband Jamie and their baby boy. And Rose and Angus of course, and I think you met Meggie, Angus's sister the other day too.' He was about to decline, it sounded like a group of long-time friends to him. But Melanie continued, 'Angus will also ask you, but Rose wanted you to know the invitation is really from her. She's keen for you and Tommy to be there.'

'Alright.' He smiled at Melanie, they were pulling up at Drum's horse yards. 'It would be rude to say no, wouldn't it?'

'You betcha.' Melanie stepped out, put her arm around Tiffany who had walked across to the car. Max strolled to the fence with them. Drum was standing in the centre of the round yard, supervising Tommy on a grey pony. Tommy was wearing a hard hat and the biggest grin. He had the reins firmly in his hands and Max knew he would have waved if he could. Billie, on tip toes, was unsaddling her horse by the fence. Tiffany followed Billie into the stables, carrying the saddle blanket for her.

'Ride over to the fence Tommy, say hi to your dad.' Drum called out from the centre of yards. Tommy turned the horse, touched his heels to its side, and trotted over to where Max stood, rising correctly in the saddle as he did. Drum strolled across too, putting one foot on the bottom rail, he patted the horse on the shoulder. 'He's a natural Max. Took to it straight away. Cowboy potential.'

Max chuckled, looking from Tommy's happy face to Drum. 'Thank you Drum. Really. Very good of you.'

'It's what we do. He's a good kid.' He turned to Tommy. 'Ride over to the gate, Billie will help you unsaddle Chippy. Then I'd like you to brush him down and give him some feed.'

'Yes Mr Murray.' Tommy turned the horse and trotted to the gate, where Billie and Tiffany had reappeared.

'Angus tells me you've lightened the load considerably. He said he's barely been into the clinic this week.' Drum chuckled as he spoke, and Max warmed to him.

'It's a good business, it's easy to work somewhere that's clean and organised.' He glanced at Melanie beside him, 'although I suspect the organised part is all Melanie.'

She laughed. 'You do all right Max Masters.'

* * *

FRIDAY AFTERNOON MELANIE PICKED TOMMY UP WITH TIFFANY, SHE WAS taking them to the library after school, then home for afternoon tea. Tommy was keen to see where Tiffany lived, they had a small farm too and some new kittens.

Max stepped out of the clinic, locking the door. Melanie wouldn't drop Tommy back for another hour, so he thought he'd pick up something from the shops for dinner. He'd bought an air fryer for the flat, so chops and chips in it, with carrots and peas done in the microwave. The fridge was tiny, so he only bought what they needed every couple of days.

With time up his sleeve, Max crossed the road, the supermarket was next to the Post Office, with a lane between them. Movement in the lane caught his eye. Meggie Hamilton was dragging a large suitcase out of the back of an old Landrover, and as he watched she tripped and fell, with the suitcase squarely on top of her.

He rushed to help her, lifting the suitcase off, holding his hand out to pull her up. He noticed how pretty she was when she blushed. 'Thanks Max. Just as well you saw me, I might have been stuck under there for days, weeks even.' She laughed, brushing herself off ruefully. Max caught his breath. She was gorgeous. Tall, thick dark hair and right now, dancing brown eyes.

He laughed with her. 'All part of the service, Ms Hamilton, Ma'am.' Doffing an imaginary hat. He looked around. 'Where are you taking this beast?' He saw another suitcase in the back of the car, and a couple of boxes.

'Upstairs. To the flat over the post office. My mum and step-father arrive on Sunday, and I've rented the flat, you know, to make more room at the homestead.' She pointed toward the staircase behind the lovely old sandstone building. 'There are back stairs, thought it might be easier than taking everything through the front entrance.'

'I'll carry these up for you.' He could see she was about to decline, obviously an independent woman, but she looked up at the stairs, then at the two suitcases.

'Okay, that's brilliant, thanks.' She picked up one of the boxes from the back seat and he followed her up the stairs with the first suitcase. She unlocked the door and stepped in, holding it open so he could bring the suitcase through. His shoulder touched hers as he entered, and he could smell her perfume, which confused him for a moment.

'Um, Max?' He turned when she spoke. She pointed to the suitcase, her smile broad. 'it's got wheels, I can take it from here.'

'Of course.' He set it down, then almost ran back down the stairs, hauling the second case out of the vehicle. She followed him down, picked up the other box, and walked up the stairs in front of him again. He took his time, watching her shapely bottom, encased in denim cut-offs, as she took each stair. Long legs, nice bum, small waist. She had turned before he reached the top. Her look was questioning. She'd caught him looking at her backside. Damn. She'd know by now that he was widowed.

He placed the case on its wheels as he walked through the door, pushing it a few feet into the room.

'Thanks Max, appreciate that.' She looked at him, and he wondered if she was going to ask about his wife. 'Where's Tommy this afternoon?'

He let out a small breath. 'Melanie picked him up with Tiffany. He's gone to see some new kittens. Much more exciting than hanging with me.'

Laughing, she turned, pushing the second case further into what looked like a laundry room. 'Kittens. They'll do it every time.'

He stood awkwardly for a moment, knowing he should leave her to unpack. He was curious about the apartment. And about her, he admitted to himself. 'Any chance I could take the tour? I love these old buildings.'

'Um. Sure. Come in.' He followed her in, and she closed the back door, leading him through a large room to the front door.

'Let's start here. You come through the door to this fabulous big room. Kitchen down on the far wall. Lots of natural light.' He was fascinated, she lit up when she spoke about the history of the building, the changes that had been made to the apartment over the years. He followed her through to the bedrooms, they were enormous, and the bathroom was relatively modern.

Back in the centre of the living area he walked to the windows overlooking the main street. 'Right across the road from the clinic.' His smile was wide. 'If I'd seen it first I might have snapped it up.'

'Yes, Angus said the flat at the clinic is very small, not much more than a motel room really. How are you and Tommy coping?' She seemed genuinely interested, so he told her.

'It's great. It works for now, with Angus soon to be away, we need someone there if we have overnight patients. The kitchen isn't much, but I bought an air fryer, so we don't eat out every night.' He chuckled, 'I'm not a great cook, but I can manage a couple of chops and chips. And it's fine for breakfast and lunch.'

'But you said you would have taken this if you'd known. Are you looking to stay, after Angus gets back?' she prompted him.

'Well. Yes, I'd like to. I like the area and Tommy is enjoying school. We're meeting people. But Angus hasn't asked me to stay, and I don't want him to feel pressured.' He suddenly felt concerned. This is a conversation he should have with Angus, not his sister.

She nudged him with her shoulder, speaking quietly. 'I get it Max. He won't hear it from me. But honestly?' He nodded and she continued. 'I think Angus is hoping you'll want to stay, so keep doing what you do, it may work out exactly the way you want it to.'

He felt suddenly lighter. While it hadn't come from Angus himself, he didn't think Meggie would say it without reason. 'Are you staying here tonight Meggie, or will you wait until Sunday when your family arrives?'

He saw the happy look on her face. 'Oh, I'm staying here. I have bedding in those boxes and some kitchen things borrowed from Rose. The fridge is on, and I have a bottle of wine cooling. I'm going to make the bed, unpack some gear, then whip up something simple for dinner,' she leaned closer, 'like a vegemite sandwich, and toast my new home.'

'Sounds brilliant Meggie.' He took another look out the window, such a great position. 'And you, Meggie. Are you settling into the area or is this just short-term accommodation until the wedding?' Her face lit up when he asked, she intrigued him in a way he hadn't felt about a woman in a long time.

'I'm staying. I'm setting up a business here. Weddings and events, and maybe festivals and such.' She pointed across the road to Evans Real Estate, a few doors up from the Vet Clinic. 'Harriet has offered me office space, and we're planning to collaborate on some things.' She glanced at Max. 'Maybe it's a fresh start, here in Barrington, for both of us.'

Her words made him happy, he didn't want to think about the reason for that, not yet anyway. He glanced at his watch. 'Thanks for the tour, Melanie will be dropping Tommy back shortly, so I'd better head across the road.'

'Thank you. For the grunt work.' She cocked her head to one side, cheekily. Something about the way she said grunt sent a rush of blood to his groin. He turned toward the door, he needed to leave. Now. But as he reached the door, he turned back to her. She was right there, in front of him.

'I'm taking Tommy to the pub for a quick dinner, you know, Friday night special. You're welcome to join us.' He really hoped she'd say yes. 'Not as good as a vegemite sandwich, to be sure, but we could share a bottle of wine and celebrate your new home.' His earlier thoughts of chops in the air fryer deserted him.

He watched as she considered his question. 'Sure. Why not. I've heard some good things about Tommy, I'd love to meet him.' He knew she was teasing him, knew too that she felt something, a connection between them.

'Six o'clock then. Want us to pick you up?'

'Ha, ha, the pub is four doors that way. Thank you, but I'll meet you there at six.' She stepped back, then added, 'don't you lads stand me up now.'

He threw back his head and laughed. 'Not a chance, Meggie, not a chance.'

15

Meggie leant against the door, hearing him clatter down the stairs two at a time. What was she thinking? He's widowed, with a young son. She should cool her jets. But she'd flirted, a little. Maybe to see if she could, you know, get a reaction from him. Had he flirted back? She thought so, but maybe he was being nice because he wants it to work out at the clinic with Angus.

She walked to the window, watched him cross the street. He didn't go through the front of the clinic but walked down the side lane to the back. She hadn't met Tommy, but Melanie said he was lovely, and friends with her daughter Tiffany and Harriet's … um, what is Billie to Harri? Step-daughter? Not quite, they're not married. But she could hear Harri's love for Billie when she spoke of her. Step-daughter works.

Max was a few years older than her, closer to forty than thirty. She'd been with an older man before, back in Napa. It hadn't worked out. She had wasted two years, ruined her career and alienated some very good work friends. And she'd lost something she may never have again. A small sob escaped her. She stepped back. Yes, she'd have dinner with him and Tommy. Get to know them, they'd be part of the fabric of her community if they stayed, but she shouldn't get involved. Wouldn't get involved.

Walking quickly to the main bedroom, she made up the bed, then unpacked one of the suitcases. She'd have a quick shower and change. She hung some dresses in the wardrobe, and noticed how most of them were short, to show her legs to best advantage, or fitted to show off her figure. She thought for a moment about Rose's wedding dress. A similar height and shape to herself, the style was something that Meggie had once dreamed of. She'd organised so many weddings, seen so many brides, but Rose in that dress, not just glamorous, but simply elegant.

It was almost six and she was still trying to decide what to wear. In the end she took a shapeless shift from its hanger. It was plain cream, sleeveless and almost reached her knees, with a row of sunflowers around the hem. Flat sandals, a touch of mascara and lip-gloss, hair in a high messy bun and she was ready. She picked up her small cross-over bag and walked down the main stairs to the street.

It was five past six when she stepped into the air-conditioned dining room at the pub. Max waved to her from a booth to one side. She waved back and walked over. He stood. Then she saw Tommy. A miniature version of his father, his hair freshly washed and brushed to one side. He stood and waited beside his dad. She was delighted.

'Hi Meggie, this is Tommy.'

Tommy held his hand out, saying, 'Hello Meggie,' as he did. She took his hand, he shook hers with a firm little grip.

'Hello Tommy, nice to meet you too. Hi Max.'

Tommy sat down and slid over, Max moved in beside him, offering Meggie the seat on the other side of the table, then handed her the wine list. 'You will know the wines better than I.' His fingers brushed hers as she took it, making her catch her breath for a moment. She wondered if he felt something too, but he didn't let on.

'It's a warm night, and I don't get too concerned about matching my wine to my meal, so I think a Sauvignon Blanc works best.' She looked up at him. 'If that suits you?'

'Excellent. I'll go to the bar while you have a look at the menu.' He leaned toward his son. 'Tommy can't decide between the lamb chops and the chicken schnitzel.'

As Max walked to the bar she glanced at the menu, then turned to Tommy. 'Have you tried both meals before?'

He nodded vigorously. 'Yup. We've eaten here eight times in two weeks, and I've tried almost everything. But they have a specials board,' he pointed to a blackboard leaning against the wall, 'and they have duck spring rolls as an entrée. I think I'll order that tonight, you know, as my main course.'

Great kid. Articulate too. She raised an eyebrow at him. 'Do you want to get the duck spring rolls as an entrée, and share them with me, then we can get a main course each too?'

His expression became serious, as he considered this. Max was returning to the table with the drinks. 'Yes please!' He reached for the glass of orange juice Max passed across, then looked over at Meggie. 'Thank you.'

Max poured the wine, offering a glass to Meggie. She lifted it to her nose, breathing in the crisp citrus tones. Max raised his glass, clinked with Tommy and then Meggie. 'What is my son thanking you for, Meggie Hamilton?' She chuckled at his use of her full name, his voice was deep, rich with emotion. She could clearly see his devotion for Tommy. It made him more attractive to her, but she shook her head slightly, telling herself to get that thought out of her mind.

'No? You don't want to tell me?' Now his words were full of laughter. Tommy nudged his father. 'I'm ordering the duck spring rolls.' Max was about to speak, but Tommy continued. 'Meggie said she'd share the entrée with me, then I'll have the kids chicken schnitty.'

'Oh, did she?' he picked up the menu Tommy handed him. 'And what would you like for main course Meggie?' He looked over the menu, meeting her eyes.

'The Caesar Salad, with chicken. But I'll get it, you've already bought the drinks.'

Max looked at his son for a moment. Tommy cleared his throat, then spoke quite seriously to Meggie. 'Masters men don't let girls pay for their own dinner.' She almost laughed.

'Really? Well in that case, thank you very much, er Masters men.'

Tommy pulled his glass closer, taking a big sip. Max slid out of the booth. 'I'll order.' She could see he was proud of his boy, was raising him to have manners. She liked that. She watched him stride back to the bar. He wore blue jeans and loafers and an open neck shirt. He looked good in those jeans from behind, and she had been trying not to stare at the size of his shoulders, and arms since she sat down. He was a giant, even taller than Angus and a fraction broader.

Focus on Tommy, she told herself. 'How was school today Tommy?'

'Good thank you.' He sipped his drink. She tried again. 'What was the best part of your day?' Tommy thought for a moment, then his face split into a broad grin. 'Playing with Tiffany's kittens. I'm going to be a Vet too when I grow up. I'll be Dad's partner.'

'Will you? That's an excellent plan.' She watched Max return. 'And do you need to do a lot of study to be a Vet?'

'Years and years. School, then uni. I'm good at maths and science, and Vet's need that.' His little face was animated. She was entranced. Max was turned slightly toward his son. He's heard this before, she was sure, but he was taking a keen interest in the boy's words. 'And I'm going to specialise in equine health.' He leaned toward Meggie. 'That's horses.'

'It's great you know what you want to do Tommy. That will keep you motivated along the way.'

Max topped Meggie's glass up. 'And you Meggie. Did you always want to go into event management?'

'I studied hotel management and communications at Uni. I really wanted to travel. And I'm very organised. I worked in hotels in Melbourne and Sydney, then London for a while. Then four years in California in the Napa Valley.'

He actively listened as she spoke. She had his full attention. 'And now, here in Barrington. It will be quieter for you, but I totally understand wanting to start your own business, be the master of your destiny. You'll make it work, I'm sure.' She was warmed by his praise, and wanted to continue the conversation, but realised it left Tommy out.

'Tell me more about the horses you like Tommy? Have you ridden very much?' He told her, in great detail, about his visit to Billie's farm and his ride on Chippy. But not just the ride, the grooming, saddling, and feeding the horses too. She loved the expressions on his face as he described his experience, and at one point Max hastily moved the half-full glass of orange juice away from his hands, as he was demonstrating how he had lifted the saddle off his horse. She found herself laughing, asking for more details. Max said very little, and she had almost forgotten his presence, until he nudged Tommy, saying, 'your entrée is here.'

While they ate Max spoke a little bit about his first two weeks in the area and told some entertaining anecdotes about some of his patients, including a very angry blue-tongue lizard. The entree came with three spring rolls, so Tommy offered a second one to Meggie. She declined, saying she wouldn't eat her main course. He then offered it to his dad. Max ruffled his hair. 'You eat it son, I've got a steak coming.'

By seven thirty they'd finished the wine, and dinner, and Tommy was starting to yawn, but covered his mouth, saying excuse me, each time.

Meggie covered her own mouth, as if yawning. 'It's been lovely, Masters men, but I need to get my beauty sleep.' They all slid out of the booth, Max and Tommy waiting for her to walk ahead of them. They strolled with her to the downstairs entrance to her flat, waiting while she unlocked the door.

'Goodnight, thank you for dinner.'

'Goodnight Meggie.' Tommy and Max spoke at the same time, then looked at each other and laughed.

'I think we're catching up again tomorrow, at Angus and Rose's house, so I'll see you there.' Meggie stepped inside.

'Bye, see you tomorrow!' This was from Tommy.

She ran quickly up the stairs, opened her front door, then dashed to the window, pulling the heavy drapes to one side. Max had his arm around Tommy's shoulders, they were almost to the other side of the street, Tommy was speaking to his father, his young face looking earnestly up at him. They reached the entrance to the side lane and Max stopped, looked up to her window. She was about to step back, but he raised his hand in a wave. She waved back, then quickly pulled the curtains closed.

16

T ommy was in bed five minutes after they got home, so Max relaxed on the sofa in semi-darkness with a cold beer and thought about the last two weeks, how quickly they had settled in at Barrington. But his mind drifted, from Barrington, to the Vet practice, to Angus, hoping Meggie was right and there was a real possibility they could stay. Maybe he could buy into the practice if Angus was interested. He'd already sold his share of the Newcastle clinic, three of his former partners had been great, made it easy for him. Not the fourth partner though. He shook his head. Don't go down that path, not tonight.

His mind rattled around for a few minutes, putting away bad memories. He chuckled, it was a game he played with himself, picturing his mind opening a new file to store new memories, good memories, locking the old ones in the bottom drawer of a virtual filing cabinet. He was almost ready to toss away the key to that drawer. It was something the therapist had suggested to Tommy, but Max thought he'd benefited more.

So now he had a bright shiny new drawer, with Meggie's name on the front. Images of her chatting with Tommy, laughing at something he said. Her long legs in cut off shorts, walking up the stairs ahead of him; laughing as he lifted the suitcase and helped her off the ground; waving from the upstairs window when he looked back. He finished his beer, placing the empty bottle in the bin. He looked at Tommy, asleep in the bed. When it first happened, the kid wouldn't sleep until Max lay down with him, would curl up against him, needing to know his dad was right there. But now, here, he was sprawled in the bed, one foot sticking out beneath the covers, sleeping soundly. As he should, Max thought, as he should.

He picked up his phone, checked for messages. Nothing. He sent one anyway.

We're loving it here, would be great to have you visit. His finger hovered over the buttons. *Love you.* XX

No reply. He didn't really expect one, but he remained hopeful.

* * *

MAX WONDERED IF HE SHOULD TAKE SOMETHING TO THE BARBECUE. HE'D asked Angus the day before, and he'd said, 'Nah, mate, it's just a steak on the barbie, sausages for the kids. The girls will have salads organised.' He wondered if he should take a bottle of wine, and definitely some beer, although he wouldn't drink much himself, he needed to drive home.

He strolled down to the café with Tommy. They'd been up early and taken a football to the park, where they'd spent a happy couple of hours kicking it around before it got too hot. When Tommy said he wanted to stop, needing a cold drink, Max happily obliged.

The café was busy, so they found a seat outside. Tommy waited there while Max walked in to order.

'Hey Max, how are you?' Debbie waved at him from the coffee machine.

'Great, thanks. You're busy today. Or is this the usual summer weekend?' He gestured to the interior of the café, humming with chatter.

'It's busier than usual, but with all the rain recently the rivers are up and there's a lot of people in town for the outdoor stuff. You know, kayaking, bushwalking to the falls.' She passed two coffees to a younger member of staff, then stepped over to the cash register. 'What would the Masters men like today?'

Max chuckled. Tommy had started it, but it was catching on. 'Tommy wants his favourite milkshake, and a big brownie.' He leaned forward. 'He emphasised big. And I'll have an Americano and apple slice please.'

'We can do that. I've got an oversize brownie out in the kitchen, two of them stuck together when Cathy baked earlier. I'll send it out.' Debbie beamed, taking his payment.

'Careful, you might set a precedent and he'll want double size every time.' Max strolled back to the table, a couple of clients said hello as he did. That hardly ever happened in Newcastle. As he sat, the phone in his pocket vibrated. It was a text. Tommy leaned closer to see it, but Max gave him a look and he sat back.

Hey Max, it's Rose. Don't bring anything tonight. But come early, around 4pm, and Tommy can visit my horses.

Nice. He liked Rose, had only met her a couple of times, but she was friendly and direct. He shook his head at Tommy. 'It's Rose. Wants us to come early to visit her horses. What do you think?'

'Answer her Dad! Tell her yes please!' Tommy fist-pumped the air.

Thanks Rose. You've made Tommy's day! See you at 4. Max.

But he wouldn't go empty-handed. He looked at Tommy. 'When we finish here, let's buy the biggest box of chocolates we can, to take there today. As a thank you.'

'Okay.' Tommy turned his attention back to the double brownie. He had chocolate on his hands and around his mouth, but he was happy, so Max quietly sipped his coffee and watched his boy enjoy himself.

17

———————

Putting the freshly made pasta salad in the fridge, Meggie turned and stretched. It was almost four and she needed to quickly change for the barbecue. Most were arriving at five, but Max was coming early with Tommy, to see the horses. Thinking about Max made her draw a quick breath, but she remonstrated with herself. *He's grieving the loss of his wife and has responsibilities while I, well, I am not ready to risk my heart again.*

She dashed to the guest room to change into the pale blue gingham shift dress she'd brought, falling almost to the knee. It was sleeveless, showing her toned, tanned shoulders to advantage. She teamed it with flat sandals, brushed her hair and applied lip gloss and mascara. Stepping back, she looked at herself in the mirror. Feminine yet casual, she didn't want to overdo it, she was sure Rose, and the others would be similarly dressed. At the last minute she lifted her hair into a messy bun on top of her head.

Voices at the front door alerted her to Max and Tommy's arrival. She walked down the hallway, joining Angus, and Rose with Charlie on her hip. Max watched her approach, his look seemed intense for a moment, then he smiled, his eyes crinkling at the corners. Rose was holding a giant box of Belgian chocolates and Angus a bottle of wine, gifts from their guests, she thought.

Tommy grinned at her, excitement evident on his face. 'Hello Meggie. The Masters men have arrived!'

Gorgeous kid. She laughed. 'I can see that Tommy Masters.' Turning to Max, she added, 'And Max.'

'Nice to see you Meggie.' Then he focussed on Angus and Rose, 'what a beautiful home you have. Late 1800's?'

Meggie watched Rose nod happily. 'It is. My great-grandfather built it. I'll give you the tour if you like.'

Max was keen, but looked down at Tommy, who had tugged on his hand. 'Perhaps we can tour the horses first, Tommy's been bursting with excitement all day.'

Rose threw her head back and laughed. 'Of course.' She looked at Tommy. 'You have your priorities right, Tommy. Horses always come first.'

Turning to Meggie, Rose moved Charlie from one hip to the other. 'Do you think you could watch Charlie while we go to the stables Megs?' Meggie had planned to walk down with them, but she immediately held out her arms for Charlie, who threw himself into them, saying 'Megs. Megs play now.'

Angus nudged her as he walked by, setting the chocolates and wine on the hall stand. Meggie suspected he had seen the look Max had given her. He would tease her later but was unlikely to say anything to embarrass his guest. She jiggled Charlie in her arms, making him giggle, then walked through to the living area where he had his blocks and farm animals. By the time she set him down on the floor, the front door had closed.

Keeping an eye on Charlie, now absorbed in a game involving horses, cows and a seemingly rogue giraffe, Meggie took the chocolates and wine to the kitchen. It was an excellent bottle of Australian red, from Tyrrells Wines in the Hunter region. She really should do a trip across there after the wedding, it was only a couple of hours away.

Back with Charlie, she lay on the floor on her tummy, loading animals in his toy truck, before driving them across his legs to the other side of the mat. He chortled each time, shouting, 'Again Megs, do it again!' She was laughing with him, enjoying the game, and didn't hear the others return. Charlie yelled, 'Daddee,' and ran as fast as his chubby legs would allow, across the room to Angus, standing shoulder to shoulder with Max, who was studying her intently. Flushed, Meggie got up from the floor as elegantly, and modestly, as she could, but her hair had come out of its bun during the game, and she knew she looked a red hot mess.

Mumbling something about, 'just fix my hair,' she dashed past, now seeing more people arriving through the open front door.

18

———————

Max turned to say hello to Ben, Melanie, Drum, Harriet, Tiffany and Billie who had arrived together in Drum's large Range Rover.

'Can we play outside please Rose?' This was Billie, dressed in shorts, tee and canvas shoes, her hair in a braid down her back. Tiffany was almost identically dressed and when Rose said yes, of course, they shot across the room and out through cedar and glass doors to the back veranda. Tommy looked bemused and remained by Max's side, but within seconds Billie re-opened the door. 'Come on Tommy, you have to see the garden out here, we're going to play cricket.' Tommy looked at Max for permission. He ruffled his son's hair and said, 'Masters men never keep the ladies waiting.' Tommy walked quickly to the door, where Billie grabbed his hand and almost dragged him outside, closing the door after him.

The adults looked at each other and laughed. Melanie nudged Max, 'he fits in well with those two. Billie is a bit of a tomboy and Tiffany loves to play sport.' Max agreed. He had wondered if he'd feel a bit uncomfortable, all these people had known each other a long time, some of them their whole lives, but the conversation was easy. Debbie and husband Jamie arrived then, their young son Warwick only just walking. He watched as Meggie and Debbie set Warwick up with Charlie on the mat with toy farm animals, then he accepted a beer from Angus and joined the men by the barbecue on the veranda. He could see the kids had set up a cricket pitch on the green lawn, and with the sun starting to go down the day had cooled.

The women joined them on the veranda, where a large table had been set at one end, with comfortable wicker chairs. Debbie and Rose moved Charlie and Warwick out to the lawn with some of their toys. Max turned around, he wanted to talk with Meggie some more, but she had disappeared inside. He turned back, to find himself face to face with Angus. He gave him a look, not unfriendly, but cautious. Max nodded to Angus, acknowledging the look, then answered a question from Jamie. Internally he noted he should be careful with Meggie. Angus was protective of his sister. But she returned from inside with two plates of cheese and crackers, setting one down on the table with the women and offered the other to the men, as she stood with them for a moment. He watched as she chatted easily among them. Smart and confident, she joined a conversation about economic development in the region, the conversation becoming animated. She fascinated him.

Harriet called out from the table, 'come on blokes. Join us over here. 'It's sooo Aussie for the men and women to segregate at barbecues, but not here, hey Rose?' The women laughed, rearranging themselves at the table to make room for the men. Max was last there and sat at the end. Meggie pulled up a chair beside him. Angus looked at her, one eyebrow raised. He watched Meggie lift her chin slightly. 'I need to be close to the kitchen.' Then she turned to add a comment to the conversation Harriet and Debbie were having about tourism.

'Dad! We need a fieldsman, and more batters.' Billie was standing at the bottom of the steps, hands on hips. Tommy and Tiffany were at each end of the pitch, bats in hands. Drum threw up his hands, looking at the other adults. 'We've been called up to play.' He pushed his chair back and stood, calling to his daughter. 'Okay Billie, pick teams, we've still got a half hour before it's too dark to play.'

Billie and Tiffany were captains. Max was pleased to see Tommy was Billie's first pick. Drum, Harriet, Max and Meggie joined her team, while Tiffany had Ben, Angus, Jamie, Rose and Melanie. Debbie laughed, saying she'd feed Warwick and Charlie their dinner, 'it's a tough job but someone has to do it.' Rose skipped past her to the lawn, giggling over her shoulder, 'good luck with that Debbie, I'm here if you need backup.'

The game was hilarious, Max hadn't laughed so much in ages. Tommy and Billie bowled to Tiffany and Melanie, with Jamie catching Melanie out after only two runs. She excused herself to help Debbie with the little ones, so Ben stepped in, to bat. At one point Max was running backwards to catch a ball and almost landed on Rose. They high-fived, brushing themselves off, before re-joining the game. It was a short over, and their team went to bat. Tommy and Billie started, making more than a dozen runs before Angus caught Tommy out. They cheered from the sidelines and by the time it got so dark they were having trouble finding the ball Meggie hit out of bounds. They gave the game up then, all collapsing on the grass or the veranda steps, seeking cold drinks.

Melanie and Debbie returned, announcing the little ones were asleep, and it was time to light the barbecue. The game had broken the ice, if there had been any to begin with, and the conversation flowed. Max had expected the three children to eat first, or at least at their own table, but was delighted when he counted the chairs around the big table, realising they were not just included, but welcomed.

Meggie asked Tommy about his visit to see Rose's horses. He was wide-eyed and serious, explaining he had patted Cotton and Calico and even said hello to the old stallion, Topper.

Angus looked across at Max. 'You may have to consider investing in some horseflesh, Max, if you stay on here.' It was the first time he'd alluded to Max staying beyond the three month contract and his heart beat a little faster with the possibility.

Ben laughed. 'I'd like to see how you and Tommy manage in the flat behind the clinic with a horse as well.'

Meggie turned to him, an overly innocent expression on her face. 'Oh Max if you're going to get a horse you'll need a dog too.' Max suddenly saw the look on Tommy's face, excitement and awe, and thought he'd better temper the conversation before his son burst.

'They're teasing us a bit Tommy. But if we stay, then we'll look for a bigger place, with room for animals.' Tommy's excitement was obvious.

'Scuse me Angus.' Tommy was looking across the table, and suddenly all chatter stopped. Max wasn't sure what his boy was going to say, and he felt his heart begin to pound. 'My Dad is a really, really good Vet.' He nodded solemnly as he spoke. 'So you'll want him to stay. Us. You'll want us to stay. I'll help before and after school too, you'll see, you won't want us to leave.' Max closed his eyes for a moment, what should he say? He didn't want to upset Tommy and he didn't want to put Angus on the spot like that.

'Well Tommy,' Angus began. 'It's like this. I can already see that your dad is a really, really good Vet and I think we work well together. I wasn't one hundred percent sure, but since you've been helping with the patients in our animal hospital, I'm convinced that you both should join the practice permanently.' Tommy clapped his hands, then pushed his chair back, rushed around to Angus and threw his arms around him. Max was shocked and hadn't a clue what to do or say. He looked from Rose to Meggie, saw their happy smiles, and back to Angus. Over Tommy's head, Angus added, 'And we've already got a succession plan, Tommy here is going to be a Vet too.' He laughed loudly, giving Tommy a hug. 'We've no idea about Charlie's aspirations however.'

Suddenly everyone was laughing and talking at once, with Angus reaching across the table to shake Max's hand. More quietly he said, 'We'll talk Max, next week. But I mean it. I want you to stay.' Max could only mouth 'Yes and thank you.' Tommy returned to Max's side grinning broadly as everyone congratulated them and shook their hands. Max felt a lump of emotion in his throat and was relieved when Tommy asked to go to the bathroom. He took the opportunity to leave the room with him, needing to draw a breath and compose himself, but he risked a quick glance at Meggie as he went. Her look was almost pensive, but she had a small smile playing around her mouth, and she cocked a cheeky eyebrow at him. He hugged Tommy to his side as they walked down the hall. 'So we're staying mate. We'll work it all out next week, but we're definitely staying.'

'I knew he'd want us Dad. Tiffany already told Billie that her Mum said we'd stay.' Max glanced at his son. It was a good move for them. He sent Tommy back to the table while he took a moment to splash his face with cold water. He wasn't sure exactly what steps would be next. Sell the house in Newcastle, look for a place big enough to keep a couple of horses, but close enough to town for the clinic. And move on from the past. Put Liliana's death behind them, start living again. He was ready. They both were. They'd been in a state of limbo for almost a year, but he was determined to change that. He pulled his phone out of his pocket, looked at the last message he'd sent. Still no response. He sighed. There were things he needed to put right, and it was time he was more proactive about it.

Back at the table, the plates had been cleared and the children were playing a noisy game in the garden of 'chasey in the dark.' Rose and Meggie brought out plates of pavlova with lashings of cream, and they sat back, discussing everything from local Council, Drum was a Councillor, to small business and the property market. Ben Evans and his father were leading real estate agents in the area and Ben mentioned he had a couple of listings Max might like to consider, when he was ready. The girls seemed to be having a separate conversation, now grouped together at one end of the table, about the wedding. It was only three weeks away and he overheard Rose and Debbie oohing and aahing over the theme and planning, which Meggie was apparently in charge of. He wondered about Meggie for a moment. She must be around thirty, absolutely beautiful and if the conversation was anything to go by, professional and hard working. He wondered why she wasn't married or partnered. Perhaps she had someone back in the United States, although she had told him the evening before that she wasn't going back. Perhaps she was harbouring a broken heart? He should tread carefully, she was Angus's sister. He'd hate to mess up the opportunity by making a social faux pas.

The children finished their game, Tommy now perched beside him, his eyes drooping. Max looked at his watch, almost ten, they'd better take their leave. Tiffany was on Ben's lap, her head against his shoulder. Billie still seemed wide awake, but she sat beside Harriet, holding her hand.

Jamie collected Warwick from little Charlie's room and speaking quietly, they all made their way out to the cars, saying goodnight and thank you and see you on Monday. As the others drove out, Max put Tommy in the car, then turned to Angus and Rose, who stood side by side, Angus with his arm around his fiancée's shoulders.

'Thank you Rose, for the invitation, for including us today.' He tried to keep the emotion from his voice. 'I'm sure Tommy will announce tomorrow that today was his Best. Day. Ever.' He tried to make light of it, but he was deeply touched by their faith in him, and their genuine welcome. Meggie had followed them out, now standing next to Rose. Max wasn't sure whether he should shake Rose's hand, but she stepped forward, drawing him into a tight embrace, saying simply, 'Welcome to Barrington Max. You and Tommy.' He hugged her quickly, then turned to Angus. He shook his hand, then found himself in a one-arm embrace. Angus released him. 'We'll nut out the details Max. I was planning to discuss this with you in the office next week, but I didn't want to wait when Tommy asked me the question. I hope you didn't mind.'

Max shook his head, 'I'd already decided I'd accept if you offered to make it permanent. We love it here. I'm glad you answered Tommy honestly. It really has been the best day, for both of us. Thank you.'

'Don't thank me mate, I'm grateful we found someone that's such a good fit for the practice, and for the area. Barrington suits you.' He took Rose's hand, glancing for a moment at his sister, still standing by Max's car. 'Goodnight, see you Monday.' They walked back to the house and Max turned to Meggie.

'It's been a lovely night Meggie, thank you.' He glanced into the car. Tommy was asleep in the front seat. He wondered if he should hug her, but she gave nothing away, so he looked at her for a moment. Long-limbed and beautiful, he wanted to kiss her.

'I have one complaint, though.' Her voice was low, a sultry tone he hadn't heard before.

'What's that Meggie?' He took half a step closer.

She leaned toward him, one hand touched his shoulder. He held her hand there with his, his heart pounding. She almost breathed the next words to him. 'I really wanted to spend all night talking to you.

Just you.' She turned her face up and he leaned down, brushing her lips with his.

'There will be talking Meggie Hamilton. You heard your brother. We're staying. You're staying. There will definitely be,' he kissed her again, lingering this time, the slightest pressure of his mouth on hers, 'talking.' He walked to the car and looked back. She stood there, one hand raised in farewell, the other, fingertips on her mouth.

19

———————

Angus and Rose were washing up in the kitchen when Meggie returned to the house. She rushed out to the veranda, to collect any dishes or glasses still out there, and if she was honest, to feel the cool air on her face.

'Meggie. We've got it all. Come inside.' Rose stood at the door, looking at her fondly. She took Meggie's hand and led her back to the kitchen.

Angus had his back against the kitchen bench, his arms folded. 'You're a grown woman Megs and it's not for us to interfere. We can see there's a connection between you and Max, and we like him. And Tommy. I'm offering Max the opportunity to buy into the practice, so once he does, he'll be staying. But we all know he's been through something, he's got baggage. So, take it slowly, be friends first.'

While she knew he'd say something, she was still annoyed. He had no idea what she'd dealt with by herself in the last couple of years, she didn't need his advice. Or approval. 'I've been making my own decisions for a long time Gus.' She raised her chin. 'Not all of them good ones, but that's life, isn't it? I'm aware of Max's position with your business and I promise I won't do anything to jeopardise that. And you're right, there is a spark between us. But we have to work out what that means for us. He's older than you Gus, so don't underestimate either of us.' Her chin was high, eyes flashing.

Angus looked at her for a moment, then opened his arms. 'Megs.' It was quietly said, and she found herself in his arms, sobbing. He was rubbing her back. After a few minutes, she stopped crying, drew back and reached for a tissue, blowing her nose loudly.

'Ha, my delicate sister!' Angus laughed. 'You always did blow your nose like a honking goose.' She laughed with him through her tears, playfully hitting him on the shoulder.

'But Megs, is there anything you want to share? Rose already said she thought you'd had some trauma in Napa. Do you want to tell us? But no pressure.' Angus glanced at Rose, who'd been hovering nearby. She hugged Meggie. 'We love you Megs. Both of us. We want you to be happy. But if there's something holding you back, we're here. No judgement, just love.'

Tears sprang to her eyes again. 'Yes. Yes I would like to tell you. I've been stupid, I've made mistakes. I've hurt others, and myself.' She looked at them both. 'More than you can imagine.'

They hugged her between them, and she let out a deep sigh. She looked at her watch. 'It's almost eleven, you must be exhausted. Yes, I will tell you what happened in Napa, but not tonight. I'll think about it over the next few days, and we'll talk.' She paused. 'Although this isn't something I want to share with Mum, and she'll be here tomorrow.' She kissed Angus on the cheek, hugged Rose again, and picked up her tote bag. 'But I feel better having said I'll share, I wasn't sure if I ever would. Thank you both.' Meggie walked to the door, looked back. 'I love you too. Both of you. And Charlie. So much.' Her voice broke as she spoke, and she ran to her car.

MEGGIE MADE SURE SHE WAS AT THE HOMESTEAD BEFORE HER MUM AND step-father, Helen and Barry arrived for lunch, helping Rose with last minute details. She hadn't met Barry and liked him straight away. He had grown children and grandchildren of his own, and she was impressed with how easily he wrangled little Charlie. They made a good team and Meggie discovered she was genuinely happy for her Mum to have found someone at this stage in her life.

Meggie surprised her mum when she told them she wasn't returning to Napa and looked for a moment like she wanted to argue with her about it. But Barry put his hand gently over Helen's at the table and gave her a look. She said no more, and Meggie was grateful. Angus and Rose supported Meggie too, saying how lovely it was to have her so close after years on different continents. Meggie could read her Mum well, relieved to see she was appeased. Thankfully, the antics of Charlie distracted her.

Meggie stayed for dinner, Helen asked about the wedding arrangements. Rose and Meggie gave her an overview and she was delighted by the simple elegance. Towards the end of the meal Helen asked about the wedding dress.

'What style have you chosen Rose? You're tall and slim, I'm sure any style would suit you.' Helen took a sip of her wine.

Meggie jumped in. 'The bride never reveals her dress and certainly not with the groom present.' Rose looked relieved, Angus curious. 'So no hints about the dress at all, but we *can* tell you, in keeping with the simple elegance of the event, Angus will be in black tie.'

Helen accepted this, clapping her hands. 'Ohh, formal, Angus will look so handsome in a dinner suit.' She turned to Barry, patting his knee. 'And so will you Baz, I brought your dinner suit and your good grey suit, just in case. You'll look very distinguished too.' She leaned across to Rose. 'I've brought two outfits, to make sure I don't clash with your bridal party. You can tell me which one, later.'

'You'll look gorgeous too Helen. Mother of the groom. But yes, Meggie and I can choose the one that will work best in the photos.' Rose gazed around the table happily.

Stifling a yawn, Meggie excused herself. 'We had a barbecue here last night Mum, it got a bit late. I'm off, but I'll meet you for coffee in town tomorrow, just let me know when you're coming in.'

Meggie drove back to her apartment, tired certainly and a bit drained from her mother's questions, but she admitted it was lovely to be in the same room with her family for the first time in years.

Upstairs in her flat, she glanced across the street to the clinic. It was Sunday, and closed, but she thought she may have caught a glimpse of Max and Tommy.

20

———————

Already hot at eight, Max looked at his son while they ate their breakfast cereal. 'Want to go down to the river today? We can swim, or even check out the kayak hire place, go for a paddle.'

'A paddle and a swim Dad. Tiffany said the river is running well and her dad, well, step-dad, took her and Billie down in a kayak last weekend.' He shovelled the last few mouthfuls of cereal in, rinsed his plate at the sink then announced he had to brush his teeth and he'd be ready to go.

Max took his time, tidying the tiny kitchen, finding their board shorts and packed drinks, snacks and sunscreen into a backpack. 'Okay, let's go. There's a kayak and a river waiting for us.'

Later that afternoon, they returned home hot and happy. Max had been impressed with how quickly Tommy mastered the kayak, and they'd ended with a swim and a picnic down near Rocky Crossing, where Drum had told them the best swimming spot was. Tommy sat on the sofa, after his shower, to finish some homework before school the next day and Max went through to the clinic hospital to check on their only patient, a border collie with a large litter of pups.

While he worked Max thought about the last few weeks. Moving to

Barrington had propelled him into a forward motion, after treading water for so long. Tommy was happy at school and Max knew the Vet practice would be a good long-term investment for him, and if Tommy fulfilled his current dream to become a Vet, for his son too.

They'd go back to Newcastle next weekend, speak to the real estate agent about listing the house. He'd originally thought he'd hang on to it, he'd definitely get a capital gain in the city, and rent in Barrington. But in his heart Max knew he was committed to stay, so he'd ask Ben Evans for a list of prospective properties and once the house sold, he'd be ready to buy. There was something else he needed to do when they went back, and he'd been putting it off for too long. Max sighed. That part of the trip might be hard. It would certainly raise some difficult memories and emotions.

Later that evening, he relaxed on the sofa. Tommy was already asleep, and Max flexed his shoulders, thinking he'd be a bit sore tomorrow from today's exercise. His mind turned to Meggie. Stunning woman, smart and independent too. She'd travelled, worked all over, but still had a bit of Aussie country girl about her. It was her attitude really. He saw it in Harriet and Debbie too, and Melanie to a lesser extent. His logical mind told him that Meggie may have romantic baggage, and he wondered what her story entailed. The connection between them, the attraction, was obvious, but was she looking for more than that? Was he even ready for that himself? He had some loose ends to fix, to feel whole again. And he should be careful, Angus is her brother and he'd hate to jeopardise the budding friendship and business relationship with a romantic mis-step. But her eyes, when he kissed her, as fleeting as it was, hinted at a deeper passion. If he was honest with himself, her untapped depth fascinated and terrified him, and he couldn't wait to kiss her again.

He took his empty glass to the kitchenette and looked around ruefully. How was he going to explore a relationship, living in a one room flat? He chuckled quietly. He had time. They had time. little steps Max, little steps.

✱ ✱ ✱

THE WEEK FLEW BY, THE CLINIC WAS BUSY WITH ANGUS MAINLY HANDLING the large animal work, although Max joined him some afternoons, taking Tommy with him after school. They'd had a business meeting on Tuesday afternoon, Melanie had taken Tommy and Tiffany to get an ice-cream after closing the clinic for the day.

The offer from Angus was better than Max had expected. Full partnership in the whole practice, with Max running the clinic full time. The price was little more than he had received for his quarter share in the city business.

'It's up to you Max, you can open the clinic longer hours if you think the work is there, although Melanie still wants to work school hours. But it's important you do some of the farm visits with me, and for me when I'm away, just as I need to keep my hand in with the clinic to an extent. We need to be able to take a break from the business.' Angus handed a bound document to Max.

'I've written a business plan, with Rose's help I might add.' Angus looked sheepish. 'If you look at the projections, next year I'd planned to have a part-time trainee Vet. There's a local, Freddie, who's studying in Newcastle at the moment, keen to do all the prac work here.'

Max studied the projections, looking back at the earnings for the last two years. 'It's do-able. When will he be in town next? Maybe we can invite him in for a chat?'

Angus laughed. 'Freddie's a girl! Frederica Campbell. She's worked here in the school holidays for a couple of years, but now she's in second year at Uni, she'll be even more useful. She's filled in out the front for Melanie too, when she's on leave.'

Laughing with him, Max looked again at the projections. 'There's a couple of new pieces of equipment we could use in the hospital.' He pointed to a column of figures. 'Even after we pay ourselves we'll have profit this financial year, with a contract signed between us within the next couple of weeks. What do you say to some capital expense before the end of the financial year? We'd get instant tax write offs, which would help offset the injection of my capital.'

'You're right Max. Let's get some reps out here to quote.' Angus frowned for a moment. 'When I first bought the practice the area was in drought, the whole town was struggling, but especially the farmers, and profits were low. In fact, a lot of clients paid me in-kind. It's how I started my beef herd. I'd like to quarantine some of your capital into an interest-bearing account, to call on if we run into hard times again.'

'Okay. Agreed. That's sensible.' Max looked at Angus. 'But mate, you need to pull some of my investment back into your personal account, you've put in the hard yards, running this by yourself with barely a break for the last few years.'

'Oh, I will. Honeymoon money.' Angus chortled. 'We're going to Scotland.'

Melanie returned with Tommy, congratulating Max on the partner-ship. She gave him a shy hug and he was warmed by her pleasure at him joining the firm. Tommy ran through to the hospital to check the pups, they were going home tomorrow. If Max had space, he would have offered to buy one from the owner for Tommy. There'd be time and other pups.

* * *

'How about a pub meal tonight Tommy? We can celebrate. Barrington Veterinary will have a new partner, officially, in about two weeks. But we agreed on everything today.' Max knew he was grin-ning madly, by the excited response from his son.

'Sure Dad. Tiff and I did our maths homework at the café already. I want a schnitty.' Tommy charged off to have a shower and change. Max picked up his phone, sending a text before he had time to consider if it was a good idea.

Barrington Vet and son request your company at pub for dinner.

A minute later his phoned beeped.

Barrington Weddings and Events accept. See you at 6.

New business name?

Yup. Registered today. Double celebration.

'Come on Tommy, don't use all the water, your old man needs a shower too!' Max's step was light as he walked to the bathroom door.

21

———————

His face lit up when she walked in, there was a bottle of champagne in an ice bucket on their table. Sliding into the seat opposite the Masters men, she winked at Tommy.

'There are three champagne glasses. Are you joining the celebration? Why wasn't I invited to your eighteenth birthday?' She laughed as Tommy giggled.

'I'm not eighteen, you're silly Meggie. I've got lemonade in mine.'

'Of course, I am silly.' She looked up, meeting Max's eyes. Her stomach fluttered at the hungry look he gave her. He was one hot Dad. Hot Vet. Hot Max.

Max handed her a glass, raising his, she saw his smile reached his eyes, making them crinkle at the corners. 'Here's to Barrington Veterinary and Barrington Weddings etc.'

'Barrington. Place of new beginnings.' She responded. Her eyes focused on his as they took their first sip. A shiver of excitement ran down her back. She saw him sip, swallow, then swallow again. Good. He felt it too.

Tommy had taken a gulp of his lemonade, but was studying the menu, completely unaware of the frisson of tension between the adults.

'I'll order if you know what you want.' Max pushed the menu toward Meggie.

'What are you having Tommy?'

'I'm having the schnitty. It's got pineapple topping today.' His enthusiasm was infectious.

'I wouldn't normally, but I am celebrating and, well, you know. Pineapple.' She winked at Max. 'I'll have what he's having.' Max grinned, and she lowered her eyes while she took another sip of champagne. Just as well Tommy was here. They had to speak in code and *keep themselves nice*, as her Mum often said.

The conversation flowed, though. Max asked her about her business start-up, and she asked him about plans for the practice. They included Tommy in the conversation, and he graphically re-told their kayaking story from the day before. Her heart melted when he said earnestly at the end of the telling, 'you need to come with us next time Meggie. They have kayaks for three and four people. You can sit at my end, I'll help you.'

Unexpected tears came to her eyes and Meggie hid behind her glass. 'I'd like that Tommy.' Was all she could manage.

At seven-thirty they strolled back to her place, Tommy walking a few steps ahead. Max brushed her hand with his and she caught his fingertips with her own, for a moment, then his enormous hand folded hers inside it and a small charge ran up her arm and lodged in her chest.

Tommy looked over his shoulder, his face a grimace. 'C'mon Dad, I need to go to the toilet.' He didn't notice their hands were clasped.

Max dug in his pocket, pulling out a set of keys. 'Here you go mate. Run ahead and open up, I'll just see Meggie safely inside.'

'Okay. Night Meggie!' They watched as Tommy crossed the road, looking both ways first, although there was no traffic at all.

Max guided her to the door of her building, leaning down, his mouth close to her ear, his breath hot. 'Open the door Megs, we've got about five minutes.'

The door opened inwards, they stepped in, and he closed it with his foot because his hands were already on each side of her face, his mouth on hers as he backed her against the wall of the entry. She opened her mouth, emitting a small moan, which only served to deepen his kiss. He had one long denim clad leg between hers and she involuntarily pushed her body against it. Her hands were around his neck, holding his mouth to hers as they kissed, hot and hard. He drew his head back for a moment, growled her name, then lowered it, kissing her again before nibbling her earlobe. She involuntarily thrust her hips towards his, moaning softly.

He let her go and stepped back, so suddenly she almost slid down the wall. 'Meggie. We need to go slow.' He looked at the back of the door. Opening his arms, he drew her to him again, hugging her gently. That was even sexier. 'There's Tommy. And we need to talk. There are things that should be said. Before. Before we do more of this.' He was breathing hard, she could see him struggling to keep himself in check.

She had trouble forming words. 'Talk. Yes. We should talk. I have stuff. We should definitely talk.' Taking a deep breath, she stepped back. 'Goodnight Max Masters. Thank you. For dinner.'

He opened the front door and stepped out, his eyes meeting hers as he closed it. She wanted to kick it open, drag him back in, but she gave him the look instead. The look that told him she wants him. He acknowledged it with a look of his own, and after he closed the door she sat on the bottom step for a moment, to gather herself. Her legs were like jelly and her heart was racing. She was warm in places she'd forgotten she had.

* * *

MEGGIE SPENT THE MORNING WITH HER MUM, WHO DECLARED SHE LOVED the apartment, and took her across to Evans Real Estate to meet Harriet and show her the office she'd set up in the rear of their business.

The three of them walked down to the coffee shop for an early lunch. Meggie knew her independent attitude irritated her mum sometimes, but the morning was fun, and she thought maybe she was maturing, and her mum was relaxing. That made her chuckle. And having Harriet with them broke the ice.

Debbie, at the café, gave them special attention and Meggie could see her mum was impressed by the friendliness of those she met.

Meggie felt validated, she'd made the right choice not to go back to Napa.

Walking back, they popped into the clinic. Melanie looked flustered, there were several people with their animals in the waiting room, and at that moment Angus stepped out of the surgery.

'Hi Mum, Megs. Harriet.' He looked harried. 'Max had to dash to Newcastle right after he opened this morning. A family thing, he said so I was a bit late starting.' He indicated the busy waiting room. 'No time to chat, sorry.'

'No problem son.' Meggie saw her mum frown as she spoke.

They turned back to the door, then Meggie strode up to the counter. Angus was already in the surgery with a client. 'Melanie, what about Tommy? Did he go too?'

'No.' Melanie leaned forward, her concern obvious and Meggie could see the people sitting closest in the waiting room were straining to hear. 'He was upset. Got a call from someone, said he had to go. Right now. So I told him to leave Tommy, I'd take him home with me. He can pick him up later tonight, or whenever he gets back. He was so relieved, Meggie, I could see it on his face.'

'Okay, thanks Melanie. If he stays away more than tonight, I can take Tommy if you like.' Meggie patted her hand, then walked through the clinic to the street, catching up with Harriet and her mum.

'I hope this Max is going to be reliable. Angus can't have him dashing off at the drop of a hat when he's on his honeymoon.' Her mother's lips were pursed, her displeasure obvious.

'It's a family emergency, Melanie said. Family comes first mum, you taught us that.' Meggie knew her tone was a bit sharp, but she was worried for Max, and wondered who, or what, could make him rush off like that. He always seemed so solid, dependable.

Harriet offered to drive Helen back to Barrington Homestead, said she had some wedding stuff to discuss with Rose. Meggie was grateful, she needed time to think. She'd message Max as soon as she was alone.

* * *

By seven that night she hadn't heard from Max. He'd given a thumbs up to her *are you alright?* message, but no more.

Around nine, she decided she'd go to bed. Melanie was keeping Tommy with her overnight. She wandered to the window overlooking the street, wondering when Max might come home. She was about to draw the curtain when she saw a faint glow from the clinic, like an interior light had come on. Max must be home. He's checking the animals.

She grabbed her keys and ran lightly across the empty street, down the side lane to the door of the flat. She was about to knock but knew if he'd gone through to the clinic he wouldn't hear her. She tried the door, it was unlocked. She stepped through the flat to the door to the practice. She did it quietly, cautiously, as it occurred to her that maybe someone else was inside. Angus most likely, looking in on the patients.

The light was coming from the hospital section, through a glass panel in the swing door. She stepped up to the door, looking through the window, then drew back in shock. A young girl was sitting on the floor, her face buried in the fur of a puppy. Meggie didn't recognise her at all.

She pushed the door open, and the girl looked up. Her face was tear-stained, she blinked once or twice.

Meggie stepped into the room. 'Hello. I'm Meggie. Who are you?' Her tone was soothing, yet wary. While the girl only looked about fifteen, she could be a thief, looking for drugs and side tracked by the puppies.

The girl raised her chin. 'I'm Indiana. My dad works here. I'm allowed to be here.' Her voice shook and she started to get up. Thoughts raced through Meggie's brain. Her dad? Is she Angus's daughter, someone she's never heard of, or Max's?

'Hi Indiana. That's okay. Who is your dad? My brother Angus owns the clinic here.' Meggie tried to keep her voice calm. The girl still looked frightened.

'Max Masters. He's my dad.' She buried her face in the puppy's fur again, before opening the enclosure and returning it to its mother and siblings. 'I can't find him. He should be here. My brother Tommy too.' She started to cry. 'I need to speak to him, I need to tell him the truth.'

Meggie was surprised more than shocked, but the girl was distressed so she stepped forward, holding her gently while she cried.

'Max went to Newcastle this morning and Tommy is staying with a friend. Family thing he said.' She grabbed some paper towel from a cupboard, handing it to Indiana. 'I expect that might be about you.' She raised an eyebrow.

Indiana nodded. 'I ran away. Last night. I was coming here. To tell him.' She sniffed loudly.

'Does he know that? That you're here? Have you messaged him?'

Indiana shook her head. 'My phone went flat. I forgot to bring my charger.' She looked up. 'Do you have one? A charger?'

Meggie placed an arm around Indiana's shoulders. 'Let's go to my place. It's across the road. We can charge your phone, and I have your dad's number, we can let him know you're here and you're safe.' She walked her from the clinic, turning out the light, then through the flat to the street. 'How did you get in? I'm curious.'

Indiana wiped her tears, her mouth curving upwards for the first time. She was pretty, fine bones, looked a bit like Tommy. Meggie couldn't see her father in her features at all. 'He always forgets to lock the door, I tried it, in case, and it opened.'

Across the street, Meggie took Indiana through to the kitchen. 'You must be hungry. Vegemite toast? Scrambled eggs? I can make a hot chocolate.'

'Can you call him? Tell him I'm here. Please?' Indiana handed her phone to Meggie, who put it on the charger.

Getting her own phone out, she found Max's number. 'Do you want to speak to him yourself?'

Indiana shook her head, her face anguished. 'I have to tell him in person. Can you ask him to come here? Please.'

'Okay. Why don't you go and find the bathroom, wash your face. I'll call him now.' She watched Indiana leave the room.

Max picked up after two rings. 'Meggie, I want to talk to you, but I can't right now.' He sounded distant, breathless.

'Don't go Max. Is it about Indiana? Your daughter? She's here. She's with me.'

There was silence for a moment, then Max's voice, sounding muffled. 'She's there? With you? She's safe?' He sounded close to tears.

'She's safe. I found her at the clinic, looking for you.' Meggie spoke quickly, hoping to ease his mind.

'Can I talk to her?' His voice broke as he spoke. He was struggling.

'I'm sorry. She wants to talk to you, but not on the phone. Says she has something to tell you, but it has to be in person. Can you come home?'

'I'll come now. I can be there before midnight.' He was silent, she wondered if he was still there. 'Meggie. Thank you. Keep her safe. Tell her I love her. Please don't let her leave.'

22

———————

Max stopped at the service station at Raymond Terrace, getting fuel and a black coffee. He'd made another call before he left, then concentrated on driving. He thought a lot about what he needed to say to Indiana. And Meggie. She needed to know the full story too, if they had any chance of a future together.

He knocked on the door downstairs shortly after twelve. She must have seen him walk across the road because she opened it straight away. He wasn't sure what to expect from Meggie. Would she accuse him of lying about having a daughter? Would she be angry?

If she was angry, she didn't show it. She looked tired. 'Max. Come upstairs.' He followed her up, stepping into the living area.

'Indiana's asleep in the second bedroom. She was exhausted. But I told her I'd wake her when you arrived. She's really distraught.' Meggie led him to the couch, drawing him down beside her. 'I don't know what's happened between you Max, but it needs to be fixed.' She glanced away for a moment. 'I'll put the kettle on, make a pot of tea. Maybe you should gather your thoughts before you speak to her. Or we can wait until she wakes in the morning?'

Max leaned back, closed his eyes for a moment, then looked sadly at Meggie. 'I can't thank you enough Meggie. For finding her, keeping her safe.' He took her hand. 'I planned to tell you the full story, wanted to start, with you, with no secrets.' She squeezed his hand in acknowledgement.

'Yes, tea would be nice, thank you. Maybe we should let her sleep.' He watched as Meggie walked to the kitchen, heard the sounds of water running, then the kettle boiling. He may have drifted off for a few minutes, then she was beside him again, the tea things on a coffee table in front of them. He took the cup she offered, took a hesitant sip. Black and sweet. He glanced at her, 'how did you know I take it black?'

'You have your coffee black. I assumed. And you need the sugar, so I made it sweet.' She sipped her own as she spoke. She was calm, but he sensed underlying tension in her body.

He drank half the tea, then set the cup down. He took one of her hands and was relieved she didn't tug it from his grasp. 'Indiana is my step-daughter, she was six when I met Liliana. I've always considered her my daughter as much as Tommy is my son. I love her. Aways have.' He drew a breath. 'She spent time with Matthew, her biological dad, over the years, but she lived with us. Then, when Liliana died it all changed. I expected to keep her, keep the arrangement with Matthew for visits.' He leaned forward, his head in his hands.

He was struggling to keep his composure. He sat back, looking at Meggie, his eyes burned with tiredness and unshed tears. 'But she hates me now. Blames me for her mother's death. For the car accident. Indiana was in the car with her, she saw her mother take her last breath. I can never make that right.' He sobbed, he couldn't help himself, and Meggie's arms were around him, rocking him.

He felt moisture on his cheeks. 'I'd found out she was having an affair. Liliana. With one of my partners. We argued. We'd been arguing a lot and I confess, I'd thought about ending the marriage too, before the affair. We weren't happy. But that day, she was taking Indiana to netball. I thought Indi was in the car, waiting, and I told Liliana it was over, I was leaving her. She walked out the door, slamming it. I looked up and Indiana was standing in the hall, crying, her water bottle in her hand. She'd come back in. She heard everything.'

He drew a breath. 'She never spoke to me again. Not at the hospital, not at the funeral. She went to Matthew and his wife. They arranged counselling. Nothing helped. She wouldn't speak to me or to Tommy. He hasn't seen his sister for a year. In the beginning he asked after her every day, but now he just looks sad sometimes and I know he's thinking about her, and his mum.'

He sat back, then saw Meggie turn her head toward the door to the bedrooms. Indiana was standing there, wearing a tee shirt he knew was Meggie's. Body aching, Max pushed himself off the couch, not caring that he was crying. He opened his arms as he walked toward her. 'Indiana. I love you.' He didn't know what else to say. 'I'm so sorry.'

Indiana threw herself into his arms and they collapsed on the sofa together, sobbing. Meggie started walking from the room. Indiana spoke, surprising him. 'Stay Meggie. I need you to stay.'

Indiana made room for her then looked at the ceiling for a moment. She turned to him. 'I don't hate you Dad. I don't blame you for the accident.' She started to sob, and Meggie rubbed her back gently, looking at him over his daughter's head, her face anguished, probably mirroring his own.

Indiana cried harder. 'The reason I don't blame you. Is. Because.' She hiccupped between words. 'Is because I killed her! I killed Mum! I took her away from all of us! From Tommy. He was only seven and I took her away from him!' She was almost screaming the words and Max and Meggie held her between them, rocking her.

He repeated, 'I love you Indi.' Over and over, until her sobs subsided. They were all crying. Finally, Indiana sat up and looked at him. 'Let me tell you dad. Let me tell you the truth. You may never speak to me again, but I have to say it.' He nodded. Meggie had her hand on Indiana's back. 'I heard what you said to Mum that day. About leaving her, about the affair. But dad, I knew already. I heard her talking to him days before, on the phone.' She straightened. 'She begged me not to tell you. Then, in the car that day, I yelled at her. I called her names, I told her I hated her. She was crying, telling me she loved me, that it wasn't about me. And she was driving fast. I didn't stop. I screamed at her over and over.' Indiana took a deep breath. 'She didn't see the lights change. She was looking at *me*. She drove straight through. I don't remember everything, someone pulled me out of the car. And I knew she was dead. I killed her dad.' He held her tightly, rubbing her back, murmuring to her.

Meggie left the room. After a while she came back, knelt in front of Indiana, a cup of hot chocolate in her hands. She spoke quietly. 'I've heard your stories, both of you. But I don't think anyone is to blame. Liliana was already upset when she got in the car that day Indi, and not necessarily because of the argument with you Max. Guilt is a powerful emotion. I expect Liliana was feeling plenty of that, just like you both feel guilty for her death. But she's gone, and you're still family.' He held her hand as she sat back on her heels. 'And think of Tommy, he needs you both. All I've really taken from tonight,' she waved her arm around them both, 'is that you love each other. As you should. Don't waste any more time on guilt. Guilt totally sucks.'

Indiana sniffed, then smiled tremulously at him. 'Guilt sucks Dad.'

'Oh Indiana. How I've missed you. Yes, guilt definitely sucks.' He kissed her forehead gently and was relieved when she kissed his cheek in return. A heavy weight was lifted from his heart, there was a way forward. It might not be easy, and he'd look into counselling, maybe together, but he had his girl back. He looked at Meggie. He saw how she handled them, how gentle and wise she was. She had a story to tell too, he was positive, and he would hear it, with the same openness she'd given him.

Looking at his watch, he said, 'it's almost two. We all need some sleep.' He looked at Meggie, but she spoke before he could ask her.

'Indiana will stay here. In the guest bed.' She nudged his daughter. 'We've got a girl thing going on here.' He heard Indiana giggle, she was looking at Meggie with open admiration. Meggie turned to him. 'You, Max Masters, can return to your man-cave and we will regroup in the morning. You need to pick Tommy up, he'll want to see his sister.'

'Yes please Dad. I saw your flat. It's tiny.' He laughed when she wrinkled her nose. 'Can I stay here for a couple of days? See Tommy. Look around a bit?' She hesitated. 'You've told Matt you found me?'

'Matt? You don't call him Dad now?' Was all he could think to say. She shook her head. 'You've been Dad as long as I can remember.'

He stood, said goodnight to Indiana. She went straight back to bed.

He looked at Meggie. She jerked her head toward the door. He followed her downstairs to the entrance. There was so much he wanted to say to her, but he was exhausted, physically and emotionally.

'It's alright Max. Go home, get some sleep. Do you want to come here for breakfast, with Tommy, or meet at the café?'

'The café. Seven? I'll call Angus first thing, explain. I'll let Tommy have a couple of days off school.' Meggie nodded as he spoke.

'See you tomorrow Max.' She stood on tiptoe and kissed him softly on the lips. He let his eyes speak for him, then opened the door, stepping out into the fresh air.

23

———————

Meggie was surprised when Indiana knocked on her bedroom door around six-thirty. They chatted a bit and Meggie made some green tea for them, before giving leggings and a San Francisco tee to Indiana to wear to breakfast. The tee was a bit big, but she loved it.

Indiana talked about her school, how she only had this year and next to go. She was interested in teaching but wanted to travel too. She asked Meggie about her career, where she had travelled. She talked about moving back in with Max and Tommy when they finished their three months in Barrington. Meggie wondered if Max would return to the city, change his mind about staying, if it meant Indiana would come home.

They walked down to the café together, Indiana peeking in shop windows and exclaiming over a display in a menswear store, about how old fashioned, but quaint, it was. Meggie liked her, could see she'd need some guidance to overcome her feelings about her mother's death, one honest talk in the middle of the night wasn't a magic wand. But it was a good start.

They neared the café and Tommy burst from inside, his legs moving so quickly he was a blur. He threw himself at his sister. She leaned down, wrapping him in her arms. She was petite and he was tall, he was going to be a man-giant like his father, Meggie observed. They hugged, laughed and hugged again. He tugged Indiana to the counter, introducing her to Debbie, ordering his favourite milkshake for them both.

Max and Meggie sat together, watching. Max looked tired, but happy, he was grinning at everyone. 'I called Angus at six, gave him the abridged version. Melanie too when I picked Tommy up. Angus said to take as long as I need.' Max shook his head. 'He's a good man, your brother.'

'The best.' Meggie pushed her chair back, standing. 'Breakfast is on me today. I'll be back in a minute.' She walked to the counter. 'Two scrambled eggs with avocado on toast please Deb. And our usual coffees. Did the kids order theirs?'

'Tommy did. Pancakes for them both.' Debbie looked at her curiously. 'I take it Indiana is a bit of a surprise?'

'There's a story Deb. But it's going to be okay.' Meggie knew Debbie wouldn't ask anything further, but she also knew that she'd share some of the story with her, and Rose, Harriet and Mel, when they had some privacy.

Back at the table, Max was telling Indiana he was buying into the practice, staying in Barrington. Her face fell, for a moment. 'You can live here too if you'd like to Indi.'

'Your place is so small.' She appeared on the verge of tears. 'But I need to finish this year and next at my school. I'm doing really well Dad.' She looked at Meggie, then to Max. 'I thought you might come back.'

Max shook his head. 'I'm going to sell the house, buy a place here. With a paddock for horses.' Indiana seemed to perk up. 'Can I have a horse? I'll come on weekends when I can and in school holidays.'

'Of course. It'll be your home whenever you want to be here.'

Tommy interrupted. 'We're going to get kayaks too, we went down the river the other day, and I'm signing up for football, and cricket next summer. You can come and watch me play Indi.' Meggie liked the way Indiana gave her little brother a playful nudge. There was no need for Tommy to know what they'd been through.

They ate their breakfast, letting Tommy lead the conversation. Indiana was quiet, but Meggie thought she was processing. And she'd be tired.

'Dad.' That was Indiana. 'I'll stay today and tomorrow, if that's okay, have a look around. But I need to be back at school on Thursday or I'll fall behind.'

'Okay Indi. I'll speak to Matt, we can drive you home tomorrow afternoon, or we can meet him in Raymond Terrace.'

Indiana turned to Meggie. 'Can I keep your things for now?' She touched the neck of the tee.

'Of course. Keep them, I have heaps. And I'll wash what you had on yesterday, so you'll have a change of clothes. You can borrow a bikini if they take you for a swim.' Meggie looked fondly at Indiana, on the verge of womanhood, yet her childhood had been stolen when her mother died.

* * *

Meggie was finishing dinner at the Homestead with Angus and Rose when Max pulled in on Wednesday evening. He asked if Tommy could watch television in the other room and accepted a beer from Angus. Helen and Barry had driven into the pub for dinner and Charlie was already asleep.

'Thank you. Angus, Meggie. Thank you for these last couple of days. I apologise for not telling you the full story. Telling you about Indiana. I honestly didn't know if she was ever going to speak to me again. And it was hard, thinking about that.' Max spoke quietly.

'It's all good Max. But I hope you haven't driven out here to tell me you've changed your mind about buying in?' Angus looked unsure as he asked.

'No. Not at all. If you'll still have me, I'm one hundred percent committed. Barrington is the right fit for us. Indiana is welcome to stay with Matt, but she knows she can come here for school if she prefers. We both love her, we've talked it over and we're happy for Indi to spend time with both of us. I don't expect her to make a decision like that in two days. And we'll be doing some more counselling.' He said this firmly.

'Whatever you need Max. If you need a day a week in the city, we'll work it out.'

Max continued. 'I'll be looking for a place of our own soon enough. The agent says the current tenants want to make an offer on our old place.'

'Good. Speak to Ben. He'll have a few listings that may suit.'

'But don't worry about the animal hospital. Tommy and I can stay there when we have patients. Have a pub dinner.' Max gave a lop-sided smile as he turned down a second beer.

'We'll have Freddie here in the holidays, she might want to move into the flat.' Angus seemed more relaxed. 'There are always options, Max.'

Max seemed relieved. The look he gave Meggie across the table was questioning. They had a connection, but she really had to tell him her own story. It might be a deal-breaker and she'd rather know now.

Meggie spoke softly, and they all turned to her. 'There's something I've been wanting to tell you.' She glanced at Angus and Rose. 'And you too Max. You should know too.'

She was nervous, her hand shook as she picked up her wine glass, taking a sip. Rose said firmly, 'nothing you tell us will make any differ-ence to us Megs. You know that.'

She spoke slowly, thinking about her words. 'I made some mistakes in Napa. Big mistakes, bad decisions. I fell in love with my boss about two years ago, we were away at a conference.' She inhaled deeply. 'He's married. We had an affair. More than an affair.' As she spoke, Max's face seemed to tighten. She pushed on. 'I knew it was wrong, but I thought.' She lifted her chin. 'I thought he loved me. Thought he would divorce her. He said he didn't love her anymore.' She wiped a tear from her cheek with the back of her hand. 'I fell pregnant. I was so happy, thought he'd divorce her for sure. We'd marry, have the baby.'

She looked at Max, his face had relaxed a bit, she wished she knew what he was thinking. Rose, beside her, was holding her hand. She was scared to look at Angus, afraid to see his disappointment. 'At the clinic, for the first ultrasound at twelve weeks, I saw his wife. She was pregnant too. About six months. She looked so happy.' She wiped another tear away. 'And that's when I knew. He'd played me. I was so stupid. He wasn't going to divorce her. Her father owned the vineyard. We'd even talked about starting our own one day, but maybe that was what *I* talked about, what *I* said.' She took the tissue Rose handed to her wordlessly. 'My workmates had warned me in the beginning, tried to tell me what he was like. I didn't listen. I lost most of my friends over it. Because of my stubbornness. I resigned. Found another job.'

She looked at Angus, he was angry. God, she didn't want Angus to turn from her, but he needed to know. 'I thought about not having the baby. I was scared, alone. But I wanted her, I really wanted her. I was planning to call you, tell you I'd be home for the wedding, pregnant.' She shook her head, tears trickling down her face. 'I went into labour at five months. The baby, my daughter, only lived a few minutes.'

Angus stood, his face dark with anger. Meggie flinched as he stalked around the table to her. He pulled her out of her chair and enfolded her in his arms, his strength seeping into her. 'That bastard! I'd knock him out if he was standing here. That rotten bastard.' He held her while she sobbed. 'But Meggie, we would have welcomed you back, pregnant, with a baby, under any circumstances.'

'Really?' Relief began to wash over her. 'It was my own fault. My stupidity. I believed his lies, even though I was warned. I didn't listen.'

Angus growled. 'It takes two Megs. It always takes two. Don't be so hard on yourself.'

'I feel your pain Meggie.' Rose murmured. 'Losing your baby, your relationship, in another country, no family, feeling friendless. How hard this must have been.' Angus released Meggie. 'You could have told us Meggie. You could have come home straight away.'

Meggie blinked as more tears threatened to fall. 'I was being independent. I got myself into trouble, I was trying to work my way out of it. Coming home for the wedding was a lifeline, after losing her. I won't go back, I've travelled enough. I want to settle. Here. Close to my family.'

Max stood. 'You've been through a lot, Meggie, you're a strong woman. And I want to talk to you about this some more, but it's after eight and Tommy has fallen asleep on the couch, and I think your mum and Barry have pulled up outside.' Meggie felt relieved, that Max still wanted to talk. And even if her story cooled his ardour, maybe they could be friends.

The flurry of activity with Helen and Barry returning as Max carried Tommy, asleep, out to his car, allowed Meggie to hug Rose and Angus. 'Don't tell mum. I couldn't bear it if she knew.'

'You will tell her yourself one day Megs. When you're ready. Go home. Get some rest.' Angus kissed her forehead and walked her to the car.

24

Max tapped his hand on the wheel as he drove. Meggie's story had thrown him, momentarily. She's been through so much, discovered her partner was playing her, followed by the loss of her baby. Thinking about Meggie's kindness to Indiana, how good she is with Tommy, he was amazed at her strength and compassion. Yet logic told him he should slow down a bit, consolidate their friendship before embarking on a relationship. And he needs to be present for Indiana, and Tommy. They'd made a good start, finally he understood why Indi had cut them off, but the grief and guilt wouldn't instantly dissolve, and it will take time to help her through it. He had to put the kids first, as much as his body, and if he admitted it, his heart, finally free, yearned for Meggie.

So much to do, sell the house in the city, investigate properties locally. He sighed. Tommy woke as he pulled in behind the Clinic, and he walked him through to the flat, helping him undress and get straight into bed. He sat on the sofa for ages, thinking about the last few days.

* * *

WITH THE WEDDING LOOMING, HE WAS BUSIER THAN EVER. ANGUS WAS spending very little time at the Clinic and Max often returned to work after Tommy was asleep to research the new equipment they needed and check on their sleepover patients. On top of that Tommy had joined the netball comp with Billie and Tiffany and they trained two afternoons a week and had a game on Saturdays. Max was surprised, and pleased, that Tommy wasn't the only boy playing netball, it was a mixed competition, and he'd made friends with a couple of the boys from school now in the same team.

They'd had a weekend in Newcastle to see Indiana and sign the contract for the sale of the house. Indi had wanted to see Meggie, but she'd been in Sydney with Debbie and Rose, something about shoes and the bridesmaid outfit. Max was pleased Indi had asked after Meggie, she'd wanted to thank her and return her clothes, and he was even happier that Meggie had seemed disappointed it hadn't worked out to catch up.

Max had been surprised, and touched, when an invitation to the wedding was handed to him by Angus days after Indiana first appeared. It was for Max, Tommy and Indiana and he accepted with pleasure. He already felt an attachment to Angus, as a friend and business partner. He hired a dinner suit for Tommy, there was no point buying one, he would grow out of it in months. Indiana was a different story, she was petite and fair, and he wanted her to have something she would love wearing. In the end they chose a sky blue floor length gown, with shoe-string straps, fitted to below the bust, then fell softly to the floor. He thought they'd need to take it up, but she chose silver strappy heels and with the shoes on the length was perfect. He hoped she knew how to walk in them but chuckled when he remembered taking girls out when he was in his late teens. They all took their shoes off after a while anyway.

He wondered what Meggie would wear. She was tall, athletically built, she'd look stunning in any gown. He hoped he'd get a chance to dance with her. The thought of holding her in his arms, swaying to music, made his heart race.

He'd barely seen Meggie for more than a few minutes in weeks. Despite their minimal contact recently, he knew his feelings hadn't changed. If anything, they were stronger, now that he was finally beginning to sort through the aftermath of Liliana's death with his kids. He was impressed Meggie hadn't pushed for more contact, giving him space to spend time with Tommy and Indi when he wasn't working.

He knew she was hyper busy with last-minute wedding arrangements too and he wondered if she had chosen to remain friends, after processing all that came with him if a relationship started. His doubts niggled him at times. He was older than Meggie by six or seven years, and he had a family. After hearing her devastation at the loss of her baby, he was sure she'd want a child of her own at some stage. Could he offer that? He decided he'd leave the ball in her court. The thought had barely formed when she messaged him.

Any chance of a pub meal with the Masters men tonight?

Love to! See you at six. X

He tossed up whether to put the kiss on the end but pushed send before over-thinking it.

Tommy's hand waving caught his attention as she walked in. They were at their usual booth. Tommy slid over, making room for her beside him. Max leaned across and kissed her cheek before she sat down. He liked the way her neck turned pink when he did.

'What have you been up to Tommy Masters? I haven't seen you properly in weeks.' He watched her focus on his son, and sat back a bit, enjoying the conversation.

'I'm playing netball Meggie. With Billie and Tiff and the Bain twins. They're in my class at school.' Tommy was excited, he was loving her attention. But who wouldn't he thought.

'Have you played netball before Tommy?' Her interest seemed genuine, his heart sped up a bit. Beautiful, smart, compassionate. What's not to like? And sexy as hell, without even trying. He leaned forward a bit, to re-focus on the conversation. Tommy was speaking again.

'… not before I came here but I'm pretty good. We play at lunchtime. We beat the team from Stroud last week. I play centre 'cos I'm taller than the others. But Billie plays wing and she's super-fast and Tiffany is goalie. It's funny, she's usually really quiet but her Mum says she's a tiger on the court.' He giggled and Meggie laughed with him.

She nudged him. 'I bet you're all terrific. What's the best part for you?'

Tommy paused, his brow crinkled as he considered her question. She shot Max an amused look and he knew he was grinning back. Try as he might, he couldn't help it. 'Well, our netball team is sort of like …' he stopped and looked at Max, then turned back to Meggie. 'It's sort of like a family. I love winning and everything, but going to practice is really fun too, 'cos, you know…' he trailed off, looking uncomfortable.

Meggie leaned closer to him, but Max heard her clearly enough. 'Friends that are like family are the best Tommy. You know, it's quite likely you'll stay friends with these kids all your school years and even beyond.' She looked up, her eyes were glistening. Was she trying to tell him something? That she merely wanted friendship?

Changing the subject quickly, Tommy announced he was hungry. 'The duck spring rolls are on again tonight Meggie. Wanna share the entrée?'

'Duck spring rolls. Yes please!' she nudged him again, then glanced at Max. Then he saw it. Her expression was unguarded for a moment. Love. She loves Tommy. Meggie adores his son.

Emotion caught in his throat, so he cleared it before speaking. 'And for main course Meggie? And what about you Tommy?'

'Maybe a kids schnitty. But I always have that.' Tommy picked up the menu again, frowning.

'There's fish and chips on tonight. Whiting fillets. But the main course would be too big for me after sharing the spring rolls. How about we order the main and share that too? I'm sure they'll bring two plates if we ask.' Meggie was pointing to the specials board, and he laughed out loud when Tommy clapped his hands.

Max chuckled and as he got out of his seat. 'I'll order. Wine for you Meggie?' She said, 'yes please' and he walked to the counter, ordered their meals and a steak for himself, then bought the drinks and returned. Tommy was talking about seeing Indi and having to wait around in *all* the dress shops while she picked a dress for the wedding.

'It's a girl thing mate, you'll get used to it when you're older.' Max raised his glass. 'To Angus and Rose.' He watched Meggie take a sip of her wine, a small smile playing around her mouth. Like she had a secret. He wondered what.

An hour later they walked Meggie back to her apartment, and despite offering the keys to Tommy to let himself into their flat, he announced he'd wait and walk home with his dad. If Meggie was disappointed, she didn't show it. She gave Max a cheeky look, like she knew he was keen for a few moments alone. So he said goodnight and kissed her cheek, then watched as she leaned down and hugged Tommy. He wondered if Tommy would pull away in embarrassment, but he threw his thin arms around her waist and hugged her tightly in return. It moved him beyond words, and as she straightened he placed his hand on Tommy's shoulder as the boy whispered, *'goodnight Meggie'* and they walked across the street. Max turned and looked back. She was standing there still, watching them. He raised his hand, and she raised hers in reply.

25

On the eve of the wedding Rose and Debbie slept over at Meggie's apartment. They shared a bottle of champagne and chatted until nearly midnight, when Debbie declared they all needed their beauty sleep. Meggie had been surprised, at first, that Rose and Debbie were happy to share the spare bedroom. Meggie had offered to sleep on the sofa. But as the night wore on, she got it. The women had been friends since school days and had shared a room many times, and she could see how their history and closeness, giggling like schoolgirls, made it more fun for them.

Meggie was first up, making healthy smoothies for breakfast, with a platter of fruit, nuts, cheese and dips to sustain them through the morning. The hairdresser and make-up artist were due at ten and the photographer at twelve. Rose and Debbie were being driven to Barrington Homestead at two in a nineteen-forty-seven white Daimler, in keeping with the theme. Meggie and the photographer would head to Barrington in her car, arriving ahead of the slow travelling vintage vehicle.

The morning was fun, and Meggie enjoyed watching the hairdresser turn Rose's thick auburn hair into an up-do. Rose didn't require heavy make-up, but they focussed on smoky eyes and bright red lips. Debbie's blonde hair was in a similar style and the navy-blue pinstripe dress fit her like a glove, the pencil skirt ending just above the ankles.

'You know I'll need help walking up the stairs at the homestead?' Debbie laughed, demonstrating how the narrow skirt made it hard to take more than a tiny step. Rose giggled, 'I'm sure Jamie can pick you up, if he needs to.'

Finally, they helped Rose into her gown. With her hair and make-up already done, she looked like a star from old Hollywood as she turned in a slow circle for the photographer. Meggie loved the way Rose grinned at Debbie, her eyes wide. 'Do you think Angus has any idea? About the style of the gown?'

'Not at all. He said something to Jamie the other night about you being a little conservative, and thought you'd have a full-length white gown, modern but modest.' They looked at each other and laughed.

'He's in for a surprise then!' Rose took Meggie's hand. 'Thank you, for organising this, I fell in love with the dress, but you've styled the whole day around it. Even the wedding car. Everyone will expect a white gown. I can't wait to see Angus' expression when he sees me.'

Meggie squeezed her hand back. 'He'll fall in love with you all over again Rose Gordon. And you know we're going to take some *first look* photos and video footage. He won't be allowed to look at you until you step fully out of the car, we'll have it arrive close to the outdoor chapel. When we give the signal, Jamie will tell him to turn around and we'll zoom in on his face. You know the rest, what you have to do.'

Meggie looked at her watch. 'You've got fifteen minutes before we leave. Sit for a moment while I quickly put my outfit on.' At Rose's insistence Meggie had her own hair in a similar style, and had help with her make-up, wearing a deep red lipstick. Secretly she thought it was a little bit Katherine Hepburn, and so was her outfit. She wasn't in the wedding party and had a lot of behind the scenes things to attend to. She hadn't shared it with Rose but hoped she'd like it.

Stepping back into the living area she cleared her throat. Rose, Debbie and the photographer turned as one. She watched Rose smile, look at Debbie, then laugh. 'You're perfect!' She turned to the photographer, 'a photo with my sister please.' Meggie's heart flipped over when Rose called her sister instead of sister-in-law. But she felt the same. Rose had become a sister to her too.

A couple of photos, then Debbie joined them. Meggie could see Rose bursting with happiness, but she didn't think it eclipsed her own. Standing there, with Rose and Debbie, laughing together, she realised she felt whole. And strong. She hadn't felt this way since before Napa. Actually, she didn't think she'd ever felt this good, ready to move on with her life. She wanted what Angus and Rose have. Is Max the one? Maybe. Tommy already filled her heart and she hoped she could build a relationship with Indi too, when they had more time together. She realised Max may not want to start another family, have a baby, he had a lot going on with his children already. Would it be deal-breaker for her? Maybe not. But if she didn't explore the possibilities with Max, she knew she'd be sorry. And she hoped they would have a friendship strong enough to withstand any outcome.

* * *

A ROSE-COVERED ARBOUR WAS SET UP IN THE GARDEN DIRECTLY IN FRONT of the grand old homestead that Rose's forebears had built. They had folding chairs on either side of a red carpet aisle and Meggie had told the driver of the Daimler to take at least fifteen minutes to give her time to get the photographer in place for the *first look* video.

Harriet and Drum were acting as ushers, standing with the celebrant and Angus and Jamie in the arbour when Meggie arrived, parking her car to one side. As she helped the photographer with his gear, she heard Jamie say quite clearly, 'we'd like all of the guests to face us at the front after the car arrives before Rose gets out. No peeking, we want Angus to be the first to see the bride. So eyes front when we tell you, especially you Angus.'

Meggie stood to one side at the back, partially hidden by rose bushes. She could see Max on the groom's side, his back broad, with Indi and Tommy beside him. It looked like Tommy had a dinner suit too, so gorgeous. And Indi was in blue. Meggie saw her Mum in the front row, wearing deep green and gold. Little Charlie was squirming on her lap. She'd be dying to peek.

The Daimler pulled in and Jamie directed all eyes to the front. Even Harriet turned around. Meggie watched as the driver opened the door for Rose. Jamie told Angus to turn around. She watched closely as her brother turned, then looked at Rose. She looked exquisite, almost regal. She carried herself with such grace. Meggie turned back to Angus, he staggered slightly, Jamie grabbed his arm. He was grinning, his face a picture of astonishment and adoration, then he wiped the back of his hand across his eyes. He mouthed 'I love you' to Rose.

Drum told the congregation they could turn. Rose walked slowly toward Angus, Debbie almost hidden behind her. Meggie heard the oohs and ahhs of the crowd, and murmurings and phones clicking. Halfway up the aisle Rose stopped, and turned in a slow circle, showing the almost backless design of the dress, held together by delicate rose gold chains. A few people clapped and someone let out a low wolf whistle. Rose kept her demeanour, taking the last few steps to Angus, placing her hands in his. The congregation turned then, to watch Debbie, a few steps behind Rose, her small steps, encumbered by the slim skirt, making her hips swing. Everyone clapped again and Jamie shook his finger at her. Meggie thought he mouthed, 'you're in so much trouble Debbie Tait.'

Debbie stood alongside Rose, and Drum and Harriet sat down on the bride's side, in the front row. The congregation were all focussed on the front and Meggie stepped forward, planning to slip into a spare seat a few rows behind Max. But he turned, saw her, and half stood up. He met her eyes. Something passed between them.

The celebrant began to speak.

26

———————

Max had been searching for Meggie, she had to be there somewhere, stage directing the event from the side perhaps, so all attention would remain on Rose and Debbie. With everyone now looking at the wedding party, he sensed movement behind and turned his head.

He saw her. Meggie. Not wearing a gown at all. She had on navy pants, some sort of silky satin fabric, fitted snugly to her waist and hips but kind of loose legs. On top she had a white shirt, the same sort of fabric as the pants, but it was a man-style shirt, the collar up and sleeves rolled to the elbow, tucked into the pants showing off her small waist. The top buttons were undone, he could see her cleavage. She had her hair done in a similar style to the bride and dark red lips. He grinned, almost stood up. Classic. The look was perfect for Meggie. She had an hourglass figure, and the long pants made her look even taller.

He returned his gaze to the ceremony, then glanced about at the decorations. He hadn't been inside the marquee yet, but he was sure it was in keeping with the theme. Meggie had done a great job, she really has flair. Even the car looked the right vintage. He'd ask her later.

***

CANAPES HAD BEEN SERVED ON THE VERANDA WHILE THE BRIDAL PARTY had their photos taken around the homestead. Tommy said they'd even gone down to the stables for a picture with the horses. Max had looked for Meggie then, but she had gone with the bridal party, probably directing the photographer.

Meggie joined them for the meal, they were on a table with Melanie, Ben, Harriet and Drum. It was the perfect table. Indi sat on the other side of Meggie, and they chatted a lot over the meal. Tommy, Billie and Tiffany had excused themselves after the main meal and were playing in the garden outside the marquee. They'd made him promise to call them in for dessert.

The official part was relatively short, although Jamie had them in stitches with his best man speech. His comments about the beauty of the bride and bridesmaid were heartfelt and Max had to cough to hide his emotion. He felt Meggie looking at him then. But kept his eyes to the front. One look, in that moment, would undo him.

Angus made a short speech, then held his hand for Rose to stand. She thanked everyone, but especially her sister Meggie, for putting the day together. He glanced at Meggie, a tear slid down her face. He took her slender hand in his and squeezed, then handed her his handkerchief.

The band struck up a waltz and Angus led Rose to the floor, dancing perfectly together, Rose elegant and sexy as she twirled with Angus. Debbie and Jamie joined them on the dance floor, Debbie having trouble with her skirt until Jamie picked her up in his arms, spun her around, then held her close, rocking slowly from side to side, making the watchers laugh. The waltz finished and the band changed to swing tunes, and within moments the dance floor was full. Meggie had left the table again, murmuring something about the cake, so Max asked Indi to dance with him.

He showed her how to do the jitterbug, and she giggled the whole time, flushed with happiness as he spun her around. Two songs later she said her feet hurt and he danced her back to the table, kissing the top of her head as she sat. He grinned when she pulled her shoes off, kicking them under the table.

Max was about to sit when Meggie reappeared. He took her hand wordlessly and led her to the dance floor, drawing her in, holding her firmly against him as he managed a foxtrot. He didn't want to let her go.

He murmured in her ear. 'You look stunning Meggie. Your outfit is perfect. It, um, shows off your …' He paused.

She leaned back, laughing. 'My?'

'Assets. Your assets.'

'Really Max Masters? You've mentioned several times already, over dinner, how much you like my hair like this, and the outfit. I think you need some new material.' She laughed, then leaned in. 'You're devastatingly Clark-Gable-ish in the dinner suit by the way.'

He chuckled. He loved her humour, her playful side. They danced through another three songs, and he sang, slightly out of tune, in her ear. He knew all the old show tunes. He could feel the warmth of her body through the fabric of her outfit. If he wasn't in a public place, he'd explore a little more with his hands. As it was, he'd caught a glare from her mother Helen when one hand slipped below Meggie's waist, touching the top of her very shapely bum.

Tommy bounded onto the dance floor to tell them dessert had arrived, so they returned to the table. The younger kids ate theirs quickly then ran onto the dance floor, dodging in and out between dancing couples. Max looked over at Drum and Ben. 'Do we tell them to stop?'

Drum glanced at Billie, running back through the tent, Tommy and Tiffany behind her. 'No mate. They're fine. Let them have fun.' Max relaxed.

The others got up to dance and Indi went in search of the bathroom, and it was only Meggie and Max at the table. Their chairs were close, legs touching, as they spoke in each other's ears to be heard over the music. 'You've got great kids Max.'

'I know. I'm really lucky. So grateful to have Indi back, Tommy was missing her as much as his mum.'

Her head was almost on his shoulder. He kissed the top of her head, then leant down. 'But I don't think I'm finished.'

She looked at him, confused. 'Finished what? Dancing? My feet are sore.'

'Kids. I don't think I'm finished having kids.'

Now she looked at him, startled, but was prevented from saying more as Jamie announced the bride and groom were leaving shortly. The guests stood in a large circle around the dance floor and Angus and Rose did a traditional country wedding goodbye, each working their way around the circle in opposite directions, thanking their family and friends for coming. The band played a soft waltz and guests chatted and laughed together.

Finally they were done, and Jamie jumped back on stage, saying into the microphone, 'the bride is going to throw the bouquet, ladies, get ready.' Max watched in amusement as the single women, and even the little girls stood together, shouting for Rose to throw them the bouquet. Meggie stood back from the group, Max a few steps behind her. Rose turned around and everyone counted down, then she tossed the bouquet over her head, high into the air.

It sailed over the heads of the noisy bunch of women and girls. Meggie reached up and almost touched a dangling ribbon as it flew by. Almost in slow motion it began its descent. Max took one step back and deftly caught it in his giant paw. The room fell silent. He looked at Meggie, his eyes drawing her to him. Almost in a daze, she stepped closer. He knelt on one knee, held the bouquet out to her. She took it, then threw herself into his arms and the room went wild, cheering and laughing.

She whispered to him. 'You said something about kids?' He kissed her for a full minute, ignoring the laughter and cheers around him. 'First things first, Meggie Hamilton. I'm coming home with you tonight. There are things to be said. And things to do.'

Rose and Angus were beside them, and he watched Meggie fall into Rose's arms, hugging her tightly. Angus pumped his hand. 'Good work mate, good work.'

Rose and Angus stepped toward the waiting Daimler, taking them to Sydney for the night, then they were off to Scotland for three weeks.

Rose whispered something to Meggie, then skipped back to Angus, sliding into the back seat before him.

'What did Rose say to you Meggie?' Max asked quietly.

'She wants hot news when she gets back. We've got three weeks.'

'Then we better start straight away.'

THE END

THE SONG

EMMA POWELL

The SONG

EMMA POWELL

To everyone who has that special song in their heart.

Emma Powell

1

If *counting cows put you to sleep then she'd be asleep for a hundred years*, Tina Lombardi mused, as she closed her eyes and leaned back against the tanned leather headrest.

'How much bloody longer Brad?' she sighed, her exasperation evident.

Brad glanced into the rear-view mirror. 'Twenty minutes, Ms Lombardi, give or take.'

Tina caught his eyes in the mirror, catching a flicker of a smile, before he turned his attention back to the seemingly endless country road ahead of them. 'Give or take what exactly?' She was in no mood for smiles, or never-ending roads or the country for that matter. But, hell, she was under contract. And as her Manager, Keith had insisted to her on the phone that morning, there was no way out.

'Give or take a few minutes. But according to the GPS we're not far away.' Brad tapped the map on the dash as if to prove his point.

None of this was Brad's fault. She knew that. She had insisted on a private plane but as it was only a three-and-a-half-hour trip by car, the production company had insisted right back that a car would be her mode of transport. And it was a nice car. They had certainly outdone themselves on that front. Very comfortable. The time would have gone so much faster if she'd driven. She liked driving. But since her win years ago she hadn't done much of it. The label always provided a car for her and because she travelled so much there wasn't much use for her own vehicle. The hotels she was put up in were always central to everything so she Ubered everywhere else when she wasn't touring. She wasn't even sure she'd know how to drive anymore. The last time she'd been behind the wheel of a car was in the US during her last concert tour.

Danny had whisked her away from some posh function where she was being handed around from promoter to politician. He'd sidled up to her and whispered that he had a car waiting and he'd meet her out front in five.

The five couldn't come fast enough and extricating herself from the adoring attention of yet another rich, boring man who spent most of his time talking to her breasts, she found Danny leaning against the bonnet of a sleek red, two-door Chevy.

He threw her the keys. 'It's all yours,' he smiled as he jumped into the passenger side.

Tina slid into the driver's seat and started her up. Her stomach churned because a left-hand drive was alien to her. She took a deep breath and just before she put the car into gear, Danny ran his hand up her thigh, his fingers playing lightly against her bare skin. 'Okay babe. Let's see what you've got!'

Glancing into the rear-view mirror she threw the car into gear and slammed her foot on the accelerator, watching in glee as her manager raced out the door after her, eventually giving up the chase and throwing his arms up in frustrated surrender.

Tina smiled at the memory, feeling the sensation of Danny's hand on her skin. She missed him. He said he missed her too. It had been too long between visits. And phone sex just didn't cut it anymore. She wanted him in the flesh. A warmth flowed through her at the thought of touching him again and him touching her. He was rather good.

'Ahh shit,' Brad muttered under his breath, pulling Tina away from thoughts of Danny.

'Ahhh shit what?' she replied, reluctantly sitting up in her seat, that really was very comfortable.

'Oh, sorry ma'am you weren't supposed to hear that. My apologies.'

'You don't need to worry about cursing around me. You really don't. So, what's the problem?'

'Sorry to say it's a give or take.'

Tina leaned forward to get a better view at the road that had turned from a faded bitumen of summer haze to a sea of pretty tanned jerseys, ambling towards them, not a care in the world. 'Shit alright.'

Brad slowed to a snail's pace as the herd bore down on them, separating like the Red Sea as they realized the big black thing heading towards them wasn't going to get out of the way. They didn't seem concerned about it, continuing to moo and chew their cuds on their way to greener, or at the very least, grassier, pastures. Although having driven three hours through the country there wasn't a lot of green or grass. Just dry, brown land. Drought was a bitch.

The mob started to thin out, with a few stragglers bringing up the rear, followed by a man on a horse and a working dog zig-zagging behind to keep the herd moving. Tina shook her head, amazed at how one little furry animal could wrangle a bunch of four-legged hooved animals ten times its weight.

Brad had to pull to a stop in the middle of the road as a few of the renegade bovines meandered across the road in front of the car.

The bloke on the horse whistled directions to his furry companion with a few added 'hups' and 'hips' and the well-trained dog went to work, rounding the recalcitrant rabble into well behaved pupils.

He urged his horse into a trot heading straight for the car, coming to stop at the driver's side and gently rapping on the window. Brad buzzed the window down, letting in a plume of dust left over from heavy hooves tramping on the sun-baked ground. A wave of heat pushed its way inside as well, making a mockery of the air conditioning that was pumping through the cabin.

'Hey mate. Sorry about that. You should be good to go now.' His voice was strong and clear. Tina couldn't help herself and leant forward. 'Well thank you *mate* for letting us pass. It's not like we had anywhere else to be. Brad! Window up please, you're letting in all the crap.' She waved her hand at invisible particles of dust and let out a cough to prove her point, before donning her latest Louis Vuitton sunnies and leaning back into the leather seat, staring straight ahead.

Brad hesitated and looked like he was about to say something to the horse dude.

'Window!' Tina got in first. She'd learnt that from Danny.

Brad nodded, buzzed the window back up and moved off, a little bit too slow for Tina's liking.

The fella on the horse dipped his well-worn hat in thanks as he passed her window and Tina could've sworn he was looking right at her. But she knew he couldn't have because the windows were fully tinted. But nevertheless, his blue eyes pierced into her, making her breath catch. His smile, genuine, made his handsome tanned face come alive and the corners of his deliciously blue eyes crinkle.

Tina turned away to focus on the road in front and she could feel her heart racing as Brad finally leaned on the accelerator, keen to make up the time.

She glanced out the rear windshield and saw the cowboy, watching them speed away. Turning around she settled back against the soft leather and closed her eyes. The cowboy's gaze sprang into her vision and she shuddered as a warmth ran down her body. It had been too long. She really needed to see Danny…and soon.

2

———————

As Clay watched the car speed away, he removed his hat and running a hand through his sweat-soaked hair, chuckled to himself. City folk were a funny bunch. They came to the country for a tree change but when that tree change got in their way, like his herd of cattle, they cracked a wobbly.

The woman in that car wasn't just any city folk though, he could tell. The car was a limo, not stretch, and the driver, Brad, as he'd ascertained from her yelling his name…twice…was wearing a suit and tie so she was important. Well, she thought she was important, that was clear. And probably on her way to another city. Although Echuca wasn't technically 'on the way' to anything. And she'd most likely have taken air travel.

He was curious. She made him curious. He wondered if she was staying in town.

A sharp bark from his mate brought him back to the task at hand.

'Okay Pup I'm coming!' he yelled back.

With a click of his tongue, he urged his horse into a canter to catch up to the herd, leaving a wider distance between him and the car that was quickly disappearing into a mirage of heat haze.

* * *

'WE'RE HERE MS. LOMBARDI.' BRAD PULLED INTO THE RIVER RUN MOTEL which sat on the main road between the Paddlesteamer Inn and The Campaspe Condos.

'A…motel?' Tina gasped. 'I am not staying in a motel.'

'Sorry Ms. Lombardi…'

'Oh for fucks sake Brad stop calling me that! Call me Tina.'

Brad cleared his throat, clearly uncomfortable with being on a first-name basis with a client. 'Alright, sorry ma'am…'

Tina groaned.

'…Tina,' Brad forced out of his mouth, 'this is the address I was told to bring you to. I'll double-check?'

'No. I'll do it.'

Tina dug her phone out of her bag. She hadn't looked at it for the whole time they'd been travelling because scrolling on her phone made her feel car sick. She'd learnt that the hard way during a trip from L.A. to San Diego in a car with her US publicist and the local promoter when a second helping of her breakfast burrito reappeared halfway through the trip. From that embarrassing moment on, her phone always went deep into the recesses of her bag until the end of any trip.

She had two missed calls from her manager, probably to apologise in advance for the motel and an explicit photo from Danny with the message; *Ready when you are babe xx*

She normally felt a rush of excitement when Danny got naughty but she was too annoyed. Also, she'd told him only yesterday that she'd be travelling that day and would be too tired to speak with him. He'd forgotten about her schedule. Again.

Firing up her earpods, she pressed return call to her manager who picked up after two rings.

'Darling!' he gushed.

'Motel!' Tina replied.

'I know. How quaint right?'

Tina glanced out the window at her surroundings. A single-story building with about twenty rooms all facing out onto a U-shaped gravel courtyard. Cars parked outside the rooms varied from large, dust-covered four-wheel drives to family sedans. Tina shuddered to think that the people who owned these vehicles were gong to be sleeping only metres away from her.

She also shuddered at the memory of the last time she'd spent a night in a motel. A night she'd rather forget. She forced the memory back down where it belonged and focused on the task at hand.

'Quaint?' she asked. It was rhetorical. 'No Keith. It's not fucking quaint. What happened to looking into Airbnb's? I thought we'd agreed on that?'

'We did honey.'

Tina rolled her eyes. She could tell from his tone he was about to platitude her to death.

'Keith. Honey. Darling. No. I will not be staying here.'

'Take a breath. We're working on it sweetie. It's only for a few nights. But you see this is the biggest thing to happen in this region for years and well they left it a bit late and there's...how shall I say it... there's no room at the inn.' He chuckled at his biblical reference, quite chuffed with himself.

Her phone dinged. Another pic from Danny. Now she was getting really cranky with these men in her life. Except for Brad, who she could see was watching her, in the rear-view mirror, trying to be discreet, concern etched on his face.

She swiped Danny's pic into the bin and took a deep breath. She'd seen it from that angle before. 'Okay Keith one night. That's it. And I want danger money added to my per diems.'

'You're not in any danger darling.' Keith replied, his voice laced with honey and condescension.

'I don't bloody care what you call it *darling*, it just needs to be extra. Got it?'

Keith took a long drag of his vape, probably to steady his nerves. Tina could be a handful. And she knew it and had been called a pushy bitch, aggressive, a slut, and every other sexist trope available to those who wished to cut her down. When she won, over the crowd favourite, Cameron, she was called everything under the sun and it had bothered her. It tainted an otherwise really exciting time in her young life. Some would even say it ruined it. But that's not what ruined her trajectory. That was something wholly different. Name-calling didn't bother her anymore. She was immune. A stint in the US, meeting Danny whose motto for everything was 'fuck 'em and the bike they rode in on' and losing her beloved father while she was away, had turned her thought process around. She needed to look after numero uno. And being a guest judge and celebrity mentor for *Sing to Win* in country Victoria was not going to stop her from demanding what *she* needed. Damn everyone else.

Another vape drag. 'Sure thing darling. I'll do my best. Always do.' Tina could hear the smile in his voice. She had always been told by singing teachers that smiling was the best way to brighten her sound. Keith was a master at it. He was most likely cursing her under his breath at the same time.

'Well if the River Runs Motel is your best you're not trying hard enough.' Tina clicked off the call always needing to have the last word.

Keith would forgive her. He always did.

She pulled her sunnies off and rubbed her eyes, a wave of weariness suddenly enveloping her. Not surprising though, considering she'd literally stepped off a twenty-four-hour flight from the US that morning and straight into Brad's limo.

At this point, she really didn't care where the bed was, and how close the guy who owned the navy blue four-wheel-drive with the *Country blokes do IT better* sticker was to her room, she needed to be horizontal.

Brad turned in his seat. 'Shall I go check us in then Ms… Tina?'

Tina gave him a tired smile to prove she wasn't going to bite his head off as well. 'Yes, thank you Brad. I'd appreciate that.'

He left the car running as he disappeared into the tiny reception area.

Moments later he returned with two keys attached to large wooden keyrings with the room numbers etched into the wood in black writing.

What self-respecting hospitality venue still used keys nowadays? Keycard all the way. Echuca, three hours and fifty years from Melbourne.

Brad drove the ten metres to the spot outside their rooms. Side by side. Rooms nineteen & twenty. Brad insisted she wait in the air-conditioned car while he unloaded the luggage and checked the rooms. Leaning her tired head against the comfy headrest Tina watched him lug her Louis Vuitton suitcases into her room. He had chosen room twenty for her as there were no other rooms next to it. He would be the only thing between her and the country bloke who does 'IT' better. A flimsy-looking aluminium table and two similarly wobbly chairs sat between their rooms with planter boxes in front of the car spots, filled with plants that looked just as weary and ready to flake out as her. She closed her eyes and images, memories, of another motel, doors side by side pushed into her mind.

Night time. Carnations in the pots. Pink ones. Sitting next to another pot filled with sand and cigarette butts. Another country town. Somewhere in New South Wales on her post-win tour. Sixty venues in seventy days. Did that even add up? Her tour manager, Billy knocked on her door at three in the morning. Drunk as usual. He wouldn't stop knocking. Not loud enough to wake anyone else up. He was too smart for that. But enough to make Tina pull the covers over her head and hum her hit song, to herself, over and over until he gave up and went to his room. Next door.

But the knocking continued in her head. Oh wait. No that was Brad knocking on her window. She'd fallen asleep against the door. She sat up, shaking the memory from her head and opened the door to the oppressive January heat of an Australian summer. It wasn't unlike the heat of a Californian summer, but she had come from winter, which although very pleasant it was still a tonne cooler than it was stepping out of that car. It reminded her of the heat in Las Vegas when she did a weekend of shows there. Dry. Hot. Dusty.

Stepping into the room she was instantly thankful for Brad, who had pumped the air con up to freezing so it had cooled the room down while she was waiting. He had placed her bags within easy reach – not hard in a 35m square room - and boiled the kettle in case she wanted a cuppa.

She turned to him as he opened the door to leave. 'Thank you Brad.'

'You are most welcome. I'm right next door if you need anything. You've got my number as well. I'll wait to hear from you once you've rested and in the meantime, I'll find a place for you to have dinner. Or if you'd rather eat in, I can arrange that for you.'

Tears of gratitude threatened to fall. Wow she must've been tired if a bloke simply doing his job was enough to make her cry. But it was his sincerity and genuine kindness that caught her by surprise. Normally it was people pretending to care, with the sneaky glance up and down her body, or inner eye roll that she could pick straight away, but Brad was different. He meant every word. She assumed he'd been doing this for a long time given he was somewhere in his mid to late sixties, a little paunchy around the middle but still with a strong posture, lots of energy and a full head of hair, albeit speckled with more grey than brown. And kind eyes.

'That sounds perfect. I definitely need a nap but don't want to go into a deep sleep. I'll save that until tonight to get my southern hemisphere rhythms back. I'll call you when I'm ready.'

Brad nodded. 'Nap well Tina.' Then stepping back, he closed the door. A force of habit, Tina latched the key chain and it wasn't until she heard Brad's door close that she breathed out. She was finally alone and she felt very safe with him next door to her. Unlike Billy all those years ago.

3

Tina didn't even remember her head hitting the pillow and not even the occasional irregular clunk of the old air conditioner woke her from her two-hour nap. It was almost too long and she still felt a little jet-lagged and woozy. But after a long rinse in the surprisingly good shower, she started to feel more like a real human being. She gave her honey tinted hair a quick blow dry before curling it into an organized mess on top of her head. She was hopeless when it came to hair and makeup and no matter how many stylists had tried to teach her the ins and outs of a beauty regime, it went in one ear and out the other. So on top of the head it went. She threw on a pair of wide-legged white linen pants and a bright orange tank top.

Slipping into a pair of sandals and grabbing a light wrap from her suitcase she rang Brad's number.

He answered immediately. 'Hello Tina. Are you well-rested? Ready for some dinner?'

At the mention of dinner, Tina's stomach grumbled and she realized the last time she'd eaten was breakfast on the plane that morning. 'I'm starving.'

Brad laughed. 'Me too. Meet you outside.'

Tina opened her door to find him standing next to the car, the back door already open ready for her. She took a step towards him then thought better of it, turned and walked to the front passenger side, opened the door and slid inside.

'Well come on Bradley! Let's eat!' She giggled feeling fresh and ready to inhale a medium to rare piece of steak.

Brad shut the back door and settled into his seat next to her. She could sense him smiling.

'Can I call you Bradley?' She glanced across at him.

'You can call me whatever you want...Christina.' He sucked in a short breath, clearly regretting his spontaneous decision to use her full birth name.

Tina on the other hand threw her head back and laughed. 'Oh touché Bradley. Tou..fucking...che!!'

He joined in with her laughter as he drove out of the River Runs Motel and onto the main road on their way to dinner.

* * *

Tina didn't think she'd ever been as hungry in her life, as she made light work of the fillet steak, beer battered chips and salad in front of her.

While she was napping Brad had done his research and found a pub, The Pevensey Tavern, that was highly recommended by the locals for its ambience and its steak. A five-star average on TripAdvisor concurred. He'd arranged for a table with a view of the river and in a spot with no-through foot traffic to avoid Tina being recognized and set upon by fans.

He needn't have worried about that however. When they walked into the pub they were greeted by Yvonne. A short woman, mid-sixties, with equally short grey hair, a smile that lit up the room and an obvious fondness for beer battered chips.

'Well, if it isn't Tina Lombardi. Voice of an angel. I loved *My heart, My home*,' she exclaimed, holding her hand to her heart and then pulling Tina into a warm embrace. Brad stepped forward to separate them, but Tina mouthed *it's okay*, which stopped him, but stayed close.

Yvonne pulled back and turned to the punters. 'Look everyone. It's Tina!'

Tina leaned into Brad. 'There goes my quiet dinner.'

'When I booked, I told her you wanted…needed privacy.'

'Occupational hazard I'm afraid,' Tina sighed, before steeling herself with a wide smile and wave to the room. Except it wasn't what she expected. Most of the patrons turned at the announcement and there was a smattering of applause with the a few *woo hoos* but that was about it.

'And so help me God if any of you lot interrupt her dinner you'll be banned for life,' Yvonne added for good measure, her sunny disposition evaporating under her authority. 'Now, keep drinking.'

There was no danger of that NOT happening as most of them had already returned to their various dinner and drinking buddies.

Yvonne turned back to them, her demeanour having returned to sunny and clapped her hands.

'Follow me.'

She led them to their table, picking up menus, a water bottle and two tumblers on the way, without skipping a beat.

Several diners smiled and nodded at Tina, an acknowledgement of appreciation and also giving her privacy.

'That was…' Tina searched for the right word.

'Unexpected?' Brad suggested.

'No…and yes. But no…that was…nice,' she smiled.

Yvonne placed the menus, glasses and water on the table and stood back to let Tina and Brad take their seats.

'Best view in town,' she declared proudly, gesturing towards the window.

Brad gave Tina the chair facing the view. And what a view. She drew a deep, audible breath. The restaurant area of the pub jutted out over the riverbank, giving diners an unencumbered view of the river from the floor to ceiling windows. Tina's nap had meant dinner was later than usual, so they'd arrived smack bang in the middle of sunset. The pinks, oranges and purples of the sky reflected off the glassy water making it look like a painter's palette with the silhouettes of the eucalypts giving texture to the pastel.

'It's beautiful,' she whispered.

'Sure is,' Yvonne smiled, 'I'll be back in a few minutes to take your order, but can I get you drinks?'

Tina tore herself away from the view and studied the wine list. Brad asked for a soda with lime and Tina insisted he order whatever he wanted but he stuck to his guns. He was on the job and there was no drinking on the job. Tina reflected that in the music industry it seemed like drinking on the job was a requirement.

Tina was keen to try something local and ordered a chardonnay from Riverbank Winery. When in Rome…

Moments later their drinks arrived and Brad raised his glass to hers.

'What shall we toast to?'

Tina lifted her glass and couldn't think of anything. It felt like a trick question. Like all the times she'd been asked in interviews what her plans for her life and her career were. If she and Danny were serious. If she was going to cancel her tour because of her dad's illness. If she was ever going to return to Australia.

Brad's glass hovered, waiting for a response.

'To peace,' she blurted out the first thing that came to her mind.

'World peace?' Brad replied, his eyes twinkling as he tried to suppress a smile.

'Sure, why not. One can dream. To peace in the world.' They clinked and Tina swirled her wine around the glass before taking her first sip. She let the cool honey liquid slide down her throat. It was good. Very good. Woody but with just enough acidity to awaken her taste buds.

'Good?' Brad asked.

Tina smiled. 'I should have ordered a bottle,' she replied, taking another sip.

Brad nodded and took a swig of his bubbly water looking slightly disappointed at not being able to share in Tina's pleasure.

Yvonne returned to the table to take their food orders. They decided on the same thing. Medium eye fillet with beer battered chips and a side of roquette and parmesan salad. Tina ordered another glass of wine.

'Where is Riverbank Winery?' she asked Yvonne.

'Not far from here. About a ten-minute drive.'

'I'd love to visit, grab a few bottles of these,' Tina declared, raising her glass.

'Well, you give me a yell when you want to go love and I'll let Nat know. She's the owner and I'm sure she'd love to give you a tour.' Yvonne picked up the menus from the table and leaned down to Tina, although she didn't need to lean very far because her head was almost level with Tina's as it was. 'It may not look like it love, but we're all so excited you're here. That the show is here. We haven't had anything like this since they filmed All The Rivers Run in this very pub back in the eighties. With the drought we need a boost. So anything, and I mean anything you need you give me a hoy.' She nodded at Tina, the love of her town evident in the brightness of her eyes and sincerity in her voice.

'I will,' Tina replied.

'Promise?'

Tina took Yvonne's hand. 'I promise.'

It looked as if Yvonne might cry, but she cleared her throat, pulled her hand away and patted Tina on the shoulder. 'I'll hold you to that young lady. Now, two of the best eye fillets you've ever had are coming your way!'

Brad and Tina smiled as they watched Yvonne scurry to the kitchen to place their order. Then in shared silence they sat back in their chairs and looked out into the fading light as nightfall came.

* * *

Yvonne wasn't wrong and Brad and Tina agreed it was bloody good meal. Tina had ordered another wine and with three in total the jet lag was starting to kick in. She should've known that alcohol would make it worse, but she was having such a lovely time she felt normal. Nobody interrupted her for a selfie or an autograph. She suspected it was out of a fear of Yvonne's warning but also from a level of respect from the locals who really didn't care that she was eating amongst them.

The company was excellent too. Brad had started to relax as well without the pressure of being the all-in-one chauffeur and bodyguard.

He opened up about his life. Ex-military, he'd taken a job as a bouncer for a mate's nightclub which led to driving limos for some of the more shady elements, as he called them, of Melbourne's nightlife. But when he was involved in a standoff between opposing syndicates and got a bullet to the shoulder, his wife, who had since passed, insisted he change careers. In the end he didn't change careers, he got a new boss. And that's how he started driving important people who weren't going to get him into the middle of a gun fight.

Tina wasn't quite as forthcoming when he'd asked about her life so far. She told him that if he's read it in the media then he's probably got all the information he needs. She could tell he didn't buy a word of it but was gentleman enough to not push. Their conversation was also interrupted by the sound of a solo singer and acoustic guitar wafting in from the main bar.

A yummy dessert of a classic Crème Brulee with a perfect snap of sugar on top and the creamiest Crème she'd ever had, finished off, she wandered out to the bar while Brad fixed up the bill. He'd insisted but she knew it would be charged back to the production company in the end anyway.

At the front of the bar area, a small triangular stage jutted out from the corner, passers-by able to see the performance through the window.

Tina propped on a stool at the corner of the bar where the lighting was low enough so as not to draw attention to herself. Force of habit. She glanced back into the restaurant to see what was taking Brad so long and saw him chatting with Yvonne next to the till. Turning around, she heard Brad let out a huge laugh and she smiled to herself. Yvonne must be a good joke teller.

She directed her attention back to the bar area. A soft light lit the stage where the solo guitarist sat, one foot balanced on the floor and the other resting on a rung of the stool so his guitar could sit comfortably on his thigh. Dressed in faded jeans, tan cowboy boots and a black tee, the performer, eyes closed, sang into the microphone, lost in the song. Tina knew that feeling. She hadn't felt it for a long time. When just the act of singing was enough. And it was enough for him, he was clearly in his happy place. She scanned his face, handsome. Rugged. A lock of dark wavy hair fell across his forehead and Tina's fingers tingled with an urge to brush it away. She found herself humming along, in harmony with him, a soft smile on her lips, as his rich, perfectly in tune voice reached deep into her. Did she know him? Did he have an album she'd heard before? He was familiar. Or maybe it was because she knew the song. A cover of a well-known ballad that he sang better, with more heart, than the original artist. And the way he played that guitar – well it was sexy. He didn't need to watch what he was doing and his rhythm was, well, it was spectacular. For a moment she was transfixed by his fingers on the strings as he felt his way through the song.

He was coming to the end and she looked back at his face. On the final note he opened his eyes and looked straight at her. Those bright, blue eyes staring right into her. Oh. Him. Then…he smiled.

4

———————

'Ok folks talk amongst yourselves. I'm on a ten-minute break for fifteen minutes. See you in twenty,' he announced, getting a laugh from the punters and a much larger round of applause than Tina had received earlier.

He placed his guitar into its stand and stepping off the stage, made a beeline straight for her, his arm raised in greeting. And that smile lighting up his face.

Tina felt the familiar sensation that came before stepping out onto stage — a buzz in her solar plexus, heart racing and a complete focus on what was in front of her. All other sounds, sights, feelings vanished, except for her eyes on the prize. In the Pevensey Tavern, that prize was striding…straight past her. Into the restaurant. She watched him walk up to a young woman, mid-teens, and pull her into a bear hug. She pushed him away, admonishing him with a glare.

'Dad.'

He held his hands up in mock surrender.

'I forgot. Not in public. How embarrassing to have a Dad who loves you. Sorry pumpkin.'

Her glare intensified, hands on hips. 'You promised.'

'No, I only promised not to hug you in public, but you'll always be my pumpkin.'

'Dad! I'm not a vegetable.'

'Well, some would say that pumpkins are fruits because of their seeds. And you'll always be my pumpkin,' he declared, tongue well and truly in his cheek. Tina squinted, trying to read the nametag on her Best Burgers uniform. Samantha.

A smile tugged at the corner of her mouth and she turned her head away so he wouldn't see it.

'Whatever. My shift is done. When can we go?'

He draped his arm over his daughter's shoulders and pulled her into him. She allowed it, her teenage impulse to rebel overruled by the obvious love she had for her dad.

'I've got one more set, then we can go. You hungry or did you eat at work?' he asked, guiding her towards a table close to the cut-off point where people under eighteen weren't allowed to go.

It was only a matter of feet which Tina thought was a bit ridiculous, kind of like no smoking zones on a plane. Eventually everyone got the cigarette smoke at some point in the flight. In the same vein, Samantha was not really shielded from what was going on in the front bar. But she would have a good view of her dad and he could keep his eyes on her too. Tina wondered why someone else, like her mum, couldn't pick her up.

Samantha screwed her nose up. 'Yuck. No, I wouldn't eat anything from there. I work there. I know things.'

Her dad chuckled and waved to Yvonne who was still deep in conversation with Brad. What the hell were they talking about?

'Hey Yvey any chance of a toastie for Sam?'

Yvonne placed a hand on Brad's arm, saying her goodbyes and for the briefest of moments a smile passed between them that Tina was going to get to the bottom of during the car ride back to the motel.

Yvonne strode over to the table. 'Of course Clay. Whatever your girl wants.'

'I'll take the lobster then thanks,' Samantha declared in her best posh English accent.

'One yabbie coming right up your highness.' Yvonne bowed in servitude, giving Samantha's dad, aka Clay, a wink. He winked back, making Tina catch her breath. Boy he was handsome. And talented. The great aphrodisiac.

As if sensing her vibes, he glanced into the bar, catching her gaze. He cocked his head and frowned, as if recalling a memory, his eyes scanning her body, taking her in with an intensity she was unused to. Tina was accustomed to thousands of screaming fans all wanting a piece of her, but she was constantly surrounded by security, managers, PA's, who always protected her from any one-on-one associations. Except for Danny. He wouldn't take no for an answer and he was the only real connection she had.

There was an intimacy with this man in this moment. Him, staring at her, if only for a few seconds, unnerved and excited her. Is this what normal life was like? Connecting in a noisy pub in the middle of nowhere with Clay, the singing cowboy. Well, if that was normal life, Tina was ready to sign up for it right then and there.

Brad broke the moment by walking between them, cutting off the line of sight. Cutting off her connection. It felt cruel. It felt like he was cutting of a lifeline. He wasn't of course. But the thought of never having Clay look at her or her not being able to look at him felt wrong. Like an axis had shifted. All of a sudden Tina felt like the ground was about to rush up and meet her. Had Clay made the earth literally move for her or was her jetlag, combined with three large – Yvonne was a generous host – glasses of wine, finally catching up with her?

Brad reached out and grabbed her arm before she fell off the stool. 'I think it's time I got you home.'

'I'll be fine Bradley,' Tina muttered, 'I'd like to watch his last set.'

'My job is to look after you so I think we should go.'

Tina yanked her arm away from his grasp. 'You're not my dad!' she barked, realizing that she sounded like a child but couldn't seem to help herself. Years of 'yes men' had turned her into a spoiled brat. 'You're the hired help so you can go if you want. I'm staying.' She gestured vigorously towards the entrance to make her point, making the stool wobble.

Knowing what was coming, she reached out, grabbing at the thin air for something to hold onto as she, and the stool, toppled to the floor.

* * *

SHE DIDN'T WANT TO OPEN HER EYES. MAINLY OUT OF EMBARRASSMENT. But also, because she knew when she opened them there would be a bunch of people recording her fall from grace with their smart phones. And no doubt popping up on gossip sites before she was even upright.

'Tina!' she heard Brad exclaim.

'I'm fine,' she replied. Then she felt a strong grip on her arm and a gentle hand lifting her head off the floor. When she opened her eyes, Clay was leaning over her. That rugged, handsome face, creased with worry, his eyes scanning her body to make sure she wasn't hurt, finally coming to rest on hers.

'Are you okay?' he asked with genuine concern.

Tina held his gaze. 'Yes. Thank you. I'm fine. A hurt ego that's all. And there's *a lot* of it,' she chuckled trying desperately to make light of falling off the proverbial pedestal. And also, to cover the rising warmth that was threatening to consume her entire body just from his touch.

She shuffled onto her side and stood up, his hand never leaving her arm. A steady support. Once upright, she pulled her arm from his and leaned on the bar. Inanimate and sturdy instead of hot blooded and sexy. Much safer.

'Are you sure you're not hurt? We can call an ambo. Or I can take you to the hospital.' Clay insisted.

'Oh my goodness that's *waaay* too much trouble. I'm fine. I mean who *hasn't* fallen off a stool after too many glasses of wine and jet lag. Terrible combo.'

The silence that followed answered her question. All of a sudden Clay reached over to a man who was filming the whole thing and grabbed the phone out of his hands.

The man was too stunned to respond and after a few quick swipes on the phone, Clay handed it back to him. 'Nothing to see here mate. Now piss off!'

The man, realizing that he had deleted the video, glared at Clay. 'Who the fuck do you think you are? The local cop?'

'Nope. No cop. But you'll wish I was by the time I'm finished with you.' Clay took a step towards him, his wide strong shoulders squared, eyes dark with anger and purpose. He was at least three inches taller than the other bloke.

'It's okay,' Tina insisted, stepping in between them, and turning to Clay, pressed her hands on his powerful chest. She could feel his heart beating through the black cotton tee. For a moment she was speechless. Clay glowered at the man over her head and she knew that if they were going to go at it there was nothing she could do. But she was determined they not fight over her the first night she was there. 'It happens all the time. I'm used to it. Part of the job.'

'Well, it doesn't happen here,' Clay muttered under his breath, as if to himself. He removed her hands from his chest and stepped around her and towards the guy who had taken a few steps back, in full realization of what was about to happen. He'd pushed his luck.

'Dad!' Samantha's young but firm voice cut through the air. It stopped Clay in his tracks.

Tina watched him blink a number of times, as if realising where he was, then his shoulders dropped and he blew out a long breath. Still keeping his eyes on the man, he pointed to the door. 'Out.'

Realising he'd been saved by a teenage girl, the bloke gave Clay a single finger salute before turning on his heels and leaving the pub.

Clay sucked in a deep breath before turning around.

'Yvey, she's not supposed to be in here.'

Yvonne shrugged her shoulders. 'You try telling her what to do love. She takes after you on that score.'

Clay smiled back and walked over to Samantha, draping his arm over her shoulder. 'Sorry you had to see that pumpkin. Did you get your sandwich?'

Samantha, still cross, held up half a toasted sandwich. 'Yes. But thanks to you being bouncer, cop and a knight in shining armour all in one, it's cold now.' She glanced at Tina, a little accusatory if she was being honest, 'Can we go home. Please? Work was so busy, with everyone here for the show. And I've got to get ready for tomorrow.'

Clay looked over to Yvonne, about to speak. She held her hand up to stop him. 'That's fine love. Go.'

'Are you sure. I've still got one more set.'

Yvonne shooed him away and took Samantha gently by the arm,

guiding her back to the restaurant. 'Go on pack up and get out of here. I'll chuck on a best of the eighties CD. This lot'll love it.' As she passed the bar, she gave Brad a nod. 'And I'll see you tomorrow Bradley.' Tina was sure she saw her blush.

'See you then,' Brad mumbled, embarrassed but with a wide smile. Clearing his throat, he looked over to Tina, the smile gone, back in business mode. 'I'll get the car. Meet you out the front in five.'

Tina nodded and gave him a smile that she hoped conveyed how sorry she was for her *hired help* outburst earlier. Based on his frown, it didn't.

Another bout of wooziness hit her and she reached out to steady herself on the bar.

'You good?' Clay reached out to offer support which she avoided by turning to him and resting against the bar.

'I'm delightful,' she declared.

He laughed and held his hand out to her. 'Hello delightful, nice to meet you. I'm Clay.'

She took his hand, even though every fibre in her body shouted at her *Danger Danger!* And sure enough a shot of electricity shot along her arm when she shook his hand. He held on for just that little bit too long and his piercing blue eyes, that were actually looking at her this time, held onto her gaze even longer.

Tina cleared her throat and pulled her hand away, rubbing it against her linen pants to stop the buzz that lingered. 'And nice to meet you too Clay. I may be delightful, but my friends call me —'

'Tina Lombardi. Yes, I know who you are. Everyone knows who you are.'

She laughed. 'Not everyone.'

'Everyone who counts.' Movement behind her caught his attention and he nodded. 'Best get moving. The boss is getting antsy.'

Tina turned to see Samantha on the restaurant side of the bar, arms crossed, brows pulled together in a frown, bag over her shoulder, ready to go.

Twisting back around she found that Clay was packing up his gear on the stage.

A pair of headlights outside the window flashed on and off. It was

Brad. And that was her cue. Walking out to the car she glanced back, and Clay was watching her through the window as he wound the microphone cord around his arm. He smiled and nodded a goodbye as she slid into the passenger seat, next to an icy reception from Brad.

The ten-minute drive back to the motel was done in an uncomfortable silence and Tina vowed to make it up to him.

Back at the motel she let herself into her room as Brad stood watch, waiting for her to be safe and sound inside. He still did his job well even if he was pissed off.

'Thanks. Goodnight, Bradley,' Tina said with another apologetic smile.

Brad dropped his head and turned to his door. 'Goodnight Ms. Lombardi.'

After latching the key chain, Tina dropped onto her bed, exhausted from, well, everything. As the alcohol pain buffer wore off, she felt an ache in her hip from the fall. She was going to be sore in the morning. Much like after the fall she had at her concert in Denver. A short get-in meant that the crew didn't have the chance to properly apply new nonslip padding to the stairs and she'd come a cropper down the last three steps during her first song. The audience had let out a collective shriek, but she'd bounced right back up and carried on with the show. After she'd yelled at the crew, out of delayed fear, which wasn't fair because they'd worked twenty-two hours straight to get the stage set up on time, her posse called her a trooper. The next day her left side was black and blue and they had to find another costume to hide the injuries. She also bought the crew slabs of beer to apologise for her outburst and suggested they join a union. It was never quite the same with them again though and she hoped she could fix it with Brad before it got to that point.

She really needed to get control of her anger or what one of her therapists had called it, privilege. She found another therapist. The irony that she was privileged enough to have a choice of therapists was not lost on her now.

After a warm shower, Tina hopped into bed and checked her phone. There was a message from Danny. No 'money shot' at least.

Hmmm was it something I said?

Tina grinned, despite still being annoyed with him for forgetting her schedule, she could imagine him with that crooked smile of his, leaning into her with a kiss on her neck and saying it as if he'd been a bad boy. She'd ignored him all day and it was the beginning of his, so she didn't want to leave him hanging. Even to prove a point. She messaged back.

So sorry. Crazy busy day in bumfuckwest. Tomorrow will be busier with auditions so we might not connect for a few days.

The three dots, meaning he was replying, blinked on her screen.

Awww babe. That's a shame.

Nothing about how busy she was. Or how she was. Or where she was. She was not in the mood for a fight. There'd been a few between them of late and she was tired and getting sorer by the minute.

Yeah. Well I'm off to bed so chat wheneves. Xx

Ohhh you're in bed. Whatcha wearing? hehe

My usual. Sleeping now. Byeeeeeeee!

Babe send me a hot pic before you go. I miss yoooouuueeee. Xx

Tina nearly threw the phone against the wall. But instead, she replied with a fire emoji.

Hot enough for you. Night.

Before he could reply she flicked the phone to airplane mode and switched the bedside light off.

She lay there for a few moments, trying to still the rising frustration that threatened to destroy her sleep. Listening to the irregular rattles of the air conditioner, which was strangely calming she realized that Danny had never stood up for her the way Clay had done in the pub. Clay didn't even know her. Why should he care? Danny on the other hand was her…boyfriend? Partner? Lover? Fuck buddy? Goodness knows what they were because they'd never actually talked about it.

Her breathing regular, the exhaustion found her and she closed her eyes. As

she drifted off to sleep, the last thing she remembered was the feeling of her hands on Clay's chest and his beating heart as he stood protecting her honour.

5

———

Tina woke before her alarm, before her breakfast arrived and before the sun had come up. Perhaps it was the fresh country air, the fact that she'd fallen asleep before 1a.m. or the nagging anxiety that sat in her solar plexus. Either way she was awake and she knew the only thing that could shift her unease was a walk.

Ten minutes later, dressed in the latest Lululemon active wear, she stepped outside, closing the door with care so as not to wake Brad, who she suspected slept lightly when he was on the job in case he was needed at some ungodly hour by a privileged rich person.

Pulling her hair up into a loose ponytail she breathed in the early morning air, already tinged with heat. It was going to be a hot day in the Riverina. Tina headed towards the river, only a five-minute stroll from the motel, stretching her upper body as she walked. The tell-tale signs of dawn flecked across the dark country sky which gave the towering gumtrees ghostly silhouettes as she approached the riverbank.

Tina was not normally one for conscious contemplation but the shimmer of the river as the sun touched it and the morning birdsong echoing through the trees made it impossible not to. She breathed deep into her anxiety and picked up her walking pace, her muscles warming up. It had been years since she'd been back in Australia and even though Keith had insisted that the public would welcome her back with open arms, she wasn't convinced. Her fanbase was mainly in the US and the UK since leaving Australia, with accusations that she wasn't really an Aussie anymore because she'd left. Escaped would've been a better word. But other major celebrities had moved overseas without any kafuffle, so why her? The melt down on national TV probably hadn't helped.

According to Keith, this show would be her way back into the hearts and minds of Oz. And much like Dorothy in Oz, Tina felt like she was on a hero's journey through difficult terrain to find her way home. The bright laugh of a kookaburra cut into her thoughts, as if having a crack at her Dorothy metaphor. Tina laughed along, the bird's merriment contagious.

'I know, I know,' she shouted into the ether, 'it's dumb.'

A chorus of shrieking cockatoos seemed to echo her sentiments as they flew down river.

Tina stopped and watched the crackle of cockies disappear around the bend, their high-pitched screeches filling the atmosphere as they flew out of sight.

She closed her eyes and took a deep breath, the smell of eucalyptus filling her senses. Nature. She'd missed it. Sure, she'd spent time on some stunning beaches in California, but nothing beat the sounds and scents of home. She felt a tear escape and roll onto her cheek. Wiping it away, she opened her eyes, feeling a renewed sense of self. She had to make this show work. She had to get people to like, no, love her again. She wanted to come home for good. She'd had enough of L.A. and the rat race. She wanted to make a career in Australia. Settle down a bit. Maybe she could convince Danny to move Downunder. He loved an adventure. She'd talk about it with him later. A buzz of excitement replaced the anxiety and she strode back towards the motel, resolved to make what had felt impossible…possible.

* * *

It was going to be a big day. After devouring her breakfast and slipping into comfortable summer pants and a tee shirt, Tina grabbed her phone and handbag and was waiting for Brad next to the car when he came out of his room.

He pulled up short. 'Oh, Ms. Lombardi I didn't expect you to be...' he trailed off realizing he was about to imply that she was lazy or what was that word again...entitled. Well, she was neither of those things. Perhaps of late she'd been disengaged, or depressed or simply couldn't give a rats, but the clarity on her walk had given her a new sense of purpose. And one of the things that purpose did was make a person on time.

'What time do you call this?' she declared, tapping an invisible watch on her wrist.

Brad shuffled and cleared his throat. Tina knew instantly she'd screwed up again. She held her hands up in apology. 'Oh no Brad that was a joke. I'm so sorry.'

For a moment Tina thought he was going to turn around and go back inside his room. Why couldn't she keep her mouth shut?

After what felt like the longest, most awkward silence he smiled. 'Very funny,' he nodded, unlocking the car with his remote and opening the back door for her. She slid into the seat and as he held the door, he looked at her, his eyes filled with a cheeky glint. 'But a word of advice Christina...don't give up your day job,' he said as the door closed.

He called her Christina! A wave of relief flooded Tina's body in the hope that he'd forgiven her for her childish behaviour the night before.

Brad slipped into the driver's seat. 'Brad,' Tina began, fighting to keep her voice steady, which surprised her, 'I really am sorry...about last night. What I said. You're not the help. You are so much more than that. You're my lion, my tin man, my scarecrow.' Tina grimaced at her use of that metaphor again and could hear the cackle of an amused kookaburra in her head.

Brad shook his head and started the car. 'Well, I am offended actually,' he said, scowling into the rear vision mirror.

'Oh...' Tina mumbled, unable to continue in case she started to cry.

Brad broke into a smile. 'You see in all honesty I consider myself more of a Toto.'

It took Tina a moment to realise he had embraced the metaphor which made her want to cry even more. She cleared her throat, pushing the emotion away.

'Well Toto,' she declared. 'we're not in Kansas anymore. Let's go do a show!'

Brad laughed and Tina joined him as he put the car in drive, heading towards the first day of shooting for *Sing to Win*.

6

Tina sat back in the chair, her eyes closed while Susie, makeup artist to the stars, worked her magic. Tina loved the feel of a makeup brush on her face, although Susie was spending an inordinate amount of time underneath her eyes with the sponge. Dibbing and dabbing at what Tina could only assume were dark circles. Travelling halfway around the world with little sleep will do that to a person. Not to mention the last few months of partying in the US, all thanks to Danny's dogged insistence. Tina would've been more than happy to have nights in with a cuddle, a good movie and a bottle of wine.

Susie spun the chair around to face the mirrors. 'All done,' she declared.

Tina almost didn't recognize the woman looking back at her and a small gasp escaped her lips. 'From now on I'll be calling you Susie the Sorcerer,' she started, 'because honey this is pure magic.'

Susie shook her head. 'It helps when I have such a great canvas to work with,' she whispered, squeezing her shoulder.

Tina blushed, which no one would be able to see under all the makeup. 'Well thank you but seriously I had an entire baggage carousel under these eyes that have disappeared.'

Susie waved her hand in the air with a flourish. 'Abracadabra! Bags be gone!'

'Poof!' Tina joined in, throwing her arms up as if she was tossing confetti.

'Who you calling a poof?' a bright voice demanded.

Tina spun around in the chair to see Carter B, third place getter from her season of *Sing To Win*, leaning against the trailer door, hands on hips, an eyebrow cocked and his lips in pout position. Which, if she was being honest, was their go to position whenever there weren't words coming out of them.

She'd been thrilled when the production company told her he'd be one of the judges on the show. Together again. He could be a bitchy queen when he wanted to be but overall, he was a good human. And extremely talented. In fact, Tina thought he should've won that season or at least come a close second. But it was when he'd introduced his life partner, Nigel, to the world, his support flatlined. Unable to bear the fact that it was because he was loud and proud and that some people were still bigots, he convinced himself and everyone else that he wasn't a good enough singer. He was wrong. But from then on, he lost confidence and slipped from being first on the leader board to fifth. It was only Kari in fourth position missing the final two performances due to laryngitis and Mikey in third who constantly head banged his way through each song, even the ballads, put his neck out badly and left the competition, that moved Carter into third.

He'd also been one of the few people who had helped her when things started to fall apart. They hadn't communicated much since she'd left the country, the odd text here and there, but he was never far from her thoughts.

So, she was thrilled to see him, except for a moment, she thought she was in trouble. She was about to defend herself for using the 'P' word as a euphemism for voila when she saw that glint in his eye. The cheeky twinkle that told her he was winding her up. His favourite game to play with her. Especially right before she was about to go on stage and sing during the competition. It was his way of trying to put her off her game.

Her turn. 'Oh will you look who's here Susie. My favourite bronze medallist. Although you didn't get a medal did you? What did you get for coming third again?'

Carter's pout twitched, he was rattled. Perhaps she'd pushed it this time. Cocking his head, his lips formed into a tight grin and he glared at her – the twinkle still evident. He wasn't done quite yet.

'Hmmm…let me think. I got twenty-five thou and anonymity. Which if memory serves me correctly was better than what you got. Yeah?'

'One-hundred thousand and a record deal totally trumps that,' I declared, giving Susie a wink who nodded her agreement. Of course, that was a better prize but Tina knew that wasn't the end and she could feel a nervous twirl in her stomach. He had a zinger coming she was sure of it.

'Oh, is that what you got sweetie?' he said as he sashayed towards her. 'I thought you got a Westfield Shopping Centre tour and a nervous breakdown…but maybe I'm thinking of someone else.'

Susie sucked in a quick breath and Tina swallowed hard, refusing to allow the truth to bite. She removed the makeup bib from around her neck and stood up nice and slow until she was level with him. She looked him up and down, nodding, a little frown creasing her well made-up forehead. Then a smile crinkled her mouth. 'Come here you!' she squealed, pulling him into a hug.

He wrapped his arms around her and they swayed side to side, clenched together like two lost souls who had found each other.

As they pulled apart Tina gasped. 'Oh shit. Sorry!' She tried to brush off the makeup stain she'd left on the shoulder of his cream linen jacket. Susie grabbed a makeup wipe and stepped forward to give it a crack.

Carter waved them off. 'This old thing. Don't worry. I've been meaning to get rid of it to be honest. But Nigel *loves* linen, so he won't let me. Now I've got a reason to dump it. You've helped me out sweetie. Big time.'

'Glad I could help. I guess.'

'But oh my God,' he shrieked, clapping his hands before pulling her into another hug, 'it's *soooo* good to see you. I missed you.'

'You could've picked up the phone doll,' Tina said as she pulled away.

'Ditto darling,' Carter chided, snapping his fingers.

Susie rolled her eyes. 'Okay a truce please. We've got fifteen minutes and I've still got to work my magic on you Carter.'

'Oh honey I won't need much,' he preened into the mirror.

Tina stifled a laugh.

'I heard that. What? What do I need? I just had my fillers done.' He pushed his fingers into his face, leaning closer into the mirror, feeling and looking for any anomalies.

'You're perfect actually,' Susie said, trying to assuage his fears and her guilt, 'I only need to do a general base. You know…for digital. It's cruel. To everyone.' She glanced across at Tina who mouthed *It's ok.*

Leaning into the mirror, Tina draped her arm around Carter's shoulders. 'Well. Now who's having the nervous breakdown.'

'Bitch!' he cried, before breaking into laughter. Tina joined in followed closely by a very relieved Susie.

Chuckling, he flopped into the makeup chair. 'Okay Susie my love. Do your worst.' He glanced across at Tina, took her hand and kissed it. 'Then you and I can go do some judging. And you know how much I love to judge.'

* * *

IT DIDN'T MATTER WHETHER SHE WAS PERFORMING AT MADISON SQUARE Gardens in front of thousands of people, or a in woolshed on the Murray to five hundred, Tina felt the nerves. Occupational hazard. But also, an occupational necessity. She knew that the minute she stopped feeling the flutter of thousands of butterflies she would quit. And although the thought of being a judge on the show that made her famous also made her feel slightly queasy, today was not the day to quit. The butterflies were well and truly whizzing around her tummy. Just like the flies were buzzing around her face. There was no air con in a woolshed. They'd set up fans because Carter, who had turned an alarming colour of red in the heat, had screamed blue murder that if they didn't, he'd walk off set and never come back. However, the fans had ruined Tina's hair and Susie was furious. Tina calmed her down by telling her that if not for the fans the makeup would be ruined from the sweat so either way it was a win/lose situation. Hair/makeup take your pick. Susie shrugged, realizing the fight was lost and turned her matted mane of dishevelment into a post-modern homage to a bird's nest.

Tina wasn't sure if it was any better but Carter and the crew *ohhed* and *ahhed* enough to make it convincing.

And anyway, she didn't really care about what she looked like to a bunch of country bumpkins. It was only the first round of auditions and she'd make sure her manager got them to edit out any crappy shots of her.

'Oh hey.' A deep, husky voice cut through her thoughts and nerves.

She turned around and came face to face with Clay. The butterflies started flapping their wings again

'Oh…hey,' she replied. *How original*

'Fancy meeting you here,' he chuckled.

'Well I am a judge on the show so…' It dawned on her that he was being ironic. She laughed and it sounded forced, because it was. All she really wanted was for the ground to open up and swallow her and her birds nest excuse for hair. 'Oh ha…I see. You're being ironic. Very cute.'

He frowned. 'No that wasn't irony.'

'Ummm yes it was.'

'No irony is when…'

'I know what irony is…'

He raised his hand to cut her off and gave a small derisive laugh. 'Please don't say rain on your wedding day. That's bad luck. Or ten thousand spoons when all you need is a knife. Unfortunate. And you can cut with a spoon if you have to. I know, I've done it.'

'I am aware…'

He ploughed on. 'What *would* be ironic is if there were heaps of spoons in the staff room of a knife factory. Or a traffic jam if you're late for work as a taxi driver. Or the theme of a wedding was *Singin' In The Rain* and it didn't rain.'

He blew out a loud breath and stared at Tina as if to challenge her to an 'irony-off'.

Maybe, like Alanis, she didn't know what irony was. But there was no way she was going to admit to that. She was the star in the room, not him.

'No fraternizing with the talent darling,' Carter declared with a wave of his hand as he strutted over to them.

Gone was the white linen jacket, replaced with something Tina was sure must've been stolen from the 90's wardrobe of Elton John. She covered her eyes with her hands. 'My eyes. My eyes!'

Carter slapped her playfully on the arm. 'Oh you've seen this before darling. And besides what doesn't kill you makes you stronger.'

'I'm not worried about it killing me, I'm worried about going blind.'

'Oh honey there are other things that will make you go blind…' He clicked his fingers and turned to Clay, raking his eyes over his body from top to bottom and back again. 'You know what I'm talking about don't you, big boy?'

Tina drew in a breath, her body tensed. Carter was harmless but she wasn't sure whether flirting with a local cowboy from a smallish country town would be seen as harmless. Sometimes the further you were from a metropolis the smaller the minds.

Clay took a step towards Carter, his mouth rigid and his eyes darkening as they returned the favour, scanning Carter's body. 'Look mate,' he growled, 'you seem like a nice bloke. But I'm into a different vibe.'

Carter gave Clay his cutest pouty face. 'Vibe is my middle name.'

Clay stifled a smile. 'Nah it's your hair.'

Carter gasped, his hand flying to his head. 'What's wrong with my hair? Is it too purple? I knew it was too much,' he whimpered.

'No, it's a lovely shade. There's nothing wrong with your hair. Hair is hair. I just prefer my *vibe* to have curly hair.' He glanced over Carter's shoulder to Tina, a cheeky smile tugging at his lips, before picking up a guitar from the stand next to him and striding away.

They both watched him go. Tina was sure that Carter would be looking at the same thing she was. His cowboy swagger. His cowboy butt. Then a realization. The talent?

'Clay wait!' she cried out to him. He turned around. The smile still in place, his eyes bore into hers, making her momentarily forget what she'd stopped him for.

'Yeah?' he prompted.

'Oh sorry. Talent? Are you in the comp?'

He laughed. 'God no! Wouldn't touch this fifteen minute of fame crap with a ten-foot pole. But my girl Sam really wanted to, so I said I'd play for her. Performing on national TV.' He shrugged. 'The sacrifices we dads make for our kids. See you out there.'

A warmth buzzed in Tina's chest. A hot cowboy, who could sing and was a great dad. Although he'd just called her job *fifteen minutes of fame*. She'd had a good ten years plus out of it so far. Next to her Carter swooned and grabbed her arm for support.

'Are you okay?' she asked, holding him up.

'Oh Tina Barina,' he sighed, 'I think I just went blind.'

Tina shoved him away, laughing. 'You're terrible Carter.'

'Well honey, if you don't go blind by the end of this trip, I'll be very disappointed and a little suspect of your sexual preferences. I mean hello!'

And with that he twirled in an Eltonesque blaze of bling and danced out onto the stage as his name was called by the M.C.

She was to be announced next and instead of the usual butterflies in her stomach all she could feel was the hammering of her heart because the only thing on her mind was Clay and thoughts of going blind.

7

————————

Talent was one thing. Knowing what to do with it was another. There was a lot of raw talent on that stage. Raw being the operative word. After being introduced, she and Carter had been ushered to their judge seats in amongst the audience. Although calling them an audience was a little generous as far as Carter was concerned.

'The great unwashed,' he complained, screwing up his nose as they took their seats.

'Oh well listen to you mister privilege. You've got your judgy hat on early today.' Tina gave his arm a punch which was harder than it might normally have been. Once Carter was off on a rant, he had to be pulled back in line quickly or it could spiral into a full-blown event. Tina smiled at the locals gathered around them, in their temporary seats. Some had brought along their own camping chairs that she had to admit went the whole nine yards. Cup holders, head rests, side pockets for snacks. One bloke even had a leg rest that folded out. All the mod cons. She shifted in her plastic chair and she could already feel the sweat gathering on the back of her legs. She made a mental note to ask for a cushion at the first break in filming.

The production company had done a nice job prepping the woolshed and its surrounds into a sound studio for the auditions. They'd draped black masking along each of the wooden walls, creating a black box effect so the only focus was the stage. The stage had been constructed to look like a four-piece hillbilly band - complete with washboard and banjo - was about to walk out any moment. The only thing they hadn't been above to cover up was the smell of lanolin, sheep and sweat from years of being a working shearing shed, where the aromas had seeped into the wood. Kind of like the smell of an old pub. Beer and memories.

'I think they've gone a bit overboard with the *country* feel don't you think? I've counted twenty-five bales so far,' Tina whispered to Carter, who was trying to move closer to her and away from the family of seven who'd set up camp near him.

'Put it this way...if I wasn't allergic to hay, I am now.'

'It's not hay, it's straw.'

'What's the difference? It's all grass to me and there's only one kind of grass I like.' Carter waved his arm towards the stage. 'And it ain't that type.'

Thankfully the lights dimmed and the first act was introduced before he could keep going. Although that didn't stop him writing notes to Tina, making fun of each act and trying to make her laugh. It didn't work, except for when a bloke called Willy, act number ten, walked on stage with a cow. He announced that his cow was going to do tricks.

Carter slipped a note to her. *Willy or won't she?*

Tina smiled and nodded to Willy, swallowing the laugh that threatened.

Willy pulled out a tennis ball from his pocket and placed it in between the cow's front legs.

'Play ball!' he yelled at the cow who stepped forward and kicked the ball across the stage. Willy kicked it back to her. She kicked it back again.

Tina glanced across at Carter who actually looked like he was starting to enjoy the farmer and cow act. His frown had disappeared and he was even smiling, a little bit.

Willy kicked it back. The cow dropped her head and Tina was sure she was about to pick it up in her mouth and 'throw' it, but instead she let out a grunt, lifted her tail and dropped one of the largest blobs of manure she'd ever seen. Granted, she hadn't seen many cow doo doos but the round of applause from the audience suggested it was an A for effort and an A for result. And the steam coming of it would've put any boiling kettle to shame.

Carter dipped his head and got to writing, slipping it across to Tina when he was done. He couldn't look at her. She shook her head at him nonetheless then glanced at the note. *She did.*

That was it. Tina lost it. She laughed so hard she snorted. And that normally only happened when she was tired or drunk, or both. Carter reached out and took her hand and they laughed together until he gave her a nod. She knew exactly what he meant. Up and out of their chairs they gave Willy and his cow a standing ovation, followed closely by the rest of the crowd. Willy smiled, an almost toothless smile and bowed. Then he tapped the cow gently on her shoulder and she dropped her head. The last time she'd done that she'd dropped something else.

'She can't possibly have anything left in there!' Tina exclaimed to Carter above the clapping and cheering.

But then the clever bovine lowered herself down onto her front knees and bowed.

The crowd went wild. Carter even jumped up and down. 'I was today years old when I found out that cows could bow!' he yelled. 'A cow bow. OMG she wins EVERYTHING!'

Tina thought it was pretty special, but she also knew that whatever Carter had popped before the filming was obviously starting to kick in, because he was overly excited about a cow bow.

Willy waved to the crowd as he led his cow offstage.

'Hey Willy!' an audience member yelled out to him, 'what's her name?'

Willy draped his arm over his cow's neck and pecked her on her cheek. 'Lily,' he announced proudly.

Carter let out a sob. 'Willy and Lily.' He turned to Tina his hand on his heart. 'So beautiful. I love what we do.' He pulled her into a hug as one of the production assistants approached, looking unimpressed.

'We're going to take a break while they clean up. I'll take you back to your trailer.'

'I think we can make it back ourselves,' Tina said, pulling away from the emotional Carter.

'It was either take you back to your trailer or clean up the shit. So, I'm taking you back to your trailer okay?' It was rhetorical.

Carter and Tina linked arms as they followed the cranky assistant back to their air-conditioned trailer, where Tina hoped she could have a change of clothes because she was a hot dripping, sweaty mess.

As she went to close the door on the heat and dust she caught a glimpse of Clay, sitting on a straw bale with his daughter, rehearsing her song. She stared at him for a moment, until he looked up, straight at her as if he'd felt someone was watching him. She shut the door, but not before she caught him smile, just for her and all of sudden, she became a whole other version of a hot dripping mess.

* * *

BREAK OVER. CHANGE OF CLOTHES. A MORE SOBER CARTER AND THE auditions continued. The M.C. was a local real estate agent who wasn't doing such a bad job. The city council had insisted that if the production wanted to film there they had to use as many locals in the show as possible. It had come down to a used car salesman or the real estate agent. Tina couldn't tell the difference but apparently the agent had more public speaking experience because he'd run for mayor the year before. He didn't win.

'So sorry for the delay but a girl's gotta do what a girl's gotta do. Am I right ladies or am I right?'

He winked at a woman in the front row who gave him the middle finger. 'Who you callin' a fucken lady Barry! Now get on with it,' she yelled back at him, receiving a hearty applause for her troubles.

He blushed and shuffled his feet. 'Awww geez Mum...' One of the assistant directors waved her arms to get his attention, then pointed to camera one. He nodded, cleared his throat and eyeballed the camera. He may not have won the election, but he sure knew how to work a camera. Tina gave him that.

'Ladies and gentlemen, it gives me immense pleasure to welcome Samantha Reynolds and our very own singing cowboy and Sam's dad, Clay Reynolds, to the stage.'

At the mention of Clay's name, Tina felt her body respond. She had no control over it. Her heart flipped flopped and as if she could get any hotter, a wave of warmth travelled the length of her body to her toes. Making a stop in between her legs along the way.

Okay Tina. Put your judging cap on. Not your lady bits hat. That's reserved for Danny anyway. Listen and do your job.

Carter let out a small whistle. 'Singing cowboy. Oh, I like that. He can slip that lasso on me anytime.'

Tina rolled her eyes. She shuffled in her chair and sat up straight with her pen in hand to take notes. She plastered her go-to-professional smile on her face, lest she give away any feelings she had for Clay for the entire country to see.

She needn't have worried because as soon as Clay strummed the first chord and Samantha started to sing, she was lost in the moment.

When a performance stops you from thinking about your shopping list, or what you were having for dinner or the sweaty plastic chair you were sitting in, it really was something. Tina couldn't remember a time when she'd become lost in a voice before. As if the singer was channelling something, or somebody through that voice. But Samantha was doing exactly that. She was special. Like her dad. Maybe even more special.

It was if Tina was in a trance because she didn't realise the song had finished until Carter gave her a nudge. It was then that she heard the roar of the crowd who had already leapt to their feet.

'You okay Tina Barina?' he asked, concern on his face, as he clapped along with the audience.

She gave her head a shake to bring herself back to the present. 'I'm fine. So fine.' She jumped to her feet and starting clapping, her arms raised as far as they could go. And she wasn't alone. The woolshed had turned into a Samantha Reynolds fan club. Had they just found the winner of this season?

And then it hit her. Samantha was too young to navigate the dangers of winning. She couldn't let another young woman be put through what she went through. Tina felt woozy and grabbed at Carter to steady herself.

'Carter,' she exclaimed, 'she can't win.'

Carter stopped clapping and stared at her. 'That's not up to you honey. And let me tell you she's going to win. I was rooting for Willy & Lily but not anymore. She will win. You and I both know that.'

'She. Can't…she…I…' Tina felt the breath leave her body as the room started to spin and the last thing she remembered was reaching for the plastic chair as she crumpled towards the floor.

8

———————

Tina felt herself swaying side to side. Like she was on a yacht. Or a swing. Or in someone's arms.

Her eyes fluttered open and sure enough she was in someone's arms. To be precise… Clay's.

A moan escaped her lips, which she hoped would be interpreted as her being in discomfort rather than the actual reason. Being in Clay's arms.

He glanced down at her and grinned. 'Welcome back.'

She smiled back. 'Pleasure to be here.'

'We've got to stop meeting like this.'

A wave of nausea hit her and she screwed up her face, willing it to go away.

'You okay?' he asked as he stepped up into her trailer, placing her carefully onto the couch.

She nodded, unwilling to open her mouth in case something other than words came out.

'The paramedics are on their way. I'll get you a water.'

She reached out and grabbed his hand not wanting him to leave her side, feeling incredibly vulnerable all of a sudden. He sat down next to her, covering her hand with his. She looked up at him and there were no words necessary. He would stay as long as she needed him to.

A kerfuffle at the door drew their attention and Tina yanked her hand out from under Clay's feeling his body go rigid at the sudden move.

A sweaty Carter dropped to his knees next to her, forcing Clay to stand. 'OMG Tina Barina…you gave me such a fright. I almost fainted in sympathy with you.'

Tina pushed herself up onto her elbows and propped against the cushions. Once comfortable she patted his arm. 'I'm so glad you're okay,' she crooned, raising an eyebrow in amusement.

'Me too,' he gushed, wiping the sweat from his brow. 'I mean you couldn't have carried us both back,' he said, looking over his shoulder at Clay who had pulled a bottle of cold water from the fridge. 'Could you?'

'Anything's possible,' Clay replied, handing the water to Tina and giving Carter a wink who reacted with an audible gasp.

Tina stifled a laugh and shook her head at Clay for winding Carter up. He shrugged and stuffed his hands in his pockets, trying, but failing, to look chastised. He looked like a hot singing cowboy who had his hands in his pockets. Tina figured he'd look good doing anything. Especially her.

Two paramedics, carrying medical bags, jostled their way into the trailer, interrupting Tina's thoughts, which was probably a good thing.

With four people plus medical bags it was starting to get a little crowded in the well decked out, but modestly sized trailer.

'I'll leave you all to it,' Clay said as he shuffled sideways towards the door. 'You're in good hands now Tina.'

Tina glanced across at Carter, who had sat down next to her, his hand grasping hers in a vice like grip. She gave him a nudge, hoping he'd read her mind and leave instead, giving Clay his spot next to her. It was to no avail as he was too busy staring at the male paramedic who was kneeling in front of her, strapping a blood pressure monitor onto her arm.

The female paramedic started asking her questions and before Tina had a chance to tell Clay thank you, he had already left. A ripple of disappointment flooded through her but dissolved as the high beep from the blood pressure monitor informed them all that it was lower than it should've been.

'Do you have a history of hypotension?' The female medic asked.

Tina shook her head.

'How much water have you had today?' hot paramedic guy asked.

Tina thought back over the day. 'Ummm none,' she muttered, sheepish, before raising the half empty bottle Clay had given her, 'except for this.'

The female medic clicked her tongue and shook her head. She wasn't old enough to be Tina's mother, it felt like she was ten years old again and had broken the vase that had been in the family for generations. That was not a good day.

'In this weather you need to keep your fluids up. I'm going to make you a hydrolyte solution and I'd like you to have that now. Take the rest of the day off and hydrate, hydrate, hydrate.'

'We still have auditions. I can't take the rest of the day off.' Tina was starting to panic. She was already screwing it up.

The female medic frowned and in that one look sent Tina 'to her room'.

'Fine. I'll work something out.' She took a swig of the hydrolyte mixture and screwed up her nose. 'No orange flavour?'

'No additives,' hot male medic said, 'better for the body.'

'Mmm hmmm,' Carter agreed, running his eyes up and down the medic's body.

'Look after yourself,' the female medic insisted as she packed up her gear and headed for the door. 'Oh, and I love your music. I'm glad you're back. Good luck with everything,' she said, leading the hot one out of the trailer.

Carter jumped to his feet and planted a kiss on the top of Tina's head. 'Get some rest hun. I'll see you later!' he trilled as he hurried out the door after the hot medic.

As appreciative as Tina was for her friend and frontline medicos, she was grateful to finally be alone.

She took another mouthful of the hydrolyte and almost gagged. But

Tina knew it was doing her good and not being a complete self-saboteur, made herself finish the whole thing.

A wave of fatigue rolled through her body. She lay down on the couch, eyes closed, hoping she wasn't going to lose her job on the first day.

She felt herself drifting off into sleep then her phone buzzed with a message. She pulled it out of her pocket and almost had to pry her eyes open they were so heavy.

Danny.

OMG hun. R U ok? Saw you collapse on Insta!!!!!!!

Bloody social media. Some random person had decided that what happened to her was the rest of the worlds' business and that she was fair game. But Tina understood that as a public figure there would be attention but what most people failed to understand was that she was also a person. A human being. With a private life that should stay private. She sighed, no chance of that.

Her fingers tapped out a quick reply.

I'm fine. It's just bloody hot. Didn't drink enough water.

Then she tapped on her Insta app – might as well check out the damage.

The audience member was filming Samantha's performance, zooming in on Clay a few too many times to be a random fan. She glanced at the insta handle. @countrygirl98. Her avatar photo was her in a bikini, blowing a kiss to the camera. She was a Clay fan and young enough to be his other daughter. Tina huffed in displeasure and focused her attention back on the video. The song ended and the crowd rose to their feet in front of the lens. Then she saw herself, from behind, reach out for support, before crumpling to the ground.

Carter threw up his hands, squealed and then swayed side to side as if about to collapse himself. Well, at least he hadn't been lying earlier about almost fainting in sympathy. It was mayhem and nobody seemed to know what to do with the motionless body sprawled on the ground. Except for one person. Clay. She watched as he placed his guitar on the chair, leapt off the stage and sprinted over to her, the crowd parting for him as if he were Moses and they the Red Sea.

It was biblical.

He reached her well before any of the production staff did. Kneeling down he brushed her hair away from her face so gently that sitting in that trailer watching it play out in front of her, she could almost feel the warmth of his hand and a tiny tremor ran all over her skin.

He leaned into her and she could tell he was saying something, but she couldn't hear with all of the background noise in the video.

Then a stupid annoying person walked in front of the video, so she missed the moment he picked her up but as the view cleared, she saw herself in his arms. Her neck supported by his wide biceps and his grip firm across her body. She heard @countrygirl98 sigh. 'I wish *I'd* fainted.'

Then the video went black.

Normally when Tina watched videos of herself, she felt like she was observing a stranger. It wasn't really her. There was a detachment. There had to be, for her own sanity. That was a little gem that Carter had taught her all those years ago. Even though he was terrible at it, it was good advice.

But she had been unable to separate herself from the one she'd just watched. An excitement fluttered deep in the pit of her stomach. There was something about Clay that made her connect. And it was then that she realized that's what she'd been missing in her life. Connection. Oh, she had *connections*. Who in the music industry didn't? Connections made that world go around. But real, deep, truthful connection was different and had been difficult to come by.

Another message from Danny dinged.

Phew! I was worried. I thought it was happening again.

Trust Danny to bring up her most embarrassing moment of her life.

Then another message.

And babe who was that dude? Prince Charming? ;-)

The feminist in her cringed at the thought. But he kinda was. She felt her skin blush and was glad they weren't on FaceTime.

She typed back quickly.

It won't happen again. And that guy is just…

Just what? Just a competitor. Just a singer. Just a cowboy. Just the best thing since sliced bread. Ugh she was having textual anxiety. She knew if Danny was staring at the three moving dots on his phone for too long, he'd know she was making something up.

It won't happen again. Prince Charming? I don't even remember him. I was out cold.

It took Danny a few minutes to respond. Danny was a likable guy and Tina didn't want to hurt his feelings but lying to him didn't sit well either. She'd make it up to him when she got back. Although, truth be told, Tina wasn't so sure about returning to the US. Her early morning walk along the river the day before had strengthened her resolve to stay.

Ding

Cool babe. Miss you xx

Miss you too x

There she was, lying again.

Drained, she turned her phone to silent and slumped back against the pillows, her head heavy and ready to rest.

She closed her eyes and fell asleep, a faint smile crinkling her lips.

9

———

Clay headed to the stage to collect his guitar, his mind elsewhere. One hundred feet away in a trailer behind the stage kind of elsewhere. She'd been on his mind quite a bit since the pub the night before. The kind of white-hot rage he'd felt when that idiot with the camera had filmed her, sprawled, on the floor, was something he hadn't felt in a long time. Perhaps ever. It had surprised him. And yet the need to protect her had felt the most natural thing in the world.

'Dad!' Samantha called out from side stage, 'is Tina okay?' She hurried across to him, her brow creased with worry and eyes glistening with unshed tears.

'She's fine.'

Relief flooded across her face and it was if she was ten-years old again, and he'd just told her that her bunny Duke, was going to be okay after having escaped his hutch and having a scary run-in with a fox. Clay opened his arms and his not-so-little-girl rushed into them, allowing the tears to flow.

'I thought…' she whispered before the sobs took over.

Clay tightened his arms around her further and he stroked her hair.

'It's not the same pumpkin. Just a bit of dehydration that's all. Typical city folk hey?'

She chuckled against his shoulder then pulled back. 'Rookie error,' she sniffed, wiping her eyes and turning back into the sixteen-year-old-too-cool-for-school girl again.

Even though it was born from trauma, Clay was thankful for the brief moment of father, daughter connection. It had been a while since they'd had that. It's why he'd agreed to help her in the competition. Any kind of positive connection was something.

Glancing around at the empty, makeshift auditorium, Samantha pushed distractedly at her hair. 'So, is that it? Show's over?'

'Just postponed until Tina's feeling better,' Clay replied, packing his guitar back into its case. 'How'd you feel about the song?'

She turned to him and her eyes lit up. 'It was good,' she breathed. 'I think?'

'You think?' he replied, raising an eyebrow in amusement.

Her mouth moved in a humble smile. 'Yeah…it was *good.*'

'Good?'

'Dad! Stop repeating everything I say,' she exclaimed, breaking into a laugh.

He laughed with her. 'It wasn't good. It was great. Terrific. Amazing. Phenomenal…'

She raised her hand to stop him. 'Okay. I get the point. You liked it.' A blush spread across her face and she tilted her head. 'Do you think I'll get to the semis?'

'Pumpk…'

Her eyes flashed.

'Look, it's between you, a cow that plays ball, Derek on his accordion and the Fontina Twins. You've got it in the bag. So, if you don't win this thing I'll eat my hat,' he declared.

'Gross,' she scoffed. But Clay could tell she was chuffed. She gazed out at the empty seats and his heart twisted in his chest, so full of love he thought it would explode. His throat muscles tightened, warning him that tears were not far away. He wasn't a fan of crying, so he busied himself with his guitar case, making sure all the clasps were closed, even though he knew they were.

He cleared his throat. 'Shall we?'

Samantha closed her eyes and drew a deep audible breath before turning to him. 'We shall.'

She linked her arm in his and they walked off the stage together. Two displays of affection in one day. Clay smiled, raised his eyes and sent a silent *thank you* skyward.

* * *

Today is another day, mused Tina, as she flung the sheets back and forced herself out of bed. Was there such a thing as dehydration hangovers? Because if there was, she had a doozy. It was tiredness on top of exhaustion on top of fatigue. Revolting. She was a shell of her former self. Thank god for makeup and camera filters.

She shuffled into the bathroom for a shower and felt a fraction more human afterwards. And maybe after a coffee she'd be a real person.

As if on cue there was a knock on the door. It was Brad with her morning coffee.

'You're a lifesaver,' she gushed as he handed it to her.

'You feeling okay?' he asked, concern etched across his face.

'I will after this.' She raised the coffee to her lips, a small groan escaping as she took the first sip of the caffeine elixir.

Brad smiled. 'Excellent. We'll head off in twenty minutes.'

'Cool,' Tina replied, starting to feel better already. She knew it was the placebo effect but didn't care. Whatever worked.

Thirty minutes, one coffee and a phone call to her manager later they arrived at the woodshed to begin filming the semi-finals.

After her rest in the trailer the day before, Carter had reappeared, having snagged the phone number of the hot paramedic – it was never in doubt – and they'd chosen the four semi-finalists.

'I just think Samantha is too young that's all,' Tina argued when Carter had insisted she be in the top four.

'She's sixteen. Under the rules she passes. She's in hun.'

'That's still too young,' she said, a hollow feeling in the pit of her stomach.

Carter took her hand in his. 'It won't happen to her. We'll make sure of it,' he said with deep affection in his voice.

Her heart clenched with emotion. 'Promise?'

'Have I ever let you down Tina Barina?' he asked.

She tilted her head and widened her eyes at him. 'Where do I start?'

He flung up his arms in mock surrender. 'Okay I can be a bit… flighty.' Then he looked at her and something flashed in his eyes. Fury. His grip tightened on her hand. 'But *that*. I will never let anything like that happen under my watch. *Ever.*'

She nodded. 'Okay then. She's in.' Her stomach still twitched in discomfort but Carter's endearing, if not rather out of character earnestness helped quell her fear.

He clapped his hands, back to vivacious Carter. 'So we've got Lily the cow, Samantha, Derek and the Fontina twins. This semi is gonna rock!'

Unfortunately, it didn't quite rock the way Carter thought it would.

Lily got stage fright or a bout of bovine bewilderment because no matter what Willy did, she refused to come out on stage. She stuck her hooves in and no amount of pushing and pulling would cajole the cow. Willy was forced to withdraw. But it wasn't all for naught as he won $10,000 from one of the sponsors for getting into the semis.

Derek's rendition of Heave Away – an Irish sea shanty – had the whole crowd clapping and singing along, Carter and Tina included. Tina had learnt during her discussions with Derek afterwards just how hard it was to play the accordion. And whenever he mentioned 'fingering' Carter broke into giggles next to her, which earned him a few sneaky whacks on the leg.

The Fontina twins wowed the crowd with some very impressive and what looked like very dangerous circus gymnastics. The brother and sister team were in sync the whole time, flowing from one move to the next, with the grand finale making the audience hold a collective breath as Despina balanced one foot on her brother's head as the music swelled to the inevitable sensational dismount. The crowd went wild.

'Well that rocked!' Carter shouted over the applause.

Tina was impressed but her thoughts were on the next and final act. Samantha. She knew Samantha could have a career in the music industry if she wanted. There was no doubt. But her thoughts were on seeing Clay again.

During their semi-final pick meeting Carter had given her a hard time about him.

'So, what's the deal with the comely cowboy?' he teased.

'Nothing,' Tina insisted, her face blushing in embarrassment.

'Hmmm. He picked you up like you weighed nothing. And you don't weigh nothing let me tell you,' he quipped, slowly raising an eyebrow. This got him a punch to his upper arm. 'Ouch, that hurt,' he whimpered.

Tina rolled her eyes at him. 'We're not here to talk about Clay. He's only here to accompany Samantha. And anyway, I'm with Danny.' Was she though? Was she really?

'All I'm saying is, if it looks like a duck and sounds like a duck it's you falling for a cowboy kind of duck,' he said with a wry little smile.

Back at the semi-finals the M.C. announced Samantha and Clay. Tina's stomach fluttered and she felt her breath catch in her throat as he walked on stage.

In the same jeans as the day before - she could tell because there was a tear in the left knee - he wore a different tee. Black this time. But just as tight as the white one, showing the shape of his wide shoulders and muscular arms. A tingle shot down her body to her core and she shifted in her seat to dispel the feeling. It was nice but it was a distraction.

'You okay hun?' Carter whispered.

'Fine,' she breathed.

He glanced across at her. 'He does look hot today.'

'Shut up!'

Her performance was even better than the day before if that was even possible. Tina could tell there'd been a shift in her. An assuredness. A knowing that she was good. That she was excellent in fact.

At one point in the song, Tina closed her eyes and just listened. Clay was singing harmonies and their blend was perfect. Father and daughter as one. Their sound felt like liquid gold. When she opened her eyes, he was looking directly at her. Holding her gaze, his eyes seared into her. Appraising her, drinking her in. She felt her pulse flutter in her throat and she couldn't look away. Then he smiled at her before breaking their gaze and giving his attention back to his daughter, pride spreading across his face.

The crowd erupted when Samantha finished and it became clear that she would be making it to the finals. There was no stopping her now.

Before the end of the day Carter and Tina had announced to the expectant crowd and contestants that it would be Samantha and the Fontina Twins who would be in the grand final in two day's time.

It was a popular decision and Tina found herself actually looking forward to it. And that was saying something because it had been a long time since she'd looked forward to anything.

10

Awhole day off. What the hell was she going to do with herself? She'd given up on moving accommodation as there where only a few more days left and she'd kind of settled into the motel room. It was simple but clean and there was something about the smallness of it that made her feel safe and secure; not rambling around by herself in a massive house built for a dozen people.

Tina liked the simplicity of it. She'd been so accustomed to the trappings of stardom she'd forgotten how much the simple life had agreed with her. A sunset. A homecooked meal – oh it had been a long time since she'd had one of those. The dinner with Brad at the Penvensy Hotel a few nights ago had come close to that. Maybe she'd see if Carter wanted to join her for dinner there tonight.

But there was eight hours to kill. She threw on her jeans and a tee, slipped into her thongs and wandered over to the motel's main office where she ran her eyes over the wall of tourist pamphlets that was a hallmark of motels & hotels all over the world.

One in particular caught her eye.

Riverbank Winery. That was where the wine she had at the pub came from. The pub's owner Yvonne had mentioned the woman's name who ran it. But for the life of her Tina couldn't remember it. She whipped one of the pamphlets out of its holder and flicked through it. The kitchen opened for lunch at noon. Tina glanced at her phone. Ten-thirty a.m. But the cellar door opened at eleven. Enough time for a quick shower, make herself look winery ready and head out.

Brad, sitting outside his room with a cup of coffee and a newspaper, waved to her.

'Good morning Tina.' He folded his newspaper neatly and placed it next to the coffee on the table.

'Hey Brad.'

He stood and offered her the other chair. 'You're looking much more rested today I must say,' he said, as his mouth moved into a smile of relief.

She waved away his offer of the chair. 'I am. I feel like a different person today. Sleep is *everything*. Did you sleep well?'

'I did thank you. When I'm on a job it's always with one eye and one ear open but I'm used to that.' He gestured towards the coffee with a little laugh. 'Hence this being my second coffee today. So far.'

'Then I'm glad you've got today off for some rest. You deserve it.'

He brushed off the comment with a flick of his hand and Tina was sure she saw a blush rise up his neck. Perhaps he wasn't used to being complimented by his clients.

'So, what are you up to today?' he asked.

'I'm going to head to the Riverbank Winery for some tastings and lunch.'

'I'll drive you,' Brad declared, gathering up his paper and coffee.

'No, you won't,' Tina said with a shake of her head. 'I can get an Uber or a Taxi. It's your day off too.'

'I need to wash the car anyway so let me drop you there and I can clean it on the way back. I saw a carwash when we arrived the other day.'

'Are you sure?'

'One hundred percent. I'd be happy to. What time?'

'Well, the cellar door opens at eleven so does fifteen minutes sound okay?'

His eyebrows came together in a thoughtful frown. 'That's early.'

Tina shrugged. 'Well, I figured it's *wine time* somewhere in the world.'

He shuffled his feet and shook his head. 'I'm sorry it's none of my business. Fifteen minutes.' And with that he disappeared into his room.

Tina blew out a slow breath and rolled her eyes at herself. She kept putting her foot in it with Brad. Never saying the right things. Two steps forward, one step back. She resolved to buy him a bottle of wine or two, to apologise – again.

The drive to the winery was uneventful and it seemed that Brad was his old self again. She sat in the front and asked what he thought about the contestants. It was no surprise that Samantha was his favourite as well. Although, much like Carter he was rather enamoured of Lily the cow and believed very strongly that if she hadn't gotten cold hooves, she deserved a spot in the finals.

Tina didn't agree but kept her mouth shut lest she put her foot in it again.

Brad turned off the main highway towards the river and as the Riverbank Winery came into view Tina felt her shoulders literally soften and drop about an inch. She'd been wearing her shoulders as earrings and hadn't even noticed.

The mighty river gums swaying lightly in the warm summer breeze framed the bright green grass that created a moat-like border around the central building and cellar door. A sign that read *Here at Riverbank, we use recycled water on our thirsty garden. Enjoy your visit*

With the river just metres away, Tina had assumed they'd use the water from that. She smiled with respect that they didn't.

Brad dropped her off outside the cellar door and told her to message him when she was ready to be picked up. He wasn't taking the day off as seriously as Tina would have liked. Although having a designated driver at her fingertips was pretty handy.

She stepped inside and removed her sunnies. It smelled of oak and tannin with the polished concrete flooring and wooden beams criss-crossing the ceiling giving it a natural cooling effect. Shelves of wine bottles and shiny glasses lined the wall behind the bar and she stepped up to it, picking up the cellar menu, running her eyes over it.

'Good morning!' a cheery voice greeted her.

Tina looked up as a woman entered from behind the bar, her smile wide, eyes bright, and her short brown curls bouncing in step with her enthusiasm. She was welcome personified.

An uncontrollable smile tugged at Tina's mouth. It was contagious. 'Yes. It is.'

The woman extended her hand. 'I'm Nat.'

Tina took her hand. 'Oh Nat. Yes. That's it. Yvonne mentioned you. I'm Tina.'

Nat laughed with delight and gave her a conspiratorial wink. 'I know who you are.'

Tina got that a lot. She was used to it. But this time it felt different. As if Nat really *did* know who she was. She tilted her head at Nat. 'You do?'

Nat leaned across the bar, glancing side to side as if checking for spies, before fixing Tina with her gaze. She'd seen those opal green eyes before hadn't she? Tina was transfixed. She'd come for chardonnay, but she now sensed she was going to get a whole lot more.

'Natalie!' A voice boomed across the polished concrete floor.

Nat lurched back as if caught in the act.

Tina spun around to see Clay striding towards them. His body language shouted trouble but the smile flickering on his face said otherwise.

'Big brother!' Nat squealed, running around the bar and pulling him into a hug. She almost disappeared into his large frame as he plastered a kiss on the top of her curly brown head.

'Sis. Are you behaving yourself?' he growled, holding her shoulders and glaring down at her.

'Of course I am,' she meowed, fluttering her lashes at him before landing a light punch to his gut and running back behind the safety of the bar. Clay grabbed his stomach and groaned in phony pain.

Straightening back up he plonked down on the bar stool next to Tina, his closeness making her stomach contract and a rush of heat flood her entire body. He gazed down into her eyes. Oh right, that's where she'd seen those eyes before. It was genetic. 'So...is she?'

'Is she what?' Tina stammered, trying her best to avoid his eyes in case he saw how she felt.

'My naughty sister. It looked like she was about to tell you state secrets.'

Behind the bar, Nat rolled her eyes as she placed a row of wine glasses in front of Tina. 'Don't be ridiculous. I was going to ask her if she thought Samantha was going to win. That's all.'

'You can't ask that!' Clay thundered, smacking his hand on the polished wooden bar. He was actually angry this time. 'Jesus Nat. You can't keep your mouth shut can you.' He kicked the stool back and stomped towards the door.

'Are you still gonna fix the fence?' Nat yelled after him.

'Of course! I said I would. I keep my promises.' He threw his arms up in frustration and disappeared outside.

Nat scowled and tossed her brown curls with disdain. 'Ugh he's such a goody two shoes. Always has been. He needs to chill out a bit.'

'Be a little naughty?' Tina suggested, trying to lighten the mood. It was her day off and all she wanted to do was taste some nice wine, eat some nice food and get an early night. She most certainly didn't want to get involved in any family dramas when she'd only just met them. And she wanted Clay to remain the perfect man in her memory when she left at the end of the show. The hot singing cowboy. That was her version of Clay and that was how she wanted him to remain.

'Yes!' Nat trilled, 'he needs to be naughty. He's had so much on his plate with the farm and Samantha after the accident he needs a bit of fun in his life.'

Clay was right, Nat didn't know how to keep her mouth shut. An over sharer. She and Carter would get along like a house on fire.

But hang on. 'Accident?'

The lightness left Nat as she poured a sample size of various wines into each glass, her face heavy with sadness. 'Yeah. On the farm. Sarah's quad bike rolled onto her.' She paused, her eyes misted with tears. 'Samantha was the one that found her.'

Tina didn't need to be a rocket scientist to work out that Sarah must've been Clay's wife, Samantha's mum. 'Oh...' she whispered, 'that's...awful. I'm so sorry.'

Nat sniffed and wiped the tears away. 'Thanks. It was tough. I didn't think Clay would get through it,' she passed one of the glasses to Tina, 'try this I think you'll like it.'

'If it's the chardi I know I already do.' Tina offered Nat a soft smile.

Nat poured a glass for herself. 'We all thought Samantha would just crumble, especially since she was the one that found...' she stopped, her breath catching in her throat. 'Sorry, I haven't talked about this for a while. No need to.'

Tina reached across the bar and placed a reassuring hand on Nat's arm. 'You don't need to talk about it, really. I was being nosy. It's none of my business.'

Nat raised her eyes and smiled at her. 'You're lovely. No wonder Clay talks about you all the time,' she said, amusement and warmth in her voice. She held out her wine and the women clinked glasses.

Tina grinned back at Nat and took a sip of the honey liquid. She closed her eyes and let it swirl in her mouth before letting it slide down her throat. She let out a soft groan and licked her lips. 'This is *good*,' she purred.

'We're just getting started,' Nat proclaimed, handing her a plain cracker and a glass of water to cleanse the palette.

'Now you're talking!' Tina laughed, taking the last mouthful of the rich woody chardonnay and suddenly feeling very grateful. At the same time her heart turned over with sorrow for Clay and Samantha and the horror they must've lived through. And all she wanted to do was draw him into her arms and never let go.

11

———————

Ugh. Women could be so bloody annoying. Clay's mind was a swirl of emotions and he took it out on the wooden post he was hammering into the earth, ramming it hard with his mallet. He could always rely on physical exertion to distract him from his feelings. It worked after the accident. It pushed the grief and the guilt down. But it wasn't working this time.

He hadn't expected to see Tina today. And he'd been disappointed, until he walked into his sister's winery. The rush of delight he'd felt seeing her standing at the bar made his body tingle from head to toe. He had stood at the door for a few moments drinking her in. Her honey-tinged hair was wound up onto her head in a messy bun with a few unruly tendrils resting against her neck. His fingers twitched with the desire to brush them away and drop soft kisses onto her smooth skin. He could see the pink hue of her bra underneath the white linen shirt and he imagined unclasping it and running his rough hands over her curves.

All she had to do was stand at a bar for him to feel the ache of his want.

He watched as Nat leaned into her which pulled him out of his thoughts. He had been dropping Tina into the conversations a lot over the last few days, not on purpose and he knew that Nat would deduce his feelings and love telling Tina all about them. He had to stop it. Which he did. But then he'd made a fool of himself by getting angry and storming off. What would she think of him now?

He shook his head at the memory and brought his mallet down hard on the wooden post again. In his frustration he had worked up a sweat. He needed to get a move on and get back to the farm before milking. Samantha was going to help him today, which she hated. But he'd promised if she helped him, they'd rehearse for the final afterwards.

The fence post now well and truly in the ground, he packed up his tools and as he turned to walk back to his ute, he saw Tina strolling down to the river's edge with a glass of wine in her hand.

She hadn't seen him. Then as she swatted a bug away from her glass she glanced across the lawn. Spotting him, she nodded, lifting her hand in a wave.

He waved back and dropped his tools in the tray of the ute. He really did have to get going but he felt rude. And he felt the need to explain his outburst.

Wiping his grubby hands on his jeans he walked down to her. A smile lit up her face as he approached and his stomach flip flopped like he was back in Year 7 when the girl he had a crush on, looked at him.

He stopped next to her, gesturing to the glass.

'So, what have you got?'

'Guess,' she teased.

'Well, it's white.'

'Uh huh,' she nodded and took a sip.

'So, it's either the Chardonnay or the Sav Blanc.'

She fixed him with her jade green eyes that held a mischievous twinkle. 'Well that narrows it down,' she said, holding the glass towards him. 'Would you like to taste?'

'Sure,' he said, their hands brushing as he reached out to take it and it felt as if an electric current had shot up his arm. He brought the glass to his lips to stop the groan that threatened.

He took a sip and swilled it around in his mouth, doing the wanky wine tasting mouth gurgling business. He made the mistake of glancing across at Tina, who's eyes were transfixed on his mouth, her own sweet lips partially open as if waiting for something. For him? He felt his groin twitch and he swallowed hard, the tanginess of the wine catching in his throat, making him splutter and cough.

Tina laughed and patted his back. 'That's not a very positive review of your sister's wine.'

He joined in the laughter, happy to be distracted from her lips and what he wanted to do with them.

'Yeah, I'm more of a beer man,' he said, clearing his throat and handing the glass back to her.

'Clearly.'

They stood in silence for a moment and then spoke at the same time.

'I should…' Clay began.

'It's beautiful…' Tina started.

The awkwardness set them off laughing again as they both offered for the other to speak first. Clay won and let Tina go first.

'It's such a beautiful part of the world here isn't it,' she breathed.

'Yeah, we're pretty lucky.'

She looked up at him, her eyes filled with…pity? They studied him, probed into him. Then she blinked and it was gone, her attention back to the river.

Clay sucked in a breath. He knew it. Nat had told her. He'd asked her not to tell people because this is exactly what he didn't want. Pity. He was well regarded in his hometown. A successful dairy farm that had been passed down through generations of farmers. Through drought and floods. He wasn't a bad singer even if he said so himself and he got tonnes of praise for that. But when people came to town and found out what had happened, they instantly looked at him with sad, sympathy eyes. Pathetic. He'd been enjoying the camaraderie he and Tina had and Nat had gone and stuffed it up. Oh well another one bites the dust. His throat tightened and he flexed his fingers trying to supress the urge to race back to the cellar door and give Nat a piece of his mind. He loved his sister more than anything but sometimes…Christ!

'Clay?'

He realised Tina had been speaking to him. 'Sorry, I was somewhere else.'

'Your turn,' she said, brushing a soft wave of hair that had escaped the top knot, out of her eyes.

Hey that was his job! He shook off his exasperation and turned his attention on Tina. After all it wasn't her fault that his sister was an over sharer. Had been since they were kids.

He cleared his throat and felt a swirl of nervous knots in his stomach. It was important what she thought of him. 'I wanted to apologise for my angry outburst earlier. Totally inappropriate.'

Tina nodded, her face crinkled in thought. After a few seconds he realised he'd been holding his breath, waiting for her response.

She rested her slender hand on his forearm. 'It's fine. No need to apologise. I get the sense that Nat can be…how do I say it…'

'Annoying?'

Her hand still on his arm and burning into his skin, she laughed. 'I was going to say candid. But I suppose to a brother annoying will do.'

She gave his arm a tender squeeze before pulling away, leaving him feeling bereft of her touch. 'And…I'm sorry,' she said, staring towards the water, unable to look at him, her voice laden with emotion.

He wanted to tell her it was okay. That he and Samantha had come through the fire, through the worst of it. That sometimes the grief and guilt crept up when he least expected it. That he should've been the one out on the quad bike that day but had instead chosen a gig over the farm. That he'd wanted to pursue a career in singing and that Sarah had been his number one fan and handing him his guitar, had pushed him out the door that afternoon. That he'd only started singing again a year ago and as penance he'd decided that pub gigs were enough. That he was living vicariously through his daughter and her talent and desire to forge a career with her voice. But mostly he wanted to tell Tina that she was the first woman to find her way into his bones since that awful day. But just having had a go at Nat for being an over sharer he figured that would be hypocritical.

Instead, he lifted his face towards the river and closed his eyes. 'Thank you,' he whispered, his voice so husky with emotion as to be almost inaudible.

They stood together that way for a few minutes, the warm summer breeze floating around them, the leaves of the river gums swaying as if to music and the most wonderful feeling of stillness and clarity Clay had felt for a long time.

He took a small sideways step towards her, their shoulders almost touching and he felt her breath quicken. He was about to reach down and take her hand in his when he heard Nat yell out from the cellar door.

'Clay! I need your help.'

Frustrated, he thrust a hand through his hair and stepped away, the moment gone. 'Well, the boss calls,' he said, reluctant to leave her side.

Tina dipped her head and he was sure he saw a look of disappointment flash across her face. She recovered well though and gave him a wide smile. Almost too wide.

'A man's gotta do what a man's gotta do. I'll see you tomorrow.' She raised her glass to him. 'Good luck.'

He frowned at her. 'It's bad luck to wish someone good luck.'

'Let's face it though, it's not about luck is it. It's about talent. And Samantha has that in spades...' she paused and took the last sip of the wine. 'As do you,' she murmured, her voice soft and shy.

Clay smiled with delight. 'Thanks. That means a lot.'

'Well I mean it,' she said, looking up at him, her eyes filled with deep admiration from one singer to another.

'Clay!' Nat's shriek cut between them and he almost jumped at the intrusion.

'I'm coming,' he yelled back. He growled under his breath, flashing Tina a *well- whadaya-gonna-do* look and headed back up the grassy hill to the cellar door.

He turned to give Tina a wave, but his hand got caught midway because she'd already turned her attention back towards the river.

That didn't last long he mused. But he guessed the Mighty Murray was more interesting than his retreating back.

12

————————

Tina watched Clay jog up the slope, thinking how sexy his toned backside looked in those well-worn jeans. They fitted him like a glove. She wondered whether he was a boxers or an undies kind of guy, feeling her cheeks redden at the thought. Then he slowed down and started to turn. She didn't want to get caught checking him out, so she whipped around just in time and stared out onto the water. She wasn't really taking in the view because she could sense his eyes on her and a tiny tremor ran across her skin.

Finally, the sound of Nat and Clay talking to each other told her that she was in the clear. His attention was elsewhere. She was a little disappointed. She enjoyed his company. Felt safe in it. Felt like she could be herself. Whoever that was. But coming back to Oz she felt like she was just starting to find that woman again.

Her phone buzzed in her pocket. Probably Brad wondering when she wanted to be picked up.

It was Carter.

OMG TEENS CHECK THIS OUT

He'd attached a link for her to click, but before she had time to press on it, he sent another message.

CALL ME AFTER YOU WATCH IT. LOVE YOU!

He texted as he lived. In capitals.

She giggled at the ridiculousness that they could be friends. They were *so* different. It was probably a silly cat video or a clip of a miniature pony that lived inside someone's home. He'd almost bought one just so he could put videos of it living with him on TikTok, but then realised with all the travelling he did it would be cruel. No kidding!

Tina clicked on the link, still chuckling to herself.

It took a moment to register that it wasn't an animal doing funny things. There were humans in it. One human in particular. Danny. With another human. A woman. In a nightclub. They seemed very cosy.

Her eyes burned with tears of fury and confusion at what she was watching.

Then they kissed. Her hand flew to her mouth and her throat contracted in pain. She clicked off the video, even though there was another few minutes left to go, not wanting to see what happened next. She didn't have to. He'd kissed her like that in nightclubs. Many times and she knew what was to come. He…and the woman, were oblivious they were being recorded.

But wait. When was it filmed? Maybe it was before they'd gotten together. She clicked back on the link and paused the video – she didn't need to see it again – scanning for when it was uploaded. Two hours ago. Damn. But that doesn't mean it was filmed two hours ago. It already had over 250,000 views.

Her mind raced, wondering how she could find out without calling Danny. She wasn't ready to talk to him, just yet.

Then it clicked. He'd gotten a tattoo of a panda on his left forearm, just before she headed back to Oz. He'd loved Kung Fu Panda when it was first released and had been wanting a tatt of him for years. But was the left arm visible in the video? She held her breath and pressed play. He was sitting against the seat as the woman whispered some-thing into his ear. Apparently, it was funny because he laughed as if he'd never heard anything that funny before. Part of his schtick. Tina had been *hilarious* at the start. She couldn't see the outside of his forearm but then he turned and wrapped his arms around her, pulling her into him. And there it was. The unmistakable image of a panda with a big smile plastered on its inky face. She'd nevver look at a panda in the same way again.

The hand holding the phone dropped listlessly to her side as a tear stole down her cheek.

She knew that Danny wasn't 'the one' but she'd trusted him. Shaking her head, she drew in a breathless sigh and squared her shoulders, wiping the wetness off her cheeks with a trembling hand.

Her phone dinged. Carter.

BABE ??

Tina didn't have it in her to debrief with Carter about this. With anyone really. She needed some time alone. She messaged him back.

Seen it. Buzz u later xx

The three dots blinked across the screen.

BASTARD! U OK THO?

I'll be ok. Just need time. Thanks bub.

WHERE ARE YOU?

STOP YELLING AT ME!

I'LL YELL AT YOU IF I WANT TO. AS LONG AS YR OK. CHAT LATERZ. LOVE YA.

Yes I'm fine. Buzz later. Mwah.

Good, that was done. Now what?

The sound of a car starting and the engine revving made her look up towards the cellar door. It was Clay in his ute. His window wound down, he waved a goodbye to her. She just stared at him, wondering if he would do what Danny had done. What many of the men in her life had done. She couldn't imagine it. Nat had said he was a goody two shoes. But weren't they always the ones that seemed too goody two shoes to be true? But where were her manners. She plastered a smile on her face and waved back, suddenly overwhelmed with a desire for more of Nat's chardonnay. Much more.

She watched him wind his window up and pull away, the tyres crunching on the gravelled driveway. He was definitely a stickler for rules as he inched along at the requested ten kilometres an hour. Safe. That's the one word that described Clay in a nutshell. Safe and sexy.

Tina allowed herself a smile because she realised that only minutes before she'd been watching her boyfriend/partner/friend with benefits making out with another woman and here she was feeling all yummy in the tummy about a bloke in a ute. Maybe she was as bad as Danny.

But she didn't have time to contemplate the intricacies of the human emotion. She had wine to drink!

13

Clay sped down the bumpy dirt driveway cursing himself for being late. Between a day of fixing fences and being distracted by Tina he'd lost track of the time and now the ladies would be getting antsy. Sure enough as the milking sheds came into view, his fifty-five Jersey girls were gathered at the gate, ready for their afternoon feeding and milking. And he was only fashionably late by ten minutes, but these girls had their own body clock which he could set his watch to.

Six a.m. and four p.m. On the dot. The herd looked towards the ute as he came to stop outside the shed. He was sure their big brown eyes held a note of accusation and if they could talk they'd be saying *About time. Where have you been?*

As if on cue, Betty the Jersey with the white heart shaped splodge between her eyes let out a loud, accusatory, moo. The rest of the ladies followed suit. They were annoyed.

He leapt out of the ute. 'Sorry m'ladies. I was talking with another lady but I'm here now.'

Betty stamped her foot. Jealous? And where was Samantha? She said she would help in return for a practice session afterwards. Of course he was always going to rehearse with her but it had been a good way to get her into the sheds.

Ever since that traumatic day she struggled with being around the farm. The main house, a quad bike ride from the sheds was far enough away for her to pretend it was just a normal suburban house with a half a kilometre driveway. He empathised with her shunning the farm, but he also thought it was important for her to face her fears. Not run away from them. And whenever he told her that, the conversation would usually end with her huffing off to her bedroom and slamming the door. He'd even convinced her to see a therapist but that didn't last long because she spent most of the session in silence. Didn't seem worth the money in the end. Then, when she was thirteen, a year after her mum's death, she'd picked up his guitar and started playing. The Rainbow Connection. The next day he took her to the local music shop and bought her a guitar. She refused to be taught by him, so he arranged lessons with a mate he sometimes jammed with.

Her guitar skills quickly improved but it was her singing that filled his soul.

She'd been musical as a kid and when she sang along with The Wiggles and Hi-Five she would always be in tune. Even as a four-year-old.

But there was something in her voice that broke his heart and filled it up at the same time whenever she sang. A yearning, a maturity, that came from a deep place in her.

But today he wanted her in that shed. To get out of her mind and get her body working. Bring her down to earth a bit after the highs of the competition. He didn't believe in ego. It really was a dirty word and he vowed to always make sure Samantha kept hers in check.

He unlatched the gate and waved the herd through, helped in part by Pup, his tan and brown kelpie who had met him at the shed. No doubt she'd heard the ute on the driveway and had been ready and waiting as he arrived.

Samantha had called her Pup when she was given to them ten years ago and she'd stayed Pup ever since. She'd been a hard one to train at the start, nipping at the herd's heels all the time, until she got a good kick in the ribs from his oldest cow, Maisy. She was bruised but bounced back quickly and kept a safe distance from that time on. And ever since between Clay and Pup they managed the herd easily. Most of the time.

Sometimes when moving between paddocks they'd get a little toey and test him and Pup, the unrest usually led by Betty. The day he'd seen Tina for the first time was one of those times.

The cattle filed into their milking stalls in their usual well-mannered, habitual way. Gosh he loved these girls.

'Hey Dad.' Clay, relieved, smiled to himself as Samantha entered the shed. But he didn't want her to see that, just yet. He pursed his lips and turned to her.

'I thought you'd have them in already Samantha,' he said in his dad voice.

'Ohhh Samantha is it? I'm in trouble,' she said to Pup, bending down to give her a scratch behind the ears.

Clay gave an audible sigh. 'No. You're not in trouble. I expected you'd be here that's all.'

Samantha stood up, squared her shoulders and looked at him, her eyes glittering with amusement. 'Well, I'm not the one who was late because he was chatting with another "lady",' she said with a brief tilt of her head.

So, she'd been in the shed the whole time. Cheeky.

'Fine, you've made your point.' Clay turned back to the cattle and started to attach the milking pumps. 'You do the feed please,' he directed at Samantha.

'Was Tina the lady in question?' Samantha asked, laughter in her voice.

'None of your business,' he replied hoping that would be the end of it. He most certainly didn't want to discuss his love life with his sixteen-year-old daughter. But it wasn't a love life. Was it? Just because she made his stomach flutter and his heart turn over every time he thought of her didn't constitute a love life.

'I'll take that as a yes. C'mon Pup.' Samantha tapped her leg and Pup followed her into the feeding shed.

Who was that young sassy woman and what had she done with his wide-eyed little girl? How he yearned for the days when she doted on him and had been his little shadow, always by his side. Helping him with the cows, hosing down the shed after each milking and always insisting on him reading her a bedtime story, twice.

He knew he was going to have to let go eventually. She was going to win the competition and that meant she would leave the farm. Leave the town. Leave him. His throat tightened. Who was going to look after her? He'd thought about selling up many times over the years since Sarah died but he couldn't bring himself to do it. She'd loved the farm. The animals. Them working together as a family.

But they weren't a family anymore. Samantha would be gone soon, he had no doubt. Then it would be just him and some young blokes he got to work on the farm sometimes. That was no life.

He raked his fingers through his hair, his future unsure. As he was contemplating that future, Maisy, who he was attaching the suctions to, let out a sharp grunt, kicked out her hind leg and caught him on the hand. He lunged back and grabbed his hand. 'Fuck!' he groaned.

It wasn't Maisy's fault. He hadn't been paying attention and had obviously mucked up the connection, causing her pain. None of his girls would do that for no reason.

'Sorry Maisy that was my fault,' he whispered, giving her a pat on her neck with his uninjured hand.

Samantha entered the shed with a wheelbarrow full of feed and registered him holding his hand. She dropped the handles of the wheelbarrow and raced to him.

'Dad what happened?' She reached out to touch his hand.

He pulled away. 'Nothing. I'm okay. Maisy got a little cranky when I screwed up the connection,' he replied, his mouth twisting into a grimace. It was throbbing now. The old girl still had a good kick in her. 'I'll go put some ice on it if you can finish up here that'd be great. And don't forget to…'

'I know what to do Dad,' Samantha said, her eyebrows scrunched with concern.

He nodded, unable to speak in case she could hear the pain in his voice and headed towards his ute.

Samantha came running out before he pulled away. 'Dad!'

'Yes pumpkin?' He really needed to get some ice on it and pop some pain killers.

She looked like she was about to cry. 'What if you can't play?'

'Play what?'

'Tomorrow night? In the final.'

Oh fuck. It was the hand that played the chords. He stretched his fingers and a sharp stabbing pain ran up his arm. Not good.

'It's only a little bruise. I'll be fine.'

'You promise?'

'I promise.'

A smile of relief lit up her face 'Love you!' She blew him a kiss and skipped back into the shed.

'Love you too,' he called out after her, as a sense of dread rolled through the pit of his stomach.

14

———————

Where were those paramedics when she needed them? If they were there, they would've told her that it was self-inflicted and to take Panadol and a Berocca and if symptoms persisted, stop drinking.

Tina rolled over in the bed and promptly fell out. Her eyes shot open on impact, a loud groan escaping her mouth as she pressed her hand to her pounding forehead.

Sound hurt. Moving hurt. Landing on floorboards hurt. Wait. What? Floorboards? The motel had carpet. Tina pulled herself onto her knees, using the bed sheets as leverage. No wonder she'd fallen out of bed. It was a single. The motel had queens. She was not in the motel. Clearly. *Fuck.*

Then where was she?

'Good morning!' A voice trilled outside the door. 'I heard a thud. You okay?'

Trilling was not good for a hangover.

'I'm fine,' she moaned, trying to give her voice some energy to prove her point. It didn't work.

The door flung open and Nat bounced in with a plate of something in her hands. Tina regarded her through narrow eyes because it hurt to open them fully.

'Oh you silly billy. Here let me help.' She placed the plate on the side table and helped Tina up onto the bed.

Tina winced and dropped her head into her hands.

'I'm glad I cut you off after the third,' Nat mused.

'The third? How am I feeling like this after three glasses?'

'The third *bottle*,' Nat said, a smile in her voice.

Tina grunted. 'Yep, that'll do it.'

Nat clapped her hands, causing Tina's head to spin. 'But never fear the cure is here.' My egg and bacon breakfast rolls never fail to do the trick,' she said, handing Tina the plate.

Tina looked down at the greasy offering and when the smell of fried egg and bacon hit her nostrils, she knew that she'd never eat again.

Tina shoved the plate back at Nat and slapped her hands over her mouth. 'Bathroom. Now!'

Nat's eyes widened with dread. She pointed towards the hallway. 'Second door on the right.'

Tina nodded, her hands gripped tightly across her mouth as if that could stop the body's need to expel the poison, and ran to the bathroom in the nick of time.

As she drove the porcelain bus, she heard Nat rap lightly on the door. 'Erm, I'll keep your breakfast warm cause you'll need a refill. There are clean towels you can use to freshen up. See you soon,' she offered, between Tina's bouts of puking.

Once she was completely empty, Tina lay on the cool tiled floor of the bathroom, the hangover shivers taking over her body but all she could think about was that Clay would find out about this over the bush telegraph. AKA Nat.

Then she remembered. Danny. She had to deal with him at some point. But she had a final to judge that night and that had to be her focus to get through the day. Danny could wait.

After a cold shower and a fresh change of clothes that Nat had left on the end of her bed – lucky they were a similar size – she was starting to feel a bit more normal. And when her tummy rumbled, she was pleased that Nat had kept her breakfast warm because it was quite possibly the best egg and bacon roll she'd ever had. The winning combination of greasy fried food and a strong, sugary coffee was all she needed to feel like she could get through the day.

* * *

THE DAY HAD OTHER IDEAS.

The positive side effects of the curative breakfast disappeared when Tina turned her phone on after breakfast. The alerts dinged immediately. She had a myriad of messages from her manager, the production company, Carter, Brad – wanting to know when she needed to be picked up - and various media outlets. How they got her number she'll never know. It seemed that Australia cared more about her love life than her music because social media had gone nuts. The video was everywhere. Curiously, Danny hadn't left a message. No text, no phone call. Nothing. Surely, he would've known he'd been caught out by now. He'd screwed up a few times since they'd started dating – although nothing as bad as this – and he'd always come grovelling back straight away.

Thinking about dealing with it all, her head started to pound and all she wanted to do was stay at the winery and stare out at the calmness of the Murray River leaving the mad world outside the gates. But she knew that was impossible and she'd have to face it sooner or later.

She was collecting her belongings when there was a soft knock on the bedroom door. 'It's me. Are you okay?'

Tina opened the door to find Clay standing in the hallway, a line of worry creasing his eyebrows.

She must've looked like she'd been ambushed because he held his hands up, palms out and took a step back. 'Nat called me. She was worried about you.' Then he chuckled. 'I mean what exactly I could do to help is anyone's guess. I'm useless with women's stuff. But she insisted and you know my sister. She's hard to say no to. Always has been. Takes after my dad. Gift of the gab, both of them.' He faded out when he registered the look of amusement on Tina's face.

'Have you finished?' she asked with a soft laugh.

'Seems so,' he replied, 'but you're laughing so my work here is done.' He clapped his hands together for a job well done.

'I appreciate your help, but you could've saved yourself a trip, I'm fine,' Tina declared as she brushed past him, his earthy combination of sweat and musk filling her nostrils, setting off a liquid heat between her thighs.

He followed her up the hallway. 'Speaking of trips why don't I drop you back into town. I have to go right past the motel on my way back to the farm. Save Brad coming to get you.'

She spun around, hands on hips, suddenly annoyed at him for trying to organise her life. 'Thank you for coming but I'm fine. Really. I'll make my own way back. What is it, a half an hour walk? A walk will do me good.'

'It's already thirty-two degrees out there. You were dehydrated just a few days ago.'

Her pulse quickened in her throat. Why was he being so insistent? She'd only just meet him days ago. 'Clay, please,' she seethed, resisting the urge to shout. Then she made the mistake of looking up at him. His blue eyes were focused intently on her face, full of genuine concern. A sob rose in her throat as hot tears welled into her eyes. She turned her head away, not wanting Clay to see her like this.

'Oh Tina,' he whispered, laying a hand on her trembling shoulder, before drawing her into his arms. She stiffened at his touch before surrendering and allowing the tears to flow. Tears of anguish, heartbreak, embarrassment, the lot.

He shushed her, his breath against her hair, his strong protective arms holding her tight.

And there was that word again. Safe. Even after she'd finished crying, she was happy to remain in his arms for just that little bit longer. She fitted perfectly there.

'You okay?' he asked.

'I think so,' she sniffed.

'You'll definitely be dehydrated after that,' he chuckled and she smiled against his shoulder before pulling away and giving him a playful slap on the arm.

'Call the paramedics. Maybe they can fix my broken heart at the same time,' she laughed.

Clay's face darkened and his hands clenched into fists. 'If I ever see that douche bag I'm gonna let him have it.'

Tina reached out and rested her hand on his arm. 'Well lucky for him you won't see him unless you're heading to the US anytime soon.'

Clay wiggled his fingers and twitched a little before letting his arms relax by his side. 'You call him lucky I call him a…'

'Clay!' Nat yelled out from the kitchen. 'I heard that. Keep it clean brother.'

Tina and Clay looked at each other and burst out laughing. True to form Nat would be listening in on it all.

'Geez sis, first I'm a goody two shoes and then when I simply express myself, I get in trouble. A bloke can't win with you,' Clay called out as he headed towards the kitchen.

Tina followed, her heart full, despite Danny's deceit, knowing that these people including Carter and Brad had her back. She was not in this alone.

'Now where's my egg and bacon roll,' Clay asked, sliding onto the stool at the breakfast bar.

Nat was already onto it and shoved a paper bag with grease spots already appearing, into his hands. 'Get going brother. You've got a final to win tonight.'

He grabbed the bag off her and winced.

'What's wrong?' Nat asked, worry flashing across her pixie like face.

He curled his fingers, in and out, which clearly caused him pain.

'Oh, Maisy got a bit cranky yesterday. Let me know about it with a hoof to the hand.'

'Maybe you should put her out to pasture, she's getting a bit old now,' Nat exclaimed, grabbing a pack of pills, popping two out and handing them over with a glass of water.

'Not her fault. I wasn't concentrating. I'll be fine. Occupational hazard.' He swallowed the pills without the water.

Tina frowned, aware that hand injuries spelled bad news for a guitarist. 'Can you play?'

Clay mimed an air guitar and smiled at her, a little too broadly. 'Does this look like someone who can't play?'

'Rock on brother.' Nat started to mime playing drums and looked at Tina, expecting her to pick up a non-existent instrument.

That was never going to happen and hoped the look on her face told them so. The other two scrunched their faces in disappointment and "dropped" their instruments.

'Party pooper,' Nat teased. 'Now eat up brother, I can't have you starving on me now can I?'

He tore open the bag with his good hand and took an enthusiastic bite of the roll, almost demolishing half of it in one go.

'Wow you are hungry,' Tina teased.

Clay locked his eyes on hers as he chewed. She couldn't tear her eyes away and out of the corner of her eye she saw Nat looking from one to the other as if at a tennis match. He swallowed, then licked a spot of barbeque sauce off his lips. 'Yes I am.'

There was no mistaking his intent. Nat got it too and she giggled, breaking the connection.

Tina slapped her hand on the bench. 'Okay I'll take you up on your offer of a ride. Let's go. You can finish that in the car,' she bossed, tossing her hair with a turn of her head. 'Thanks for your hospitality Nat. See you at the show tonight?'

'Wouldn't miss it for the world,' Nat beamed. 'Where do you want the boxes of wine you bought last night?'

Tina's stomach churned at the thought. 'I bought wine last night?'

'Three cases my friend.'

Clay had already finished his roll and jumped off the stool, brushing crumbs off his legs. 'I'll pop them in the ute. Which ones Nattie?'

'In the coolroom. Labelled Tina.'

'Righto. See you outside,' he said as he strode towards the cool room, out the back of the building.

Nat started to sing.

Clay and Tina sitting in a tree, K.I.S.S.I.N.G

Tina gave Nat a death stare, but her lips quivered, trying not to laugh.

Nat trotted around the breakfast bar and pulled Tina into a hug before planting a kiss on her cheek and pulling back with a wink. 'What's that expression? To get over a man you need to get another one under you. Well, you have my permission. See you tonight,' she sing songed as she waved her hand in the air and scooted out of the kitchen.

Tina opened her mouth to yell something witty back at her, but she was rendered speechless. A smile crinkled her mouth and she shook her head in affectionate disbelief until she realised what was facing her once she stepped back out into the world.

Taking a deep breath, she squared her shoulders and headed outside to Clay's ute, almost keen to see what that world was going to throw at her.

15

During the ten-minute car ride back to the motel Tina called Carter, mainly so she didn't have to chat with Clay. She was a little afraid of what she'd say. Something like, *pull over and make mad love to me right now.* Something like that. So instead, she spent the ten minutes making Carter feel better. He seemed to be more upset about Danny's infidelity than she was.

She sensed Clay's eyes dart across at her a few times as she explained to Carter that she didn't even know if they were a couple. They had kind of talked about exclusivity, but it had never been signed sealed and delivered. She had just assumed that's what it had become. The morale of the story – never assume anything when it comes to the heart.

At one point when Tina told Carter she wasn't angry with Danny, Clay let out a snort of disapproval and out of the corner of her eye she saw him shake his head. It was very lucky for Danny that Clay would never set eyes on him.

She clicked off the call as Clay pulled to stop outside the motel. He kept the car idling.

'Thanks for, well, everything.' Tina pushed the door open and a wave of hot air rushed into the cabin. It had to be hotter than thirty-two by now surely.

'No worries Tina. Anytime,' Clay replied, checking the rear-view mirror to make sure he wasn't going to get a semi-trailer up his backside.

'See you tonight and I won't wish you luck this time. Break a leg.'

'Well, I just might if I don't get out of this loading zone,' he chuckled. Then he glanced over her shoulder. A flash of fury passed across his face and his jaw clenched. Tina turned to see what the cause of the sudden change was.

'Baby!'

Tina's breath left her body as Danny picked her up and spun her around, landing kisses all over her face and neck.

'I missed you,' he breathed.

Tina's head began to spin, then she met Clay's eyes which steadied her. The knuckles of his hands gripping the steering wheel had turned white and she knew he was trying hard not to get out and punch Danny in the face. She pleaded with her eyes for him to not make trouble.

Nodding he broke their eye contact and put the car in gear. 'See you tonight,' he said, the words seeming to drag themselves from his throat. He leaned across the console pulling her door closed before he sped off, leaving a sea of dust behind him.

'Jesus buddy!' Danny shouted after him, getting a mouthful of dust as a reward. He released his hold on Tina as he spluttered and carried on.

'Come on let's get you a glass of water,' Tina sighed, grabbing his hand and leading him towards her room.

'They put you here babe?' he coughed, really milking it.

'I don't mind it. It's clean. Cute. And not where people would expect me to be. Carter on the other hand is living it up at a swish place on the river but there are fans camping out there all day to get his autograph. But of course he loves that.' She was rambling now. Just to talk about something other than the reason he was there.

Once inside, he gulped down a large glass of pristine country tap water – he'd insisted on bottled water and she told him Oz had some of the best water in the world and that there wasn't any bottled water anyway. After he finished, he moved to her, sliding his arms around her waist. She wanted to slap them away but felt frozen in place. He brushed a lock of hair off her neck and dropped soft kisses along her skin. 'I've missed you babe,' he groaned.

Oh, his lips felt good. Her pent-up feelings about Clay, about how much she wanted him made her body shiver under the physical touch. The memory of being back at the winery in his arms gripped her heart and she moaned.

'Yeah babe, moan for me,' Danny crooned, gliding his hands down to her bottom and giving it a squeeze while he tugged on her earlobe with his teeth.

He knew she liked that. But she didn't want it from him. In a flash she stepped back and slapped him across the face.

She caught her breath, shocked at what she'd done. But not as shocked as Danny. He held his hand to his cheek that was starting to redden, eyes wide with horror. 'Babe,' he pleaded. Then he started to cry. 'I'm sorry. She means nothing to me. I was so fucking high I didn't know what I was doing.' It was pathetic. Snot started to seep from his nose as tears streamed down his face.

She couldn't look at him. Bile rose into her throat. Not again. No.

Her eyes narrowed and she resolved then and there no man was ever going to underestimate her ever again.

Turning to Danny who was wiping his nose on his sleeve, classy, she fastened her eyes on him, a fierceness surrounding her. 'Get out,' she said, her voice hard as steel.

'Babe!' Danny pleaded, literally dropping to his knees. 'You're the only one for me.' He shuffled towards her. 'I flew all the way to this,' he waved his hand in the air, 'shithole. Just for you. For us.'

He pushed himself off the ground and sat on the bed, his head in his hands.

'What about *get out* don't you understand Danny?' Tina marched to the door flinging it open.

Defeated, Danny shuffled to the door, then made one last attempt by grabbing Tina's hand showering her palm with kisses. She yanked it back. 'Out!'

'Fuck you,' he shot back, his eyes now glittering with anger. 'You'll regret this. You'll miss Danny I can guarantee it. And where are you gonna find a cock like mine?'

To accentuate his point, he grabbed his groin and gave it a good shake. Then he spun on his heels and walked out of her life, down the dusty motel driveway and into the country heat.

Good riddance. Relief flooded Tina's body and something between a laugh and a sob escaped from her mouth, which she quickly supressed.

She had a job to do. No point crying over spilt milk or men.

16

Clay drove straight to the milking sheds where he was to meet Gordo and Dicko, two young lads who would often help with the milking when he needed them. They were going to take care of everything so he could get ready for the final.

They were good blokes and he knew he could trust them with the job.

The pain killers that Nat had given him hadn't kicked in yet. His hand ached and a nice bluey tinge had started to develop across his wrist. Made sense. If it was only a few fingers that Maisy had hit there wouldn't be the kind of generalised pain that ran up his arm every time he moved his hand. He probably should've gone to the doctor, but he already knew that his wrist was fucked. And he didn't need a doc to tell him that. But he wasn't going to let that stop him from accompanying Samantha in the final. He just had to get through two minutes and forty-four seconds. And he knew it was that long because he'd tried to play the song late last night after Samantha had gone to bed and it was two minutes and forty-four seconds of excruciating torment.

He'd made the excuse of having to deal with an emergency with the bloke who collected their milk, to get out of rehearsing. Promising that they'd go through the song before the performance the next day. Although after his own private practice he was worried he wouldn't even be able to do that.

And when he'd seen that dickhead Danny scoop Tina up at the motel, he was this close to jumping out of the car and landing a punch but it was his punching hand that was injured. And he knew that if he used his 'good' hand it would feel like a pathetic slap in the face. So that desire would have to be put on hold.

And it looked like his desire for Tina would have to be put on hold or completely let go as well. She seemed surprised to see Danny but not unhappy. Maybe they were making up right now. Him planting her with kisses and making love to her, running his hands over her smooth skin and looking deeply into her eyes. *Argh he was sounding like a romance novel.* He shook his head to dispel the thoughts and got out of the ute as Gordo and Dicko strolled towards him, their well-worn baseball caps pulled low on their heads.

'Mate!' they shouted in unison.

Clay gave them the same greeting and together they walked into the shed to start the preparation.

* * *

In the makeup chair, Tina listened patiently to Carter sitting next to her.

'You slapped him? O. M. G I would've given *anything* to see that,' he squealed, clapping his hands and bouncing in his chair.

Susie, the makeup artist, pushed down on his shoulders. 'Keep still Carter,' she pleaded for about the fifth time. 'Do you want lopsided hair?'

'I've had worse. But okay I'll try.' He locked eyes on Tina in the mirror. 'Then what?'

'He started to cry.'

Carter's hand flew to his mouth. 'Oh that poor baby.'

'What!' Tina and Susie exclaimed at the same time.

'I mean you. You poor baby,' he said, a blush starting to creep up his neck.

Susie clocked the red heat rising. 'Would you like some powder on that faux pax?' she said, her voice deadpan, but her eyes twinkling with mirth.

Carter pouted his lips at her. 'Funny. And no,' he sulked, crossing his arms over his chest.

Tina and Susie shared a smile in the mirror.

'I saw that!' Carter squealed.

'You were supposed to,' laughed Tina.

'Fine then.' He sucked in a dramatic breath. 'Keep going.'

'Not much to add. He went through the five stages of grief in about thirty seconds. He blubbered, got mad, said I'd miss him and he said that in third person,' Tina rolled her eyes, 'then, that I'd regret it and finally he asked me how I'd ever find a cock like his.'

'Hmm fair point,' Carter mused.

'Which one?' Tina raised a brow to him.

'Well honey you did say he was…you know…impressive in the manhood department. It would be shame to let that go wouldn't it?'

'Seen one, seen 'em all,' Tina teased, waving her hand dismissively.

He didn't bite. 'Well good riddance I suppose. Onto greener pastures. Or more specifically a singing cowboy.' It was his turn to share a knowing smile with Susie.

'Stop it you two,' she exclaimed, her face blushing in embarrassment.

Carter rubbed his hands together in glee. 'Now who looks like she needs some powder.'

Daneesh, one of the production assistants poked her head into the trailer saving Tina from having to participate in the conversation anymore.

'Ten minutes until filming. Let's get you two set up,' she said, touching her hand to the wired earbud as a call came through. 'Getting them now.' Nodding to Tina and Carter, the sign that hair and makeup was done, she waited for them to join her outside.

Carter slipped his arm through Tina's as they followed Daneesh to the stage. It was his way of apologising and telling her he was on her side. She leaned over and kissed him on the cheek. They were okay. She'd missed him and vowed to keep in touch. When she'd run away to the U.S., she lost touch with many of her Aussie mates. They didn't stop trying, she did. It was her way of trying to forget the trauma of her abuse at the hands of her tour manager and the subsequent minimising of her experience by the powers that be. She was so young, she sucked it up and then the trauma reared its ugly head during the last performance she ever did in Oz. Waves and waves of it finally rushing up like a ball in the water when you've been holding it down for too long.

But she was a different person now, she knew that. Well at least she was trying. Coming back was the first most terrifying step. Then getting Danny out of her life another move forward. A lightness touched her. Possibility. A future she could look forward to. In whatever form that took.

And maybe that form was in the shape of the man standing in front of her.

* * *

CLAY TURNED TO SEE TINA AND CARTER WALKING TOWARDS THEM ARM IN arm. Carter was a weird one, but he had warmed to him and loved how much he loved Tina. Wasn't hard to do he admitted to himself.

He nodded a hello. Tina raised his eyes to him and mouthed *break a leg,* followed by the most incredible smile he had ever seen. It held an openness he hadn't seen in her until now. He wanted to cup her divine face in his hands and kiss the sexy little crease at the edge of her lips that appeared every time she smiled.

Instead, he gave her the thumbs up, a stupid goofy smile, finishing off with a click of the tongue and a wink.

'Smooth,' Samantha chuckled. 'My dad the Casanova.'

Clay rolled his eyes at her. 'It's been a while. Give the old man a break.'

'So, you do admit you like her?' Samantha asked, an excited catch in her voice.

'She's alright.' He shuffled his feet, uncomfortable with where the conversation was headed. He was nervous enough about getting through the next few minutes let alone declaring his feelings for a woman other than Samantha's mother. It felt weird and wrong, like he was cheating. 'Let's just get through this okay?' He squeezed his injured hand and formed a chord with his fingers, causing him to grimace.

'Dad…'

'I'm okay. Low pain threshold,' he joked, trying to alleviate his anxiety as much as hers. She had enough to worry about.

They were given their five-minute call to get ready to go on, setting off a flip flop in his gut If he was feeling like this goodness knows what Samantha was feeling. Even if she didn't win, he was sure with all the exposure she would get as runner up, her career was about to take off. A recording contract, a national tour and whatever else lay ahead of her. He thought perhaps he'd be jealous. But he wasn't. He was so incredibly, ridiculously proud of the young woman she'd become. His body was such a hot mess. With his heart swelling with love and the butterflies in his stomach, he thought he might actually vomit. But there was no time for that. *Suck it up sunshine.*

Just as the M.C. was introducing them Samantha turned to him. 'Dad. If I win, will you come with me?'

'Come with you where sweetheart?'

'Everywhere,' she said, her young face soft and a little scared. The last time she'd looked at him like that was when he'd told her her mum was gone, forever.

'Of course I will pumpkin,' he replied gently, reaching out with his injured hand and squeezing hers. He didn't feel a thing.

'Promise?'

'Promise.'

A deep resolve planted itself inside him in that moment. He was a goody two shoes bloke who kept his promises.

'And Dad,' she continued, 'let's do the song.'

'Which song?'

'*The* Song,' she smiled, her eyes glistening with tears.

17

———————

As the sun was beginning to set, the warm summer breeze wafted into the woolshed through the slats in the walls, having been built with hard working shearers in mind who needed good airflow to reduce their heat levels. Thankfully, the production company, having seen the error of their ways, had removed the black masking on the walls that had given it a 'studio' look but had turned it into a sauna. It was much more comfortable.

And fairy lights now adorned the shed giving it a more romantic quality rather than a flashy mainstream talent competition feel. Tina preferred that. It felt earthy, real. There was a celebratory feeling amongst the crowd. She'd been anxious about what they would all think of the Danny situation, but she was welcomed by many of them with a simple nod of the head, a tip of an Akubra hat or a small wave, as if they had no idea what had transpired. She knew they had but was grateful that they didn't give a shit.

The M.C. warmed the crowd up before introducing act number one. The Fontina Twins who wowed again with their spine-tingling physical tricks that had her covering her eyes and watching through the gaps in her fingers.

They really couldn't have put on a better performance and the crowd agreed, going wild at the end. This brother and sister act would be entertaining people all over the world she had no doubt. She could see them landing a residency spot in Las Vegas.

As the M.C. did his over winded introduction for Samantha and Clay, he really did love the sound of his voice, Carter reached across and took her hand and until then she hadn't realised it had been trembling.

After what had happened to Clay and Samantha, she so desperately wanted something wonderful to happen for them.

And then they were in position. Clay strummed the first chord. Samantha held out her hand to stop him. Confusion spread across his face and he mouthed, *You okay?* She nodded, then stepped up to the microphone and cleared her throat.

'Hello,' she squeaked, her voice a mere whisper. The microphone squealed.

'Speak up honey!' someone in the crowd yelled.

She smiled at them and continued. 'Hello,' her voice stronger now; the crowd yelled *Hello* back to her, which made her giggle. She composed herself. 'Anyway, you all know me and my dad.' She gestured to him and the crowd clapped with a few whoo hoos thrown in.

Clay looked like he wanted the ground to open up and swallow him. This was clearly not planned and like everybody else he had no idea where it was going.

'Well, he wrote a song a few years ago. It's a good song. He wrote it for Mum.'

There was a sad, respectful silence in the crowd, the air thick with emotion and Tina felt tears slipping from the corner of her eyes.

Clay stood up, walked over to Samantha and leaned in, whispering something into her ear. Oh how Tina wished it was a multi directional microphone because it may have picked up what he said. But it didn't seem to matter, because Samantha shook her head and it was clear her mind was made up.

'So, without any further ado I give you, my Dad. My hero. Clay Reynolds to sing The Song.'

That was when the crowd released every single emotion they were holding inside. They were on their feet and it felt like the roof was going to be lifted off the one-hundred-year-old woolshed.

A sob mixed with a cheer fell out of Tina's mouth and she had no idea when she'd leapt to her feet, but she couldn't stop clapping and crying.

Carter was next to her weeping his beautiful gay, flamboyant heart out.

Tina could see the production crew waiting for instructions because this was definitely not what they expected to happen. They were also sobbing like little babies. It didn't matter to Tina whether they filmed it or not. She knew that's not why Samantha did what she did. There was no doubt she had already won the night.

Samantha pulled her dad into her arms and kissed him on the cheek. He shook his head, incredulous and dropped a quick kiss on her head as she pulled away and ran off the stage.

Silence came over the crowd and they took their seats. Clay stood at the microphone and he'd never looked more alone. For a moment Tina thought he might run off after his daughter. Then he closed his eyes and let out a long breath. When he opened them, he adjusted to the light and sought her out.

Her heart blossomed and her breath quickened.

A smile touched his lips and in the moment she knew he was singing it to her too.

Carter, got it as well and squealed under his breath. 'Oh my God. This is soooo fucking romantic I'm gonna die.'

Then Clay sang. To her. For her. And for his wife. Samantha's mother.

Tina couldn't tear her eyes from him. Nobody could. His voice deep and husky, told her everything he needed to say. Held every emotion he'd been unable to express over the years. She couldn't take in all the lyrics because her head was swimming with the sound of him. But she heard words like *sink, swim, love, soul, forever*. But the words didn't seem to matter. It was as if there was an invisible chord between them, stretching from the stage to where she sat.

Halfway through the song, Daneesh brought Samantha to sit with her. No words were needed as Tina took her hand and together, they listened to her dad sing his soul in front of millions of people.

After the last chord was strummed and the last note sung the crowd didn't so much applaud as give thanks. Sure, they were clapping and cheering but it was more than that. It was a community of people embracing one of their own. Taking his grief from him so he could live and love again.

Clay muttered a thank you into the microphone and left the stage and that's when Tina was able to look around. She caught Nat's eyes and they smiled through their shared tears of love. Yvonne from the pub was a complete mess, hugging anyone who was near her. One of them being Brad, who pulled out a handkerchief and offered it to her. Of course he carried a handkerchief.

Daneesh tapped Tina on the shoulder. 'He's asking for you,' she said.

Tina looked to Samantha. 'You should go. Not me.'

Samantha squeezed her hand. 'No, it's you. It's always been you. Go.'

Tina hesitated.

'For God's sake woman. GO!' Carter cried out, in capitals.

She threw her hands up in mock surrender. 'Okay I'm going. I'm going.' At the same time her stomach muscles fluttered and goosebumps covered her skin.

Daneesh led her to the side of the woolshed where production crew were already starting to bump out the equipment into awaiting trucks. Time was money.

It was dark by now, but it was a cloudless night and the three-quarter moon provided enough light for her to see Clay's figure standing by the river's edge.

He had his back to her and his guitar sat on a nearby hay bale. Should she say his name? Or walk up next to him? Or slide her arms around his waist? Or…

He turned, knowing she was there.

'Tina,' he breathed.

Her heart pounded in her chest as she walked towards him, her legs feeling shaky and unstable on the rough earth, her thoughts swimming madly making it nearly impossible to breathe.

Clay stepped into her, folding his arms around her waist. Gazing up at him, her eyes blazing with emotion, she felt her core tighten and pulse.

'Tina…I…'

A small breathless whisper escaped her lips. 'I do too.' Tina felt raw to her bones and in that instance everything cracked open.

She melted into him and he moved his hand over the back of her neck. Dipping his head, his sweet warm breath lingered just above her lips before he kissed her. A lingering, tender, soft hello.

The clapping of hands pulled them out of the moment. Carter stood only metres away, tears streaming down his face. 'Oh my God this is so fucking romantic.'

'Carter!' Tina exclaimed, unable to stop the bubbles of laughter from escaping her mouth. Clay joined in and Carter saw that as his cue. He rushed towards them and pulled them into a bear hug.

'Ouch,' Clay yelped. Carter had jammed his injured hand between them.

'Dad.' Samantha joined them, bringing an ice pack with her. 'I thought you might need this after playing…oh looks like I'm right on time.'

'Thanks pumpk…Sam,' he corrected himself, giving her a peck on the forehead.

'Wedding at the winery?' Nat yelled as she trotted towards them, as inappropriately splendid as always.

'We can use my car,' Brad declared as he too joined the throng, his arm linked with Yvonne's, who wore a wide smile like the cat that got the cream.

Tina and Clay looked at each and smiled, both completely fine with the posse of crazy family and friends they'd gathered along the way.

As the gang chatted about the imaginary upcoming nuptials, Clay pulled Tina into the shadows of the giant river gums and pressed her up against one of the ancient trees. She felt his powerful masculinity against her thigh and she smiled to herself. Then he bent down and kissed her again, his tongue dipping between the seam of her lips. A deep sensual kiss and a promise of what was yet to come. She moaned into his mouth and as Tina felt her womanhood start to tremble and smoulder, she hoped that Clay really was a man who kept his promises.

THE END

ABOUT THE AUTHORS

Rhonda Forrest is an Australian author who writes captivating contemporary and historical fiction about relationships, family life and social issues. Over the last ten years she has published ten novels, all set amidst beautiful and uniquely Australian landscapes.

Rhonda teaches English and History to high-school students and along with her husband, divides her time between Tamborine Mountain and a 100-year-old cottage, overlooking the waters of the Whitsundays.

She continues to write and document stories that bring to life the remarkable characters and settings that make up our wonderful Australian heritage.

https://www.rhondaforrest.com/

https://www.facebook.com/valeenapress

https://www.instagram.com/rhondaforrestauthor/

bookbub.com/author/rhonda-forrest

Louise Forster is the author of bestselling novels in the Tumble Creek series, with the 5th book well on its way, titled, Tumbling Back. She lives on the far north coast of New South Wales, Australia, five minutes from the Pacific Ocean with her childhood sweetheart, extended family and a menagerie of pets. She loves writing edgy romance with a touch of humour, mystery, and loving, sensual passion.

Louise enjoys writing from a hero's point of view, resilient, straightforward men who love their women unconditionally. They can also fix anything, including a broken heart.

Her sassy heroines are strong and stand up for their beliefs, even when they feel vulnerable.

www.louiseforster.com

https://www.facebook.com/profile.php?id=100070056198721

https://www.instagram.com/louise.forster.author/

bookbub.com/authors/louise-forster

Leanne Lovegrove is a lawyer, wife and mother and a lover of romance and reading. Her law career created an addiction to coffee but provides countless story ideas. She is the author of four romance novels, and this is her third novella and second anthology. Leanne writes sweeping love stories with happily-ever-afters with strong female heroines and set in the beautiful landscape of Australia. She lives in Brisbane, Australia with her husband and three children.

To find out more about Leanne's books, you can find her here:

www.leannelovegroveauthor.com

www.facebook.com/leanne.lovegrove.545/

www.instagram.com/leannelovegroveauthor/

www.bookbub.com/profile/leanne-lovegrove

Susan Mackie is the author of Amazon best-selling novels *Charlie's Will*, and *A Place to Start Over*. Her third full length novel, *The Bee Whisperer*, is due out later in 2022. Susan writes romance novels filled with vibrant, authentic characters and a touch of mystery, set in Australian country towns. Oh, and there's often a horse or two, and maybe a dog, in her stories. This is her second novella and anthology participation. Susan also edits and publishes for other authors, under her *Small Town Publishing* imprint. Susan has two grown daughters and lives in Warwick, Queensland, with Bloke.

www.susanmackie.com

https://www.instagram.com/susanmackieauthor/

https://www.facebook.com/susanmackieauthor

bookbub.com/authors/susan-mackie

Emma Powell, author of all things romance, funny and female lives in Melbourne, Australia with her human kid and fur babies. Her hobbies include, chicken chips, reading, true crime docos, politics and sleeping. Her other career is as a theatre actor which she has done for the last three decades. So as an actor and a writer she is able to do what she loves best - tell stories. So far, Emma has released five feel-good fiction books, with ore to come!

Emma has three romance books available:

https://www.emmapowell.com.au/

https://www.facebook.com/Emma-Powell-588701104921778

https://www.instagram.com/emmapowellauthor

bookbub.com/authors/emma-powell

Support for Independent Authors

The authors hope you enjoyed reading Love in a Sunburnt Land as much as we enjoyed writing each story within. As independent authors, we rely on readers rating and reviewing our books, and we would love you to leave a rating and/or review on your preferred retailer.

Thank you.